THE
SWITCH

Also by Beth O'Leary

The Flatshare

THE
SWITCH

BETH O'LEARY

Quercus

First published in Great Britain in 2020 by

Quercus Editions Ltd
Carmelite House
50 Victoria Embankment
London EC4Y 0DZ

An Hachette UK company

A CIP catalogue record for this book is available
from the British Library

HB ISBN 978 1 78747 499 4
TPB ISBN 978 1 78747 500 7

This book is a work of fiction. Although some of the
settings are real, the people depicted, businesses,
organisations, places and events described are
fictitious and any resemblance to actual
persons, living or dead, events or
locales is entirely coincidental.

10 9 8 7 6 5 4 3 2 1

Typeset by Jouve (UK), Milton Keynes

Printed and bound in Great Britain by Clays Ltd, Elcograf S.p.A.

Papers used by Quercus are from well-managed forests and other responsible sources.

For Helena and Jeannine,
My brave, brilliant, inspiring grandmothers.

1

Leena

'I think we should swap,' I tell Bee, bobbing up into a half-squat so I can talk to her over my computer screen. 'I'm bricking it. You should do the start and I'll do the end and that way by the time it gets to me I'll be less, you know . . .' I wave my hands to convey my mental state.

'You'll be less jazz hands?' Bee says, tilting her head to the side.

'Come on. Please.'

'Leena. My dear friend. My guiding light. My favourite pain in the ass. You are much better than I am at starting presentations and we are not switching the order of things now, ten minutes before our key client stakeholder update, just like we didn't switch at the last programme board, or the one before that, or the one before that, because that would be madness and quite frankly I haven't a bloody clue what's on the opening slides.'

I sag back into my chair. 'Right. Yes.' I bob up again. 'Only this time I am *really* feeling—'

'Mmm,' Bee says, not looking up from her screen. 'Absolutely. Worst ever. Shaking, sweaty palms, the lot. Only as soon as you get in there you'll be as charming and brilliant as you always are and nobody will notice a thing.'

'But what if I . . .'

'You won't.'

'Bee, I really think—'

'I know you do.'

'But this time—'

'Only eight minutes to go, Leena. Try that breathing thing.'

'What breathing thing?'

Bee pauses. 'You know. Breathing?'

'Oh, just normal breathing? I thought you meant some kind of meditative technique.'

She snorts at that. There's a pause. 'You've coped with way worse than this hundreds of times over, Leena,' she says.

I wince, cupping my coffee mug between my palms. The fear sits in the hollow at the base of my ribs, so real it feels almost physical – a stone, a knot, something you could cut out with a knife.

'I know,' I say. 'I know I have.'

'You just need to get your mojo back,' Bee tells me. 'And the only way to do that is to stay in the ring. OK? Come on. You are Leena Cotton, youngest senior consultant in the business, Selmount Consulting's one-to-watch 2020. And . . .' she lowers her voice, 'soon – one day – co-director of our own business. Yes?'

Yes. Only I don't *feel* like that Leena Cotton.

Bee's watching me now, her pencilled brows drawn tight with concern. I close my eyes and try to will the fear away, and for a moment it works: I feel a flicker of the person I was a year and a half ago, the person who would have flown through a presentation like this without letting it touch her.

'You ready, Bee, Leena?' the CEO's assistant calls as he makes his way across the Upgo office floor.

I stand and my head lurches; a wave of nausea hits. I grab the edge of the desk. Shit. *This* is new.

'You OK?' Bee whispers.

I swallow and press my hands into the desk until my wrists start to ache. For a moment I don't think I can do it – I just don't have it in me, God, I'm so *tired* – but then, at last, the grit kicks in.

'Absolutely,' I say. 'Let's do this.'

Half an hour has passed. That's not an especially long time, really. You can't watch a whole episode of *Buffy* in that time, or . . . or bake a large potato. But you *can* totally destroy your career.

I've been so afraid this was coming. For over a year now I've been fumbling my way through work, making absent-minded slip-ups and oversights, the sort of stuff I just don't *do*. It's like since Carla died I've switched my writing hand, and suddenly I'm doing everything with my left, not my right. But I've been trying so hard and I've been pushing through and I really thought I was getting there.

Evidently not.

I honestly thought I was going to die in that meeting. I've had a panic attack once before, when I was at university, but it wasn't as bad as this one. I have never felt so far out of my own control. It was like the fear got loose: it wasn't a tight knot any more, it had ten-drils, and they were tightening at my wrists and ankles and clawing at my throat. My heart was beating so fast – faster and faster – until it didn't feel like part of my body any longer, it felt like a vicious thrashing little bird trapped against my ribcage.

Getting *one* of the revenue numbers wrong would have been for-givable. But once that happened the nausea came, and I got another wrong, and another, and then my breathing started coming too fast and my brain was filled with . . . not fog, more like bright, bright light. Too bright to see anything by.

So when Bee stepped in and said *allow me to—*

Then when someone else said *come on this is laughable—*

And when the CEO of Upgo Finance said *I think we've seen enough here don't you—*

THE SWITCH | 4

I was already gone. Doubled over, gasping, quite sure I was about to die.

'You're OK,' Bee's saying now, her hands gripping mine tightly. We're tucked away in one of the phone-call booths in the corner of the Upgo offices; Bee led me here, still hyperventilating, sweating through my shirt. 'I've got you. You're OK.'

Each breath is coming in a jagged gasp. 'I just lost Selmount the Upgo contract, didn't I?' I manage.

'Rebecca's on a call with the CEO now. I'm sure it'll be fine. Come on, just breathe.'

'Leena?' someone calls. 'Leena, are you all right?'

I keep my eyes closed. Maybe, if I stay like this, that will not be the voice of my boss's assistant.

'Leena? It's Ceci, Rebecca's assistant?'

Gah. How did she *get* here so fast? The Upgo offices are at least a twenty-minute tube ride from Selmount headquarters.

'Oh, Leena, what a mess!' Ceci says. She joins us in the booth and rubs my shoulder in nagging circles. 'You poor little thing. That's right, cry it out.'

I'm not crying, actually. I breathe out slowly and look at Ceci, who is wearing a couture dress and a particularly gleeful smile, and remind myself for the hundredth time how important it is to support other women in business. I really, fully believe that. It's a code I live by, and it's how I plan to make it to the top.

But women are still, you know, people. And some people are just awful.

'What can we do you for, Ceci?' Bee asks, through gritted teeth.

'Rebecca sent me to check you're all right,' she says. 'You know. After your . . .' She waggles her fingers. 'Your *little wobble*.' Her iPhone buzzes. 'Oh! There's an email from her now.'

Bee and I wait, shoulders tensed. Ceci reads the email inhumanely slowly.

'Well?' Bee says.

'Hmm?' says Ceci.

'Rebecca. What did she say? Has she . . . Did I lose us the contract?' I manage.

Ceci tilts her head, eyes still on her phone. We wait. I can feel the tide of panic waiting too, ready to drag me back under.

'Rebecca's sorted it – isn't she a marvel? They're retaining Selmount on this project and have been *very* understanding, considering,' Ceci says eventually, with a little smile. 'She wants to see you now, so you'd better hotfoot it back over to the office, don't you think?'

'Where?' I manage. 'Where does she want to meet me?'

'Hmm? Oh, Room 5c, in HR.'

Of course. Where else would she go to fire me?

Rebecca and I are sitting opposite each other. Judy from HR is beside her. I am not taking it as a good sign that Judy is on her side of the table, not mine.

Rebecca pushes her hair back from her face and looks at me with pained sympathy, which can only be a very bad sign. This is Rebecca, queen of tough love, master of the mid-meeting put-down. She once told me that expecting the impossible is the only real route to the best results.

Basically, if she's being nice to me, that means she's given up.

'Leena,' Rebecca begins. 'Are you all right?'

'Yes, of course, I'm absolutely fine,' I say. 'Please, Rebecca, let me explain. What happened in that meeting was . . .' I trail off, because Rebecca is waving her hand and frowning.

'Look, Leena, I know you play the part very well, and God knows I love you for it.' She glances at Judy. 'I mean, Selmount values your . . . gritty, can-do attitude. But let's cut the crap. You look fucking terrible.'

Judy coughs quietly.

'That is, we wonder if you are a little run-down,' Rebecca says, without missing a beat. 'We've just checked your records – do you know when you last took a holiday?'

'Is that a . . . trick question?'

'Yes, yes it is, Leena, because for the last year you have not taken *any annual leave.*' Rebecca glares at Judy. 'Something which, by the way, should not be possible.'

'I told you,' Judy hisses, 'I don't know how she slipped through the net!'

I know how I slipped through the net. Human Resources talk the talk about making sure staff take their allotted annual leave, but all they actually do is send you an email twice a year telling you how many days you have left and saying something encouraging about 'wellness' and 'our holistic approach' and 'taking things offline to maximise your potential'.

'Really, Rebecca, I'm absolutely fine. I'm very sorry that my – that I disrupted the meeting this morning, but if you'll let me . . .'

More frowning and hand-waving.

'Leena, I'm sorry. I know it's been an impossibly tough time for you. This project is an incredibly high-stress one, and I've been feeling for a while that we didn't do right by you when we staffed you on it. I know I'm usually taking the piss when I say this sort of thing, but your well-being genuinely matters to me, all right? So I've talked to the partners, and we're taking you off the Upgo project.'

I shiver all of a sudden, a ridiculous, over-the-top shake, my body reminding me that I am still not in control. I open my mouth to speak, but Rebecca gets there first.

'And we've decided not to staff you on any projects for the next two months,' she goes on. 'Treat it as a sabbatical. Two months' holiday. You are not allowed back in Selmount headquarters until you are rested and relaxed and look less like someone who's spent a year in a war zone. OK?'

'That's not necessary,' I say. 'Rebecca, please. Give me a chance to prove that I—'

'This is a fucking gift, Leena,' Rebecca says with exasperation. 'Paid leave! Two months!'

'I don't want it. I want to work.'

'*Really?* Because your face is saying you want to *sleep*. Do you think I don't know you've been working until two in the morning every day this week?'

'I'm sorry. I know I should be able to keep to regular working hours – there have just been a few—'

'I'm not criticising you for how you manage your workload, I'm asking *when you ever bloody rest*, woman.'

Judy lets out a little string of quiet coughs at that. Rebecca shoots her an irritated look.

'A week,' I say desperately. 'I'll take a week off, get some rest, then when I come back I'll—'

'Two. Months. Off. That's it. This isn't a negotiation, Leena. You need this. Don't make me set HR on you to prove it.' This is said with a dismissive head-jerk in Judy's direction. Judy draws her chin in as though someone's clapped loudly in her face, perhaps, or flicked her on the forehead.

I can feel my breathing speeding up again. Yes, I've been struggling a little, but I can't take two months off. I can't. Selmount is all about reputation – if I step out of the game for eight whole weeks after that Upgo meeting, I'll be a laughing stock.

'Nothing is going to change in eight weeks,' Rebecca tells me. 'OK? We'll still be here when you get back. And you'll still be Leena Cotton, youngest senior, hardest worker, smartest cookie.' Rebecca looks at me intently. 'We all need a break sometimes. Even you.'

I walk out of the meeting feeling sick. I thought they'd try to fire me – I had all these lines prepared about unfair dismissal. But . . . a sabbatical?

'Well?' Bee says, appearing so close in front of me I have to stumble to a stop. 'I was lurking,' she explains. 'What did Rebecca say?'

'She said I . . . have to go on holiday.'

Bee blinks at me for a moment. 'Let's take an early lunch.'

As we dodge tourists and businessmen on our way down Commercial Street, my phone rings in my hand. I look at the screen and falter, almost running into a man with an e-cig hanging out of his mouth like a pipe.

Bee glances at the phone screen over my shoulder. 'You don't have to answer right now. You can let it ring out.'

My finger hovers over the green icon on the screen. I bash shoulders with a passing man in a suit; he tuts as I go buffeting across the pavement, and Bee has to steady me.

'What would you tell me to do if I was in this position right now?' Bee tries.

I answer the call. Bee sighs and pulls open the door to Watson's Café, our usual haunt for the rare, special occasions when we leave the Selmount offices for a meal.

'Hi, Mum,' I say.

'Leena, hi!'

I wince. She's all breezy and faux casual, like she's practised the greeting before making the call.

'I want to talk to you about hypnotherapy,' she says.

I sit down opposite Bee. 'What?'

'Hypnotherapy,' Mum repeats, with slightly less confidence this time. 'Have you heard of it? There's someone who does it over in Leeds, and I think it could be really good for us, Leena, and I thought perhaps we could go together, next time you're up visiting?'

'I don't need hypnotherapy, Mum.'

'It's not hypnotising people like Derren Brown does or anything, it's . . .'

'I don't need hypnotherapy, Mum.' It comes out sharply; I can hear her smarting in the silence that follows. I close my eyes, steadying my breathing again. 'You're welcome to try it, but I'm fine.'

'I just think – maybe, maybe it'd be good for us to do something together, not necessarily therapy, but . . .'

I notice she's dropped the 'hypno'. I smooth back my hair, the familiar stiff stickiness of hairspray under my fingers, and avoid Bee's gaze across the table.

'I think we should try talking maybe somewhere where . . . hurtful things can't be said. Positive dialogue only.'

Behind the conversation I can feel the presence of Mum's latest self-help book. It's in the careful use of the passive voice, the measured tone, the *positive dialogue* and *hurtful things*. But when it makes me waver, when it makes me want to say, *Yes, Mum, whatever would make you feel better*, I think of the choice my mother helped Carla to make. How she let my sister choose to end treatment, to – to give up.

I'm not sure even the Derren Brown kind of hypnotherapy could help me deal with that.

'I'll think about it,' I say. 'Goodbye, Mum.'

'Bye, Leena.'

Bee watches me across the table, letting me regroup. 'OK?' she says eventually. Bee's been on the Upgo project with me for the last year – she's seen me through every day since Carla died. She knows as much about my relationship with my mum as my boyfriend does, if not more – I only get to see Ethan at the weekends and the odd midweek evening if we can both get away from work on time, whereas Bee and I are together about sixteen hours a day.

I rub my eyes hard; my hands come away grainy with mascara. I must look an absolute state. 'You were right. I shouldn't have taken the call. I handled that all wrong.'

'Sounded like you did pretty well to me,' Bee says.

'Please, talk to me about something else. Something that isn't my family. Or work. Or anything else similarly disastrous. Tell me about your date last night.'

'If you want non-disastrous, you're going to need to pick another topic,' Bee says, settling back in her chair.

'Oh no, not good?' I ask.

I'm blinking back tears, but Bee kindly ploughs on, pretending not to notice.

'Nope. Odious. I knew it was a no as soon as he leaned in to kiss me on the cheek and all I could smell was the foisty, mouldy man-towel he must've used to wash his face.'

That works – it's gross enough to startle me back to the present. 'Eww,' I say.

'He had this massive globule of sleepy dust in the corner of his eye too. Like eye snot.'

'Oh, Bee . . .' I'm trying to find the right way to tell her to stop giv-ing up on people so quickly, but my powers of pep-talking seem to have deserted me, and in any case, that towel thing really is quite disgusting.

'I am on the brink of giving up and facing an eternity as a single mother,' Bee says, trying to catch the waiter's eye. 'I've come to the decision that dating is genuinely worse than loneliness. At least when you're alone there's no hope, right?'

'No hope?'

'Yeah. No hope. Lovely. We all know where we stand – alone, as we entered the world, so we shall leave it, et cetera, et cetera . . . Whereas dating, dating is *full* of hope. In fact, dating is really one long, pain-ful exercise in discovering how disappointing other humans are. Every time you start to believe you've found a good, kind man . . .' She wiggles her fingers. 'Out come the mummy issues and the fra-gile egos and the weird cheese fetishes.'

The waiter finally looks our way. 'The usual?' he calls across the café.

'Yup! Extra syrup on her pancakes,' Bee calls back, pointing at me.

'Did you say *cheese* fetishes?' I ask.

'Let's just say I've seen some photos that've really put me off brie.'

'Brie?' I say, horrified. 'But – oh, God, brie is so delicious! How could anyone corrupt brie?'

Bee pats my hand. 'I suspect you'll never have to find out, my friend. In fact, yes, if I'm supposed to be cheering you up, why aren't we talking about *your* ever-so-perfect love life? Surely the count-down's on for Ethan to pop the question.' She catches my expression. 'No? Don't want to talk about that either?'

'I've just got . . .' I flap my hand, eyes pricking again. 'A big wave of the horror. Oh, God. Oh God, oh God.'

'Which life crisis are you oh-godding about, just so I know?' Bee asks.

'Work.' I press my knuckles against my eyes until it hurts. 'I can't believe they're not staffing me for two whole months. It's like a . . . like a mini firing.'

'Actually,' Bee says, and her tone makes me move my hands and open my eyes, 'it's a two-month holiday.'

'Yes, but . . .'

'Leena, I love you, and I know you've got a lot of shit going on right now, but please try to see that this could be a good thing? Because it's going to be quite hard to continue loving you if you're going to spend the next eight weeks complaining about getting two months' paid leave.'

'Oh, I . . .'

'You could go to Bali! Or explore the Amazon rainforest! Or sail around the world!' She raises her eyebrows. 'Do you know what I'd give to have that kind of freedom?'

I swallow. 'Yes. Right. Sorry, Bee.'

'You're all right. I know this is about more than time off work for you. Just spare a thought for those of us who spend our allotted holiday at dinosaur museums full of nine-year-olds, yeah?'

I breathe in and out slowly, trying to let that sink in. 'Thank you,' I say, as the waiter approaches our table. 'I needed to hear that.'

Bee smiles at me, then looks down at her plate. 'You know,' she says casually, 'you *could* use the time off to get back to our business plan.'

I wince. Bee and I have been planning on setting up our own consultancy firm for a couple of years – we were almost ready to go when Carla got sick. Now, things have kind of . . . stalled a little.

'Yes!' I say, as cheerily as I can manage. 'Absolutely.'

Bee raises an eyebrow. I sag.

'I'm so sorry, Bee. I want to, I really do, it just feels . . . impossible, now. How are we going to launch our own business when I'm finding it so hard just holding down my job at Selmount?'

Bee chews a mouthful of pancake and looks thoughtful. 'OK,' she says. 'Your confidence has taken a hit lately, I get it. I can wait. But even if you don't use this time to work on the business plan, you should use it to work on *you*. My Leena Cotton doesn't talk about "holding down a job" like that's the best she can do, and she definitely doesn't use the word "impossible". And I want my Leena Cotton back. So,' she points her fork at me, 'you've got two months to find her for me.'

'And how am I doing that?'

Bee shrugs. '"Finding yourself" isn't really my forte. I'm just doing strategy here – you're on deliverables.'

That gets a laugh out of me. 'Thank you, Bee,' I say suddenly, reaching to clutch her hand. 'You're so great. Really. You're phenomenal.'

'Mmm, well. Tell that to the single men of London, my friend,' she says, giving my hand a pat and then picking up her fork again.

2

Eileen

It's been four lovely long months since my husband made off with the instructor from our dance class, and until this very moment I haven't missed him once.

I stare at the jar on the sideboard with my eyes narrowed. My wrist is still singing with pain from a quarter of an hour trying to wrench off the lid, but I'm not giving up. Some women live alone all their lives and *they* eat food out of jars.

I give the jar a good glare and myself a good talking-to. I am a seventy-nine-year-old woman. I have given birth. I have chained myself to a bulldozer to save a forest. I have stood up to Betsy about the new parking rules on Lower Lane.

I can open this wretched jar of pasta sauce.

Dec eyes me from the windowsill as I rummage through the drawer of kitchen implements in search of something that'll do the job of my increasingly useless fingers.

'You think I'm a daft old woman, don't you?' I say to the cat.

Dec swishes his tail. It's a sardonic swish. *All humans are daft,* that swish says. *You should take a leaf out of my book. I have my jars opened for me.*

'Well, just be grateful your tea for tonight is in a pouch,' I tell him, waggling a spaghetti spoon his way. I don't even like cats. It was Wade's idea to get kittens last year, but he lost interest in Ant and Dec when he found Miss Cha-Cha-Cha and decided that Hamleigh was too small for him, and that only old people keep cats. *You can keep them both*, he said, with an air of great magnanimity. *They suit your lifestyle better.*

Smug sod. He's older than me, anyway – eighty-one come September. And as for my lifestyle . . . Well. Just you wait and see, Wade Cotton. Just you bloody wait and see.

'Things are going to be changing around here, Declan,' I tell the cat, my fingers closing around the bread knife in the back of the drawer. Dec gives a slow, unimpressed blink, then his eyes widen and he swishes out of the window as I lift the knife with both hands to stab the lid of the jar. I let out a little *ha!* as I pierce it; it takes me a few stabs, like an amateur murderer in an Agatha Christie play, but this time when I twist the lid it turns easily. I hum to myself as I triumphantly empty the contents into the pan.

There. Once the sauce has warmed through and the pasta's cooked, I settle back down at the dining-room table with my tea and examine my list.

Basil Wallingham

Pros:

- Lives just down the road – not far to walk
- Own teeth
- Still got enough oomph in him to chase squirrels off birdfeeders

Cons:

- Tremendous bore
- Always wearing tweed
- Might well be a fascist

Mr Rogers

Pros:

- Only 67
- Full head of hair (very impressive)
- Dances like Pasha off of *Strictly* (even more impressive)
- Polite to everyone, even Basil (most impressive of all)

Cons:

- Highly religious man. *Very* pious. Likely to be dull in bed?
- Only visits Hamleigh once a month
- Shown no signs of interest in anyone except Jesus

Dr Piotr Nowak

Pros:

- Polish. How exciting!
- Doctor. Useful for ailments
- Very interesting to talk to and exceptional at Scrabble

Cons:

- Rather too young for me (59)
- Almost certainly still in love with ex-wife
- Looks a bit like Wade (not his fault but off-putting)

I chew slowly and pick up my pen. I've been ignoring this thought all day, but . . . I really ought to list *all* the unattached gentlemen of the right age. After all, I've put Basil on there, haven't I?

Arnold Macintyre

Pros:

- Lives next door
- Appropriate age (72)

Cons:
- Odious human being
- Poisoned my rabbit (as yet unproven, granted, but I know he did)
- Cut back my tree full of birds' nests
- Sucks all joy from the world
- Probably feasts on kittens for breakfast
- Likely descended from ogres
- Hates me almost as much as I hate him

I cross out *likely descended from ogres* after a moment, because I ought not to bring his parents into it – they might have been perfectly nice for all I know. But I'm leaving the part about kittens.

There. A complete list. I tilt my head, but it looks just as bleak from that angle as it does straight on. I have to face the truth: pickings are very slim in Hamleigh-in-Harksdale, population one hundred and sixty-eight. If I want to find love at this stage of my life, I need to be looking further afield. Over to Tauntingham, for instance. There's at least two-hundred people in Tauntingham, and it's only thirty minutes on the bus.

The telephone rings; I get to the living room just in time.

'Hello?'

'Grandma? It's Leena.'

I beam. 'Hold on, let me get myself sat down.'

I settle back into my favourite armchair, the green one with the rose pattern. This phone call is the best part of any day. Even when it was bitterly sad, when all we talked about was Carla's death – or anything but that, because that felt too painful – even then, these calls with Leena kept me going.

'How are you, love?' I ask Leena.

'I'm fine, how are you?'

I narrow my eyes. 'You're not fine.'

'I know, it just came out, sorry. Like when someone sneezes and you say "bless you".' I hear her swallow. 'Grandma, I had this – I had a panic attack at work. They've sent me off on a two-month sabbatical.'

'Oh, Leena!' I press my hand to my heart. 'But it's no bad thing that you're getting some time off,' I say quickly. 'A little break from it all will do you good.'

'They're side-lining me. I've been off my game, Grandma.'

'Well, that's understandable, given . . .'

'No,' she says, and her voice catches, 'it's not. God, I – I promised Carla, I told her I wouldn't let it hold me back, losing her, and she always said – she said she was so proud, but now I've . . .'

She's crying. My hand grips at my cardigan, like Ant or Dec's paws when they're sitting in my lap. Even as a child, Leena hardly ever cried. Not like Carla. When Carla was upset, she would throw her arms in the air, the very picture of misery, like a melodramatic actress in a play – it was hard not to laugh. But Leena would just frown and dip her head, looking up at you reproachfully through those long, dark eyelashes.

'Come on, love. Carla would have wanted you to take holidays,' I tell her.

'I know I should be thinking of it as a holiday, but I can't. It's just . . . I hate that I messed up.' This is muffled, as if she's speaking into her hands.

I take off my glasses and rub the bridge of my nose. 'You didn't *mess up*, love. You're stressed, that's what it is. Why don't you come up and stay this weekend? Everything looks better over a mug of hot chocolate, and we can talk properly, and you can have a little break from it all, up here in Hamleigh . . .'

There's a long silence.

'You haven't been to visit for an awfully long time,' I say tentatively.

'I know. I'm really sorry, Grandma.'

'Oh, that's all right. You came up when Wade left, I was ever so grateful for that. And I'm very lucky to have a granddaughter who calls me so often.'

'But I know chatting over the phone isn't the same. And it's not that I . . . You know I really would love to see you.'

No mention of her mother. Before Carla's death, Leena would have come up to see Marian once a month at least. When will this end, this miserable feud between them? I'm so careful never to mention it – I don't want to interfere, it's not my place. But . . .

'Did your mother call you?'

Another long silence. 'Yes.'

'About . . .' What was it she'd settled on in the end? 'Hyper-therapy?'

'Hypnotherapy.'

'Ah, yes.'

Leena says nothing. She's so *steely*, our Leena. How will the two of them ever get through this when they're both so bloody stubborn?

'Right. I'll stay out of it,' I say into the silence.

'I'm sorry, Grandma. I know it's hard for you.'

'No, no, don't worry about me. But will you think about coming up here at the weekend? It's hard to help from so far away, love.'

I hear her sniff. 'Do you know what, Grandma, I will come. I've been meaning to, and – and I really would love to see you.'

'There!' I beam. 'It'll be lovely. I'll make you one of your favourites for tea and clue you in on all the village gossip. Roland's on a diet, you know. And Betsy tried to dye her hair, but it went wrong, and I had to drive her to the hairdresser's with a tea towel on her head.'

Leena snorts with laughter. 'Thanks, Grandma,' she says after a moment. 'You always know how to make me feel better.'

'That's what Eileens do,' I say. 'They look after each other.' I used to say that to her as a child – Leena's full name is Eileen too. Marian named her after me when we all thought I was dying after a bad bout of pneumonia back in the early nineties; when we realised I wasn't at death's door after all it got very confusing, and so Leena became Leena.

'Love you, Grandma,' she says.

'You too, love.'

After she hangs up the telephone, I realise I've not told her about my new project. I wince. I promised myself I would tell her the next time she called. It's not that I'm embarrassed to be looking for love, exactly. But young people tend to find old people wanting to fall in love rather funny. Not unkindly, just without thinking, the way you laugh at children behaving like grown-ups, or husbands trying to do the weekly shop.

I make my way back to the dining room and, when I get there, I look down at my sad little list of eligible Hamleigh men. It all feels rather small now. My thoughts are full of Carla. I try to think of other things – Basil's tweed jackets, Piotr's ex-wife – but it's no use, so I settle down and let myself remember.

I think of Carla as a little girl, with a mass of curls and scuffed knees, clutching her sister's hand. I think of her as the young woman in a washed-out Greenpeace T-shirt, too thin, but grinning, full of fire. And then I think of the Carla who lay in Marian's front room. Gaunt and drawn and fighting the cancer with all she had left.

I shouldn't paint her that way, as if she looked weak – she was still so Carla, still fiery. Even on Leena's last visit, just days before she died, Carla would take no nonsense from her big sister.

She was in her special hospital bed, brought into Marian's living room one evening by a group of gentle NHS staff, who put it up with astonishing efficiency and cleared out before I could make them so much as a cup of tea. Marian and I were standing in the doorway. Leena was beside the bed, in the armchair we'd moved there once and never shifted back. The living room didn't centre around the television any more, but around that bed, with its magnolia-cream bars on each side of the mattress, and that grey remote control, always lost under the blankets, for adjusting the bed's height and shifting Carla when she wanted to sit up.

'You're incredible,' Leena was telling her sister, her eyes bright with tears. 'I think you're – you're incredible, and so brave, and . . .'

Carla reached out, faster than I'd thought she could, now, and poked her sister in the arm.

'Stop it. You'd never say that sort of thing if I wasn't dying,' she said. Even with her voice thin and dry, you could hear the humour. 'You're way nicer to me these days. It's weird. I miss you telling me off for wasting my life away.'

Leena winced. 'I didn't . . .'

'Leena, it's fine, I'm teasing.'

Leena shifted uncomfortably in the armchair, and Carla raised her eyes upwards, as if to say, *Oh, for heaven's sake.* I'd grown used to her face without eyebrows by then, but I remember how strange it had looked at first – stranger, in some ways, than the loss of her long brown curls.

'Fine, fine. I'll be serious,' she said.

She glanced at me and Marian, and then reached for Leena's hand, her fingers too pale against Leena's tanned skin.

'All right? Serious face on.' Carla closed her eyes for a moment. 'There is some stuff I've wanted to say, you know. Serious stuff.' She opened her eyes then, fixing her gaze on Leena. 'You remember when we went camping together that summer when you were back from uni, and you told me how you thought management consultancy was the way to change the world, and I laughed? And then we argued about capitalism?'

'I remember,' Leena said.

'I shouldn't have laughed.' Carla swallowed; pain touched her features, a tightening around the eyes, a quiver of her dry lips. 'I should have listened and told you I was proud. You're shaping the world, in a way – you're making it better, and the world needs people like you. I want you to kick out all the stuffy old men and I want you to run the show. Launch that business. Help people. And promise me you won't let losing me hold you back.'

Leena was crying, then, her shoulders hunched and shaking. Carla shook her head.

'Leena, stop it, would you? Jesus, this is what comes of being serious! Do I have to poke you again?'

'No,' Leena said, laughing through her tears. 'No, please don't. It actually kind of hurt.'

'Well. Just know that any time you let an opportunity slip, any time you wonder if you can really do it, any time you think about giving up on *anything* that you want . . . I'll be poking you from the afterlife.'

And that was Carla Cotton for you.

She was fierce, and she was silly, and she knew we couldn't manage without her.

3

Leena

I wake up at six twenty-two, twenty-two minutes after my usual alarm, and sit bolt upright with a gasp. I think the reason I'm freaked out is the strange silence, the absence of my phone alarm's horrendous cheery beeping. It takes me a while to remember that I'm not late – I do not have to get up and go to the office. I am actually not *allowed* to go back to the office.

I slump back against the pillow as the horror and the shame resettle. I slept terribly, stuck in a loop of remembering that meeting, never less than half-awake, and then, when I did fall asleep, I dreamt of Carla, one of the last nights I spent at Mum's house, how I'd crawled into the bed and held Carla against me, her frail body tucked to mine like a child's. She'd elbowed me off, after a bit. *Stop getting the pillow all wet*, she'd told me, but then she'd kissed me on the cheek and sent me off to make midnight hot chocolate, and we'd talked for a while, giggling in the dark like we were kids again.

I haven't dreamt of Carla for a good few months. Now, awake, reliving that dream, I miss my sister so much I cry out with a little, strangled, *Oh God*, remembering the gutting sucker-punches of grief that floored me in those first few months, feeling them again for a heart-splitting instant and wondering how I survived that time at all.

This is bad. I need to move. A run. That'll sort me out. I throw on the Lululemon leggings Ethan got me for my birthday, and an old T-shirt, and head out the door. I run through the streets of Shoreditch until dark bricks and street art give way to the repurposed ware-houses of Clerkenwell, the shuttered bars and restaurants on Upper Street, the leafy affluence of Islington, until I'm dripping with sweat and all I can think about is the inch of pavement in my eyeline. The next step, next step, next step.

When I get back, Martha's in the kitchen, attempting to wedge her very pregnant body into one of the ridiculous art deco breakfast stools she chose for the flat. Her dark-brown hair is in pigtails; Mar-tha always looks young, she's got one of those faces, but add the pigtails and she looks like she should not legally be bearing a child.

I offer her an arm to lean on as she clambers up, but she waves me away.

'That's a very lovely gesture,' she says, 'but you are far too sweaty to be touching other people, my sweet.'

I wipe my face with the bottom of my T-shirt and head to the sink for a glass of water. 'We need proper chairs,' I tell her over my shoulder.

'No we do not! These are *perfect*,' Martha tells me, wriggling back-wards to try to fit her bottom into the seat.

I roll my eyes.

Martha is a high-end interior designer. The work is flashy, exhaust-ing and irregular; her clients are nightmarishly picky, always ringing her out-of-hours to have lengthy breakdowns about curtain fabrics. But the upside is that she gets discounts on designer furniture, and she has dotted our flat with an assortment of very stylish things that either serve no purpose – the W-shaped vase on the windowsill, the cast-iron lamp that barely emits the faintest glow when turned on – or actively don't fulfil their intended function: the breakfast stools you can hardly sit on, the coffee table with the convex surface.

Still, it seems to make her happy, and I'm so rarely in the flat it doesn't bother me much. I should never have let Martha talk me into renting this place with her, really, but the novelty of living in an old printworks was too good to resist when I was new to London. Now this is just a very expensive space in which I can collapse into bed, and I don't notice that what we're doing is, apparently, 'artisan warehouse living'. When Martha leaves I really should talk to Fitz about the two of us moving somewhere more reasonable. Aside from the weird old cat lady next door, everyone who lives in this building seems to have a hipster beard or a start-up; I'm not sure Shoreditch is where we belong.

'You manage to speak to Yaz last night?' I ask, getting myself another glass of water.

Yaz is Martha's girlfriend, currently touring a play out in America for six months. Yaz and Martha's relationship causes me high levels of vicarious stress. Everything seems to involve incredibly complex logistics. They're always in different time zones and sending one another important documents transatlantically and making crucial life decisions on WhatsApp calls with really patchy signal. This current situation is an excellent example of their style: Yaz will be returning in eight weeks' time, taking possession of a house (which has yet to be bought) and moving her pregnant girlfriend into it before the baby is scheduled to come a few days later. I'm sweating again just thinking about it all.

'Yeah, Yaz is good,' Martha says, idly rubbing her bump. 'Talking at four-hundred miles an hour about Chekhov and baseball games. You know, Yaz-like.' Her fond smile stretches as she yawns expansively. 'She's getting skinny, though. She needs a good meal.'

I suppress a smile. Martha may not be a mother yet, but she's been mothering everyone within reach for as long as I've known her. Feeding people up is one of her favourite forms of benevolent attack. She also keeps insisting on bringing friends from her Pilates class around for tea in the blatant hope that they might make an honest man of Fitz, our other flatmate.

Speaking of Fitz – I check the time on my fitbit. He's on his fourth new job of the year; he really shouldn't be late for this one.

'Is Fitz up yet?' I ask.

He wanders in on cue, pushing up his collar to put on a tie. As per usual, his facial hair looks like it was cut against a ruler – I've lived with him for three years and am still no closer to understanding how he achieves this. Fitz always looks so misleadingly *together*. His life is in a permanent state of disarray, but his socks are always perfectly ironed. (In his defence, they *are* always on show – he wears his trousers an inch too short – and they are more interesting than the average person's socks. He has one pair covered in a SpongeBob SquarePants motif, another speckled like a Van Gogh painting, and his favourite pair are his 'political socks', which say 'Brexit is bollocks' around the ankle.)

'I'm up. Question is, why are *you* up, holidayer?' Fitz asks, finishing off knotting his skinny tie.

'Oh, Leena,' Martha says. 'I'm sorry, I'd totally forgotten you weren't going to work this morning.' Her eyes are wide with sympathy. 'How're you feeling?'

'Miserable,' I confess. 'And then angry with myself for being miserable, because who feels miserable when they've been given a paid two-month holiday? But I keep reliving the moment in that meeting. Then all I want to do is curl up in the foetal position.'

'The foetal position is not as static as people think,' Martha says, grimacing and rubbing the side of her belly. 'But yeah, that's totally natural, sweetheart. You need to rest – that's what your body is telling you. And you need to forgive yourself. You just made a little mistake.'

'Leena's never made one of those before,' Fitz says, heading for the smoothie maker. 'Give her time to adjust.'

I scowl. 'I've made mistakes.'

'Oh, please, Little Miss Perfect. Name one,' Fitz says, winking over his shoulder.

Martha clocks my irritated expression and reaches to give my arm a squeeze, then remembers how sweaty I am and pats me gently on the shoulder instead.

'Do you have plans for your weekend?' she asks me.

'I'm going up to Hamleigh, actually,' I say, glancing at my phone. I'm expecting a text from Ethan – he had to work late last night, but I'm hoping he's free this evening. I need one of his hugs, the really gorgeous long ones where I tuck my face into his neck and he wraps me right up.

'Yeah?' Fitz says, making a face. 'Going back up north to see your mum – *that's* what you want to do right now?'

'Fitz!' Martha chides. 'I think that's a great idea, Leena. Seeing your granny will make you feel so much better, and you don't have to spend any time with your mum if you don't feel ready. Is Ethan going with you?'

'Probably not – he's on that project in Swindon. The delivery deadline's next Thursday – he's in the office all hours.'

Fitz gives the smoothie machine a rather pointed whir at that. He doesn't need to say anything: I know he thinks Ethan and I don't prioritise each other enough. It's true we don't see each other as much as we'd like to – we may work for the same company, but we're always staffed on different projects, usually in different godforsaken industrial parks. But that's part of why Ethan is so amazing. He gets how important work is. When Carla died and I was struggling so much to stay afloat, it was Ethan who kept me focused on my job, reminding me what I loved about it, pushing me to keep moving forward so I didn't have the chance to sink.

Only now I don't have any work to keep me going, not for the next eight weeks. Two enormous months gape ahead of me, unfilled. As I think of all those hours of stillness and quiet and time to think, the bottom seems to drop out of my stomach. I need a purpose, a project, *something*. If I don't keep moving those waters will close over my head, and the very thought of that makes my skin prickle with panic.

I check the time on my phone. Ethan's over an hour and a half late – he probably got cornered by a partner as he was leaving work. I've been cleaning the flat all afternoon, and finished up in time for his arrival, but now an extra two hours have passed, during which I've been pulling out furniture and dusting chair legs and doing the sort of excessive cleaning that gets you a spot on a Channel Four documentary.

When I finally hear his key in the door I wriggle my way out from underneath the sofa and brush down my gigantic cleaning-day sweatshirt. It's a *Buffy* one: the front is a big picture of her face, doing her best kick-ass expression. (Most of my clothes that aren't suits are gigantic nerdy jumpers. I may not have much time to indulge in cult telly shows these days, but I can still show my loyalties – and frankly it's the only kind of fashion I consider worth spending money on.)

Ethan does a dramatic gasp as he enters the room, spinning on his heels at the transformation. It *does* look great. We keep the place fairly tidy anyway, but now it's sparkling.

'I should've known you couldn't even manage one day off without some sort of frenzied activity,' Ethan says, swooping in to kiss me. He smells of rich, citrussy cologne and his nose is cold from the chilly March rain. 'The place looks great. Fancy doing mine next?'

I swat him on the arm and he laughs, tossing his dark hair back from his forehead with his trademark lopsided flick. He bends down and kisses me again, and I feel a flash of envy as I sense how buzzed he is from work. I miss that feeling.

'Sorry I'm late,' he says, moving away and heading for the kitchen. 'Li took me aside to talk through the R and D numbers for the Webster review and you know what he's like, can't take a hint for love nor money. How are you holding up, angel?' he calls over his shoulder.

My stomach twists. *How are you holding up, angel?* Ethan used to say that to me on the phone each night, when Carla was barely holding on; he'd say it on my doorstep, turning up just when I needed him, with a bottle of wine and a hug; he said it as I wobbled my way to the front at Carla's funeral, gripping his hand so tightly it must have hurt. I couldn't have got through it all without him. I'm not sure how you can ever be grateful enough for someone leading you through the darkest time in your life.

'I'm . . . OK,' I say.

Ethan comes back in, his socked feet looking a little incongruous with his business suit. 'I think this is a good thing,' he says, 'the time off.'

'You do?' I ask, sinking down on the sofa. He settles in beside me, pulling my legs over his.

'Absolutely. And you can keep your hand in anyway – you're always welcome to chip in on my projects, you know that, and I can drop in with Rebecca how much you're helping me out, so she knows you're not losing your edge while you're away.'

I sit up a little straighter. 'Really?'

'Of course.' He kisses me. 'You know I've got your back.'

I shift so I can look at him properly: his fine, expressive mouth, that silky dark hair, the little string of freckles above his high cheek-bones. He's so beautiful, and he's here, right now, when I need him most. I am beyond lucky to have found this man.

He leans to the side to grab his laptop bag, slung down by the sofa arm. 'Want to run through tomorrow's slide deck with me? For the Webster review?'

I hesitate, but he's already flicking the laptop open, settling it across my legs, and so I lean back and listen as he starts talking, and I realise he's right – this is helping. Like this, with Ethan, hearing his soft, low voice talk revenue and projections, I almost feel like myself.

4

Eileen

Things are rather a rush on Friday afternoon – Dec left mouse entrails on the doormat. It was a kind gesture in cat terms, I'm sure, but a bother to wipe off the bottom of my favourite shoes. I arrive at the village hall just in time for the Neighbourhood Watch meeting, and a little out of breath.

The Hamleigh Neighbourhood Watch is an unofficial association, but a thriving one. Crime is something that very much concerns the inhabitants of Hamleigh-in-Harksdale, despite the fact that in the last five years the only crime I remember occurring was the theft of Basil's lawnmower, which turned out to have been borrowed by Betsy, who swears she asked Basil first. Whoever you believe, it's hardly an epidemic of illegal activity, and a weekly two-hour meeting is almost certainly a bit much.

Thankfully, I am now in charge of the Neighbourhood Watch, with Betsy as Deputy Watcher (it was agreed that Betsy could not be Lead Watcher, given her aforementioned criminal history). We've made the meetings much more interesting. Since we're not *technically* a Neighbourhood Watch, just people who like watching our neighbours, there's no need to stick to any rules or regulations. So we stopped pretending to talk about crime, and just focused on gossip, village scandal, and complaints about rival hamlets. Next, we introduced lots of free biscuits, provided cushions for the seats, and created a sign saying 'Members Only' for the door of the village hall when we're meeting, which has had the effect of making everybody who isn't a member of the Neighbourhood Watch jealous, and everyone who is a member feel smug about being 'in the club', as it were.

Betsy calls the meeting to order by tapping her gavel on the village hall coffee table. (Goodness knows where Betsy got that gavel from, but she'll take any given opportunity to tap it. The other day, when Basil was being particularly belligerent at bingo, she tapped him on the forehead with it. That shut him up. Though Dr Piotr did pull Betsy aside later to explain that, given Basil's recent stroke, head injuries would be best avoided.)

'What's our first order of business?' Betsy calls.

I hand her the agenda.

March 20th Neighbourhood Watch Meeting

1. Welcome
2. Tea round, biscuits
3. Dr Piotr: parking outside the GP surgery
4. Roland: are we still boycotting Julie's? Move to reassess – no other good places to buy bacon sandwiches
5. Betsy: clarification on whether culottes are indeed 'back in'
6. Biscuits, tea
7. Eileen: golden oldies film night – move to ban all films with Jack Nicholson in them, can't stand any more, there must be another older gentleman who can act
8. Basil: update on the War on Squirrels
9. Any crime?
10. Biscuits, tea
11. AOB

Basil does the teas, which means they're all atrociously weak and half of us still have teabags floating in our mugs because he's too short-sighted to notice which ones he's not fished out. Betsy has brought a very good range of biscuits, though. I munch my way through a ginger snap while Piotr talks earnestly about 'those of us who park our mobility scooters across two car parking spaces' (he means Roland) and 'consequences for other patients' (he means Basil, who always complains about it).

I think of the list on my dining-room table and idly try to imagine making love to Dr Piotr, which results in a piece of ginger snap going the wrong way and the Neighbourhood Watch meeting briefly descending into panic as everyone thwacks me on the back. Betsy is just preparing to do the Heimlich manoeuvre when I get my voice back and inform them that I'm quite all right. And that, should a time arise when I am actually choking, I'd prefer it if Piotr was the one doing the manoeuvres. We exchange an amused glance over Betsy's head as I say it. With a flicker of hope I wonder whether the look might even be a little flirtatious, though it's been a while and I'm not exactly sure how you're supposed to tell.

Betsy gets predictably miffed at my comment, but is soon distracted by the discussion of whether culottes are fashionable. This one arose because last week Kathleen told Betsy they were all the rage, and Betsy bought six pairs off of the shopping channel. (Kathleen, at thirty-five, brings down the average age of the Neighbourhood Watch considerably. With three children under six she's so desperate to get out of the house she's signed up for every village activity going.) Betsy has had a crisis of confidence about her new purchases and needs a poll to be conducted. This is her favourite way of ensuring nobody can judge her for doing something – if it's decided democratically, it's everybody's fault.

The Neighbourhood Watch rules that culottes are indeed back in, though I believe Basil thinks they're some sort of French vegetable, and he was the deciding vote.

After round two of biscuits I make my case regarding Jack Nicholson films, but am overruled: Penelope is a surprisingly ardent fan. Next Basil blathers on about squirrels for a while, which is always a good part of the meeting in which to catch some shut-eye if you need it, and then it's time for more biscuits and the most important point on the agenda: 'any crime'. Otherwise known as 'new gossip'.

'Eileen, Betsy says you've sold your car?' Penelope says, blinking owlishly at me across the circle. Penelope is built like a tiny little bird; she looks so frail I'm always nervous she'll snap something, but really she's made of pretty strong stuff. I saw her shoot a cat with a water pistol the other day when it was after her bluetits' nest – she got it right in the eye.

'I think it's very wise of you to call it a day on the driving, Eileen,' Betsy says.

'I'm still driving,' I say, sitting up straighter. 'I'm just sharing Marian's car.'

'Oh, you *are* still driving?' Betsy says. 'Gosh. Aren't you brave, after that mishap on Sniddle Road!'

Betsy is a kind soul, and a very dear friend, but she is also excellent at saying rude things in a tone of voice that means you can't object to them. As for my 'mishap' on Sniddle Road, it's hardly worth mentioning. I'll admit it wasn't my best attempt at parking, but who would've thought that man's four-by-four would dent so easily? The thing looked like a ruddy tank.

'Given up on your latest project, then, have you?' Basil asks, rubbing biscuit crumbs out of his moustache. 'Weren't you ferrying lost dogs around in that car?'

'I was helping the kind folks at the Daredale dog rescue centre,' I say, with dignity. 'But they have their own transportation, now.'

'I'm sure you'll be on to something else soon enough!' Basil says with a chuckle.

I narrow my eyes.

'Have you given up on getting us a sponsor for May Day yet?' he goes on. 'No big businesses willing to lend their name to a little village fete?'

I grit my teeth. As it happens, I *have* struggled to find a sponsor for the May Day festival. I'd hoped we could use any funds raised for the cancer charity that did so much for Carla, rather than for covering the costs, as we usually do. But these days it's hard to even get somebody to speak to you at the big companies in Leeds, and the local businesses I tried are all tightening their belts and don't have any money to spare.

'Funny that!' Basil chortles.

'I shan't apologise for wanting to make a difference in this world, Basil,' I say icily.

'Quite right, quite right,' Basil says. 'And it's very brave of you to keep at it against the odds, I say.'

Conversation shifts, mercifully; Penelope turns to Piotr, discussing Roland's latest ailment, and I take the opportunity to snatch a word with Betsy.

'Have you spoken to your daughter again, love?' I ask her in a low voice. 'About visiting?'

Betsy purses her lips. 'I tried,' she says. 'No luck.'

It's Betsy's husband who's the issue. Her daughter won't be in a room with him any more. I understand – Cliff's a nasty piece of work, and I don't know how Betsy's borne it over all these years. Even Wade couldn't stand the man. But cutting Betsy off from her family is surely only going to make everything worse. Still, it's not my place to interfere; I give her hand a squeeze.

'She'll come when she's ready,' I say.

'Well, she better not leave it too long,' Betsy says. 'I *am* eighty!'

THE SWITCH | 34

I smile at that. Betsy's eighty-five. Even when she's trying to make the point that she is old, she can't help lying about her age.

'. . . Knargill buses are down to one a day,' Basil's saying to Roland on the other side of me. 'Can't help thinking that's part of the problem.'

Basil's favourite things to complain about are, in this order: squirrels, transport links, weather conditions, and the state of the nation. You shouldn't get him started on any of these topics, but it is particularly worth avoiding the last one, as it becomes very hard to like Basil once he starts talking about immigration.

'And there she was,' Basil's saying, 'drowned in her leek and potato soup! Ghoulish sight, I expect. Poor young lady who found her had just come round to see if she wanted new double glazing, found the door unlocked, and there she was – dead a week and nobody knew it!'

'What's this, Basil?' I ask. 'Are you telling horror stories again?'

'Lady over in Knargill,' Basil says, sipping his tea complacently. 'Drowned in her bowl of soup.'

'That's awful!' says Betsy.

'Were there flies and maggots by the time they found her?' asks Penelope, with interest.

'Penelope!' everybody choruses, then we all immediately turn to Basil for the answer.

'Likely,' he says, nodding sagely. 'Very likely. Poor lady was only seventy-nine. Husband died the year before. Didn't have a soul in the world to care for her. The neighbours said she'd go months without speaking to anyone but the birds.'

I suddenly feel peculiar, a little light-headed, maybe, and as I reach for another ginger snap I notice my hand is trembling more than usual.

I suppose I'm thinking this poor lady was the same age as me. But that's where the similarity ends, I tell myself firmly. I'd never choose leek and potato soup, for starters – so bland.

I swallow. Yesterday's incident with the jar was an unpleasant reminder of exactly how easy it can be to stop coping. And not coping can turn drastic quickly when you're on your own.

'We should do more for people like that,' I say suddenly. 'With all the bus timetables getting cut down and the Dales Senior Transport lot having funding trouble, it's hard for them to get anywhere even if they want to.'

Everyone looks rather surprised. Usually if the inhabitants of Knargill are mentioned in a Neighbourhood Watch meeting, it's followed by some mischievous cackling from Betsy, who will then declare 'it serves them right for living in Knargill'.

'Well, yes, I suppose,' Penelope says querulously into the silence.

'Let's put it on the next agenda,' I say. I make a note on my printout.

There's a slightly awkward pause.

'You know, over in Firs Blandon they're talking about setting up a rival May Day celebration,' Basil says, looking at me shrewdly, as if he's testing my loyalties.

'They're not!' I say, *tsking*. Basil ought to know I'd never side with Firs Blandon. A decade or two ago, when Hamleigh lost power for three days after a big storm, all the other villages offered funds and spare rooms to help those who couldn't manage without their heaters. Not a soul in Firs Blandon lifted a finger. 'Well,' I say staunchly, 'a Firs Blandon May Day will never be as good as ours.'

'Of course it won't!' Betsy declares, and everybody relaxes now we're back on safe ground. 'More biscuits, anybody?'

The rest of the meeting passes as normal, but my nasty peculiar feeling nags me all day. I'm glad Leena's coming tomorrow. I'm rather worn out, and it's an awful lot easier to be independent when there's somebody else there with you.

5

Leena

Hamleigh-in-Harksdale is as cute as it sounds. The village is cosied between two hills in the south of the Yorkshire Dales; I can just see its rooftops and wonky chimneys between tawny crags as the bus rattles along the valley road.

I didn't grow up in Hamleigh – Mum only moved there when Carla got sick. There are two versions of the village in my mind: half my memories have a sweet, sepia-toned childhood nostalgia to them, and the other half are darkly painful, raw with loss. My stomach clenches. I try to remember how I felt here as a child, the joy of coming around this bend in the road to see Hamleigh's roofs ahead of us.

Even when we were teenagers, always at each other's throats, Carla and I would make peace for the duration of a visit to Grandma's and Grandpa's house. We'd grouch about the parties we'd be missing as Mum drove us up from Leeds, but as soon as we got to Hamleigh we remembered who we were here. Illicit cider and kissing with sixth-form boys would seem slightly absurd, like something from someone else's life. We'd be outside all day, collecting blackberries together in old Tupperwares with cracks in their lids, not caring about the scratches on our newly shaven legs until we were back home and had them on show under school skirts rolled up at the waist.

I watch the colours of the Dales streak by through the grubby bus window: russets, greens, the sandy grey of drystone walls. Sheep lift dozy eyes our way as we pass. It's drizzling lightly; I can almost smell it already, the way the rain makes the earth smell bright, as if it's just woken up. The air is fresher here.

Not here on the bus, of course. The air on the bus smells of stale sleep and somebody's chicken tikka sandwich. But as soon as I step out, I know that first breath in will be beautiful.

Hamleigh itself is made up of just three streets: Lower Lane, Middling Lane, and Peewit Street, which really ought to have been called Upper Lane, but there we are, that's quirky village life for you. The houses are mostly squat limestone cottages with higgledy slate roofs, but to the furthest edge of Middling Lane there's a new development – it stands out like a cold sore on the corner of the village, all brash orange brick and black-edged windows. Grandma despises it. Whenever I point out to her that Britain is in desperate need of new affordable housing, she says, 'only because buggers like you keep spending so much on shoebox flats in London', which I have to concede is a pretty sound point, economically speaking. I only wish I was one of the buggers who'd actually got around to doing that instead of choosing to spend tens of thousands on renting the artisan warehouse lifestyle.

I head straight from the bus stop to Grandma's house. I find myself averting my eyes as I walk past the turning on to Mum's street, like when you pass a traffic accident on the motorway, horribly aware of it pulling at the corner of your vision.

My grandmother's house is the most beautiful one in the village: Clearwater Cottage, No 5 Middling Lane. A wibbly old slate roof, wisteria climbing up the front wall, a ruby red door . . . It's a fairy-tale home. That knot of anxiety lodged between my ribs loosens as I walk up the garden path.

I lift the knocker.

'Leena?' comes Grandma's voice.

I frown. I look right, then left, then up.

THE SWITCH | 38

'Grandma!' I shriek.

My grandmother is halfway up the apple tree to the left-hand side of the front door. She's almost as high as the upstairs windows, each foot wedged against a branch, dressed in khaki trousers and a brown top, both of which merge very effectively with the greenery. If it weren't for the shock of white hair, I might not have spotted her.

'What the hell are you doing up that tree?'

'Pruning!' Grandma calls. She waves a large, sharp implement at me. I wince. I am not reassured by this.

'You're very . . . high up!' I say, trying to be tactful. I don't want to say she's too old for this, but all I can think about is that episode of *24 Hours in A&E* where an elderly lady fell off a chair and broke six bones. This tree is considerably higher than a chair.

Grandma begins to shimmy down. Really. *Shimmy.*

'Take it slow! Don't rush on my account!' I call, nails biting into my palms.

'There!' Grandma even hops the last bit of the drop, brushing her hands on her thighs. 'If you want something done well, do it yourself,' she tells me. 'I've been waiting for the tree man to come for months.'

I look her over. She seems unscathed. Actually she looks well, if a little tired – there's some colour in her cheeks, and her brown eyes are bright behind her green-rimmed glasses. I reach forward to pull a leaf out of her hair, and smooth it back into its usual loose, wavy bob. She takes my hand and squeezes it.

'Hello, love,' she says, face melting into a smile. 'Hot chocolate?'

Grandma makes hot chocolate the proper way: on the hob, with cream and real chocolate. It's pure decadence in a mug. Carla used to say that if you have more than one you won't have room for meals for the rest of the day, and it is my absolute favourite thing.

I make myself useful, putting away the dishes from the drainer by the sink as Grandma stirs the chocolate. It's been months since I've been here – I came up last when Grandpa Wade left, at the end of last year – but everything still looks exactly the same. That orange wood of the skirting boards and kitchen units, the faded, patterned rugs, the wonky family photos in frames on the walls.

You can't even tell that Grandpa Wade has gone – or, rather, that he was ever here. I don't think he took anything with him except clothes. Clearwater Cottage has always felt like Grandma's house, not his. Grandpa just used to occupy an armchair in the corner of the living room, listening to talk radio and ignoring everyone. It was such a shock when he left with that ballroom dance teacher – not because I'd thought he loved Grandma, just because I'd never imagined he had it in him to run off with anybody. He's the sort of person who likes to have something to complain about, but never actually *does* anything. I could only conclude that the dance instructor did most of the legwork on the seduction front.

'I'm so glad you're here, love,' Grandma says, looking over her shoulder at me as she stirs the hot chocolate in its special pan.

'I'm sorry. I should have been back sooner.' I fiddle with the magnets on the fridge.

'I don't blame you for staying in London,' Grandma says. 'I'd have done the same at your age, if I could have.'

I glance up at her. Grandma doesn't often talk about the past – she always says she prefers to look forwards than backwards. I do know she'd had a job lined up in London before she met Grandpa, when she was in her twenties. Then they got married, and they settled here, and that was that. That's how she's always put it: *that was that.*

Though it occurs to me now that didn't *have* to be that.

'You could still go to London,' I tell her. 'You could even move there, if you wanted to, now Grandpa's not here to hold you back.'

Grandma pours the hot chocolate into mugs. 'Oh, don't be daft,' she says. 'I can't be jetting off to London, not when your mother needs me.'

I wince. 'She'd cope, Grandma. She's not as fragile as you think she is.'

Grandma gives me a look at that, as if to say, *And you'd know, would you?*

I turn away and spot Grandma's project diary open on the table. This project diary goes everywhere with her – she treats it the way I treat my phone, always horrified if she discovers it's not in her handbag, even if she's just nipping out for some milk from the shop.

'What's on today's to-do list, then?' I ask, then frown. '*Own teeth?*' I gasp. '*Likely to be dull in bed*? What *is* this?'

Grandma snatches up the diary. 'Nothing!'

'Are you blushing?' I don't think I've ever seen my grandmother blush before.

Her hand flies to her cheek. 'Don't be ridiculous,' she says. 'We did away with blushing in the 1960s.'

I laugh and reach to take her hand from her cheek. 'Nope, definite rosy hue,' I inform her. 'Are you going to tell me what's going on? Is this some new project? They're not usually *this* weird.'

She presses her lips together, her peachy lipstick gathering in the folds.

'Oh, God, sorry, Grandma.' I lead her over to sit down at the table. 'Is this something important, and I'm being an idiot?'

'No, no,' Grandma says, very unconvincingly.

I attempt to prise the diary from her hand; after a moment, reluctantly, she lets go.

I skim over the list she's made. It's pretty obvious what it is, now. My heart goes a gooey, bittersweet sort of warm just reading it, because as well as being lovely, as well as being *so* very Grandma, this list is also kind of sad.

Grandma's shoulders are tensed; she's watching me warily, and I kick myself for being so insensitive.

'Well,' I say, 'this won't do at all.' I look back down at the list.

'Basil's the one with the moustache and the Britain First sticker on his bumper, isn't he?'

'Yes,' Grandma says, still looking wary.

'Do you like him?'

'Well, I . . .' Grandma trails off. 'Not really,' she confesses. 'He's a bit of a bigot.'

I reach for a pen and cross Basil off the list.

'Wait!' Grandma says. 'Maybe I could . . . grow to like him . . .'

Her tone makes me wince. She sounds so weary. As if Basil is the best she can hope for. She's not being herself – Eileen Cotton would never settle for a man like Basil. Well, she settled for Grandpa Wade, I suppose, but I always got the impression she'd known that was a mistake and just stuck with him out of a stubborn sort of loyalty – their relationship was more a partnership they'd reconciled themselves to than a marriage. When he left her she seemed to see it not as a betrayal so much as an act of extreme rudeness.

'Rule number one of dating,' I tell Grandma, in the tone of voice I use when Bee is flagging and considering going back to one of the crappy dates she had the week before. 'You cannot change a man. Even if he does have his own teeth. Next: Mr Rogers. Isn't that the vicar's dad?'

'He's a lovely man,' Grandma says rather hopefully. I'm pleased to see her shoulders have loosened up a bit.

I scan her pros and cons. I can't help but let out another little half-laugh, half-gasp when I read her comments on Mr Rogers – then I catch her expression and shake myself. 'Right. Clearly you're looking for something more . . . physical than Mr Rogers is willing to offer.'

'Oh, lord, this is a peculiar conversation to have with your grand-daughter,' Grandma says.

'And once a month isn't nearly often enough. It'll take for ever to get to know him, only seeing him every four weeks.' I cross Mr Rogers off the list. 'Next: oh, I remember Dr Piotr! But you've hit rule number two of dating, Grandma – never go after a man who's emotionally unavailable. If Dr Piotr still loves his ex-wife, you'll only be signing yourself up for heartbreak.'

Grandma rubs her chin. 'Well, a man can . . .'

I hold up one finger. 'I sincerely hope you are not about to say "change".'

'Umm,' says Grandma, watching me cross Piotr off the list.

'And finally . . .' I read on. 'Oh, Grandma, no, no, no. Arnold from next door? Jackson Greenwood's stepdad?'

'Ex stepdad now,' Grandma tells me, with the fiendish little eyebrow twitch she employs when she's in gossip mode.

'The world's grumpiest man?' I continue firmly, not to be sidetracked. 'You deserve *so* much better.'

'I had to be fair and write everybody down,' Grandma explains as I scribble through Arnold's name. 'He's the only other single man in Hamleigh who's over seventy.'

We both stare at the list of crossed-out names. 'Well,' I say, 'it's always good to start with a clean slate.'

Grandma's shoulders are drooping again, so I reach for her hands.

'Grandma, I'm *so glad* you're looking to find someone new,' I say. 'You had a miserable time married to Grandpa and you so deserve to meet somebody lovely. I will absolutely do everything I can to help you.'

'That's sweet of you, but there's not a lot you *can* do. The fact is, I don't know any eligible men,' Grandma says, reaching for the tissue up her sleeve and blowing her nose. 'I thought maybe . . . I could go to Tauntingham and see if there's anybody there . . .'

I have visions of Grandma roaming the lanes of sleepy Tauntingham with her project diary out, making notes as she hunts for elderly gentlemen.

'I'm not sure that's the most effective method,' I say carefully. 'Have you thought about Internet dating?'

She makes a face. 'I wouldn't know where to start.'

I stand up. This is the best I've felt in ages. 'I'll get my laptop,' I say, already heading out of the door.

I do a quick half-hour of research before I start on Grandma's dating profile. Apparently, what makes for a successful profile is honesty, specificity, humour and (more than any of those other things I just said) a good profile picture. But as soon as it's set up, I realise we have a problem.

There is not a single person her age registered to the site in under an hour's drive from here. It's not just that Grandma doesn't know any eligible gentlemen in the area – there aren't any. Bee bemoans the lack of good men in London, but she has no idea how lucky she is. When there are eight million people in your city, there's going to be *someone* single.

I turn slowly in my chair to look at my grandmother.

When I think of Grandma, I always think of her as an absolute force of nature, bending the world to her will. I can't imagine there's a more youthful old lady out there. Her boundless energy has never shown any signs of running out as she enters her late seventies – she really is extraordinary for her age.

But she doesn't look like that Grandma right now.

She's had a truly terrible year. The death of one of her only two granddaughters, supporting my mum through losing her daughter, then Grandpa Wade walking out on her . . . It hits me quite suddenly that I think of my grandma as invincible, but that's so ridiculous – *nobody* could go through what she's been through unscathed. Look at her, sitting here, contemplating dating Basil the bigot. Things are not right at Clearwater Cottage.

Which I'd already have known, if I'd come home once in a while.

I reach for the laptop again. Every time I remember that I can't go to work on Monday I feel wretched, useless, afraid. I need something to *do*, to *help*, to stop me thinking about all the ways I've messed up.

I change the search area on the dating site, and suddenly: hello, four-hundred men between the ages of seventy and eighty-five, looking for love.

'I have an idea,' I tell her. 'Hear me out, OK? There's *hundreds* of eligible men in London.'

Grandma turns her empty mug between her hands. 'I told you, Leena – your mum needs me here at the moment. I can't come down to London.'

'Mum will be fine.'

'Oh, she will, will she?' Grandma says.

'You need a break, Grandma. You *deserve* a break. Come on. Tell me: why was it you wanted to go to London when you were younger?'

'I wanted to change the world,' Grandma says, with a little smile. 'I suppose I thought London was the place where the . . . big things happened. And I wanted an adventure. I wanted to . . .' she waves her arms grandly '. . . to hail down a cab with a dashing stranger and let him take me home. To walk across London Bridge on a mission with the wind in my hair. I suppose I wanted to be somebody important.'

'Grandma! You *are* important! Hamleigh would fall apart without you, for starters. How many times have you saved the village shop, now? Five?'

She smiles. 'I'm not saying I never did anything useful. I made your mother, and she made you and Carla, and that's enough for me.'

I squeeze her hand. 'What was the job? The one you turned down, for Grandpa?'

Grandma looks down at the table. 'It was for a charity. They set up community centres for youngsters in deprived areas. It would have been typing and fetching coffee, I expect. But it felt like the start. I had chosen a flat, too, not far from where you live now, though the area was rather different back then.'

'You were going to live in Shoreditch?' I say, fascinated. 'That's so . . .' I can't imagine what my grandmother would have been like if she'd taken that job. It's such a strange thought.

'Hard to believe?' she asks wryly.

'No! It's so *great*, Grandma. You have to come and stay with me! We can have an adventure in Shoreditch, just like you wanted to.'

'I'm not leaving your mother, not now,' Grandma says firmly. 'And I've got far too much on my plate here to be going away. That's that, Leena.'

There she goes again, *that's that*-ing. I'm feeling a little buzzy, the way I used to feel at work; I haven't felt this rush for ages. I *know* this is the right thing for Grandma – it's exactly what she needs.

I think suddenly of what Bee said, about finding myself, getting myself back. I've been hiding in London, buried in work. I've been avoiding my mother. I've been avoiding it all, really. But I've got two months to sort myself out. And given that I can't even *look* at the house where Carla died . . .

It feels like this might be the place to start.

'Grandma . . . what if we swapped?' I say. 'What if I came up and looked after all your projects, and you had my flat in London, and I stayed here?'

Grandma looks up at me. 'Swapped?'

'Swapped places. You do the London thing! Try dating in the city, have your adventure . . . remind yourself of who you were before Grandpa Wade. And I'll come up here. Switch off for a bit in the countryside, try to – to get my head around everything that's happened, and I'll look after your little projects, and . . . help Mum out if she needs it. I'll do whatever it is you do for her, you know, any errands and stuff.' I feel a bit dizzy, all of a sudden. Is this a good idea? It's quite extreme, even by my standards.

Grandma's eyes turn thoughtful. 'You'd stay here? And be there for Marian when she needs you?'

I can see what she's thinking. She never says as much, but I know she's been desperate to get Mum and me talking again ever since Carla died. As it happens, I think Mum is coping a hell of a lot better than Grandma thinks – she certainly doesn't need to be waited on hand and foot – but if Grandma needs to feel I'll do everything she does for Mum, then . . .

'Yeah, sure, absolutely.' I twist the laptop her way. 'Check it out, Grandma. Four-hundred men just waiting to meet you in London.'

Grandma pops her glasses back on. 'Gosh,' she says, looking at the pictures on the screen. The glasses come off again and her gaze drops to the table. 'But I have other responsibilities here too. There's the Neighbourhood Watch, there's Ant and Dec, there's driving the van to bingo . . . I couldn't ask you to take all of that on.'

I suppress a smile at Grandma's grand list of responsibilities. 'You're not asking. I'm offering,' I tell her.

There's a long silence.

'This seems a bit crackers,' Grandma says eventually.

'I know. It is, a bit. But I think it's genius, too.' I grin. 'I will not take no for an answer, and you know when I say that, I one hundred per cent mean it.'

Grandma looks amused. 'That's true enough.' She breathes out slowly. 'Gosh. Do you think I can handle London?'

'Oh, please. The question, Grandma, is whether London can handle *you*.'

6

Eileen

Leena travelled back to London the next day, packed her bags, and returned to Hamleigh. She can't have stayed there longer than an hour. I couldn't help wondering whether she was afraid that if she did, she'd come to her senses and change her mind.

Because this swap is a mad idea, of course. Barmy.

But it's brilliant, too, and it's the sort of idea *I* would have had, once. Before I got so used to my favourite seat at Neighbourhood Watch meetings and my green armchair in the living room and the comfort of seeing the same people, day in, day out. Before Wade squashed all the barmy, brilliant ideas out of me.

The more Leena talks about strolling through Hyde Park and visiting her favourite coffee shops in Shoreditch, the more excited I get. And to know that Leena is here, in Hamleigh, with her mother – well, I'd go a lot further than London if it meant those two spending some time together at last.

I smooth down a fresh page in my project diary, settling back in my chair. The key to all this will be making sure Leena stays busy while she's here. Her boss might think she needs to slow down for a while, but the last time Leena did anything slowly was in 1995 (she was *very* slow learning to ride a bike) and if she's not got anything to do, there's a danger she'll go to pieces. So I'm leaving her a list of a few of my projects. She can look after them in my absence.

<u>Projects</u>

1) Walk Jackson Greenwood's dog Wednesdays 7 a.m.
2) Drive van to bingo on Easter Monday, 5 p.m. More detail on p. 2.
3) Attend Neighbourhood Watch meetings Fridays 5 p.m. (Write notes, otherwise nobody will remember what you've discussed by next week. Also, take extra biscuits if it's Basil's turn – he always brings out-of-date broken bags of digestives from the pound shop, and they're no good for dunking.)
4) Help plan May Day Festival. (I'm chair of the committee, but best speak to Betsy about joining, she likes to handle that sort of thing.)
5) Spring clean the garden. (Please start with the shed. It's under the ivy somewhere.)

There. That's *plenty* to be getting on with.

I glance at the dining-room clock: it's six o'clock in the morning, and today I'm off to London. No use waiting around thinking about it, Leena says. Best just dive in.

Beneath my excitement there's a thrum of nerves. I've felt plenty of dread, this last year or so, but I haven't felt the thrill of not knowing what's to come for a long, long time.

I swallow, hands jittering in my lap. I hope Marian will understand that some time alone with Leena is the right thing for them both. And if she goes through another of her difficult times, I know Leena will look after her. I have to trust that she will.

'Are you all packed?' Leena says, popping up in the doorway in her pyjamas.

She looked so worn out when she arrived on Saturday: her skin, usually warm and golden, was sallow and greasy, and she'd lost weight. But today the dark smudges under her eyes have lightened, and for once her hair is loose, which makes her look more relaxed. It's such a beautiful long chestnut mane, but she's always scraping it back and covering it in lotions. The frizz Leena complains about catches the light like a halo from here, framing her little face with its button nose and those dark, earnest eyebrows – the only good thing that father of hers gave her.

I know I'm biased, but I think she's quite breathtakingly beautiful.

'Yes, I'm all packed,' I say, and my voice wobbles a little.

Leena crosses the dining room to perch next to me, giving me a one-armed hug. 'Is this my to-do list?' she asks, looking amused as she scans the paper in front of me. 'Grandma, are there . . . how many pages *is* this?'

'It's just extra information,' I explain.

'Is this a labelled diagram of the television remote?'

'Yes. It's complicated.'

'And . . . Grandma, are those all your passwords? Is that your PIN?'

'In case you need my emergency money card. It lives in the dresser. I can write that down too, if you like?'

'No, no, this is more than enough documentation of your personal data, I'd say,' Leena says, tugging her phone out of her pyjama pocket and glancing at the screen. 'Thanks, Grandma.'

'One more thing,' I say. 'I need that.'

'Pardon?' she asks, then follows my pointing finger. 'My phone? You need to borrow it?'

'I want it for these two months. You can have mine. And I'll have that nifty little portable computer of yours, too. You can use my computer. This swap isn't just for my benefit, you know. You need to leave your London life behind you, and that means getting rid of those contraptions you're always glued to.'

She gawps. 'Give you my laptop and phone for *two* months? But . . . I couldn't . . .'

'You can't do it? Can't you cope without them?'

'I *can*,' she says quickly. 'I just don't see . . . I'm all for a break, but I don't want to cut myself off from all humankind, Grandma.'

'Who do you really want to speak to? You can just send them a text message, can't you, and tell them you've got a different telephone number for two months. Go on, we can go through now and choose the people you want to tell.'

'But . . . what about . . . emails? Work . . .'

I raise my eyebrows. She breathes out slowly, cheeks puffing.

'It's a phone, Leena, not a limb,' I say. 'Come on. Hand it over.'

I tug at it. She grips tighter, then, perhaps realising how ridiculous she's being, lets it go. She doesn't take her eyes off it as I fetch my mobile phone out of the drawer of the dresser and turn it on.

'That,' she says, 'looks like something from the Neolithic era.'

'It calls and texts people for you,' I say. 'That's all you need.'

I glance at the clock again as the phone gets itself going. Only three hours until my train. What shall I wear? I wish I'd thought more seriously about the question of whether culottes are 'in' now. I quite like the new pair Betsy let me borrow, but I don't want to look decades out of date.

'Is someone knocking?' Leena asks, looking startled.

We sit in silence for a moment, the two mobile phones on the table between us. There's an insistent tapping sound coming from somewhere, but it's not the front door.

I huff. 'It'll be Arnold. He always knocks on the kitchen window.'

Leena wrinkles up her nose. 'Why?'

'I don't know,' I say testily, getting up. 'There's a gate in the hedge between my garden and his, and he seems to think it gives him the right to trespass whenever he likes.'

'What an arse,' Leena says airily as we head for the kitchen.

'*Shh!*'

'Oh, isn't Arnold going deaf?'

'No, that's Roland, Penelope's husband.'

'Oh. Well. In that case: what an arse,' Leena repeats in a stage whisper, making me snigger.

When we round the corner into the kitchen, Arnold's face looms very large in the window. The glass is clouded with his breath, but I can still see his hawkish nose, straggly flying hair, and bottle-thick glasses. I narrow my eyes.

'Yes, Arnold?' I say, pointedly refusing to open the window. Every conversation is a battle of wills when it comes to Arnold. You have to stand your ground on every point, even the really insignificant ones you don't actually mind about.

'Those cats!' he yells.

'I can hear you perfectly well at normal volume, thank you,' I say, as icily as I can. 'You are well aware this house isn't double-glazed.' He's always on at me about that too.

'Those cats of yours ate all my pansies!'

'That's ridiculous,' I tell him. 'Cats don't eat pansies.'

'Yours do!' Arnold says furiously. 'Would you just open the window or invite me in, so we can have a proper conversation like civilised adults?'

'Of course,' I say, with a polite smile. 'Do come around to the front door and knock, and we'll see if I'm in. Like civilised adults.'

In the corner of my eye I can see Leena staring at me with her mouth a little open.

'I can see you're in,' Arnold says, eyebrows drawing together in the thunderous frown that means I'm really getting to him. 'Just let me in the side door, would you?'

My polite smile is still in place. 'It's jammed.'

'I saw you walk in and out of there just this morning to put the rubbish out!'

I raise my eyebrows. 'Are you *watching* me, now, Arnold?'

He blusters. 'No,' he says, 'of course not. I just . . . it's slippy out when it's been raining. You really ought to get a grab rail put next to that door.'

I bristle. Grab rails are for old ladies who can't keep steady on their feet. When I reach that stage, I hope I shall gracefully accede to the horrors of stair lifts and standing aids, but given that I am currently able to swim twenty lengths in the Daredale swimming pool and can even manage a jog if I'm late for the bus, I do not like the suggestion that I'm so doddery I need a grab rail.

This, of course, is precisely why Arnold has suggested it. The old sod.

'Well,' Leena says brightly, 'this has been a constructive conversation thus far, but we've got a lot to do this morning, so perhaps we could push on. Did you actually *see* the cats eating the pansies, Arnold?'

Arnold considers lying. He's a dreadful liar – he can't manage to come up with a fib without a lengthy pause beforehand.

'No,' he admits eventually. 'But I know it was them. They're always at it, eating my flowers just when they're in bloom.'

Leena nods sagely. 'Well, Arnold, as soon as you have some evidence of that, do give us a call. I'll be house-sitting for Eileen for the next two months, so it'll be me you'll be dealing with.'

Arnold blinks a few times. I try not to smile. Leena is using her work voice, and she sounds wonderfully intimidating.

'OK?' Leena says.

'Just keep an eye on those cats,' is Arnold's parting shot, and then he's striding off to the gate between our gardens again.

'You need to replace that gate with a large fence,' Leena says, rolling her eyes at Arnold's back. 'You were *hilarious*, Grandma – I've never seen you being bitchy before.'

I open my mouth to protest but find myself smiling instead.

'You're going to do just fine in London,' Leena says, giving me a squeeze. 'Now. Let's find you the *perfect* outfit for your debut as a London lady, shall we?'

I stand in the hallway of my daughter's house and hold her too tightly. I can see the living room over her shoulder; Carla's bed is gone, but the chairs still arc around the space where it lay. The room has never really gone back to its old shape.

'I'll be absolutely fine, don't you worry,' Marian tells me firmly as we pull apart. 'This is a lovely idea. You so deserve a break, Mum.'

But she's tearing up again. It's been so long since I've seen those brown eyes clear; there are dark blots underneath them now, like little bruises. She was always so beautiful, Marian – boys chasing her down the street, girls copying her hairstyle, parents looking at me and Wade and wondering where we got her from. She has the same golden-toned skin as Leena, and her wavy hair is streaked through with honey, the envy of hairdressers everywhere. But there are new lines on her face, tugging down at the corners of her mouth, and through the tight yoga leggings she's wearing I can see how thin she's become. I don't want to leave her for two months. Why am I even considering this?

'No, don't you even think about it,' Marian says, shaking a finger at me. 'I'm *fine*. I'll be fine. And Leena will be here!' She gives me a wry smile, and there's a hint of the old Marian there, mischievous and impulsive. 'I have to say, I didn't think even you could persuade Leena to come up and stay within a one-mile radius of her awful mother for two whole months, Mum.'

'She does *not* think you're an awful mother. And it was her idea!'

'Oh, was it now?'

'It was!' I protest. 'But I do think it'll be good for you both.'

Marian smiles, more faintly this time. 'It's wonderful, Mum. I'm sure by the time you're back, she and I will have sorted ourselves out again, and everything will be better.'

Marian – ever the optimist, even in the depths of grief. I squeeze her arms and kiss her on the cheek. This is the right thing to do. We're stuck, the Cotton family. If we're going to get anywhere, we need to give things a shake.

To my surprise, most of the members of the Neighbourhood Watch are waiting on the platform when we arrive at Daredale station – Dr Piotr drove them down in the school minivan, bless him. It's a long journey for them all to take from Hamleigh, so I'm touched. When a rather teary Betsy presses her home phone number into my hands – 'in case you haven't got it written down anywhere' – I find myself wondering why on earth I'm leaving Hamleigh-in-Harksdale at all. Then I look at Dr Piotr, and at Basil with his Union Jack pin on his tweed lapel, and at Leena, standing alone, thin and drawn. My resolve returns.

This is the right thing for my family. And besides, I'm turning eighty this year. If I'm going to have an adventure, it has to be now.

Leena helps me on to the train and hefts my luggage on to the rack, extracting promises from various fellow travellers that they'll help me get it down when we reach London. We hug goodbye, and she slips out of the train doors just in time.

I wave to my friends from the window, watching Yorkshire slide away, and as we streak through the fields towards London I feel a sudden flush of life, a quickening, a new kind of hope, like a greyhound just let out of the gate.

7

Leena

My mum's house is on Lower Lane, semi-detached, with a dove-grey door and a brass knocker. I wait on the doorstep for a moment, then fish out the key Grandma gave me – I left mine in London. Definitely a Freudian slip.

It feels weird letting myself into Mum's house, but it feels weirder to knock on the door. A year and a half ago I would have barged in without blinking.

I stand on the threshold, trying to keep my breathing steady. The hall is horrible in its sameness: the faint smell of cleaning products, the old wooden side table, the plush carpet that makes you feel like you're walking across a sofa. Mum's always liked houses – she's an estate agent – but it occurs to me now that this place actually feels a little out of date: she never changed the previous owners' decor, and the warm yellow-cream on the walls is nothing like the bold wallpaper of the house where I grew up. This house was bought for convenience – it was bought for Carla, not for Mum.

It's awful, being back here. I feel that same lurch in the gut that you get when you spot an ex-boyfriend at a party, a sense of your two lives colliding horribly in the present.

And there it is at the end of the hall: the living-room door. I swallow. I can't look at it. Instead I focus on the huge framed photograph of Carla on the table at the bottom of the stairs. Mum put it there when Carla died, and I hate it – it makes coming to Mum's house feel like arriving at the wake. Carla looks nothing like herself: she's dressed up to go to her prom, her hair pinned back with two straightened stripes falling forwards à la Keira Knightley in *Love Actually*. She'd removed her nose piercing, and the photo was taken before she had the eyebrow ones done; she looks weird without them. She always said her face never looked right without a few studs here and there. *It'd be like you going out without five coats of hairspray*, she'd say teasingly, giving my ponytail a tug.

Mum appears at the top of the stairs. She's dressed in a loose jumper and jeans, and as she comes down the steps there's a slightly frantic air about her, as though I've just caught her in the middle of preparing a meal with many courses or rushing out of the door to meet someone important.

'Leena, hi,' she says, stopping short at the bottom of the stairs. She's so much thinner than she used to be, all elbows and knees. I swallow, glancing away.

'Hey, Mum.'

I don't move from the doormat. She approaches me cautiously, as if I might bolt. I can see two versions of my mother at once, like layered tracing paper. There's this one, frenetic, fragile, on the edge of breaking; the woman who helped my sister die and wouldn't listen when I told her we had a choice, options, drug trials and private treatments. And the other, the mother who raised me, a whirlwind of honey-streaked hair and big ideas. Impulsive and bright and unstoppable, and always, always in my corner.

It alarms me how angry I feel just looking at her. I hate this feeling, how it blooms in my gut like ink in water, and it hits me now what a stupid idea this was, forcing myself to come back here for eight whole weeks. I want to stop feeling angry – I want to forgive her – but then I see her and I remember, and the emotions just *come*.

Fitz was right: this was the last thing I needed after last week's panic attack.

'I don't really know how we do this, to be honest,' Mum says. She lifts her mouth in an apologetic smile. 'But I'm very glad you're here. It's a start.'

'Yeah. I just wanted to come and say, you know, like Grandma said, I'll help out any way you need. With errands, or whatever.'

Mum gives me a slightly odd look at that. 'Did Grandma say I needed help with errands?'

Actually, Grandma has never been especially clear on what helping Mum involves, though she always makes it sound very important.

'Just whatever you need,' I say, shifting uncomfortably. That tight, anxious knot is back between my ribs again.

Mum tilts her head. 'Won't you come in?'

I don't know yet. I thought I'd be able to, but now I'm here I'm not sure I can. I reach for a distraction, something to say, and my gaze settles on Mum's favourite picture on the wall, an Indonesian temple with a supple yogi doing a tree pose in the foreground. She's changed the frame, I think – interesting that she's updated that and nothing else. She used to point at that picture when she'd had a bad day at work, or when Carla and me were doing her head in, and she'd say, *Right, girls: for ten breaths, I'm going there.* She'd close her eyes and imagine it, and when she opened them again, she'd say, *Here I am. All better.*

My gaze shifts to the table's surface. It's absolutely covered in – little rocks? Crystals?

'What's with all the stones?' I point.

Mum's instantly distracted. 'Oh, my crystals! They've been won-derful. I bought them online. This one is snowflake obsidian – it helps with grief, it cleanses you – and that one there, that's aqua-marine, for courage, and . . .'

'Mum, you . . .' I swallow the sentence. I shouldn't tell her it's a load of crap, but God, it's frustrating watching her go through these phases. At first she's like this, all bubbly, sure it'll fix everything. Then, when obsidian – surprise surprise – does not magic away the pain of having lost one's daughter, she falls apart again. Grandma thinks there's no harm in it, but I think it's cruel, getting her hopes up over and over. There's no elixir for this. All you can do is keep moving forward even when it hurts like hell.

'I got you this, actually,' she says, reaching for a rock towards the back of the heap. 'Moonstone. It enhances intuition and brings buried emotions to the surface. It's for new beginnings.'

'I'm not sure anyone wants my emotions brought to the surface at the moment.' It's meant to sound like a joke, but doesn't come out quite right.

'It feels like it will break you, when they come,' Mum says. 'But it won't. All my episodes, they've helped, in their way. I truly believe that.'

I look at her, startled. 'What episodes?'

Mum frowns slightly, eyes flitting to mine. 'Sorry,' she says, stepping towards me. 'I assumed your grandmother would've mentioned something to you. Never mind. Take the moonstone, Leena, will you?'

'I don't want a moonstone. What episodes?'

'Here,' she says, stretching the moonstone out further. 'Take it.'

'I don't want it. What do I even do with it?'

'Put it by your bed.'

'I'm not taking it.'

'Take it, would you? Stop being so closed-minded!'

She shoves it into my hands, and I pull back; it falls on to the doormat with a small, underwhelming *thud*. We stand there for a while, staring down at the ridiculous little stone between our feet.

Mum clears her throat, then bends to scoop it up again. 'Let's start over,' she says more gently. 'Come in. Have a cuppa.'

She gestures towards the living room and I baulk.

'No, I should go. Grandma's left me this whole to-do list, and I . . . I should get on with stuff.'

There is a long silence.

'Well. Can I at least have a hug goodbye?' Mum asks eventually.

I hesitate for a moment, then open my arms. She feels fragile, her shoulder blades too sharp. The hug isn't quite right – it's not a real hug, it's an arrangement of limbs, a formality.

Outside, I find myself breathing hard, as if I was holding my breath in there. I walk back to Grandma's house fast, faster, then I run, past her front door and out along the A-road. At last I feel that inky anger subsiding and the misery, the pity, that eases too.

It's only when I get back to the house that I realise my mother has slipped the moonstone in the pocket of my jacket. You've got to give it to her – when she's made her mind up about something, when she's decided that's the right way, she doesn't give up. I get that from her.

I suppose that's part of the problem.

Normally, when I'm feeling like this, I'd do some work. Top choice would be something data-heavy: numbers are just better for clearing your head than words. It's the crispness of them, like fine pencil versus charcoal.

In the absence of any work to do, I have taken to Grandma's list as a solution. I am trying gardening.

So far, I'm not a fan.

It's so . . . endless. I filled two bags with ivy and then I realised it was all around the other side of Grandma's shed too, and up the trees, and running its nasty dark green tendrils underneath the shed, and now I've discovered that there is actually more ivy than shed, so if I remove it, what will be left?

I rub my shoulder, looking out at the hills behind the old stone wall at the end of the garden; the clouds are a very ominous shade of grey. What an excellent excuse to stop confronting the enormity of this task.

I head back inside. It's strange being at Clearwater Cottage without Grandma, making tea in her patterned china mugs, moving around like it's my place. But Ethan will be coming up to stay at the weekends, so that'll stop it ever getting too lonely. I actually think this trip is going to be the perfect thing for us after such a tough year – weekends together, cosying by the fire, talking about sweet nothings, and never mentioning Selmount . . .

Gah, Selmount. Banned word. All thoughts of Selmount are to be left at the door of Clearwater Cottage; they cannot pass the threshold. Like vampires. And Arnold, according to Grandma's notes.

There's a knock – definitely the front door this time, not the kitchen window. I glance down at myself. My favourite *Buffy* sweatshirt is covered in soil and bits of . . . whatever this is, dead leafy foliage stuff. I'm not really in a state for visitors. I consider pretending not to be in, but this is Hamleigh – whoever it is has probably had a call from Arnold confirming I'm out in the garden. I shake the worst of the debris out of my hair and head to the door.

The person on the other side is the sort of elderly lady who turns out to be an alien in a *Doctor Who* episode. Just *way too* perfectly old-lady-ish. Permed grey–white hair, neat little neck scarf, glasses on a chain, handbag clutched in front of her in both hands. I remember her being part of the gaggle of old people who'd come to see Grandma off at Daredale station, and I'm sure I saw her around at Grandma's and Grandpa's when I was little. Betsy, I think?

'Hello, dear,' she says. 'How are you getting on without Eileen?'

I blink. 'Well, umm,' I say, 'it's been one day, so . . . I've been fine. Thanks.'

'Managing all her projects, are you?'

'Yes, yes, I think I'm on top of everything. If Grandma can do it, I'm sure I can cope.'

Betsy looks at me very seriously. 'There's nobody quite like Eileen.'

'No, of course not. I just mean . . . Oh!'

Somehow, without me really moving aside, Betsy is in the hallway and heading quite determinedly for the living room. I watch her go for a moment, puzzled, before I remember my manners.

'Would you like a cup of tea?' I say, shutting the door behind us.

'Black, two sugars!' says Betsy, settling herself down in an armchair.

I shake my head as I go into the kitchen. Imagine one of my neighbours inviting herself into my flat in London like that. I might genuinely call the police.

Once Betsy and I are both sitting down with our teas, silence descends. She looks expectantly at me, but I haven't a clue what I'm meant to talk about. It's easy talking to Grandma, she's *Grandma*, but actually I don't really know what chitchat with elderly people entails otherwise. The only other old person I know is Grandpa Wade, and he's an arse, so I mostly just ignored him.

I try to imagine this is a new client meeting and reach around for the small-talk skills I usually manage to conjure up in times of dire necessity, but Betsy gets there first.

'How *are* you then, Leena, dear?' she asks, taking a sip of her tea.

'Oh, I'm very well, thanks,' I say.

'No, *really*,' she asks, and she pins me there with those watery blue eyes, all earnest and intent.

I shift in my seat. 'I *really* am fine.'

'It's been . . . gosh, over a year, now, hasn't it, since you lost Carla?'

I hate that phrase, *lost Carla*. Like we didn't take enough care of her and let her get away. We don't have any good words for talking about death – they're all too small.

'Yes. A year and two months.'

'What a dear girl she was.'

I stare down at my tea. I doubt Betsy really liked Carla much – my sister was too bold and brash to be the sort of young woman Betsy would approve of. I grit my teeth, surprised to feel the heat around my eyes that means tears are coming.

'And your mother . . . She's found it very hard, hasn't she?'

How did this conversation get so personal so quickly? I drink a few more gulps of tea – it's too hot and scalds my tongue.

'Everyone processes grief differently.' I find this line very useful for conversations like this. It usually shuts things down.

'Yes, but she did rather . . . collapse in on herself, didn't she? Is she *coping*, that's what I wonder.'

I stare at Betsy. This is personal to the point of rudeness, surely?

'Can't we do something?' Betsy offers, setting her tea down. 'Won't you let us help?'

'What would you be able to do?' It comes out too sharply, an emphasis on *you* that I didn't mean to place there, and I see Betsy recoil, offended. 'I mean . . . I don't see . . .'

'I quite understand,' Betsy says stiffly. 'I won't be any use, I'm sure.'

'No, I mean . . .'

I trail off, and her phone rings, ear-piercing in the silence. Betsy takes for ever to answer it, fumbling with the leather case.

'Hello?'

A tinny voice rattles through the phone, indistinct but definitely very loud.

'There's ham and cheese in the fridge, if you want a sarnie,' Betsy says.

More tinny rattling.

'Well, I just put the mayonnaise on one side, and . . . Yes. I'm sure you – all right, Cliff, love, I'll come home. Yes. Absolutely. I'll be there as soon as I can.'

I wince. Has he actually just summoned her home to make him a sandwich? That feels so ridiculous – if Ethan tried to do that, I'd . . .

I'd probably laugh, actually, because it would be so absurd I'd know he would have to be joking. Presumably it's different for Betsy's generation, though – it wouldn't be strange for a woman to make all her husband's meals fifty years ago, I suppose.

Betsy puts her phone back into her handbag, then tries to get up too quickly and doesn't quite have the momentum for it. She rocks back into the chair, helpless, like one of those dolls with a weight in the bottom.

'Do stay,' I say, conscious I've said all the wrong things. 'I'm sure your husband can wait, if you want to have a—'

'My husband *cannot* wait,' Betsy says sharply. 'I have to be off.'

I move to help her up.

'No, no, I'm quite all right,' she says. Once standing, she fixes me with another very serious look. 'I hope you understand what you're taking on here in Hamleigh, Leena.'

I can't help it – my lip twitches. Betsy's frown deepens.

'I'm sure it all looks very easy for someone like you, but Eileen does an awful lot around here, and we need you to step up. You'll be taking on her responsibilities for the May Day Planning Committee, I gather?'

'Yes, absolutely,' I say, managing to look serious this time.

'Good. Well. I'll drop around your task list in due course. Goodbye, Leena,' she says, and then, with what I would genuinely describe as a flounce, she heads for the door.

8

Eileen

It's a miracle that I'm still here, quite honestly. So far, since arriving in London, I have brushed with death five times.

1) I was nearly crushed by what I have now learned to be a 'pedibus': a strange vehicle propelled by a lot of whooping young men cycling and drinking beer at the same time. I had to really dash across the road to avoid them. I'm a little concerned about how my knees will feel tomorrow, but at least they're still attached to the rest of me.

2) I stood on the left on an escalator (not the done thing, I've learned.)

3) I ate a 'stir fry' cooked by Fitz (dreadful cook. Awful. I'll try and teach him a thing or two while I'm here.)

4) I changed trains at Monument station (the map *says* it's the same station as Bank, but I'm not convinced. The walk from one train to the next seemed to go on for yonks. My legs were already jiggered after my run-in with the pedibus; I had to have a sit-down next to a busker playing a ukulele. He was very understanding. He gave me his amp to sit on.)

5) I met the cat that lives next door, a feral tabby with half an ear missing. It launched itself down the stairs at me, hissing, and then immediately conked itself out on the banister. Small mercies.

I'm loath to admit it, but I'm exhausted, and more than a little shaken. London is all so fast, and everybody is so miserable. One man on the underground swore at me for getting on too slowly; when I stopped to get a map out in Oxford Street a lady bashed right into me and didn't even say sorry. Then once I was back at Leena's building, I ran into the neighbours from downstairs, a young, arty couple wearing socks and sandals, and when I tried to make conversation, I saw the woman roll her eyes at her husband.

I'm very out of place here. I've only seen three other people who looked over the age of seventy all day, and one of them turned out to be a street artist wearing an Einstein costume.

I must say it's crossed my mind that it would be a little easier if I weren't on my own – if I had Wade with me, say – but Wade would never have come to Oxford Street. I don't miss him, but I sometimes miss the idea of a husband, someone whose arm I could lean on for a tricky step down off the bus, who might take hold of my umbrella while I paid for my cup of tea.

I must stay positive, though. My adventure is only just starting, and it was bound to feel difficult at first. I just need to keep busy. Tomorrow night, Leena's friend Bee is coming to the flat to help me with my 'online dating'. Leena says Bee is a real expert. Who knows, perhaps by Thursday I'll have myself a date.

The milk in Leena's fridge has begun to coagulate; I pour it down the sink with a sigh, and get my handbag for another trip out. This time, without the distraction of rude neighbours in socks and sandals, I take a proper look as I get to the bottom of the stairs. There's a large open area between the stairway and the door to the building; it's got three sofas at strange angles, one stained with something suspiciously dark, the others with something suspiciously light. The carpet is worn, but there are two lovely big windows sending sunlight streaming in. It was designed as a communal area, I expect – what a shame nobody's done anything with it.

When I get back from the shops, the feral tabby hops off the dark-stained sofa and pads over to rub its head against my legs. It's not quite walking straight. I hope it didn't give itself some sort of brain injury with that banister incident. I spotted the cat's owner this morning, heading out of the building with her trolley bag. She's a hunched old lady, going bald. I hesitate, watching the cat meander its way to the stairs.

If it was Ant or Dec, I'd want someone to tell me. Things may be done differently around here, but a good neighbour is a good neighbour, wherever you are.

I head up the stairs and knock on the cat-owner's door, setting my shopping bag down between my feet.

'Yes?' comes a voice.

'Hello!' I say. 'I'm Leena's grandmother.'

'Who?'

'Leena's grandmother.'

'Whose grandmother?'

'Leena. Your next-door neighbour,' I say patiently. Perhaps the lady is losing her marbles a little. It's started happening to Penelope – terribly sad, though on the plus side she seems to have forgotten that she can't stand Roland. It's been something of a second honeymoon for the two of them.

'Which one's that?' the woman asks. Her voice grates as if her throat needs clearing. 'The lesbian or the natty dresser or the other one?'

I blink. Martha's definitely the lesbian – she told me all about her girlfriend after I rather put my foot in it asking who the baby's father was. And, as much as I love my granddaughter, if she's not wearing a suit, she seems to be wearing something with an iron-on picture of a television star on the front. Not exactly a natty dresser. Which leaves . . .

'The other one?' I hazard.

'The woman with all that mousey scraped-back hair? Short, runs everywhere, always frowning?'

'Leena's hair is lovely,' I say sharply, and then bite my tongue. 'But . . . yes. That'd be the one.'

'Oh. Well. Thank you, but I'm not interested,' says the lady, and I hear her shuffling away from the door.

'In what?' I ask, startled.

'Whatever it is you want,' the lady says.

I frown. 'I don't want anything.' I'm beginning to understand why Arnold gets so cross when I don't let him in the house. This is not a comfortable way to have a conversation. 'I came to talk to you about your cat.'

'Oh.' She sounds warier than ever, but I hear her shuffle back to the door, and then it clicks open by an inch or two. Two large brown eyes blink at me through the gap.

'I'm afraid she had a run-in with the banister,' I say apologetically. 'That's to say, well, she ran into it.'

The eyes narrow.

'Kick her, did you?' the woman asks.

'What? No! I'd never kick a cat!' I say, aghast. 'I have two of my own, you know. Two black cats called Ant and Dec.'

The eyes fly open, and the door inches wider. 'I love black cats,' the lady says.

I smile. 'Well then, I'm sure we'll be the best of friends,' I say, sticking my hand through the gap in the door to shake hers. 'I'm Eileen.'

She takes such a long time to take my outstretched hand that

I almost drop it, but then, at last, her fingers close around mine. 'Letitia,' she says. 'Would you . . . I don't suppose . . .' She clears her throat. 'I don't suppose you want to come in? Just to tell me about the cat,' she adds hurriedly.

'I'd love to,' I say, and step inside.

Letitia's home is just as peculiar-looking as Letitia, but not at all as you'd expect. She has a rather . . . homeless look about her, but inside her flat is an altogether different story. The place is *full* of antiques and curiosities. Old coins, arranged in spiralling patterns on the tops of oak tables; feathers in glittering gold and peacock blue, hanging from pegs along a washing line; delicate china bowls stacked carefully inside cabinets with spindly legs and wrought-iron handles. It's quite extraordinary. A cross between an antique shop and a very cramped museum – and, perhaps, a child's bedroom.

I nurse the third cup of tea I've had since walking through Letitia's door and beam at her across the collection of pots and vases occupying most of her dining table. I'm feeling better than I have all day. What a *fascinating* woman to have found living just next door! It's a real wonder Leena never mentioned her – though it seems the two of them didn't cross paths very often. I find that hard to believe, given that there's only a very thin wall dividing their lives, but from what I can gather, Letitia doesn't speak to any of the neighbours. Or rather, none of the neighbours speak to Letitia.

'Nobody?' I ask. 'Not a single person came to introduce themselves when they moved into the building?'

Letitia shakes her head, sending her long earrings rattling. They drag at the lobes of her ears; it makes her look rather mystical. 'Nobody talks to me,' she says, without particular rancour. 'I think you're the first person I've said a word to since . . .' she pauses, 'last Friday, when I got my Iceland delivery.'

'Oh, love. What about that communal area downstairs? Have you tried setting yourself up down there? Then people will say hello as they come by.'

'I tried, once,' Letitia says. 'But someone complained. They said it was bad for the building's image. So I just sit up here, now, where I can't bother anyone.'

'That's awful! Don't you get lonely?' I ask, then catch myself. 'I'm sorry, that's ever so personal of me.'

'I do get lonely,' Letitia says after a moment. 'But I've got Solstice. The cat. Who always walks a bit funny, by the way,' she adds. We did *start* by talking about her cat, but then got talking about other things, and now three hours have passed.

'Well. I'm very sorry our Leena didn't ever pop by.'

Letitia shrugs her shoulders. I notice the stains on her tunic dress and wince a little.

'She's hardly in, from what I can gather, and when she is, she's with that man of hers. The one with the shiny hair. I don't like him. I think he's . . .' Letitia waves a hand, sending a dreamcatcher spinning above her head, which in turn sends a purple and silver wind chime tinkling. 'I think he's *wet*.'

Ooh, I *do* like Letitia.

She looks into my cup. We're drinking loose leaf tea; there's a collection of black tea leaves in the bottom of my cup. 'Would you like me to read them for you?' she asks.

'You read tea leaves?'

'I was a fortune teller,' Letitia says. 'I used to sit in Trafalgar Square and read palms, once.'

Letitia might be the most interesting woman I've ever met. And to think of her stuck in here, day in day out, with not a soul coming to speak to her! How many more fascinating people are pocketed away in these little flats around the city, I wonder?

'How exciting! Please, read away,' I say, pushing the teacup towards her.

She waves it back to me. 'Lift it with your left hand and swirl, three times at least,' she says.

I do as I'm told, watching the leaves shift in the last mouthful of tea at the bottom of the cup. 'Like that?'

'Yes, that's right.' She reaches for the teacup and then carefully tips the remaining liquid into the saucer, leaving just the leaves in the cup. She turns it back and forth very slowly, breathing deeply, absorbed, and I realise I'm holding my breath. I'm not sure I quite believe in reading the future in somebody's teacup, but then, what do I know? I wonder fleetingly what Wade would say – he'd be *very* scathing about this – and then push the thought away. Bother what that old sod would think.

'Hmm,' says Letitia.

'Yes?' I say hopefully.

Letitia presses her lips together, *hmms* again, and then glances up at me rather apologetically.

'Are you not . . . getting anything?' I say, trying to peer into the cup.

'Oh, I'm getting something,' Letitia says, rubbing her chin. 'It's quite . . . clear.'

She pushes the cup back towards me, turning it so the handle points towards her.

I look down into the tea leaves. Letitia's shoulders start shaking before I see what she sees; by the time I start laughing, she's whooping, really going for it, tears in the corners of her eyes, stained tunic bouncing with each gulp of laughter.

The tea leaves look like . . . genitals. Male genitals. It couldn't be more distinct if I'd tried to arrange it that way on purpose.

'And what does *that* mean, eh?' I say, when I've finally got my breath back.

'I think it means good things are coming your way,' Letitia says, wiping her eyes. 'That, or it's telling me the tea leaves game is a load of cock and balls.'

I put my hand to my mouth at her language, then burst out laughing again. This is the best I've felt in . . . well. I can't remember how long.

'Will you come around again?' Letitia says.

I reach across the table for her hand, dodging between vases. 'As often as you'll have me.' I nod towards the teacup. 'I expect you'll want to stick around and find out what comes of that little prediction, won't you?'

'There's nothing little about it,' Letitia says, and sets us both off again.

9

Leena

It's six twenty-two, and I'm awake. This seems to be my new pattern. I nip to the loo, then attempt to go back to sleep, but I left the bedroom door ajar and it takes Ant the cat approximately twenty seconds to find his way in and locate my face for sitting on.

I shove him off with a growl and get up. Oh, that was Dec, not Ant. Naming her indistinguishable cats Ant and Dec is just the sort of long-term, mischievous joke my grandmother enjoys, though I suspect, if questioned, she will feign innocence and insist it was Grandpa Wade's idea.

Downstairs, after feeding Ant/Dec – who chain-meows all the way down the stairs, barely pausing for breath between plaintive yowls – I blink sleepily at the array of teas behind the kettle, all stored in carefully labelled old biscuit tins. God, I miss Fitz's coffee machine. There's a particular itch that tea and even instant coffee just cannot scratch.

It's Wednesday today, which means I'll be walking Jackson Greenwood's dog; I was up late last night baking homemade dog treats out of whatever I could find in Grandma's fridge. I did a bit of research on dog-walking, and apparently treats are a crucial part of the process. By the time I realised that, the shops – or rather, the shop singular – were closed, so I had to hustle a bit and figure something out. Now there are some squishy cubes of mince, egg, and crushed-up Weetabix sitting in a sandwich bag on the sideboard. They look disgusting.

While the kettle boils, I stare at the dog treats and take a brief moment to wonder what the hell I'm doing with my life right now, and then – because those thoughts rarely lead to anything fruitful, and it's a bit late to change this plan – I make a cup of tea.

I wander into the hall with my tea and spot a letter on the door-mat. It's addressed to *Leena Cotton* in large, wobbly writing. Inside is a handwritten list, headed:

May Day Planning Committee responsibilities, to be passed to Leena Cotton while Eileen Cotton, longstanding co-chairperson of the Committee, is on leave.

On leave! I nearly choke on my tea.

1) *Glitter*
2) *Lanterns*
3) *Trees cutting back – arrange*
4) *Food stalls*
5) ~~*Get sponsor*~~
6) *Garlands*
7) *Portaloos*
8) *Signs*
9) *Parking*
10) *Parade costumes*

My interest is officially piqued. This actually sounds like quite a fun project – I've never managed an event before, and by the looks of this list, Grandma handles lots of the logistics for this one: parking, signs, food stalls. And . . . glitter. Whatever *that* involves. I'll have to ask Betsy.

That buzz alights in my belly, the flicker of excitement that used to spark whenever a new project was coming my way at work, and I think suddenly of my beautiful, colour-coordinated business plan for *B&L Boutique Consulting*. The files are on Dropbox; I could get them up on Grandma's computer later. The buzz brightens, and I finish my tea with one gulp, scanning the list again.

Get sponsor is crossed through. I remember Grandma mentioning that she was hoping to get sponsorship for the May Day festival, so that profits from tickets could be given to the cancer charity that gave us so much support when Carla was sick. Had she given up? I frown, grab a pen from the hall table, and asterisk it on Betsy's list.

One more cup of tea, and I'm out the door. I'm quite curious to see Jackson Greenwood again. When I visited my grandparents as a kid, I saw him a fair bit, as he lived with Arnold – he was this quiet, sullen boy, always loping around the garden with their old dog at his heel. Jackson was the sort of child who everyone regarded as a 'problem', but who hadn't actually ever done anything wrong, specifically. He was just maungy.

Apparently Jackson is now a teacher at the local primary school. It just . . . doesn't compute. In my head, primary school teachers are smiley and bouncy and say things like 'What a good try!', whereas Jackson just used to glower, mostly.

These days he lives in one of the newbuild blocks on the corner of Hamleigh; as I approach the development, I'm struck by how weirdly two-dimensional it seems against the shadowy backdrop of the Dales, like it's a computer-generated image of what a block of flats might look like when it's done. The gardens are grey and uniform in the light from the streetlamps, all stubby lawn and gravel, but Jackson's front garden is a bustling tangle of vegetation. He's turned it into a vegetable patch. God knows what the next-door neighbours think – their gardens are much more in keeping with the block, with terracotta pots of rosemary and little tame vines trailing up trellises by their doors.

My knock on the door is met by a loud, excited barking, which stops very abruptly. I make a face. I suspect somebody just got told off.

When Jackson opens the door I don't have time to look at him, because a large bundle of black fur – lead flying between its legs – has hit me in the gut and sent me sprawling.

'*Oof!*' I've whacked my tailbone, and my wrist took the brunt of the fall, but the main thing I'm dealing with right now is the dog very enthusiastically licking my face. 'Hello, you – would you – Christ . . .'

It's sitting on top of me and has got my necklace between its teeth. Oh, and now it's started playing tug of war with it, brilliant, that's –

'Bollocks, shite, sorry.' A large hand reaches down and hauls the dog up by the collar. 'Hank. Sit.'

Hank scrabbles off me and lands in a sitting position. Unfortunately, he takes my necklace with him; it hangs between his teeth, pendant swinging on the broken chain. I follow Hank's adoring gaze upwards towards his owner.

It's strange, looking at Jackson. He's definitely the kid I knew, but it's as though he used to be crumpled up tight and now someone's smoothed him out – the tense jaw's eased, the hunched shoulders have loosened, and he's opened up into a broad-shouldered, dozy-eyed giant of a man with a mop of messy brown hair. There's what looks like coffee down the front of his T-shirt, and a very large hole in the left knee of his jeans. On the arm that's now holding Hank's lead, there's a white strip where his watch ought to be – his fore-arms are slightly sunburned, a real achievement in the English springtime.

At a push I'd say his expression is somewhere between bewilder-ment and bashfulness, but he's got one of those unreadable faces that either means you're deep and mysterious or don't have much to say, so I'm not completely sure.

'You're not Eileen Cotton,' he says. His Yorkshire accent is stronger than it was when he was younger – or perhaps I've been away too long.

'Actually, I kind of am. I'm Leena. Remember me?'

He blinks. After a few moments his eyes widen. 'Leena Cotton?'

'Yep!'

'Huh.' After a few very long seconds Jackson shifts his gaze to the horizon and clears his throat. 'Umm,' he says. 'You got . . . different. As in, you look different.'

'So do you!' I say. 'You're so much more . . .' I flush. Where am I going with this sentence? The first word that's popped into my head is *manly*, which is not a thing I'm going to say out loud. 'I hear you're a primary school teacher now?' I say quickly.

'Aye, that's right.' He scrubs a hand through his hair. It's half standing on end now.

'Well!' I say, looking down at Hank, who has dropped my necklace and is now attempting the presumably quite frustrating task of trying to pick it up again without opposable thumbs. 'I guess this is the dog!'

I'm exclaiming too much. Why am I exclaiming so much?

'Aye,' Jackson says, clearing his throat again. 'This is Hank.'

I wait. 'Great!' I say eventually. 'Well. Shall I walk him, then?'

Jackson pauses, one hand still on his head. 'Eh?'

'The dog. Shall I walk him?'

Jackson looks down at Hank. Hank gazes back at him, tail now methodically swiping my necklace back and forth on the doorstep.

'Where's Eileen?' Jackson asks after another long, bewildered pause.

'Oh, she didn't tell you? She's gone to London for two months. I'm housesitting for her and looking after all her projects – the little things she does around the village, you know.'

'You've got big wellies to fill, there,' Jackson says, scratching the back of his neck. It's a gesture another guy might use as an excuse to show off his biceps, but it seems genuinely unselfconscious. There's a shambolic sort of sexiness to Jackson, actually, helped by a pair of very blue eyes and that classic rugby-player nose, crooked to one side from having been broken.

'I'm sure I'll manage!' I say.

'You ever walked a dog before?'

'No, but don't worry, I am very well prepared.' No need to tell him that I've extensively researched dog-walking, the Labrador breed, and the exact route of the walk Grandma instructed me to take.

'He's only eight months,' Jackson says, scrubbing at his hair again. 'He's a bit of a handful, still. I really only ask Eileen to walk him on Wednesdays because she was so good with him, and it gives me a chance to go in early, get some lesson planning done before the kids get in . . .'

I reach to take back my necklace; Hank lets out a little yip and immediately tries to catch my hand in his mouth. I yelp despite myself, pulling my hand back, and then swear. That's exactly what you're *not* meant to do, I *knew* that. I should have reached forward with the back of my hand out first.

'Hank! That isn't polite. Sit.'

Hank sits, the picture of shame and dejection, head hung low. I'm not convinced there's any real remorse going on there. Those hang-dog eyes are still watching the necklace.

I clear my throat. 'So I just bring him back in an hour?'

'Thanks. If you're sure. I'll be at the school. Here,' Jackson says, handing me a key. 'Just pop him in the conservatory and lock up after.'

I stare down at the key in my hand. I know we're not exactly strangers, but I've not had a conversation with Jackson in about ten years, and I'm a little surprised that he's willing to give me perman-ent access to his home. I don't have long to think about it, though, because soon Hank is contemplating the possibility that the key might be a treat and is jumping up at me to investigate.

Jackson pulls Hank back into a sit. 'Little bugger. I've never met a dog that's such a devil to train,' he says ruefully, shaking his head, but rubbing Hank behind the ears all the same.

Oh, good. A devil dog.

'You sure you're up to this?' Jackson asks, perhaps catching my expression. He's looking doubtful.

After the near-biting incident I *am* slightly less excited about walking this dog, but if Jackson thinks I can't do it, I'm obviously going to have to do it, so that's that, really.

'We'll be just fine, won't we, Hank?'

Hank jumps up at me ecstatically. I squeal and lose my footing. I'm starting to think Google has not *entirely* prepared me for this.

'Off we go, then!' I say, as confidently as I can manage. 'Bye!'

'See you soon,' Jackson calls as we shoot off down the path. 'If you have any problems just . . .'

I think Jackson is still talking, but I don't hear anything after this point because Hank is *very* keen to get going. Christ, I hardly need to use any momentum for this walk, Hank's dragging me along – oh, feck, he's in the road, he's in the – all right, back on the – what's that he's eating? Where's he got that from?

The journey through the village to the open fields is the longest ten minutes of my life. We also pass *literally everybody* in Hamleigh-in-Harksdale – it seems they have all chosen right this very moment to be outside their houses, watching me get towed down the pavement by an extremely excited Labrador.

An old man tries to overtake me on his mobility scooter for the whole length of Middling Lane. He's mostly obscured by a large waterproof cape to keep off the drizzle; through the plastic, he calls, 'You ought to keep Hank to heel!' at me.

'Yes!' I call. 'Thank you!'

'That's what Eileen does!' the old man yells, now alongside.

'That's good to know!' I say brightly, as Hank attempts to dislocate my shoulder. 'Heel, Hank,' I try, in a spritely, talking-to-a-dog-or-baby voice. Hank doesn't even glance around at me.

'I'm Roland!' calls the man on the scooter. 'You must be Leena.'

'Yes, that's right. Heel, Hank! Heel!'

Hank stops abruptly, smelling something interesting, and I promptly fall over him. He licks my face while I'm down. Meanwhile Roland takes this opportunity to complete his overtake triumphantly, which I find incredibly annoying, because even though I hadn't consented to this being a race, I clearly just lost.

When we're finally through the village and out of sight of prying eyes, I drag Hank to a stop and lean against a tree. Bloody hell, this is more like route-marching than walking. How on *earth* did my grandmother manage this beast?

I look around the field – I remember this spot. It looks different in the grey weather, but Carla and I used to picnic here as kids; she got stuck up this tree, once, and burst into noisy tears, which didn't stop even as I talked her down one step at a time.

Hank brings me back to the present with a yank of the lead. He's straining so desperately he's managed to lift his front paws off the ground. I'm pretty sure the Internet said not to let the dog strain at the lead – I'm meant to encourage him back to me, aren't I?

I fish out one of my homemade treats and call his name; he shoots over, gobbles up the treat, then he's straight back to the business of lead-straining. This happens three more times. The homemade treats have turned to mush in the sandwich bag; I can feel the residue of mincey egginess under my fingernails.

Defeated, I strike out again and powerwalk around the perimeter of the field. Every so often I try out an optimistic 'heel' or haul Hank back to my side, but I am largely, if we're honest, getting taken for a walk by this dog.

Ironically, given Jackson's 'big wellies to fill' comment, I am actually wearing Grandma's wellies right now – I don't have a pair of my own, and me and Grandma have the same size feet. The wellies have been rubbing my heels ever since I stepped out of Clearwater Cottage, and now there's an enormous stone in the toe of one, too. I make an ineffectual attempt at getting Hank to stop, and then bend down to remove the offending boot.

I am definitely holding the lead. Of *course* I am. You wouldn't loosen your hold on the lead with a dog like Hank. Except . . . somehow, in the confusion of hopping on one leg and my welly falling over, and trying not to step my socked foot in the mud, I seem to let go of it.

Hank's gone like a bullet. He's running full pelt, back and front legs almost crossing in the middle, bolting with single-minded focus for the fields beyond.

'Fuck! Fuck!' I'm already sprinting, but I've only got one welly on, and running with one welly is very tricky – a bit like doing a three-legged race on your own – and it only takes a few paces for me to stumble and fall again. Hank is streaking away from me. I scrabble to my feet, panicked and breathless, oh God, oh God, he's out of sight now – he's – he's – where *is* he?

I dash back for the welly, yank it on, and run. I have never run harder in my whole entire life. After a few minutes of entirely random sprinting, my crisis-control impulse kicks in and I realise I'd be better off running in at least a *slightly* methodical pattern, so I work my way in a zigzag across the fields, gasping for breath. At some point I start to cry, which does not make it easier to run at speed, and eventually, when almost an hour has passed, I collapse underneath a tree and sob.

I've lost Jackson's dog. Filling in for my grandma was supposed to be easy, and restful, and something I *could not suck at*. But this is awful. God knows what could happen to Hank out there. What if he reaches a main road? What if – what if something eats him? Does anything in the Yorkshire Dales eat puppies? Oh, God, why the hell am I crying so much?

I get up again after a few moments, because sitting still is even worse than running. I yell his name over and over, but it's so windy I can barely even hear myself. One week ago, I was standing in a boardroom delivering a sixteen-point plan for ensuring stakeholder buy-in when facilitating a corporate change initiative. Now, I am weeping in a field and screaming the word *Hank* over and over into the wind with my feet rubbed raw and my hair – no doubt an absolute fecking bird's nest by now – hitting me repeatedly in the face. I can't help thinking that I am coping with this extraordinarily badly. I'm normally good in an emergency, aren't I? I'm sure Rebecca said that in my last appraisal?

I cling to this thought. I breathe as steadily as I can. There's nothing else for it: I have to go back to Hamleigh. I don't have Jackson's number (*huge* oversight – what was I thinking?), and he needs to know what's happened.

I feel sick. He's going to hate me. Obviously. *I* hate me right now. Oh, poor Hank, out there in the fields – he probably hasn't a clue what to do with himself now he's realised he's lost me. I'm *really* sobbing – it's quite hard to breathe. I need to get a grip on myself. Come on. Come *on*, what's the *matter* with me?

I thought the walk through Hamleigh was bad on the way here, but this is a hundred times worse. Silent eyes watch me from windows and doorways. A child points at me across the street and yells, 'It's Stig of the Dump, Mam!' Roland whirs by on his mobility scooter again, then double-takes when he comes level with me.

'Where's Hank?' he calls.

'I lost him,' I choke.

He gasps. 'Good God!'

I grit my teeth and keep walking.

'We must send out a search party!' Roland says. 'We must call a village committee meeting at once! I'll speak to Betsy.'

Oh, God, not Betsy.

'I need to speak to Jackson,' I say, wiping my face with my sleeve. 'Please. Let me talk to him before you speak to Betsy.'

But Roland is busy performing a very slow three-point turn and doesn't seem to hear me.

'Let me speak to Jackson first!' I yell.

'Don't you fret, Leena, we'll find Hank!' Roland calls over his shoulder, then he buzzes off again.

I swear and trudge on. I'm trying to run through exactly what to say to Jackson, but it turns out there is absolutely no good way to tell somebody you have lost their dog, and running the conversation over and over is making me feel more and more nauseous. By the time I get to his front door I am in the exact state of nervous tension I enter just before a big presentation, which, based on recent form, presumably means I'm about to have a panic attack.

I ring the doorbell, then belatedly remember the key in my pocket. Oh, God, Jackson's probably already left for work – am I going to have to go to the village school to tell him I lost his dog? This is not a conversation I want to have in front of a classroom full of small children.

But, to my surprise, Jackson opens the door.

I have an overpowering sense of déjà vu. Scrabble of paws, falling backwards, dog licking face, owner looming over us –

'*Hank!*' I shriek, burying my face in his fur and holding him as tightly as I can, given he's moving like a bucking bronco. 'Hank! Oh, my God, I thought . . .'

I become aware of Jackson's eyes on me. I look up.

He looks very big. He was big before, but now he's really . . . *owning it.* He doesn't look like an affable giant now, more like a man who could end a bar brawl with one low, careful word.

'I'm so, so sorry, Jackson,' I say, as Hank clambers all over me, paws smearing new layers of mud on my filthy jeans. 'Please believe me. I didn't let him off on purpose, he just got away from me. I'm sorry. I thought I was prepared, but . . . I'm so sorry. Are you late for school now?'

'I called in when the vicar phoned to say she'd seen Hank trotting down Peewit Street. The head's covering my class.'

I bury my face in Hank's fur.

'Are you all right?' Jackson asks.

'Am I all right?' I say, voice muffled.

'You seem . . . a bit . . . err . . .'

'Of a fucking state?'

Jackson's eyes widen fractionally. 'Not what I was going to say.'

I look up; his expression has softened, and he leans against the doorframe.

'I'm fine,' I say, wiping my cheeks. 'I really do feel terrible – I should have been more careful.'

'Look, no harm done,' Jackson says. 'Are you sure you're OK?'

Hank begins a very thorough survey of my wellies, sniffing wildly, and intermittently whacking me with his tail.

'You don't have to be nice,' I say, dodging the tail. 'You can be angry with me. I deserve it.'

Jackson looks puzzled. 'I was angry, but then . . . You said sorry, didn't you?'

'Well yeah, but . . .'

Jackson watches as I push myself up and make a vague attempt to brush the dirt off my jeans.

'You're forgiven, if that's what you're after,' he says. 'Hank's a little bugger anyway, shouldn't have let him loose on you.'

'I'll make it up to you,' I say, trying to pull myself together.

'You don't have to.'

'No,' I say, with determination. 'I do. Just name a job and I'll do it.

Cleaning classrooms at the school? Or do you need any help with admin? I'm really good at admin.'

'Are you looking for some sort of . . . detention?' he asks, tilting his head, bemused.

'I really messed up,' I say, frustrated now. 'I'm just trying to fix it.'

'It's fixed.' Jackson pauses. 'But if you really want a job to do, one of the classrooms does need a lick of paint. I could do with a hand on that.'

'Yes, absolutely,' I say. 'Just name a time and I'm there.'

'OK. I'll let you know.' He ducks down to crouch beside Hank, scratching his ears, then glances up at me. 'You're all right, Leena. It's fine. He's all under control again, see?'

Hank might be back under control, but I don't feel like *I* am. What was the matter with me out there in the fields, crying like that, screaming into the wind, running in circles? Bee's right: things aren't how they should be. This just isn't me.

10

Eileen

When Bee waltzes into the flat, I find myself rather tongue-tied. She's simply the most glamorous person I've ever seen. Her face is breathtaking, though – or perhaps because – it's asymmetrical, one eye higher than the other, one corner of her mouth curving a little more. Her skin is a beautiful creamy brown and her hair is extra-ordinarily straight and shiny, like black water sluicing over a dam. For a moment I try to imagine what life must be like when you're that young and beautiful. You could do anything, I think.

Half an hour with Bee and I am astonished to discover that this is apparently not the case at all.

'Can't find a man in this godforsaken city,' Bee says, refilling our wine glasses. 'They're all shit – excuse my language. Leena keeps telling me that there are good men out there, that you have to kiss a few frogs, but I've been smooching amphibians for almost a year now and I am *losing. The. Will.*' This last part is emphasised by several long swigs of her drink. 'Sorry – I don't want to dishearten you. Maybe the over-seventies is a better market.'

'I doubt that,' I say, heart sinking. This is daft. I'm embarrassed even to be discussing my love life with someone like Bee; if she can't find a man, how on earth am I meant to do it? I couldn't even keep my own husband.

Bee catches my expression and puts down her glass. 'Oh, don't listen to me. I'm just worn out and sick of crappy dates. But you! You have a whole *world* of fun ahead of you. Let's take a look at your dating profile, shall we?'

'Oh, no, don't you bother yourself with that,' I say weakly, remembering all the embarrassing things Leena wrote on there. *Loves the outdoors! Young at heart! Looking for love!*

Bee ignores my protests and flips open her laptop. 'Leena gave me your login,' she says, tapping away at the keys. 'Ooh, there's already a few gents messaging you!'

'Are there?' I lean forward, nudging my glasses up my nose. 'Gosh, does that – oh my lord!'

Bee snaps the laptop shut. 'Ooh,' she says, widening her eyes. 'Well. That's a landmark moment for you right there. Your first dick pic.'

'My first *what*?'

She makes a face. 'Wow, this is worse than telling my daughter where babies come from. Umm.'

I start laughing. 'It's quite all right,' I tell her. 'I'm seventy-nine. I may seem like an innocent old lady to you but that means I've had fifty extra years to see the horrors the world has to offer, and whatever that was, it's got nothing on my ex-husband's warty behind.'

Bee descends into giggles. I don't have time to reflect on the fact that's the first time I've said *ex*-husband out loud, because Bee's opened the laptop up again, and there's a very large image on the screen.

I tilt my head. 'Gosh,' I say.

'Looking pretty spritely for a man of eighty,' Bee comments, tilting her head the opposite way from mine.

'And sending this photo is meant to do what?'

'Excellent question,' Bee says. 'I believe it's meant to make you want to have sex with this man.'

'Really?' I ask, fascinated. 'Does that ever work?'

'It's a great mystery. You'd think not, but then, why do they keep doing it? Even rats can learn that ineffective mating techniques should be abandoned, right?'

'Maybe it's like flashers in the park,' I say, squinting at the screen. 'It's not about whether *you* like it – they just like showing their todgers.'

Bee bursts out laughing again. 'Todgers!' she repeats, wiping her eyes. 'Ah, Leena was right, you are a gem. Now. Shall we block this particular gentleman from communicating with you further?'

'Yes, please,' I say, thinking of Letitia's tea leaves yesterday. 'That's enough todgers for now, I'd say.'

'How about this guy?' Bee asks.

I look rather warily at the screen, but this time it's a smiling face staring back at me. It's a very handsome gentleman, actually, with silver hair swept back from a heavy, important brow, and excellent teeth. The photo looks like it might be professional.

'Is he real?' I say. You hear all about these people on the Internet who turn out to be strange ladies in Texas.

'Good question, especially with a headshot like this.' She taps away on the keyboard for a while. 'OK, I've searched by image and the only other place this picture is used is here. Same name, the bios match up . . . He's an actor, I guess!' Bee shows me a website for a theatre; the picture appears beside a description of Tod Malone, apparently playing the role of Sir Toby Belch in *Twelfth Night* at the St John's Theatre. 'Hmm, he sounds fun. Shall we message him back?'

'What's he said?' I ask, peering over Bee's shoulder.

'*Hi there, Eileen! It sounds like you're in London on an exciting adventure – I'm fascinated to hear how that came about . . .*' Bee reads.

'May I?'

Bee pushes the laptop my way; I start typing.

'*My granddaughter wanted a break in the countryside, and I wanted some excitement in the city,*' I write. '*So we swapped lives . . .*'

'Ooh, I *like* it,' Bee says approvingly. 'That dot dot dot! Very mysterious.'

I smile. 'Why, thank you.'

Bee clicks to send the message. 'Now we wait,' she says, reaching for the wine again.

'Why don't we look at your dating profile in the meantime?'

'Mine? Oh, God, no, you don't want to see that.'

'I've shown you mine!' I point out, taking a sip of my drink. I've not drunk wine for a very long time, but it seems to be a feature of life in Leena's flat. There's a stack of bottles underneath the television, and always at least one white wine in the fridge.

'I use an app, actually, not a site like this one,' Bee says, nodding at the laptop. 'So it's on my phone.'

'I can cope with looking on a phone,' I say patiently.

Bee makes an apologetic face. 'Yeah, sorry.' She chews her bottom lip, then, after a moment, pulls her phone towards her across the counter and types in a series of numbers. 'Here.' She scrolls through the pictures of herself. There's a short description underneath: *Busy working mum. Short on time, low on patience, high on caffeine.*

Oh, goodness. If I thought Bee was intimidatingly glamorous in person, it was nothing on how she looks here. All her pictures look like they're from a glossy magazine – 'Oh, yeah, I did a bit of modelling work last year, just on the side,' she tells me airily – and her description of herself could not be much more uninviting.

She shows me how to swipe left and right, and the page where she can message all the different men.

'There are so many!' I look closer. 'Why haven't you answered them? That one's very handsome.'

'Ah, that guy was one of those super successful CEO types,' she says dismissively. 'Not my scene.'

I frown. 'Why not?'

'I don't like dating guys who earn more than me,' she says, lifting one shoulder. 'It's one of my rules.'

'What are the other rules?' I ask, mulling this over.

She ticks them off on her fingers. 'Must be sporty, can't work in consulting or finance, got to be a good dancer, must be exceedingly hot, can't have a weird surname, must like cats, can't be posh or have rich parents, mustn't have boring man hobbies like cars and playing darts, has to be feminist, and I mean *properly* feminist not just when it suits, must be open-minded about Jaime – my kid . . .'

'Oh! Tell me about your daughter,' I say, distracted despite myself.

'Jaime,' Bee says, flicking around on her phone so fast I lose track. 'She's with her dad tonight.' She's scrolling through photos now, and eventually settles on a picture of a young girl with dark-brown hair cropped short, beaming at the camera through a pair of wide-rimmed glasses. 'Here she is,' Bee says proudly.

'What a lovely girl!' My heart squeezes, not so much at the child – though she's ever so sweet – but at the expression on Bee's face. The woman has *melted*. She loves this child more than anything, you can see it in seconds.

'She's going to be a world tennis champion,' Bee says. 'She's already top in her age category at the club.'

'Gosh.'

'She also likes dinosaurs and reading about brains,' Bee adds. 'And she's vegan. Which is really annoying.'

'Oh, yes,' I say sympathetically, 'my friend Kathleen has that.'

'Has what, sorry?'

'Veganism.'

Bee giggles. She has such a charming laugh – hearing that, and having seen her face when she looked at Jaime, I suddenly feel I know her an awful lot better, and like her much better too. That's the trouble with dating on the Internet, I suppose. There's no way for anybody to hear your laugh or see the way your eyes go dreamy when you talk about something you love.

I watch Bee as she flicks through more pictures of her daughter, and think to myself: I may not know anything about online dating, but I think I can do a better job of finding Bee a man than Bee can.

I reach for my new project diary. I picked one up at Smith's yesterday – Leena has mine, in Hamleigh.

Communal area – spruce up is top of my list. I spoke to Martha about it this morning; she got quite excited and starting waving paint-colour charts at me on her way out of the door. I know things are different around here, but I can't help thinking this building could do with *some* sense of community.

Below this note, I carefully write, *Find Bee a man.*

'Ooh, your silver-haired thespian has replied!' Bee says. She swivels the laptop towards me.

Todoffstage says: Hi, Eileen. Now I'm more intrigued than ever. What an exciting idea! How is your granddaughter finding life in the country? And how are you getting on in London? Is it a shock to the system?

I smile and start typing.

EileenCotton79 says: My granddaughter has gone very quiet on me, which either means it's going very well, or she's burned the house down! And I'm a little overwhelmed by London. It's hard to know where to start!

'Oh, Mrs Cotton,' Bee says. 'Now *that* is brilliant.'

Todoffstage says: Well, I've lived in London for sixty-five years . . . so if you'd like a little bit of advice from an old hand, I could show you a few places worth visiting? Starting with a coffee shop, perhaps?

I reach for the keyboard, but Bee waves my hand away. 'Make him stew!' she says.

I roll my eyes. 'That sort of nonsense is for young people,' I tell her.

EileenCotton79 says: That would be lovely. How about Friday?

11

Leena

Friday afternoon, in the quiet of the house, with Ant and Dec twin-ing their way between my feet, I sit down at Grandma's computer and log in to my Dropbox. It's all there. *B&L Boutique Consulting. Pricing strategy. Market research. Operations and logistics.* I settle in, not touching anything yet, just reading it all through again. In the end I get so deep I lose track of time. It's the Neighbourhood Watch meeting at five – I have to bomb it down on the bike I dug out of Grandma's ivy-shed, and I nearly send myself flying when turning into Lower Lane.

It's only when I'm walking through the door to the village hall that I realise I'm not entirely sure what the Neighbourhood Watch actually *is*. Are we ... fighting crime? Is this a crime-fighting society?

I take one look around at the motley crowd gathered in the centre of the hall and decide that either these guys are in the best super-hero disguises ever or this cannot possibly be a crime-fighting society. There's Roland, the over eager search-party organiser; Betsy, wearing a bright pink scarf, matching lipstick, and a pair of culottes; and Dr Piotr, much portlier than I remember from my childhood, but still clearly the man who stitched up my knee when I was nine and once extricated a dried pea from Carla's ear.

Then there's a tiny bird of a woman who looks as if she's built of matchsticks, a squinty moustached man I recognise as Basil the bigot, and one very harassed-looking young woman with what I think is baby vomit on her sleeve.

'Oh, bother,' this woman says, following my gaze to her arm. 'I really meant to clean that.'

'Leena,' I say, holding my hand out for her to shake.

'Kathleen,' she tells me. Her hair is streaked with highlights that need re-doing, and there's a flaking smear of toothpaste on her chin – she has exhausted mum written all over her. I can't help wondering why on earth she's bothered to come to this meeting instead of, I don't know, having a nap?

'I'm Penelope,' says the little bird lady. She holds out her hand the way royalty might – top of the hand first, as though I'm meant to kiss it. Unsure what to do, I give it a shake.

Betsy stops short when she sees me. Her smile comes too late to be genuine. 'Hello, Leena,' she says. 'I wasn't sure you'd come.'

'Of course!' I say. 'I brought the sign, for the door.'

'Room for one more?' says a voice from the doorway.

'Oh, what a treat!' Betsy trills. 'Jackson, I didn't realise you'd be able to make it today!'

I look up and feel myself flush. Jackson lopes in wearing a rugby shirt and a worn-out old cap. I was such a mess when he last saw me; every time I remember myself sweaty and snotty on his doorstep it makes me want to crawl right back to London. I try to meet his eye, but he's preoccupied: all the elderly ladies have gravitated Jackson's way, and he's now wearing a woman on each arm like Hugh Hefner, only with all the relevant people's ages swapped over. Basil is urging a cup of tea on him. Nobody has offered me one yet, I notice with discomfort. That's not a good sign, is it?

'Well, now that Leena's finally here, shall we begin?' Betsy asks. I resist the urge to point out that I wasn't the last to arrive, Jackson was – but everyone is too busy passing him biscuits to notice that. 'Seats, please!'

It's hard not to wince as the elderly in the room shuffle themselves in front of their chairs and then – starting slowly at first, then picking up speed – they bend at the knees as best they can until they land somewhere on their seats with a thump.

'Jackson usually sits there,' Roland says, just as I bend to sit down.

'Ah.' I look around, still in a squat. 'Jackson, do you mind if . . .'

Jackson waves a large, affable hand. 'Course, sit yourself down.'

'No,' Roland says sternly, just as my bum touches the seat. 'No, no, that's *Jackson's* seat.'

Jackson laughs. 'Roland, it's fine.'

'But you like that seat best!' Roland protests.

'Leena can have it.'

'What a thoughtful young man he is,' Penelope says to Betsy.

'Mmm. And he's been *so* kind about the incident with the dog, hasn't he?' Betsy replies, folding her hands in her lap.

I grit my teeth and straighten up. 'Here's an idea. How about we *all* swap seats, see how it changes our perspective?' I suggest. 'You'll be amazed how much difference it makes.'

They all stare at me blankly, except Jackson, who looks to me like a man trying very hard not to laugh.

'This is where I sit,' Basil declares firmly. 'I don't want to change my perspective, thank you very much. I like it right here.'

'Oh, but–'

'Do you know how hard it was to get into this chair, young lady?' says Roland.

'But I can help you get–'

'Besides, this one's nearest the gents,' says Basil.

'Yes,' Penelope says, 'and when Basil needs to spend a penny, he *needs to spend a penny*, dear, there's nothing else for it.'

'Right. OK,' I say.

They look pleased. They have defeated my attempt at a basic change-management exercise with their talk of bladder control.

'You'd better have this seat, Jackson,' I say, and make my way to a different chair. Best to pick one's battles; this does not feel like the right hill to die on.

'I really don't mind,' Jackson says mildly.

'No, no,' I say, more sharply than I should. 'You enjoy your favourite chair. I'm perfectly fine here.'

Once we've got going, I spend most of the meeting wondering what the meeting is, which is not an uncommon feeling – I'd say eighty per cent of the client meetings I attend are spent this way – but does make it hard to engage with the discussion.

The main thing that's confusing me is the total lack of any mention of crime. So far we've talked about: bacon sandwiches (Roland has discovered that Mabel at No 5 Peewit Street makes excellent ones, so he's back to boycotting Julie's, which I gather is a café in Knargill), squirrels (Basil is very anti), and whether potatoes are fattening (I think it's the bacon sandwiches they ought to be worrying about, really). Then everyone spends twenty minutes complaining about Firs Blandon, a local village that has apparently caused havoc by moving a farmer's fence two feet to the left to reflect what they believe to be the boundary between parishes. I lose the plot a bit at this stage and just dedicate myself to eating biscuits.

I glance down at the agenda. Only one more point to discuss before we reach 'any crime?', which will, I am assuming, finally cover some actual crime.

'Oh, yes, this was Eileen's latest little project, wasn't it?' Betsy says. 'So you'll be taking it on, will you, Leena?'

'Pardon?' I ask, midway through what must be my one hundredth biscuit.

'Helping the elderly and isolated of Knargill by providing

transport,' Betsy reads. 'I'm not sure how she plans to manage that, but . . .' Betsy blinks expectantly at me.

I consider the point. This seems fairly straightforward.

'How many of you have cars?' I ask. 'Aside from Jackson and Piotr and Kathleen, obviously, who can't spare the time – but the rest of you are retired, aren't you? Can you fit in, oh, a drive every other day?'

Everyone looks very alarmed – except for Jackson, who is looking more amused than ever.

'Where do you think would be a good place to take them for the odd trip out? Leeds is too far,' I say, looking back at Betsy. 'but maybe Daredale?'

There is a lengthy silence. Eventually Dr Piotr takes pity on me.

'Ah, Leena, most of the team here are . . . Though many of them do *have* cars' – this said with a slight air of resignation – 'they're not all encouraged to drive as far as Daredale.'

'Not to say that we *can't*,' Betsy says. 'I still hold a licence, you know.'

'And Dr Piotr can't stop me driving until I've gone officially doo-lally,' Penelope says, with relish.

'Ah. Right,' I say. 'Well, I've been meaning to sort myself a car for a while, anyway, what with Grandma's one being . . .'

'Out of action?' Betsy supplies.

'Damaged beyond repair?' Basil says at the same time.

'Do any of you have a car that you would like to lend me while I'm here?'

There is silence.

'Penelope!' I say brightly. She strikes me as the best option. The men aren't going to budge, and I'm certainly not going to get any support from Betsy. 'Could I borrow your car every now and then?'

'Oh, but I . . . Well, I still . . .' Penelope trails off, then, without much good grace: 'Oh, I suppose so.'

'Brilliant, thanks, Penelope!' I say. I wait until she's looked away before giving Dr Piotr a quick wink. He gives me a thumbs-up in return.

So now I've got Dr Piotr on side, at least. And a car.

'That's that, then!' says Betsy, with a clap. 'Moving on . . . May Day! I know this isn't an official committee meeting, but as the committee is all present, and there are some urgent matters that can't wait until next meeting, perhaps we could cover one or two things here?'

Everybody nods. I'm pretty sure the May Day Committee is comprised of exactly the same people as the Neighbourhood Watch Committee, so I *could* point out that two separate meetings are not entirely necessary. Better not, though, on reflection.

'Theme! I assume we're all happy with Jackson's suggestion? *Tropical*?'

'Tropical?' I say, before I can stop myself.

Betsy swivels in her chair to glare at me. 'Yes, Leena. Tropical. It's perfect for a sunny spring festival. Don't you think?'

'Well, I . . .'

I glance around the circle, then look at Jackson, who is raising his eyebrows a little, as if to say, *Oh, do go on.*

'I'm just not sure it plays to our strengths. People will be attracted to this as a quaint village fair that they can bring their kids to. "Tropical" feels a bit . . . night out in Clapham.'

I am faced with a circle of blank stares.

'Do suggest an alternative theme if you would like, Leena,' Betsy says frostily.

I glance at Jackson again. He's leaning back in his chair, arms folded, and there's something so very cocky about that posture that my plan to forbear and win this lot around before I make any changes goes right out the window.

'How about "Medieval"?' I say, thinking of *Game of Thrones*, which

I've been re-bingeing since I got to Hamleigh. Ethan always laughed at me for collecting my favourite shows on DVD, but who's laughing now that I'm in the land of no superfast broadband? 'We could serve mead, and have storytelling "bards" for kids to listen to, and the May King and Queen could wear beautiful gowns with flowing sleeves and flower wreaths, like King Arthur and Queen Guinevere.' I'm not actually sure that King Arthur was medieval, but this isn't the time for pedantry. 'And we could have falconry and jousting, and the music could be all harps and lutes. I'm imagining flower garlands draped between lamp posts, stalls overflowing with fresh fruit and sugary treats, bonfires, hog roasts . . .'

'Hmm. Well. Shall we have a vote, then?' Betsy says. 'Leena's plan to drag us all back to the Middle Ages, or Jackson's idea that we'd all by and large settled on last week?'

I let out a disbelieving laugh. 'That's kind of a leading question, Betsy.'

'Hands up for Leena's idea,' Betsy says, very deliberately.

Everyone looks at each other. Nobody raises their hand.

'And hands up for Jackson's idea,' says Betsy.

All hands go up.

'Well! Good try, Leena,' Betsy says with a smile.

'Give me a couple of weeks,' I say. 'I'll do a proper thought shower, come up with concrete ideas, pull together something to show you all. Let's vote on it properly at the next official May Day meeting. After all, *can* May Day business be settled at a Neighbourhood Watch meeting?'

Betsy's smile wavers.

'That is a good point,' says Roland. 'It wouldn't be proper.'

'Wouldn't be proper,' I echo. 'Absolutely, Roland.'

'All right, then. Two weeks,' Betsy says.

I glance at Jackson. This isn't about point-scoring, obviously, but I totally just scored one, and I'd quite like him to have noticed. He looks back at me, still sitting back in his chair with his legs apart like a manspreader on the tube, looking just as amused and unfazed as he has all session.

'That's all, everybody,' Betsy says. 'And Leena, remember you're bringing biscuits next time.'

'Absolutely. No problem.'

'And that's your chair,' Roland says, nodding helpfully at me. 'Remember that, too.'

'Thanks, Roland. I will.'

'Oh, and Leena?' says Betsy. 'I think you forgot to put Eileen's bins out yesterday.'

I breathe out slowly through my nose.

They're only trying to help. Probably.

'Thank you, Betsy,' I say. 'Good to know.'

There's a general scraping of chairs and shuffling of feet as everyone stands and makes their way to the door. Beside me, Kathleen wakes with a start.

'Shit.' She scrabbles to check her watch. 'Where've we got to? Have we done the war on squirrels?' She clocks my grumpy expression. 'God,' she says, 'did the squirrels win?'

12

Eileen

This just won't work. I'm going to call Leena and tell her it was daft of us to think we could swap lives like this, and then I'm going home. We can have hot chocolate and laugh about it, and we'll go back to where – and who – we ought to be.

I am absolutely settled on this plan until Fitz walks into the living room.

'Holy guacamole,' he says, stopping stock still. 'Eileen! You look stunning!'

'I'm not going,' I tell him firmly, bending to begin unlacing my shoes. 'It's silly.'

'Whoa, whoa, whoa!' Fitz swipes my slippers up from beneath the coffee table before I can put them on. 'You are not wasting that killer blow-dry on an afternoon in,' he says, waving a warning finger at my hair. 'You look like a million dollars, Mrs Cotton, and you *have* to meet this Tod guy!'

I told Fitz about my impending date last night. Or rather, this morning – I was getting up to start the day and he was coming in from an evening out on the town. He seemed rather the worse for wear – it *was* half past five in the morning – so I'd assumed he wouldn't remember the conversation, but unfortunately his memory is better than I'd hoped.

I shift uncomfortably on the sofa, my best pleated skirt digging into my hips. My back twinges. 'I'm too old for this,' I tell him. 'I can't be doing with these . . .' I wave a hand at my stomach.

Fitz smiles slyly. 'Butterflies?' he says.

'Oh, nonsense,' I tell him, but I can't come up with a better alternative.

He shifts up next to me on the sofa. 'Now, I don't know you very well, Eileen, but I know Leena, and the impression I get is that many of Leena's qualities come from you. And Leena *hates* failing at things.'

'This isn't failing!' I protest.

'You're right,' Fitz says, 'you've got to *try* in order to fail. And you're not even trying.'

I bristle. 'I know what you're doing,' I tell him.

'Is it working?'

'Of course it bloody well is. Now hand me those shoes, please.'

I nearly lose my nerve again on the journey to the café. I even open my mouth to tell the cab driver to turn back. But as we crawl through the traffic, a woman cycles by with dark curls beneath her helmet, and I think of Carla. She'd love seeing her old grandma going on a date. And I bet she'd tell me it'd be a crying shame to let a handsome West End actor slip through my fingers.

I worry about finding Tod in the café, but in the end he's not difficult to spot. He stands out the way wealthy people stand out everywhere: his clothes hang a little too perfectly from his frame, and his skin has a glow to it, as though he's wearing make-up.

Oh, he *is* wearing make-up. Well I never – I suppose he must have just come from the theatre, but still . . . What *would* Wade say?

'Eileen?' he asks me. I realise I am peering at his face, and feel myself blushing. That's the second time I've blushed this week. I must get a grip on myself.

'Yes,' I say, stretching my hand out to shake his.

He gets up to pull my chair out for me. He moves very nimbly for a man of his age, and I catch a waft of cologne as he comes past me. It smells of woodsmoke and oranges, and I'd say it's probably every bit as expensive as his dark wool coat.

'You are just as beautiful as your picture,' he says, settling back in the chair across from me with a smile. His teeth are startlingly white.

'Now, I know that's not true, because my granddaughter chose that picture, and it's at least ten years out of date,' I say. I wince at how prim I sound, but Tod just laughs.

'You've not aged a bit,' he assures me. 'Coffee?'

'Oh, I'll . . .' I reach for my purse, but he waves me off with a frown.

'My treat. Please, I insist. A flat white?'

'A . . . Sorry, I beg your pardon?'

'Would you like a flat white?'

'I haven't a clue what you're talking about,' I tell him.

He roars with laughter. 'Oh, I think you are going to be very good for me, Eileen Cotton.'

I really don't see what's funny, but I smile anyway, because he's very handsome when he laughs. And the rest of the time, too. At first the make-up is a little disconcerting – his skin looks rather strange, being all one colour like that. But I seem to be getting used to it.

'A flat white is a type of coffee,' Tod explains, waving down a waiter with one expert hand. 'Trust me, you'll love it.'

'I'll give it a go, then,' I say, and Tod orders the drinks. He's much less intimidating than I expected, and I feel myself relaxing as he jokes with the waiter, smoothing his hair back from his forehead as he speaks.

'Now,' Tod says, turning his attention to me. He flashes an extremely charming smile. 'As far as I'm concerned, we're too old to mess about. I'm going to put my cards out on the table.'

'Oh, right,' I say. 'Well, that's good?'

'I'm not looking for a serious relationship,' Tod says. 'I was married once, to a truly wonderful woman, and they were the happiest years of my life – I have no interest in trying to replicate them because they cannot be replicated.'

'Oh,' I say, rather moved, despite his perfunctory tone. 'Well, that's very romantic, actually.'

Tod laughs again. 'What I'm looking for, Eileen, is a bit of fun.'

'A bit of fun?' I narrow my eyes slightly. 'In the interests of putting our cards out . . .' I tap the table between us. 'Could you be a little more specific?'

He reaches to take my hand across the table. 'May I?' he says quietly.

'Yes,' I say, though I'm not quite sure what I'm agreeing to.

He turns my hand over and presses his thumb very gently to the soft skin between my wrist and my palm, and begins to stroke in slow, languid circles.

My breath quickens.

'Specifically,' he says, 'I would like us to enjoy good coffee, and good food, and good wine, and then I would like us to go to bed together.'

'To . . . bed,' I repeat, dry-mouthed. 'Together.'

He inclines his head. 'A casual fling, as it were. Non-exclusive. Purely sensual. Just for the duration of your stay in London, and then we say goodbye with no regrets.' He slowly lets go of my hand. 'How does that sound, Eileen?'

'That . . . sounds . . .' I clear my throat, rubbing at my tingling palm with the other hand. I'm tingling everywhere, in fact. I'm surprised you can't hear me creaking like a radiator that's just warming up. 'That sounds fun,' I finish, and I bite my lip to keep from smiling.

'The date was very nice,' I tell Leena, in my firmest end-of-discussion voice. I settle myself on the sofa, tucking a cushion behind my back. 'How was your first Neighbourhood Watch meeting?'

'Oh, all fine, all fine,' Leena says. 'Come on, you have to tell me more about this mystery man!'

'A lady never tells,' I say. 'And Marian? How is she getting on?'

'Grandma! Did you sleep with him?'

'I beg your pardon! No! What sort of question is that to ask your grandmother?' I splutter.

'Well, when people say "a lady never tells", that's usually what they mean,' Leena says, sounding amused. 'Are you *really* not going to tell me anything about this Tod?'

'No, I don't think I am,' I decide.

I told Fitz all about it, but I swore him to secrecy, and he said he wouldn't pass anything on to Leena. I just don't much want to discuss my new 'casual fling' with my granddaughter.

'Well,' Leena says grudgingly, 'I suppose I *did* tell you to go and do something for yourself.' She pauses. 'Grandma . . . Can I ask you something?'

'Of course.'

'Has anything happened to Mum? Anything you've not told me?'

'What do you mean?' I ask carefully.

'She mentioned "episodes".'

I close my eyes. 'Ah.'

'What happened?'

'She's just had a few . . . wobbles.'

'Wobbles like getting tearful on the bus? Or wobbles like she had to go to the doctor?'

'The second one, love.'

'How could you not tell me that?'

'I did keep telling you she was struggling, Leena.'

'Yeah, but I thought you meant – I thought she was – I didn't realise she'd been having *breakdowns*.'

'I thought she'd tell you herself, if she wanted to. I didn't want to interfere.'

'And when you left me here to look after Mum, you didn't think it was worth mentioning that she might have one of these "episodes" at any moment? What happens? Do I need to check in on her more? How bad are we talking? What did the doctor say?'

I rub the bridge of my nose. 'Dr Piotr gave her some tablets a couple of months ago.'

'Antidepressants?'

'I think so.'

'Is she taking them?'

'I think so.'

'OK. All right. God, Grandma. It's – I appreciate you not wanting to interfere, but . . . I wish you'd told me.'

'Would it have changed how you felt? Would you have come home sooner?'

There's a long silence. 'I like to think it would, but I – I know I've been . . . a bit weird about Mum lately. But I want things to be better. Bee says I'm not myself, and she's right, and I think it's partly that, you know, the distance between me and Mum, how angry she makes me . . . I want to fix that. For me, as well as for her.'

I smile slightly. And, well, if interfering is allowed, now . . .

'She wants that too, love. She misses you desperately.'

Leena sniffs. There's a moment's silence, and then: 'Got to go, Grandma – there's a man calling on your mobile to talk to me about falconry.'

'Pardon?' I say, but she's already gone.

I sigh. Now I'm worrying about Marian more than ever.

I'm just about to turn off Leena's telephone when a message pops up at the top of the screen. It's from someone called Ceci. I'm sure I remember Leena mentioning her. Wasn't she the awful, catty one from work?

Hey Leena! Just wanted to let you know the Upgo project is going really well in your absence, going from strength to strength really, in case you were worrying about it! Let me know if you're going to be down in London anytime soon, Cx

I frown. Leena doesn't need to be reminded about that Upgo project, and she's not given Ceci her new phone number, which means she didn't want to hear from her while she was away. I seem to remember Leena describing this woman as 'eighty per cent leg, twenty per cent bad intentions'; something tells me she doesn't have Leena's best interests at heart. I *tsk* and close the message.

I'm fidgety after that phone call with Leena; I look around for a job to keep me busy. I'm just eyeing Fitz's washing up when I spot Leena's laptop on the breakfast counter and perk up. Perhaps Tod is available to talk.

There is a new message waiting for me on the dating website, but it's from someone new.

OldCountryBoy says: Hello, Eileen. I hope you don't mind me saying hello?

OldCountryBoy's profile picture is photograph of him as a young man, dressed in a loose white vest with a cap on his head. He was certainly handsome then, but that doesn't mean a lot now. Though I don't mind so much about handsome. After all, Wade was a real looker, and see how he turned out.

EileenCotton79 says: Of course! I'm on this website to meet people.

I hesitate, and then, after a moment's thought, add a smiling face, like Leena does when she's texting. It's a bit flirtatious – I think – but why not, eh? Tod and I are being 'non-exclusive', after all. And twenty-something Eileen Cotton, with her big plans for a London adventure . . . She would *certainly* have imagined there'd be more than one man in the mix.

13

Leena

'Are you sure you don't want to just buy them a cake?' Ethan says.

I'm balancing the phone on top of Grandma's vintage stand mixer while I try to bake please-like-me brownies. I've decided Roland and Penelope will be my first target in winning the May Day Committee around to my medieval theme. If a team have banded together against you, the best approach is to divide and conquer, and I sensed weakness from Penelope. Separated from Betsy's influence, I think she might be quite friendly. She is letting me borrow her car, after all.

'No! I'm having a rural idyll up here in Hamleigh, remember? Baking is very idyllic and rural.' The knife slips across the cold block of butter and stabs me in the thumb. I try very hard not to swear, so as not to ruin the general air of domestic goddessery I'm trying to evoke here.

'Baking is also quite hard,' Ethan says mildly, 'especially if you've never done it before.'

'I have a comprehensive blog post guiding me through,' I tell him, squinting down at the printout beside the mixing bowl and sucking my sore thumb. I open the pack of flour and it tears, sending a snowfall of self-raising down my jeans. 'Gah.'

'Angel, come on. Just buy some brownies, put them on a plate, and do something interesting instead. Hey, I've been staring at this system requirements traceability matrix for hours and I'm getting nowhere. Want to dig your teeth into that?'

I brush down my jeans. I actually really *don't* want to get my teeth into that – it's been surprisingly great forgetting about Selmount while I'm up here. Also, even I don't like system requirements traceability matrices.

'Do you mind if I don't?' I say tentatively. 'Sorry, I just feel like I need a break.'

'Whoa, turning down a spreadsheet! That's got to be a first.'

'Sorry!'

'No worries. I should go, though – this is hours of work if I'm going it solo.'

'Oh, right. Sorry. You're still coming this weekend, though, aren't you?'

'Yeah, for sure, if I can get away. All right, angel, speak soon!'

'Good–'

Oh. He's gone already.

That evening, Penelope answers the door and stares at the plate of very, very dark brown brownies that I have thrust towards her.

'Umm. Hello?' she says.

'Hi! I made brownies!'

I am relying on the 'it's the thought that counts' principle here, because these brownies are clearly burned.

'Look, I'm a horrible baker,' I confess, 'but I really wanted to bring something around to say thanks for letting me share the car.'

Penelope stares at me blankly for a moment. 'Roland!' she yells, so loudly I let out a little surprised *eep*. 'Sorry,' she says, noticing. 'His ears, you know. Roland! Roland! Marian's girl is here, she wants to talk about the car!'

'Perhaps I could come in and speak to you both?' I suggest, as

Penelope continues to shout over her shoulder. She has impressive lungs for a woman so small and frail looking.

'Umm,' Penelope says, suddenly rather shifty.

'Penelope, dear!' calls a familiar voice from inside the house. 'Come and look at these tropical cocktails Jackson's made, they're ever so fun!'

That was definitely Betsy.

My mouth drops open. Jackson appears in the hall behind Penelope.

'Oh. Hi,' he says. He is holding a cocktail in what I think may be a knickerbocker glory glass. It even has a small yellow umbrella in the top.

A small yellow umbrella takes *planning*.

'Are you having a May Day pitch meeting without me?' I say, fixing him with my steeliest glare, the one I usually reserve for men caught mid-perv on the tube.

Jackson steps back slightly. 'No,' he says. 'No, no, really not. I'm just making tea for Penelope and Roland, I do it every week, and sometimes Basil and Betsy come along, and we just . . . got talking about cocktails.'

'You just got talking, did you?'

'Why don't you come in, Leena?' Penelope says.

I step inside. The house is like a time capsule from the sixties: an autumnal patterned carpet in oranges and browns, dark oil paintings, three china ducks flying their way up the hall wall and past the stair lift. It's stiflingly warm and smells of potpourri and gravy.

Roland, Betsy, Basil and Penelope are sitting around the dining table, all clutching cocktails with variously coloured umbrellas and slices of pineapple adorning their glasses.

'Hello,' I say, as pleasantly as I can manage. 'So. What's on the menu tonight?'

'Just a roast,' Jackson says, disappearing into the kitchen.

Oh, sure, *just a roast.*

'And brownies for pudding,' he says.

I'm glad he's no longer able to see my expression because I'm confident I have not managed to disguise my dismay at this news. I quietly set down my plate of blackened brownies on the Welsh dresser by the dining-room door, wondering whether there's somewhere I can hide them so Jackson doesn't see them. That's quite a large pot plant over there. The brownies could definitely pass for soil if I put them around the base.

'What was it you wanted to talk about, dear?' Penelope asks, making her way back to her spot at the table.

'The car!' I say, after a moment of trying to remember what my cover story was for bringing around my please-like-me brownies.

'Oh, yes. Serving you well, is it?' Roland asks.

'Yes, I just wanted to say thanks – it's been brilliant,' I lie.

That car is an absolute wreck. I have discovered in the last week of driving it that the air conditioning switches inexplicably between sauna hot and see-your-breath cold, and no amount of reading the manual online can help me figure out why. It is definitely making me a more dangerous driver. I now regularly remove or put on clothing while at the wheel, for example.

'Let's hope for Penelope's sake that you're better at parking than Eileen,' Basil chortles.

I frown at that, but Betsy's snapped back before I have the chance.

'At least Eileen's got enough sense to tie her shoelaces before she marches down the street, Basil,' she says tartly.

Basil scowls, rubbing his knee. 'That fall was no laughing matter, thank you. And it *wasn't* my shoelaces, it was the potholes on Lower Lane. They'll be the death of us, I know they will.'

'It's true,' Roland says. 'I nearly toppled my scooter down there the other day.'

'Cocktail?' Jackson says, reappearing from the kitchen with the oven gloves over his shoulder and a fresh cocktail in his hand.

I eye the cocktail. It does look excellent. And it's good to sample the competition. 'Yes, please. Though if any future May Day pitching sessions are occurring, I would appreciate an invite,' I tell him, raising my eyebrows.

'It wasn't a . . .' He sighs. 'Fine. No more tropical cocktail-tasting without your knowledge. Happy?'

'Perfectly.' A thought occurs. 'Whilst I've got you all, actually, I've been meaning to ask something. Getting a sponsor for May Day – had Grandma decided against it, for some reason?'

'Ah,' Basil says, 'Eileen's latest project. She didn't get anywhere with that one either, from what I remember.'

'And now she's off in London, I thought we'd take it off your plate,' Betsy says, sipping her cocktail.

Basil shakes his head incredulously. 'Eileen has some strange ideas, but taking off to London has to be her strangest. You know she's living with a lesbian?' he tells Betsy. 'And a *pregnant* one at that? Can you believe it?'

'Yes,' I interrupt. 'That pregnant lesbian happens to be my flatmate and one of my closest friends. Do you have a problem with lesbians, Basil?'

Basil looks startled. 'What?'

'Or perhaps you have a problem with lesbians having children?'

'Oh, I . . .'

'Well, you might be interested to learn that children fare just as well if raised by a same-sex couple in a stable environment as those raised by a heterosexual couple. What matters, Basil, is being *there* for your child, loving them, looking after them – that's what makes you a parent.'

I'm about to continue when Jackson stands abruptly and leaves the table, startling me into silence.

I watch him go. Did I offend him? Is Jackson secretly homophobic? That's . . . disappointing?

'Jackson doesn't have the privilege of being there for his child,' Betsy says quietly into the silence.

I turn to her. 'What?'

'Jackson's daughter. She lives in America.'

'Oh, I . . . I didn't know.' My cheeks burn. 'I didn't mean you can't be a good parent if you're – let me – I should go and apologise –'

Penelope stands and puts a hand on my arm. 'Better not,' she says, not unkindly. 'I'll go.'

'Grandma! How did you not tell me Jackson has a kid?' I ask as I walk home from Penelope's house, cheeks still hot.

'Oh, the Greenwood family have had a *very* interesting few years,' Grandma tells me, dropping into the lower-octave, this-is-really-juicy voice she reserves for her finest pieces of village gossip. 'When Jackson's mother left Arnold she . . . Sorry,' Grandma says, 'I'm getting a message on my phone, let me just . . .'

Dial tone. I sigh, wait ten seconds, and call her back.

'Did I cut you off, love?'

'Yeah, but don't worry – you were saying, Jackson's mum . . .' I say, turning on to Lower Lane. Basil's right, actually, these potholes are dangerous; I make a mental note to call the council about sorting them.

'Ooh, yes. So she ditched grumpy old Arnold and went off with Denley from Tauntingham. You know, the one with the house in Spain that he probably bought with dirty money from his father's used-car business?'

I laugh. 'Grandma, I'm only just getting a handle on the gossip in Hamleigh. I can't broaden my range to the whole of the Dales just yet.'

'Oh, you'll get the hang of it all in no time, just have Betsy around for coffee once a week. She can fill you in on everything you need to know.'

I make a face to myself. I don't get the impression Betsy wants to come for coffee once a week. 'Go on, Grandma – Jackson's kid?'

'At this point Jackson was living with Arnold – I never got to the bottom of that, but Jackson's always seemed strangely fond of Arnold – and so I knew he was stepping out with a bouncy blonde girl called Marigold from Daredale who fancied herself the next Hollywood starlet. I knew she was a wrong'un,' Grandma says, suddenly sounding a lot like Betsy. 'She wore these awful high-heeled shoes that were always getting stuck in the mud on the driveway and she'd squeal until Jackson heaved her out.'

'Wearing high heels, eh,' I say. 'Whatever next!'

'Oh, don't try and make me sound old-fashioned,' Grandma says. 'I'll have you know Fitz took me out shopping yesterday and I bought all sorts of trendy things. *And* I borrowed your high-heeled boots to go out for cocktails afterwards.'

I widen my eyes in alarm. Is she steady enough on her feet to be wearing my heeled boots?

'But this girl went everywhere in stilettos and tight skirts she could hardly move in. Jackson was always opening doors and helping her into cars and carrying her bags and she never liked to lift a finger for him. Then they ended things, or at least I think they did because she stopped coming by, and *then* she turned up six months later round as a Rolo.'

That makes me laugh. 'A Rolo?'

'Exactly,' Grandma says with relish. 'Pregnant! Then next thing we know, Jackson's off to Daredale half the time looking after the baby. This was all, ooh, three or four years ago, maybe? Then – and this is the real gossip – Marigold moved to LA for her big break as an actress, and she took the little girl with her. Jackson hardly gets to see her now.'

Oh, God. Poor, poor Jackson. I feel so bad about what I said at Penelope's house that I don't even feel angry with him about the sneaky cocktail-making any more.

Well, not *very* angry about it, anyway.

My phone buzzes. This phone is a relic from the era of floppy discs and Game Boys, and it takes me a while to realise what's happening: I'm getting another call.

'Got to go, Grandma – speak soon, love you.'

'Oh, bye, love,' she says, and I hang up and switch to the call waiting.

'Hello?' comes a wavering voice from the other end of the line. 'Is that Leena Cotton?'

'Yes, this is she.' I definitely just did my work voice. It felt a bit weird.

'My name is Nicola Alderson,' the lady says, 'and I'm calling about an advert I saw in the grocery store, about lifts?'

'Oh!' I drove out to Knargill and posted a few flyers (well, print-outs from Grandma's computer) yesterday – I'd not expected quite such a speedy response. 'Hello, Nicola, thanks for calling.'

'Are you *sure* it's free?' Nicola asks. 'This is all very . . . good. My grandson's always warning me about those emails that say you've won some money, and an offer of free lifts might come under the same category, I'd say. No such thing as a free lunch, and all that.'

I nod. This is a fair point – actually, I wish my grandma was this suspicious about these sorts of things. We had a scare a few years ago where she mistook some junk mail for an official letter from the bank and almost transferred her savings to a mysterious Russian bank account.

'Absolutely. So basically, my grandma had this idea about helping isolated people get around more, and I'm staying at her place at the moment, looking after all her projects, and . . . I just thought this was the simplest way to help. I've got a car and I've got time, so . . .'

'Is there some way I can check you're not about to drive me off into the woods and eat me?'

I splutter out a laugh. 'Well,' I say, 'I could ask you the same, really.'

'That's true enough,' she muses.

'I do have a DBS certificate, if that would make you feel better?'

'I haven't a clue what that is,' Nicola says. 'But I think I'd probably be able to judge by looking at you. Shall we meet at the church? You'd have to be a real piece of work to murder me there.'

'Lovely,' I say. 'Just tell me when.'

14

Eileen

It is ten o'clock at night. I am kissing a man on his doorstep. I'm wearing high-heeled boots. Tod's hands slide beneath my jacket, and his thumb trails along the zip of my long linen dress, as though finding its way for later.

Since meeting Tod I've felt like I've opened a door to a part of myself I'd entirely forgotten about. Yesterday I caught myself *giggling*. I'm not sure I giggled even when I was a young woman.

It's lovely. It really is. But underneath it all there's a dark, guilty whispering in my belly. I've been doing so well putting Wade behind me, but ever since Tod and I have started stepping out together, I haven't been able to put him out of my mind quite so easily.

I think it's just a matter of breaking the habit. After all, I've not kissed a man who wasn't my husband for fifty years. Tod's lips feel so different; even the shape of his head, his neck, his shoulders seem strange under my palms after so many years learning the lines of Wade's body. It's like trying on somebody else's clothes, kissing Tod. Strange and disconcerting, yes – but fun.

I pull away from his arms reluctantly.

'You won't come upstairs?' Tod says.

'Not yet.' I smile at him. 'We're only on date three.'

That was my stipulation. I agreed to all Tod's terms for this relationship of ours, but I said I wouldn't go to bed with him until we'd been on five dates. I wanted the time to decide if he was a good enough man for that. I'm all for a bit of fun, but I don't plan on – what was it Fitz called it? – 'getting played'. Sex does mean something to me, after all, and I don't want to share it with a man I don't much like.

As it happens, though, I seem to like Tod very much. So much that this rule feels rather . . .

He quirks an eyebrow. 'I know a wavering woman when I see one,' he says. He gives me another long kiss on the lips. 'Now get yourself in a cab home before we do something we might regret, hmm? Rules are rules.' He winks.

Good lord, that wink.

I'd better get myself a cab.

I sleep late the next morning and don't wake until eight. When I walk out of Leena's bedroom, I find Martha on the sofa in tears.

'Oh, Martha!' I hesitate in the doorway. I don't want to march in and embarrass her. But she turns her tear-stained face my way and waves me over.

'Please, come and sit with me,' she says, rubbing her belly. 'Crying alone is a new low for me. Normally I have Leena to weep on.' She sniffs as I settle myself down beside her. 'You look well, Mrs Cotton. Ooh, were you out with your silver fox last night?'

I feel myself flush. Martha smiles.

'Don't get too attached, remember,' she says, wiping her nose. 'Though I'm only saying that because you told me to remind you. Personally, I think he sounds like a catch.'

'Don't you worry about me. What's the matter, love?' I hesitate. 'If you don't mind me asking?'

'Yaz and I are close to exchanging on a house,' she says. 'I don't like it, but she says we don't have time to be picky now, and I said it's such a huge decision I don't want to rush it, and . . .' She's crying again; the tears drip off her chin. 'I'm so worried I won't be able to do this – that I'm not ready for a baby – and Yaz being all Yaz about the other stuff isn't helping. The baby will be here soon, and Yaz just thinks we can still be how we were before. But we can't, can we? Everything's going to be different. And scary. And we've *really* not got everything ready. Oh, god . . .'

I try to remember the bittersweet panic of discovering I was pregnant. That time was a complicated one for me and Wade. We weren't married when Marian was conceived. Not even engaged, actually. I did a very good job covering the baby bump in the wedding photos, so now nobody's the wiser – not even Marian – and I prefer it that way. But I remember, in amongst the chaos, those moments of pure panic that sent me spinning, just like Martha is now.

It was the change of plan that upset me the most. There would be no job down in London now, no changing the world, no adventures – or rather, the biggest adventure, but one I'd be undertaking at home. There was no question of leaving Hamleigh now. And as for men . . . well, it would be Wade, for ever. He did the honest thing and proposed, and I was grateful. Who knows what my mother and father would have done with me if he hadn't.

I take Martha's hand. 'You know what you need, love?' I tell her. 'You need a *list*. Let's get a pen and paper and sort through all the projects that need doing before the baby comes, then we can make a plan, and a back-up plan.'

She smiles at that. 'I can see where Leena gets her Leena-ness from, Mrs Cotton.'

'Call me Eileen, would you?' I say. 'I don't much feel like a Mrs any longer.'

I pull out my new project diary to start on Martha's list.

'Oh! Have you spoken to the landlord about the communal area?' I ask, catching sight of *spruce up* on my last to-do list.

Martha sits up straighter, wiping her face. 'Yeah, I meant to say:

he loved the idea. Said he'd even give a bit of money towards it. Only five-hundred quid, but . . .'

'Five-hundred pounds?' I gawp. 'That'll be *plenty*!' I pause, looking at Martha. She looks like she's been worrying here on the sofa for a while. 'I don't suppose you fancy getting started on it? We can work on that list of yours afterwards.'

'Actually, yes, do you know what – let's do it. I've done quite enough wallowy weeping.' She stands up, rubbing her eyes. 'I was thinking we could try the antique place down the road, see if we can get some nice furniture without spending too much?'

I smile. 'I've got a better idea.'

'Oh. My. God.' Martha clutches her throat. 'This place. It's a treasure trove. It's – is that *a genuine Chesterfield*? Behind that other armchair?'

She starts clambering over one of Letitia's many coffee tables in her eagerness to get to the armchairs; I reach out to steady her, laughing.

'Easy, love. We're going to need some help moving all this.'

'And you're *sure* we can use it downstairs?' Martha asks Letitia, wide-eyed.

Letitia shrugs. 'Why not?' she says. 'As long as it doesn't go walk-about, I don't mind lending it. Especially if it . . .' She swallows. 'I like the sound of a communal area. It might be a nice way to meet people.'

I pause in thought, fiddling with one of Letitia's bowls of trinkets. There must be lots of people like Letitia out there. I can't imagine other apartment blocks are any better at getting people together than this one. It must be hard, living alone in this city, especially for the elderly.

'Do you think the landlord would let us use the space for something . . . a bit . . . bigger?' I ask Martha.

'Why, what are you thinking?'

'I'm not quite sure,' I say. 'But . . . Letitia, do you happen to have a few spare dining tables?'

'I've got some in storage,' she says. 'In the basement.'

Martha looks like she's about to faint. 'Storage!' she says. 'There's storage!'

'Lead the way,' I say to Letitia. 'And we need to collect some assistants en route. I have *just* the people.'

The rude sandal-wearers who rolled their eyes at me are called Rupert and Aurora, I have discovered (thanks to thin party-walls). I knock firmly on their door, with Letitia and Martha on either side of me.

Rupert answers and looks immediately wrongfooted. He pats absently at his rounded belly and tucks his hair behind his ears.

'Umm, hi,' he says. 'I'm afraid I've forgotten your name – Isla, was it?'

'Eileen,' I say. 'Eileen Cotton. This is Martha, and Letitia. And you are?'

'Rupert,' he says, offering me his hand. It's splattered with paint.

I shake it, but only after a beat or two. There's neighbourly, and then there's having no backbone.

'Listen, Eileen, I've been meaning to catch you and apologise,' Rupert says, looking abashed. 'My girlfriend can be a little grouchy when she's working on a new piece – she's a sculptor. She was grappling with some tricky ironwork when we first met you and she'd not eaten for almost a day and . . . she was pretty rude. I'm really sorry. She is too.'

My smile becomes somewhat less haughty. 'Well. We can all be bad-tempered when we're hungry,' I say graciously. 'And if you're looking to make amends, we have just the job for you. Come on.'

'What . . . now?'

I turn to look at him again. 'Busy, are you?'

'No, no,' he says hurriedly. 'Let me just get some shoes. I'm all yours.'

We're standing in a loose circle at the centre of our soon-to-be communal space, a hodgepodge of furniture on all sides, sunlight streaming through the beautiful old windows.

Now that they're all looking at me so expectantly, my confidence is wavering. I felt like my old self for a moment there; now I'm reminded of that blank-faced circle in the village hall whenever I suggest a new idea at a Neighbourhood Watch meeting.

I swallow. Nothing ventured, and all that, I remind myself. What would Leena do?

'I thought we could have a club,' I say, fidgeting with the strap of my handbag. 'There could be activities – dominoes, card games, Scrabble, that sort of thing. And a hot meal, if we can find a way to pay for it. Being here in London, at my age, it's making me realise it might get lonely, for some older people.'

There's a long silence.

'It's probably a terrible idea. Basil is always telling me my projects are too ambitious. But – I – once, when I was younger, I was going to come to London and work on something a bit like this, but for young people. And now I think it would be . . . well, it would feel very special for me to be able to create a community here, only for older people.' I shrug rather helplessly. 'Perhaps it can't be done. I don't really know where I'd even begin.'

'Floorboards,' Martha says suddenly.

We all look at her.

'Sorry,' she says, bouncing slightly on her toes. 'But I *think* underneath this mangy carpet there are floorboards, and I just thought that might be the place to start if we want to make the place feel more inviting. And then we can have board games tables there, card games here – maybe bridge, my granddad loves bridge. And a long table here, along the back of the space, for everyone to eat together.' She smiles at me. 'I love your idea, Eileen. It's brilliant. And it's not too ambitious at all.'

'There's no such thing,' Fitz says. 'Or so Leena always tells me when I'm trying to make excuses not to apply for jobs.' He winks at me. Fitz walked in just as we were dragging a large trestle table up from Letitia's storage area, and – bless him – he dropped his bags and rolled his sleeves up and got stuck right in. He's been moving furniture ever since.

'What do you think, Letitia?' I ask, rather nervously. 'Do you think anyone would come?'

'I would,' she says after a moment. 'And I think there are other people like me, out there, though I've never been very sure how to find them.'

That's the next challenge, certainly. I unzip my handbag and pull out my project diary, itching to get started on a new list.

'I'll speak with the landlord again, and then I'll email around the building to check they're all happy,' Martha says.

Letitia pulls a face. 'Do we have to ask everyone in the building? Whoever complained about me sitting here before, they probably don't want a whole lot of oldies pottering around down here for a club, do they?'

My face falls. 'Oh.'

'Someone *complained* about you sitting down here?' Fitz says, straightening up from where he's trying to pull up a corner of the carpet on Martha's instruction. 'Jeez, that's awful!'

Letitia shrugs.

'Well,' Fitz says, 'whoever it was, they've probably moved out by now. I'm pretty sure Leena and Martha and me are the longest running residents here these days.'

'I've lived here for thirty years,' Letitia says helpfully.

Fitz gawps at her. 'Oh. Wow. You win.'

'I could run an art class,' Rupert says suddenly, gazing at the corner of the room Martha has yet to allocate to any purpose. 'For the club. Aurora and I could do it together. We've got loads of old bits and bobs, spare paints and chalks, that sort of thing.'

I beam at him, heart lifting again. 'Wonderful!'

'And the guy in Flat 17 is a magician. I bet he could do the odd show, or even a workshop,' Rupert offers.

I click my pen, beaming more broadly than ever. 'Right,' I say. 'Step one: floorboards. Step two . . .'

After an exhausting and wonderful day of planning, painting, and directing furniture about the place, I collapse into bed and sleep more deeply than I have in years. When I wake, it strikes me that I didn't think to thank Letitia for donating all that furniture. It was incredibly generous of her. I am seized by a sudden urge to return the generosity, and I swing my legs out of bed with such alacrity I have to take a moment to recover before getting up.

'You want to go shopping?' Letitia says suspiciously when I turn up outside her door with my most comfortable shoes and my largest shopping bag. 'For what?'

'New clothes! My treat, to say thank you!'

'Oh, you mustn't spend any money on me,' Letitia says, looking horrified.

I lean in. 'My ex-husband hasn't a clue of all the savings I've squirrelled away over the years, and I plan on spending them before he notices and tries to get his hands on them. Come on. Give me a hand.'

That gets a grin out of Letitia. 'I'm not fussed about fashion,' she says. 'And where would we shop?' Her grin fades; she looks slightly nervous. 'Not Oxford Street or something?'

I have no plans to repeat the experience of visiting Oxford Street. I got stabbed by an umbrella, shouted at by an angry American tourist, and, oddly, followed around Primark by a security guard.

'No, we're going to the charity shops,' I say. 'There's five within a ten-minute walk of the building and they're packed full of the bargains fancy London sorts have thrown out.'

Letitia brightens. I suspected charity shops would be more her cup of tea than those high-street places that only seem to sell clothes for tall people with gigantic bosoms and tiny waists. And even though this part of London seemed a little scary at first – what with all the graffiti, the tattoo parlours, the motorbikes – I much prefer it to the noise and bustle of London's centre now.

Since Fitz took me out shopping, I have learned all about 'makeovers'. Fitz had me trying on all sorts of ridiculous things – skirts that showed my knees, shoes that you couldn't wear stockings with. But I realised afterwards it was all a clever ploy to make me more adventurous. Once I'd tried on a short denim skirt my comfort zone was so severely stretched that it didn't seem too much of a leap to buy myself the long-sleeved linen dress I'd worn for my third date with Tod, for example, and after forcing my feet into heeled sandals, the lovely leather boots he persuaded me to borrow from Leena seemed quite comfortable.

I try this with Letitia, only I go a bit too far and she almost bolts from Save the Children when I attempt to wrestle her into a fitted pink blouse. I take a new tack and talk to her about her taste, but she stubbornly insists she has no interest in fashion and is perfectly happy in her navy-blue tunic and it doesn't need washing as often as people think.

At last, just when I'm about to give up, I catch her eyeing an embroidered jacket in Help the Aged. The penny drops. I remember what an extraordinary cove of oddities Letitia's flat is, and I take a closer look at her.

'What are you looking at?' she asks suspiciously.

'Your earrings,' I say. 'They're beautiful. And the last pair I saw you in were lovely, too.'

'Oh.' She looks pleased. 'Thank you. They're 1940s – I found them at a flea market and polished them up myself.'

'What a find!' I hustle her out of Help the Aged towards the gigantic Oxfam where Fitz found himself three floral shirts. 'Look,' I say, as casually as I can, 'they have a vintage rail. Gosh, look at the *curious* ivy pattern on this skirt!'

If Letitia were a cat, her ears would be pricking up. She sidles closer and reaches to stroke the fabric.

I need to change how Letitia views clothes. She's a magpie, she collects beautiful things – so why not decorate herself with them too? If she paid half as much attention to herself as she does to her home, well. She might still look *odd*, but at least she'd be taking some pride in her appearance.

'Shall I . . . try this on?' Letitia says nervously, holding the ivy-patterned skirt.

'Why not?' I ask, already pushing her towards the changing room.

15

Leena

Ant/Dec wakes me, as has become our routine; I am actually becoming quite fond of a furry head in my face first thing. It's much nicer than an alarm.

As he jumps down from the bed, he knocks Mum's moonstone from the bedside table. I pick it up slowly, rolling it between my fingers. It's tinged with blue, kind of alien-looking. I wonder who decided it meant 'new beginnings'.

Hesitantly, I reach for my phone. There's a goodnight message from Ethan, sent at one a.m., with four kisses instead of the usual three. He's had to miss *another* weekend visit because of work – I've been here three weeks now and he's not visited once. I get it, but it's still frustrating.

I scroll through my contacts. Mum wakes up even earlier than me – she's usually up by five.

I hit dial. I've sent Mum a text most days, just checking whether she needs anything, but she always says no. I should definitely have called her or dropped around again by now, but . . .

'Hello? Leena? Is everything OK?'

The panic in her voice takes me right back there. It's only because my phone rings so often that I've chased away the shadow of that instant, gut-dropping dread I'd feel every time it rang when Carla was dying, that conviction that this time it would be the worst news in the world. Now, as I hear that dread in my mother's voice, the emotions start boiling in my stomach. I get up from the edge of the bed to pace, sweating, immediately desperate to end the call before I've even said a word.

'Hi, sorry Mum, all fine!' I say quickly. 'I was just ringing to say hello – and – it's bingo tomorrow night, I wondered if you wanted to come? I'll be driving the van.'

There's a short pause. 'Oh, I . . . Yes, why not? If you want me to come?'

She waits.

'Yes!' I say, too shrill, and I press one fist at the point between my ribs where the emotions are roiling. 'Yeah, totally, come along! Five p.m. OK. Great!'

If I hang up then this feeling of panic will go, but I've not said what I wanted to say, not really.

'Leena, take a deep breath,' Mum says.

I close my eyes and slow my breathing. The prickling sensation on my chest and face subsides a little, until it feels less like pins-and-needles, more like light rain on the skin.

I open my eyes and take one final deep breath. 'Mum, Grandma told me you'd been to see the doctor and he'd given you some antidepressants.'

There's a long pause. 'Yes,' she says.

'I didn't realise things were . . . that bad,' I say. 'I – I'm sorry.'

'That's OK, love.' Her voice is quieter now.

'And they're helping?'

'They are, actually. Though it's hard to tell whether it's the anti-depressants or the crystals, really.'

I roll my eyes.

'Did you just roll your eyes?'

'No?'

I hear her smile. 'You're so sure about the world, Leena. But I'm not like that. You know the best way for you to heal, and you've been doing it: working hard, taking time away from me and your grand-mother. I haven't worked out how to heal. So I'm trying everything. That's *my* way.'

I twist the moonstone between my fingers again.

'I'm not sure I do know the best way to heal,' I say quietly. 'I'm not sure I'm doing very well at it, actually.'

'Is that why you're here?' Mum asks. 'In Hamleigh?'

'Maybe.' I swallow. 'So I'll see you at bingo?'

'See you at bingo.'

I shake out my arms after the phone call – they're tense, as though I've been gripping the steering wheel after a long, difficult drive. I'm too hot. I take myself out for a run, just a short one; by the time I get back and make a coffee, I'm breathing normally, feeling more in control, but even so I pace around the dining room with my mug cupped between my hands, unable to sit for more than a moment or two. I need a distraction.

There is an insistent knocking on the kitchen window.

I groan into my coffee. Not *that* distraction, please. It's only seven thirty in the morning – what could Arnold want now? Maybe I'll just pretend to be asleep.

'Hello?' Arnold yells. 'I can see your lights are on! Hello?'

Maybe I sleep with the lights on. This is a big, old house, I might find it very spooky.

'Hello? The kettle's still steaming, you must be up. Hello?'

Well, maybe I made myself a cup of tea and went back to . . .

'Leena? Hello? I saw you come back from your run! Hello?'

Christ, why isn't this man in the Neighbourhood Watch? He's made for it. I grit my teeth and head for the kitchen. 'Hello, Arnold,' I say, as pleasantly as I can manage. 'What seems to be the problem?'

'Your car,' Arnold says. 'It's in the hedge.'

THE SWITCH | 128

I blink. 'My . . . Sorry, what?'

'Your car,' Arnold says patiently. 'The hedge. It's in it. Do you want a hand getting it out?'

'Oh, God,' I say, leaning forward to look past Arnold and craning to see the driveway. 'How did it get into the hedge? Which hedge?'

'Did you put the handbrake on?' Arnold asks.

'Of course!' I say, trying to remember whether I put the handbrake on. Until this week it's been a while since I've driven – obviously I don't have a car in London, because you only have a car in London if you are looking for an opportunity to induce road rage or practise some really high-stress parallel parking. 'Oh, God, have I wrecked Penelope's car?'

Arnold rubs his chin, looking off towards the driveway. 'Let's dig it out of the leylandii and find out, shall we?'

I did not, it transpires, put the handbrake on firmly enough.

Arnold, who is a lot stronger than he looks, has helped me to push the Ford Ka far enough out of the hedge that I can get in the driving seat. I inch the car backwards, wheels squealing, and receive a double thumbs-up from Arnold when I make it over the verge and on to the gravel. I hope Grandma doesn't mind that her right-hand hedge now has a large car-shaped dent in it, and two long, dark lines running through the grass where the wheels had been.

'She's a good girl, that car,' Arnold says, as I climb out and slam the door behind me. 'What's her name?'

'You've not named her?' Arnold asks, wiping his hands on his trousers. He looks energised. With a loose T-shirt and wool cardigan instead of his usual moth-eaten sweater, and a cap covering his comb-over, he's taken a decade off himself. I watch him as he rubs at the car window with a tissue from his pocket.

'I haven't,' I say. 'Any ideas?'

'Mine's called Wilkie,' he says.

'What, like Wilkie Collins?'

Arnold straightens, looking delighted. 'You like him?'

'Grandma got me *The Moonstone* one Christmas. I loved it. She was always giving me books.'

Arnold looks interested. 'I never knew she was a reader.'

'Oh, sure. Agatha Christie's her favourite. She loves detective stories.'

'Most nosy people do,' Arnold says dryly. 'It's good validation.'

I laugh, surprised. That was actually quite funny. Who knew Arnold could be funny?

'Let's call the car Agatha, then, in Grandma's honour,' I say, giving it a pat on the bonnet. Then, on a whim: 'I don't suppose you fancy coming in for a morning coffee?'

Arnold's glances towards Grandma's house. 'In?'

'Yeah, for a coffee? Or a tea, if you prefer?'

'Eileen's never invited me in,' Arnold says.

I wrinkle up my nose. 'Never?' That's not like my grandma at all. She's always inviting *everybody* in, and if they come under the category of 'neighbour' they pretty much get their own key.

'Your grandma and I don't really see eye to eye,' Arnold says. 'We got off on the wrong foot a long time ago and she's loathed me ever since.' He shrugs. 'No skin off my nose. The way I see it, if you don't like me, you can sling your hook.'

'That's often a very admirable sentiment,' I say, 'but sometimes also an excuse for being grumpy and unreasonable.'

'Ey?' Arnold says.

'I've seen you, in the mornings, out looking after Grandma's plants.'

Arnold looks embarrassed. 'Oh, well, that's just . . .'

'And here you are, helping me fish my car out of a hedge.'

'Well, I just thought . . .' He scowls. 'What's your point?'

'Just not sure I believe the grumpy act, that's all.' I lock the car and head over to the bench under Grandma's apple tree; after a moment, Arnold follows. 'Besides, it's never too late to change – just look at my grandma. Grandpa's gone, and what's she done? Set off on an adventure in London and started online dating.'

Arnold's eyebrows shoot up above his glasses. 'Online *dating*? Your grandma?'

'Yup. I think it's great. She so deserves a story of her own, you know, and a break from looking after us all.'

Arnold looks a little disturbed at the thought. 'Online dating,' he says eventually. 'Fancy that. She's a force to be reckoned with, that woman.' He shoots me a look. 'Seems it runs in the family.'

I snort. 'I don't know where you've got that impression. Ever since I got here all I've done is screw up. Actually, scratch that: all I've done for the last *year* is screw up.'

Arnold narrows his eyes at me. 'From what I hear, while you've been coping with your sister's death, you've held down an all-hours city job, supported your partner, put Betsy in her place, and got Penelope to stop driving.'

I pause, startled into silence. Everyone here talks about Carla's death so openly, as if it happened to all of us – I'd have thought I'd mind it, but somehow it's better.

'I didn't mean to put Betsy in her place,' I say. 'Is that what people are saying?'

Arnold chuckles. 'Ah, anyone can see you've got her goat. But don't worry, she needs pulling in line sometimes. Look up busybody in the dictionary and there Betsy'll be.'

I actually think there's more to Betsy than that. There's something defensive about her bossiness, like she's getting in there first, telling you how to live your life before you can tell her how to live hers.

'What's the story with Cliff, her husband?' I ask.

Arnold looks down at the ground, scuffing one foot. 'Mmm,' he says. 'Nasty piece of work, that one. Wouldn't wish a man like that on any woman.'

'What do you mean?' I frown, remembering how quickly Betsy had got up when Cliff had summoned her home from Clearwater Cottage. 'Does he – does he treat Betsy badly?'

'I wouldn't know about that,' Arnold says hastily. 'People's marriages are their own business.'

'Sure, but . . . only to a point, right? Have you ever seen anything that's got you worried?'

'I ought not to . . .' Arnold glances sideways at me. 'It's not my business.'

'I'm not trying to gossip,' I say. 'I'm trying to make sure Betsy's all right.'

Arnold rubs his chin. 'There's been the odd thing. Cliff is a stickler for how things are done. He gets angry if Betsy gets it wrong. These days he doesn't get out much – she's at his beck and call, from what I can gather, but if you walk past their house with the windows open at the wrong moment you'll hear how he talks to her, and it's not . . .' Arnold shakes his head. 'It's not how you ought to talk to a woman is all I'm saying. It wears away at her. She's not who she used to be. But we all do what we can for her. There's nobody in this village who wouldn't take her in if she needed it.'

Does she know that, I wonder? Is anyone saying it out loud, or are they all doing what my grandma does – keeping quiet, not interfering? I make a mental note to try harder with Betsy. I'm not exactly someone she'd trust to confide in, but maybe I could be.

Arnold suddenly slaps his forehead. 'Bugger. I was meant to ask you something. That's why I dropped by in the first place. You're not busy this morning, are you? We need a favour.'

'Oh?' I say warily, wondering who 'we' might be.

'Do you know what day it is?'

'Err.' In all honesty, I have slightly lost track of the days. 'Sunday?'

'It's Easter Sunday,' Arnold says, getting up from the bench. 'And we need an Easter bunny.'

'Jackson. I should have known you'd be at the bottom of this.'

Jackson looks perplexed. The shoulders of his jumper are splattered with raindrops, and he's holding a wicker basket full of foiled chocolate eggs. We're at the village hall, which has been decorated with special Easter bunting and large signs declaring that this is the starting point for the annual Hamleigh-in-Harksdale Easter egg hunt, kicking off in exactly half an hour.

'At the bottom of this . . . free event for children?' he says.

'Yes,' I say, eyes narrowed. 'Yes, exactly.'

He blinks innocently at me, but I am not fooled. He is one hundred per cent trying to mess with me. I made some real headway with Dr Piotr the other day, in the queue at the village shop – he all but promised me he'd vote for my May Day theme. Then I caught sight of Jackson browsing the newspapers behind us, *clearly* eavesdropping.

This, surely, is his revenge.

'Doesn't Leena look the bee's knees?' Arnold asks from behind me.

I am wearing white fleece trousers with a bunny tail sewn on; they're about six sizes too big for me and held on with a leather belt borrowed from Arnold. I am also sporting a patterned waistcoat with (in case things weren't clear) bunnies all over it. Also, bunny ears. Aren't bunny ears meant to be sexy? I feel like an actual clown.

'Shut up, Arnold,' I say.

A smile tugs at Jackson's lips. 'Even better than I expected. It suits you.'

There is a loud, dramatic gasp behind me. I spin and am faced with the sight of an outrageously cute little girl. Her blonde hair is in lopsided pigtails, there is a long streak of what looks like permanent marker on her cheek, and one of her trouser legs is rolled up to reveal a long, stripy sock. She has both hands on her cheeks, like the shocked-face emoji, and her blue eyes are wide – and very familiar.

'The Easter bunny,' she breathes, gazing up at me. 'WOW.'

'Samantha, my daughter,' Jackson says from behind me. 'She's a *very firm believer* in the Easter bunny.'

This is a clear warning. What does he think I am, a monster? I may despise being dressed as a ridiculous rabbit, but there is clearly only one appropriate way to respond to this situation.

'Well, hello there, Samantha,' I say, crouching down. 'I'm *so* glad I've found you!'

'Found me?' she says, eyes like saucers.

'I left my burrow early this morning and I've been hopping all over the Yorkshire Dales looking for somebody who might be able to help me, and I think you could well be just the person, Samantha.'

'Me?' Samantha breathes.

'Well, let's see, shall we? Do you like chocolate eggs?'

'Yes!' Samantha says, with a little jump.

'Are you good at hiding things?'

'Yes!' Samantha says.

'Like my left shoe,' Jackson says dryly from behind me, though I can hear he's smiling. 'Which you did a very good job of hiding this morning.'

'A *very* good job,' Samantha says earnestly, gaze fixed on my face.

'And – now, this one is very important, Samantha – can you keep secrets? Because if you're going to be the Easter bunny's helper, you're going to know where *all* the chocolate eggs are hidden. And all the other children will be asking you for clues.'

'I won't tell!' Samantha says. 'I won't!'

'Well then,' I say, straightening up and turning back to Jackson. 'I do believe I've found my special helper.'

Jackson grins at me. It's the first full smile I've ever seen him do – he's got dimples, proper ones, one in each cheek. He swoops in and grabs Samantha by the armpits, swinging her up on to his hip.

'What a lucky young lady,' he says, burying his face in her neck until she's almost choking with giggles.

Something flips in my tummy at the sight of Samantha in his arms – it's a sort of sudden-onset fuzziness, as though my brain's gone as fleecy as my trousers.

'Thank you,' Jackson mouths at me. He bends and picks up the basket of eggs, handing it to Samantha. She leans her head against his shoulder with the perfect trust of a child. 'Ready?'

Samantha wriggles out of his arms and runs towards me, stretching her free hand up to take mine. As Jackson lets her go his face softens into an expression of such vulnerability, as if he loves her so much it hurts, and it's so raw and personal I turn my eyes away – it doesn't feel like something I'm meant to see. That fuzziness in my belly intensifies as Samantha's little fingers grip my hand.

Jackson bends to give her a quick kiss on the forehead, then opens the door to the village hall.

'Better get going, you two,' he says. 'Oh, and Leena?'

'Yeah?'

'The Easter bunny skips. Everywhere she goes. Swinging the basket. Just a reminder.'

'Does she now?' I say, through gritted teeth.

He flashes me another grin, but before I can say anything else, a skipping Samantha is dragging me down the steps and out into the rain.

16

Eileen

I feel like the woman in one of those perfume adverts on the television. You know the sort: the one who swans along with her feet a few inches off the ground, draped in chiffon, beaming ecstatically, perhaps while passers-by burst spontaneously into song.

I spent the night in Tod's bed. He really is an extraordinary man. I haven't had sex – by any definition – in about twenty years, and it's certainly changed somewhat, now that I'm seventy-nine, but it's still bloody wonderful. It did take me a little while to get back in the swing, and I'm rather achy in some peculiar places, but lord, it's worth it.

Tod is clearly a very experienced gentleman. I don't mind if the lines he spun about my beautiful body and my glowing skin were just that, lines – they did the trick. I haven't felt this good in years.

I'm meeting Bee this morning for a cup of coffee. She wants to hear all the gossip on Tod, she says. I think she's rather missing Jaime, who's with her father's family for Easter, but still, I was rather touched to receive her message.

The coffee shop where we're meeting is called Watson's Coffee, and it's very trendy. Two of the walls are painted green and the other two are painted pink. There are fake stag horns above the coffee bar and a collection of neon candles half melted at the centre of each steel-grey table. The overall effect is vaguely ridiculous, and it's horribly busy – it's Easter Monday, so of course nobody is at work, and around here if you're not in an office it seems you've got to be in a coffee shop.

Bee has managed to get us a table. She smiles up at me as I approach, that warm, open smile I glimpsed when she showed me the pictures of her daughter. It has an astonishing effect, that smile, like a warm spotlight pointing your way. Her hair is pinned back behind her ears, showing off a striking silver necklace sitting at her collarbone; she's dressed in a beautiful turquoise dress that's somehow more provocative for covering almost everything up.

'Good morning!' she says. 'Let me get you a coffee – what do you fancy?'

'A flat white, please,' I say, feeling very pleased with myself.

Bee raises her eyebrows and grins. 'Very good!' she says. 'Back in a tick.'

I pull my phone out of my handbag as she gets up to give our order. It's taken me a while – and several lessons from Fitz – to get used to Leena's phone, but now I'm starting to get the hang of it. I know enough to tell I've got a new message from Tod, for instance. And there are those butterflies again . . .

Dear Eileen, What a splendid evening. Let's repeat soon, shall we? Yours sincerely, Tod x

'OK, I know it's wrong to snoop, so I'm just going to come out and say right away that I totally read that message,' Bee says, sitting down again and placing a tray on the table. She's got us both muffins, too. 'Lemon or chocolate?' she says.

Bee isn't at all as I expected. She's very thoughtful, actually. I'm not sure why I assumed she wouldn't be – perhaps because she's so beautiful, which is a little uncharitable of me.

'Chocolate,' I hazard, guessing she wants the lemon. She looks pleased and pulls the plate her way. 'And I forgive you for snooping. I'm always doing it to other people on the underground. That's the one advantage of being squashed so close together.'

Bee giggles. 'So? Is Tod the one?'

'Oh, no,' I say firmly. 'We're just casual. Non-exclusive.'

Bee gawps at me. 'Seriously?'

'Is that such a surprise?'

'Well, I . . .' She pauses to think, chewing a mouthful of muffin. 'I guess I just assumed you'd be looking for something serious. A life partner.'

I attempt a nonchalant shrug, then wince as the movement pulls on a newly stiff muscle in my back. 'Maybe. Really, I'm just in it for the adventure.'

Bee sighs. 'I wish I was. Looking for a future father to your child really takes the fun out of a first date.'

'Still no luck?'

Bee makes a face. 'I knew the over-seventies' market would be better. Maybe I should be going for an older man.'

'Don't you be straying into my dating pool, young lady,' I say. 'Leave the old men for the old ladies or we'll never stand a chance.'

Bee laughs. 'No, no, they're all yours. But I do wonder if I might be a *bit* too picky.'

I busy myself with my muffin. I ought not to interfere, really – Bee knows herself, she knows what's good for her.

But I have been around a lot longer than Bee has. And she's been so open with me. Perhaps there's no harm in speaking my mind.

'May I say what I think when I hear your list of rules?' I say.

'Absolutely,' Bee says. 'Please do.'

'I think it sounds like a recipe for spinsterhood.'

She bursts out laughing. 'Oh, please,' she says. 'My list is totally achievable. As a society we have painfully low standards of men, do you know that?'

I think of Wade. I so rarely asked anything of him, especially once Marian was grown. All I expected was fidelity, though even that was giving him too much credit, as it turns out. And Carla and Leena's father, what did Marian ask of him? He used to sit around all day in jogging bottoms, watching obscure sports on strange channels, and even then she bent over backwards to keep him. When he finally left, he never looked back – he saw the girls once a year at best, and now he and Leena aren't even in touch.

Perhaps Bee has a point. But . . .

'While I'm all for a good list, I think you might be going about this the wrong way. You need to stop thinking and start doing.'

I finish off my coffee and stand up, chair rasping on the bare concrete floor. This café feels like a neon-painted war bunker. It's making me uncomfortable.

'Start doing what? Where are we going?' Bee asks as I get my bags together.

'To find you a different sort of man,' I say grandly, leading her out of the coffee shop.

'The *library*?' Bee looks around, bemused. 'I didn't even know there was a library in Shoreditch.'

'You ought to become a member,' I say sternly. 'Libraries are dying out and it's a travesty.'

Bee looks rather chastened. 'Right,' she says, peering at the nearest shelf, which happens to be paperback romance novels. She perks up. 'Ooh, I'll take that man,' she says, pointing to a shirtless gentleman on a Mills & Boon cover.

I take her by the arms and steer her towards the crime and thriller section. She's unlikely to find a man if she's dawdling next to the romances; the only other person in sight is a shifty-looking lady who has clearly given her husband the slip for a couple of minutes and plans to make the most. Ah yes: there's a blond-haired gent in jeans and a shirt browsing the John Grishams. Well, he's certainly a contender to look at him.

'What do you think?' I whisper, retreating behind some cookery books and gesturing for Bee to take a look.

She leans past to look at the blond gentleman. 'Ooh,' she says, cocking her head in thought. 'Yeah, maybe! Oh, no, wait, those shoes . . . Boat shoes are a shorthand for preppy Oxbridge boy,' she tells me in a regretful whisper. 'I predict a six-figure salary and a toxic inferiority complex instilled by helicopter parents.'

'Be open-minded,' I remind her. 'Do you trust me, Bee?'

'Oh, I . . . Yeah, I do, actually.'

I straighten my sleeves. 'In that case,' I say, 'I'm going in.'

'Do you believe a woman should take a man's name when she marries?'

'Oh, err, well actually I think that's a very personal choice, so –'

'What about helping out around the house? Good at Hoovering, are you?'

'I'm . . . proficient, I'd say? Sorry, can I ask what it is you're –'

'Would you say you're a romantic?'

'Yeah, I reckon so, if you –'

'And your last relationship, dear. How did it end?'

The young man stares at me with his mouth slightly open. I look back at him expectantly.

You can get away with an awful lot when you're an old lady.

'She just . . . fell out of love with me, really.'

'Oh, gosh, how sad,' I say, patting him on the arm.

'Sorry, how did we . . .' He looks baffled. 'We were talking about John Grisham novels, and then you were . . . asking questions . . . and now . . . those questions have become . . . extremely personal . . .'

I hesitate as I try to remember the word. Fitz mentioned it at tea the other night. 'I'm *wingmanning*,' I say.

'You're . . .'

'For my friend, Bee. Bee!'

She appears around the shelves, *shush*ing me. 'Eileen! Oh, my God, I'm *so* sorry, this is so embarrassing,' she tells the gentleman. 'Come on, Eileen, let's just go, we've taken enough of this man's time . . .'

She flashes him a muted version of her disarming smile. The blond man's eyes widen and the book he's holding drops a few inches, as though he's forgotten he's meant to be holding it up.

'No worries,' he says. 'Umm.'

'Bee, this young man would like to take you for coffee in that lovely café over the road,' I say. 'Wouldn't you, dear?'

'Actually,' the blond man says, beginning to blush rather fetchingly, 'I would, quite.'

When I return home, Fitz gets up from the sofa, sombre-faced. 'Eileen, I have some rubbish news.'

I clutch my chest. 'What is it? What's wrong?'

'No, no, not that bad! Just about our Silver Shoreditchers' Social Club.'

Martha, Fitz and I chose this name for our club last night after a large glass of wine. I think it's fabulous. We also all decided we were going to try going for a jog the next day, which was *not* a fabulous idea, and which was swiftly abandoned because of my knees, Martha's late-stage pregnancy, and Fitz's 'general morning malaise', whatever that is.

'Almost everyone loves the idea, and we've got sign-off from the landlord too, as long as numbers don't exceed twenty-five and nothing gets broken. But there's a lady in Flat 6 who isn't happy about it,' Fitz says, helping me out of my jacket. 'She says she doesn't agree with giving so many strangers access to the building.'

I scowl. 'And I suppose she moderates everybody's birthday parties on the same grounds, does she?'

Fitz snorts. 'Good point. I'm going to send her an email and explain why . . .'

I wave him away. 'None of this emailing nonsense. I'll go and speak to her.'

Fitz blinks, holding my jacket limp in both hands. 'Oh,' he says. 'OK.'

But she's not home. I think about pushing a note under the door, but no, that's hardly better than an email. I want this lady to look me in the eye and explain exactly why she doesn't want a few old ladies and gents to have a nice art class and lunch in a space that's *ever so slightly* near her flat.

I'm cross. I huff my way back along the corridor to Leena's flat again. Fitz pushes Leena's laptop towards me across the breakfast counter as I settle down in my seat.

'This'll cheer you up,' he says. 'It's been beeping away with new messages.'

The dating website is already on the screen. I've been visiting it quite often, lately, mainly writing to Old Country Boy, who's really called Howard, and who seems very sweet. The other day I was going back through our conversation and I was surprised to see that we've already exchanged reams of messages.

OldCountryBoy says: How are you today, Eileen? It's been a quiet day here. Not a lot going on, you know.

OldCountryBoy says: I keep reading back through our messages and thinking about you. We've known each other such a short time, but it feels like we're old friends!

OldCountryBoy says: I hope that's not too forward for me to say! I just feel very lucky to have met you on here. On a quiet day like today, it's wonderful to be able to go back to our chat.

I sigh. Howard is a bit over the top, bless him. I'm not used to men talking about their feelings quite so much. I'm not sure how I feel about it.

Then I think of Letitia, hunched at her table amongst her wind-chimes, waiting for her Iceland delivery, and I wonder if he's perhaps just very lonely. And it *is* lovely, the way he values the time we spend talking.

> *EileenCotton79 says: Hello, Howard. I'm sorry you're not having a good*
> *day. Do you have neighbours you can talk to?*
> *OldCountryBoy says: They're all young and trendy! They wouldn't be*
> *interested in talking to me.*

I hesitate. Would it be too forward to mention the Silver Shoreditchers' Social Club?

Oh, bother it. Why not?

> *EileenCotton79 says: I'm trying to set up a social club that you might*
> *like. It's for over-seventies in my area. We're having some trouble get-*
> *ting it off the ground at the moment, but once it's up and running,*
> *would you be interested in coming along? I know you're in West*
> *London, aren't you, but you'd be more than welcome all the same!*

There's an unusually long delay before Howard replies, and I start to feel a little silly. Perhaps *more than welcome* was a bit much. But then, at last . . .

> *OldCountryBoy says: I would love to come along! Will you be*
> *there?*
> *EileenCotton79 says: Of course!*
> *OldCountryBoy says: Then I can't wait for us to meet in person* ☺

I smile, but before I can reply, another dot dot dot lights up the screen.

OldCountryBoy says: Maybe I could even help out somehow. I'm good at making websites – I used to do it as part of my job. Would you be interested in me creating one for your social club?

EileenCotton79 says: How exciting! Yes, that sounds wonderful. At the moment we need to get permission from one other person in the building, but we should have that soon.

OldCountryBoy says: I can't wait to be involved!

I beam. An alert pings, making me jump.

One new user has viewed your profile.

I hover over the notification, distracted, then remember what Bee showed me about how you can keep the conversation open in another box. I click.

Arnold1234. No profile picture, no description, nothing. That's quite unusual on this website. My profile tells you all sorts of things, from my favourite holiday locations to my favourite books.

I narrow my eyes suspiciously. Of course, there are lots of Arnolds in the world. It's not an uncommon name.

But I can't help thinking . . .

I press the message button on the screen.

EileenCotton79 says: Hello, Arnold! I notice you were looking at my page and I thought I would say hello.

I go back to my conversation with Old Country Boy. It would be very easy to get confused here and message the wrong man. Not that I'm complaining about juggling men, mind.

OldCountryBoy says: I'm going to spend my evening with a good book, I think! What are you reading at the moment?

EileenCotton79 says: I'm working my way through Agatha Christie's plays again. I never get tired of her!

Meanwhile, in the other window:

Arnold1234: Eileen? It's Arnold Macintyre from next door.

I *knew* it! What's that old sod doing on my dating page? I press 'my profile' and read it again as if through Arnold's eyes. I cringe. It sounds awfully boastful all of a sudden, and very silly. How could I say that I was *full of life and looking for a new adventure*?

EileenCotton79 says: What are you doing on here Arnold???

I regret the triple question mark as soon as I've pressed send. It doesn't convey the haughty higher-ground attitude I usually try to take when it comes to dealing with Arnold.

Arnold1234 says: Same as you.

I huff.

EileenCotton79 says: Well, good for you, but you can stay off my page!

Arnold1234 says: Sorry, Eileen. I was just looking for some ideas of what to say on mine. I'm not very good at this sort of thing.

I soften slightly. I hadn't thought of that.

EileenCotton79 says: I had Leena's friend help me with mine. Why not ask Jackson for help?

Arnold1234 says: Ask Jackson for advice? I'll end up with some floozy called Petunia or Narcissus or something.

I snort with laughter.

EileenCotton79 says: You should be so lucky, Arnold Macintyre!

Oopsie, I'd forgotten about Howard for a moment there. I frown, clicking back to the right conversation. I don't want to get distracted with old Hamleigh folks.

OldCountryBoy says: I've never tried Agatha Christie, but I will now that you have recommended her! Which book should I start with, Eileen?

I smile, already typing. Now, *this* is more like it.

17

Leena

I glance at my watch, fingers tapping on the steering wheel. I am sitting in the driving seat of the school van, which is apparently lent to my grandmother every so often so she can drive the gang to bingo. Beside me is Nicola, my new – and only – client in my role as voluntary taxi driver for the Knargill elderly. She's got to be at least ninety-five – I've never seen anybody with so many wrinkles – but her brown hair is only just threaded with grey, and she has magnificently bushy eyebrows, wiry like an eccentric professor's. So far, she's spent most of our journeys together coming up with elaborate unfounded judgements about any driver we pass on the road; she is very rude and absolutely hilarious. I've informed Bee that I have a new best friend.

As well as being very old, and very judgemental, Nicola is also very isolated. She told me when we first met that she didn't know what loneliness meant until her husband passed away four years ago; now she will go days, sometimes weeks, without even so much as meeting eyes with another soul. There's nothing like it, she says. It's a kind of madness.

I've been trying to work out a good way to get her out of the house for days, and then I finally hit on it after Mum asked me to pick her up for bingo. Bingo is *perfect*. And the more the merrier, frankly, now that I have made the decision to invite my mother, with whom I have yet to really have a proper conversation for the last year and two months.

'Why are you so tense?' Nicola asks, squinting at me.

'I'm not tense.'

She says nothing, but in a pointed sort of way.

'It's my mum. We don't . . . we've not been getting on that well. And she's late.' I look at my watch again. Mum's been to her yoga class in Tauntingham and asked me to pick her up from there, which is *quite* out of my way, but I'm trying very hard not to find that annoying.

'Fallen out, have you?'

'Sort of.'

'Whatever it is, I'm sure it's not worth arguing with your mother over. Life's too short for that.'

'Well, she wouldn't let me convince my sister to try a potentially life-saving cancer treatment. And now my sister's dead.'

Nicola pauses. 'Right,' she says. 'Golly.'

At that moment the van door slides open and my mum climbs in. I notice, with a wince, that the window on Nicola's side is wide open.

'*Potentially life-saving treatment?*' Mum says. My stomach drops at the tone of her voice – it's clipped with fury. She's not spoken to me like that since I was a child. '*What* potentially life-saving treatment, Leena?'

'I showed you,' I say, gripping the steering wheel, not turning around. 'I showed you the research, I gave you that pamphlet from the medical centre in the States –'

'Oh, the *pamphlet*. Right. The treatment that Carla's doctors advised against. The one everyone said wouldn't work and would merely prolong her pain and –'

'Not *everyone*.'

'Sorry, everyone but your one American doctor who wanted to charge us tens of thousands of pounds for some false hope.'

I slam my hand against the steering wheel and turn to face her. She's flushed with emotion – it's dappling the skin of her chest, flaring on her cheeks. I feel a wave of almost-fear, because we're really doing this, we're really having this conversation, it's happening.

'*Hope. A chance.* You always said all my life *Cotton women don't quit,* and then when it mattered more than anything else in the world you let Carla do just that.'

Nicola clears her throat. Embarrassed, Mum and I glance in her direction with our mouths open, as though we've both been caught mid-word.

'Hello,' Nicola says to Mum. 'Nicola Alderson.'

As if she's pierced a bubble, we both deflate.

'Oh, hi, sorry,' Mum says, sitting back in her seat and putting on her seat belt. 'So sorry. How rude of us to – to – I'm so sorry.'

I clear my throat and turn back to the road. My heart is pounding so hard it almost makes me feel breathless, as if it's working its way up my throat. I'm late to pick up the rest of the bingo lot, now; I turn the key in the ignition and pull away.

. . . and straight into a bollard.

Fuck. Fuck. I knew that bollard was there, I made a mental note when I parked here – I thought to myself, *When you pull away, don't forget about the bollard that's just out of your line of sight.*

For fuck's sake.

I leap out of the van and grimace, covering my face with my hands. The bottom right side of the bonnet is badly dented.

'Actually, no,' Mum says, jumping out of the van behind me and pulling the door closed with a slam. 'I'm sick of half-having these sorts of conversations with you. I'm sorry, Nicola, but we're not done.'

'That's all right,' Nicola calls. 'I'll wind the window up, shall I?'

'How *dare* you act like I gave up on my daughter?' Mum says, her fists clenched at her sides.

I'm still processing the dented bonnet. 'Mum, I–'

'You didn't see her day in day out.' Mum's voice is climbing. 'The emergency admissions, the endless, brutal, wrenching vomiting, the times she was so weak she couldn't make it to the toilet. She put on a brave face when you visited – you never saw her at her worst!'

I let out a small gasp. That *hurt*. 'I wanted to be there more.' My eyes are stinging, I'm going to cry. 'You know Carla didn't want me to leave my job, and I – I couldn't be here all the time, Mum, you know that.'

'But I *was* here all the time. I saw it. I *felt* it, what she felt. I'm her mother.'

Mum's eyes narrow, catlike, frightening. She's speaking again before I can respond. The words come spilling out of her in a voice that's raw and rising and doesn't sound like my mum.

'Is this why you left us and cut us out of your life? To punish me, because you think I didn't try hard enough for Carla? Then let me tell you something, Leena. You cannot *imagine* how much I wanted your American doctor to be right. You can't *imagine* it. Losing Carla has made me wonder what the hell I'm living for every minute of every day, and if there was any way I believed I could have saved my little girl, I would have taken it.' Her cheeks are wet with tears. 'But it wouldn't have worked, Leena, and you know it.'

'It *might* have worked,' I say, pressing my hands against my face. 'It *might*.'

'And what kind of life would Carla have had? It was *her* choice, Leena.'

'Yeah? Well, she was wrong too!' I yell, dropping my hands to my sides, clenching my fists. 'I *hate* that she stopped fighting. I hate that you stopped fighting for her. And who are *you* to say I *left you* anyway? Who are you to say I cut myself off?' The emotions are boiling hot and rageful in my belly, and this time I don't push them down. 'You fucking *disintegrated*. I was the one who held it together, I was the one who sorted the funeral and dealt with the paperwork and you *fell apart*. So don't talk about me leaving you. Where the fuck were *you* when I lost my sister? Where the fuck were you?'

Mum backs up slightly. I'm really yelling. I've never shouted at anybody like this in my life.

'Leena . . .'

'No,' I say, swiping at my face with my sleeve and wrenching the driver's door open. 'No. I'm done.'

'You,' Nicola says, 'are in no fit state to drive.'

Fingers trembling, I turn the key in the ignition. The van splutters and revs, coming to life. I sit there, staring at the road ahead, feeling completely and utterly out of control.

Nicola opens her door.

I look at her. 'What are you doing?' I say, my voice thick with tears.

'I'm not bloody well letting you drive me anywhere,' she says.

I open my door too, then, because Nicola can't climb out of the van without help. My mum is still standing where I left her, her arms folded against herself, fingers wrapped around her ribs. For a moment I want to run to her and let her stroke my hair the way I would when I was a child.

Instead I turn away and help Nicola climb down from the passenger seat. I feel bodily exhausted, as if I've spent hours at the gym. The three of us stand there, Mum and me looking this way and that, anywhere but at each other. The wind whistles around us.

'Righto,' says Nicola. 'So.'

More silence.

'No?' Nicola says. 'Nobody's going to say anything?'

The idea of saying anything seems entirely beyond me. I stare at the tarmac, my hair drawing wet trails on my cheeks.

'I don't know anything about your family,' Nicola says, 'but what I do know is that it's about to start chucking it down and we're going to be stood here like lemons in the middle of the road until Leena's calm enough to drive, so the sooner we can sort all this out the better.'

'I'm calm,' I say. 'I'm calm.'

Nicola gives me a sceptical look. 'You're shaking like a leaf and there's mascara on your chin,' she says.

Mum moves then, holding one hand out. 'Give me the keys, I'll drive.'

'You're not insured.' I hate how my voice sounds, all wobbly and weak.

Mum steps towards us as a bus turns the bend and heads our way.

'Well, I'll call the insurance people then,' she says.

'I'm not sure I fancy you driving any better than her,' Nicola says, looking my mother up and down.

'Bus,' I say.

'Hmm?' says Nicola.

I point, then wave an arm, then wave both arms. The bus comes to a stop.

'Flipping heck,' says the driver as she pulls up alongside us. 'What happened here? Are you all all right? Has there been a crash?'

'Only in a symbolic sense, dear,' Nicola says, already getting on. 'You're stable, then, are you? Not about to start blubbering?'

'Umm, I'm all right, ta?' says the driver.

'Good, good. In you get then, ladies. Off we go.'

Mum and I end up sitting across the aisle from one another, each looking straight ahead. I settle slowly in the bus seat, tears easing. Blowing my nose seems to make me feel a lot better, like it's a formal end to all the crying, and as we wind our way towards Hamleigh, that terrifying sense of being out of my own control eases away, loosening the tightness in my ribs and the pounding in my throat.

I'm not entirely sure what just happened, really, but there's not a lot of time to dwell on it now – the bus driver is kindly taking a detour from her usual route to drop us in the village, but even so, we're late.

The bingo regulars are gathered at the corner of Peewit Street and Middling Lane, in front of the village shop; the rain started coming down a few minutes ago and most of the gang are only half visible inside enormous mackintoshes and rainproof ponchos.

'What are we going to do?' Nicola asks from beside me, as we approach the gaggle of bingo-goers. 'We've not got a van to take them to the bingo hall. Shall I tell them it's off?'

'Excuse me?' I say, wiping my face. 'It is *not* off. All that's required here is a bit of innovative thinking.'

'Are you sure you're up to . . .' Mum trails off on seeing my expression. 'Right,' she says. 'What do you need?'

'Felt tips,' I say. 'Chairs. And a face wipe, for the chin mascara.'

'Twenty-seven! Two and seven! Thirty-one! Three and one, that's thirty-one!'

My voice is hoarse from shouting after all that crying. Thank God for Grandma's printer – it may have taken half an hour of slow, painful chugging, but it eventually produced fifteen bingo sheets. Sometime during that time my mother disappeared (probably for the best), but the rest of the Hamleigh bingo fans are sitting in every chair that exists in my grandmother's house, plus three from Arnold's. After some initial grumbling, the bingo players looked grudgingly impressed with the set-up, and when I cooked up a few party platters Grandma had stored in the freezer and handed out some ciders, the mood of the room improved considerably.

We've rearranged the living room so I can stand at the front, where the telly is, and the bingo gang can all see me. And, in theory, hear me, but that's not going so well.

'Eh?' yells Roland. 'Was that forty-nine?'

'Thirty-one!' Penelope yells back.

'Twenty-one?'

'Thirty-one!' she calls.

'Perhaps Penelope should sit next to Roland?' I suggest. 'So she can tell him what I've said?'

'We wouldn't be having this problem in the bingo hall,' Betsy points out primly.

'Cider isn't this good at the bingo hall,' Roland says, happily swigging from the bottle.

'And those mini spring rolls are delightful,' says Penelope.

I suppress a smile and return my gaze to the random number generator on Kathleen's phone. My phone – previously known as Grandma's phone – is too rudimentary to have such features, but Kathleen came to my rescue and lent me her smartphone. 'Forty-nine!' I yell. 'That's four and nine!'

'I thought you already said forty-nine!' calls Roland. 'Didn't she already say forty-nine?'

'She said thirty-one!' Penelope shouts back to him.

'Thirty-seven?'

'Thirty-three,' calls another voice. It's Nicola. She's behind Roland, and I catch her wicked look and roll my eyes.

Not helping, I mouth at her, and she shrugs, totally unapologetic.

'Did someone say thirty-three?' asks Roland.

'Thirty-one!' Penelope yells cheerily.

'Forty–'

'Oh, bloody hellfire, Roland, turn your fucking hearing aid up!' Basil roars.

There is a short, horrified silence, and then a cacophony of outraged noise from the group. I rub my eyes; they're sore from crying. The doorbell rings and I wince. I know who that's going to be.

I didn't feel I could tell Jackson over the phone that the school van he kindly lent me had a dented bonnet and was currently abandoned just outside Tauntingham. It felt like an in-person sort of discussion.

I hurry to the door, which is not an easy task when there's an obstacle course of chairs and walking sticks to get through.

Jackson's got a sloppy grey beanie hat on, half-covering his left ear, and the shirt he's wearing under his jacket is so crumpled it looks like he's actively ironed the creases in. He gives me a smile as I open the door.

'You all right?' he says.

'Umm,' I say. 'Won't you come in?'

He steps obediently into the hall, then cocks his head, listening to the commotion from the living room. He shoots me a curious look.

'Bingo plan change,' I say. I squirm. 'That's . . . sort of what I need to talk to you about. There was a bit of an accident. With the van. That you let me borrow.'

Jackson absorbs this. 'How bad?' he says.

'I'll pay for it all, obviously, if it's not covered on insurance. And I'll walk up to where it's parked and drive it back to you or straight to the garage or whichever is best for you as soon as this lot have left. And I know I'm already coming to help paint your classroom this weekend, but if there's anything else I can do to make up for – for seemingly causing havoc in your life wherever I am able then . . .'

I trail off. He's looking amused.

'S'all right.'

'Really?'

He pulls off his hat and scrubs at his hair. 'Well, not really all right, exactly, but you're harder on yourself than I could ever be, and it sort of takes any pleasure out of having a go at you.'

'Oh, sorry,' I begin, then laugh. 'No, not sorry. But thanks. For not being rightfully furious. It's been a crappy day.'

'And now you have bingo players in your living room.'

'Yes. A crappy day that has taken a very odd turn. Do you want to come and join in?' I say. 'There's cider. And miniature foods wrapped in cardboard-like pastry.'

'Cider,' Jackson says. 'Not mead?'

'Hmm?'

A dimple appears in one cheek. 'Well, I just wouldn't put it past you to make use of this opportunity to showcase the joys of a medieval-themed evening, that's all.'

'I would *not* stoop to such levels!' I exclaim.

'Then what's that?' he says, pointing at the pile of swatches on the side table.

Feck. 'Err . . .'

He holds up a couple of the little fabric squares. I'd been showing them to Penelope while the spring rolls cooked. They're gorgeous – they look like they've come straight from Winterfell. The one currently in Jackson's hand is a lovely gold colour with a repeat pattern of a dragon on a coat of arms.

'I'm thinking of . . . redecorating,' I say, ushering him towards the living room.

'Redecorating your grandmother's house? With dragons?'

'You know Grandma!' I say. 'Loves her mythology!'

He looks amused, but hands the swatch back to me. We walk side by side to the living room; he stops in the doorway and surveys the chaos, his face unreadable.

'Do you think Grandma would have a fit if she knew I'd messed up the living room like this?' I ask. 'Is that what you're thinking?'

'Actually,' he says, smiling a little, 'I was thinking what a very Eileen Cotton thing this is.'

It feels like I've only just turfed the Neighbourhood Watch out of Grandma's cottage when I'm seeing them again the next day at the village hall. It's our second May Day Committee meeting. This is an important meet-up.

I've prepared handouts. I've brought samples of honey-roasted nuts and sugared fruits and roasted meats. I've mapped out our key demographic for the May Day festival and detailed how perfect the medieval theme is for those fair-goers.

'All those in favour of Leena's idea?' says Betsy.

No hands.

'Sorry, dear,' says Penelope. 'But Jackson knows best.'

Jackson has the decency to look slightly abashed. He didn't bring handouts. He didn't even bring food samples. He just stood up, looked all shabbily sexily charming, and said some stuff about coconut shies and sunhats and throw-the-ring-over-the-pineapple. And then, his *pièce de résistance*: *Samantha's really set her heart on coming dressed as a satsuma.*

Oh, hold on . . .

There's one hand up! One hand!

Arnold is standing in the doorway with his arm in the air.

'I vote for Leena's idea,' he says. 'Sorry, son, but hers has falcons.'

I beam at him. Jackson, as is his wont, just looks amused by everything. What *does* it take to rile that man?

'I wasn't aware you were part of the May Day Committee, Arnold,' Betsy says.

'Am now,' he says comfortably, loping in and pulling up a chair.

'Well, it's still a strong majority in favour of Jackson's theme, as I'm sure you're aware, Leena.'

'All right,' I say, as graciously as I can manage. 'That's fine. Tropical it is.'

I'm smarting, obviously. I wanted to win. But pulling all that information together was the most fun I've had in ages, and at least I got Arnold on my team – and turning up to a village committee, too. Wait until Grandma hears that Arnold the village hermit has been chipping in for the greater good.

I mouth *Thanks* at Arnold as the meeting moves on, and he shoots me a quick grin. Once Basil's started droning on about squirrels again, I switch chairs to sit next to Arnold, ignoring Roland's visible dismay at my change to the seating plan.

'What possessed you to come along?' I ask him quietly.

Arnold shrugs. 'Felt like trying something new,' he says.

'You're turning over a new leaf!' I whisper. 'You are, aren't you?'

He reaches into his pocket to pull out a small paperback: *Murder on the Orient Express*. Betsy looks on in horror as he sits back and opens it up to his page, despite the fact that Basil is mid flow.

'Don't get carried away, now,' Arnold tells me, oblivious to the stares from the rest of the committee. 'I mainly came for the biscuits.'

Whatever. Arnold is basically Shrek: a grumpy green ogre who's forgotten how to be nice to people. And I plan on being his Donkey. I've already invited him around for tea again this week, and he's actually said he'll come, so we're definitely making progress.

If Grumpy Arnold can come to a village committee meeting, anything's possible. As the meeting comes to a close, I watch Betsy make her way slowly to the coat stand, smoothing her silk scarf against her throat. So we got off on the wrong foot. So what? It's never too late to change things, that's what I told Arnold.

I stride over, chin lifted, and join her as she leaves the hall.

'How are you, Betsy?' I ask her. 'You must pop around for tea sometime. You and your husband. I'd love to meet him.'

She looks at me warily. 'Cliff doesn't like to go out,' she says, pulling on her jacket.

'Oh, I'm sorry – is he unwell?'

'No,' she says, turning away.

I walk beside her. 'I know you must be missing having Grandma here to talk to. I hope that if you – if you ever needed help, or someone to speak to, you could come to me.'

She looks at me incredulously. 'You're offering to help me?'

'Yes.'

'And what would *you* be able to do?' she asks, and it takes me a moment to realise she's mimicking what I said to her that first time she came around.

'I'm sorry,' I say frankly. 'That was rude of me, when I said that. I'm just not used to people offering help and meaning it, not when it comes to Carla's death. People usually don't like to talk about her so directly. I was taken aback.'

Betsy doesn't speak for a while. We walk silently down Lower Lane.

'I know it was you who got the council to fill in these potholes,' she says eventually, nodding to the pavement ahead.

'Oh, yeah, it was no big deal. They should have done it ages ago. I just made a few calls.'

'It hasn't gone unnoticed,' she says stiffly, as we part ways.

18

Eileen

It takes me five attempts to pin down the uncharitable woman who lives in Flat 6. She's so rarely in, goodness knows why she gets uppity about what people do in the building.

The advantage to the lengthy delay before meeting her is that by the time we are face to face, my irritation has cooled, and it's not nearly as much effort to pretend to be polite.

'Hello,' I say, when she answers the door. 'You must be Sally.'

'Yes?' Sally says, in an aggrieved sort of way. She's dressed in a suit and not wearing any make-up; her black hair is pulled back in a lopsided ponytail. 'Who are you?'

'I'm Eileen Cotton. I'm living with Fitz and Martha, over in Flat 3.'

Sally does a double take. 'Are you?' she says, and I get the strong impression that she thinks I shouldn't be.

'I'm here because I hear you objected to our idea of running a small social club in the *unused* downstairs area of the building. May I come in so we can have a chat about it?'

'I'm afraid not. I'm very busy,' she says, already moving to close the door.

'Ex*cuse* me,' I say sharply. 'Are you *really* going to shut the door in my face?'

She hesitates, looking a little surprised. As she stands there, with her door half open, I notice there are not one but three locks on its side.

I soften. 'I understand your concerns about letting strangers into the building. I know it can be frightening living in this city. But our lunch clubs will be for very respectable old ladies and gentlemen, and we will still keep the front door shut when the club is going on, so any Tom, Dick or Harry won't be able to walk into the building. Only elderly people.'

Sally swallows. I think she may be younger than I'd assumed – I find it tricky to tell people's ages, these days, and the sternness and the suit have thrown me off.

'Look,' she says, in a brisk, no-nonsense tone, 'it's not that I don't like the idea. But just because a person's elderly doesn't mean they can't be dangerous. What if someone comes in, and doesn't leave when everyone goes, and then they're just lurking in the building?'

I nod. 'All right. How's about we make sure to take names, then, and count everyone in and out so nobody lingers?'

She tilts her head. 'That's . . . Thank you,' she says stiffly. 'That sounds sensible.'

There's a somewhat steely silence.

'So you'll give your permission for the club to go ahead?' I prompt. 'You're the only person we're waiting for.'

Her eyes twitches. 'Fine. Yes. Fine, as long as we count everyone in and out.'

'Of course. As agreed.' I shake her hand. 'It's been a pleasure meeting you, Sally.'

Pleasure is a bit of a stretch, but needs must.

'You too, Eileen.'

I march back to Leena's flat.

'All sorted with Sally in Flat 6,' I tell Fitz, sweeping past to Leena's bedroom.

Fitz watches me go by with his mouth hanging open.

'How do you *do* that?' he says.

A few nights later, Tod and I are side by side in the bedroom of his very grand townhouse, propped up on the pillows. Lying tangled in each other's arms becomes slightly less practical when you've both got bad backs. That's not to say this isn't delightfully intimate: Tod's arm is pressed against mine, his skin warm from lovemaking, and he's shifted the blankets over to my side because he knows how chilly my toes get.

It's dangerously intimate, in fact. I could get quite used to this.

A phone rings; I don't move, because it's always Tod's, and it's usually somebody very important on the other end of the line – a producer, or an agent. He reaches for the phone on the bedside table, but its screen is black. I glance over at mine: *Marian calling.*

I scrabble to reach it.

'Hello?'

'Mum?' says Marian.

She starts to cry.

'Marian, love, what is it?'

'I'm sorry,' she says. 'I've been trying so hard to give you some space. But . . . I just . . . I can't . . .'

'Oh, love, I'm so sorry.' I slide my feet out from under the covers and try to reach for my clothes. 'You've not had . . .'

'No, no, nothing like that, Mum. And I've been looking after myself, I promise – I've been eating properly, doing my yoga . . .'

I breathe out. It's not for me, all that standing on one leg and bowing, but yoga has helped Marian enormously. It's the one fad that's stuck, not just for months but for years – she started when Carla was first diagnosed. When Marian stops doing yoga, I know things are bad.

'That's good, love. Has something happened with Leena, then?'

'We had this awful shouting match in the middle of the road on

Monday night, and all week I just haven't been able to stop thinking about how she . . . she's so *angry*, Mum. She hates me. I wasn't there when she needed me, and now – now I've lost her.'

'She doesn't hate you, love, and you've not *lost* her. She's hurting and angry and she's not acknowledging it yet, but she'll get there. I'd hoped this time with the two of you together would help, but . . .'

I sort through the pile of my and Tod's clothes in a frenzy, frustrated with my slowness, trying to keep the phone to my ear with one hand.

'I'll come home,' I say.

'No, no, you mustn't do that.' Her voice is thick with tears. 'I'm all right. I'm not – having one of my, you know, my moments.'

But who's to say she won't, any day now? And if Leena's shouting at her in the street, who's going to be there to keep Marian in one piece?

'I'm coming back and that's that. See you soon, love.' I hang up before she can protest.

When I turn, Tod is looking at me with raised eyebrows.

'Don't say anything,' I warn him.

He looks taken aback. 'I wasn't going to interfere,' he says.

'No talking about family,' I say. 'We both agreed. Boundaries.'

'Of course.' Tod pauses, watching me carefully as I dress. I wish I could move more quickly. 'But . . .'

I pick up my bag from the chair by the door. 'I'll call you,' I say, as I pull the door closed behind me.

Once I'm outside Tod's house, I find a park bench and settle down to take a breath. Tod lives in a posh part of town called Bloomsbury – there are lots of green spaces edged with black iron fences, and expensive cars with tinted windows.

I can't fathom a version of the Cotton family where we have screaming matches in the street. That's not how we do things. How have we come to this?

I should never have left them alone together. It was pure selfishness, this trip to London, and I'm glad Marian's brought me to my senses before she gets any worse up there in Hamleigh without me.

The pigeons tap around my feet as I rummage in my handbag until I find my diary. Well, Rupert's invited us for drinks at his and Aurora's flat tonight, to celebrate getting permission to launch the Silver Shoreditchers' Social Club. I can't back out of that now, Letitia won't go unless I do, and she needs this. I'll leave tomorrow. That's that. I'll call Leena in the morning.

I'm not sure I can hold my temper if I speak to her now.

When Letitia opens the door I can tell right away how nervous she is. Her shoulders are drawn up to her ears, her chin down to her chest.

'Come on,' I say bracingly. I'm not in the right frame of mind for this event either, but we made a commitment, and besides, I *am* proud of what we're doing with that space downstairs, even if I won't get to see the Silver Shoreditchers' Social Club come to life.

'Do we have to?' she says mournfully.

'Of course we do!' I say. 'Come on. The sooner we go, the sooner we can leave.'

Martha and Fitz are coming too, though I'm not sure Martha can get down the stairs these days, with that enormous bump of hers. She can't manage the journey into the office now, so she's usually set up on the sofa with her feet on the coffee table and her laptop balanced precariously on her stomach. And there's still no word from Yaz on when she's coming home. I purse my lips as we head down towards Rupert and Aurora's flat. I'd quite like to give that Yaz a piece of my mind.

'Mrs Cotton!' Aurora says as she throws open the door to the flat. 'I owe you an *abject* apology for my hangry behaviour when we first met.'

'Oh, hello,' I say, as she sweeps me in for a hug. She has a strong Italian accent; perhaps 'hangry' is an Italian term, although it doesn't really *sound* like one.

'And you must be Letitia,' Aurora says, cupping Letitia's face in her hands. 'What magnificent earrings!'

Letitia's eyes dart towards me with unmistakable panic. I think the face-touching might have been a little much for her. I take Aurora's arm and give it an encouraging tug.

'Do show me around your lovely flat, won't you?' I say.

'Of course! Your flatmates are already here,' she says, gesturing to the stylish grey sofa, where Martha has already settled, feet up in Fitz's lap. I feel a startling pang of fondness as I watch the two of them bickering idly with one another. I've not known them long. I ought not to have got so attached; tonight, I'll have to tell them I'm leaving.

'This is my latest sculpture,' Aurora is telling me, and I give a little squawk as I follow her gaze. It's a gigantic penis made out of marble, with a marble parrot sat on the top. Or the . . . tip, I suppose I mean.

I can't help myself. I glance over at Letitia. 'A sign from the beyond,' I whisper to her; her lips twitch and she disguises a giggle as a cough.

'Marvellous,' I say to Aurora. 'So . . . evocative.'

'Isn't it?' she enthuses. 'Now, if you follow me into the kitchen, I'll mix you up a cocktail . . .'

'No,' Fitz says firmly. 'Absolutely not.'

'What do you mean, no?'

'You can't leave!'

He points an olive on a toothpick at me. Aurora and Rupert make very good cocktails, though I was a bit suspicious about the toothpick olives, at first. Fitz says they're 'ironic'. Now I've got that floaty perfume feeling again, tucked between Martha and Fitz on the sofa, a martini glass in my hand.

'Mrs Cotton – Eileen,' Fitz says. 'Have you done what you set out to do?'

'Well,' I begin, but he waves me off.

'No you have not! The Silver Shoreditchers' Club has barely begun! You've not met your swoony Old Country Boy! And you are *definitely* not done with sorting *my* life out,' he says.

Hmm. I didn't realise he'd noticed I'd been doing that.

'Are Eileen Cottons quitters? Because the Eileen Cottons *I've* met don't strike me as quitters.'

'Not this again,' I tell him, smiling. 'I have to go, Fitz.'

'Why?' This comes from Martha.

I wouldn't give an honest answer to a question like that, usually. Not if it was Betsy or Penelope asking. But I think of Martha waving me over in tears and telling me how afraid she was about the baby coming, and I tell her the truth.

'Marian needs me. She can't cope on her own, and Leena's only been making things worse.' I stare at my martini. I might be a bit sloshed. That was *very* indiscreet. 'She's been rowing with her mother. Shouting at her in the street! That's not how we do things.'

'Maybe it should be,' Martha suggests mildly, swirling her 'mocktail'.

'Yeah, totally,' Fitz says. 'Those two needed to clear the air. Half the problem is Leena bottling everything up for the last year. Have you seen her on the phone to her mum? Twenty seconds of small talk and then she gets this frozen-rabbit face of total panic' – he demonstrates, quite uncannily well – 'and then she's bailing on that chat like a sailor with a hole in his boat.' He pauses. 'Did that simile work?' he asks Martha.

She screws up her nose.

'Leena's mad at Carla as much as she's mad at Marian,' Fitz says definitively. 'And more than *either* of them, she's mad at herself, because when did Leena Cotton ever come across a problem she couldn't fix with a lot of effort and, what does she call it, a thought shower?'

'It's good that they're expressing their feelings,' Martha says. 'A row is cathartic, sometimes.'

'But Marian is *fragile*,' I tell them. 'She's grieving. How is shouting at her going to help?'

'*Is* she fragile?' Martha asks gently. 'She's always struck me as very strong.'

I shake my head. 'You don't know the whole story. This past year, she's had these – patches. Episodes. It's awful. She won't let me in the house. I knock and I knock and she pretends she's not there. The last time was the worst – she wouldn't come out for days. In the end I used my key to get inside, and she was just sitting there on the carpet with one of those God-awful tapes playing, the ones with some man droning on about how grief is a prism and how one must let the light enter one's being or some such tripe. It was like . . .' I trail off, noticing Martha's pained expression. 'What? What did I say?'

'No, no,' Martha says, hand to her belly. 'Absolutely not.'

'Absolutely not what?' Fitz asks.

'Oh, dear,' says Letitia. She hasn't spoken in so long we're all a bit surprised; she looks rather startled herself. She points at Martha's stomach. 'Was that a contraction?'

'Don't worry,' Martha says, breathing through her nose, 'I've had them since lunchtime. They're not real contractions.'

'No?' Letitia says, eyeing Martha. 'How can you tell?'

'Because Yaz isn't back yet,' Martha says, 'and I'm not due for another three weeks.'

'Right,' Fitz says, looking at me with raised eyebrows. 'Only I'm not sure the baby necessarily knows your schedule.'

'Yes it does,' Martha says through gritted teeth. 'It is – *oooh, oww, oww!*'

She grabs Letitia's hand, which happens to be nearest. Letitia yelps.

'OK,' Martha says, leaning her head back against the sofa again.

'OK, fine. Done. What were we saying? Oh, yes, Eileen, go on – Marian's episodes?'

We all stare at her.

'What?' she says. 'It's fine. I mean, I only go to the hospital if the contractions are . . . if the contractions are . . .' She leans forward again, face twisting. She lets out an alarmingly animal sort of groan. I recognise that sound.

'Martha, love . . . those look very much like real contractions,' I tell her.

'It's too soon,' Martha gasps once the contraction has passed. 'Not . . . can't . . .'

'Martha,' Fitz says, placing his hands on her shoulders, 'you know when you say a client is being totally ridiculous and can't see what's right in front of them? Like that woman who thought her drawing room was big enough to take a picture rail?'

'Yeah?' Martha pants.

'You're being that woman,' Fitz says.

Ten minutes later and the groans are more like screams.

'We need to get her to the hospital,' Fitz tells Rupert and Aurora. I'll give them their due, they're not shying away from getting stuck in. Aurora is dashing around fetching water and typing questions into Google Search; Rupert, who did a spell as a paramedic in his youth, is desperately reciting the advice he remembers about child-birth, which is not calming Martha, but is making the rest of us feel a bit better.

'What was Martha's plan for when the baby came?' I ask Fitz.

'Yaz,' he says, pulling a face. 'She's got a car, she'd drive her to the hospital.'

'But she's not here,' I say. 'What was the alternative plan?'

Everyone blinks at me.

'I have a motorbike?' Rupert offers.

'A scooter,' Aurora corrects him. Rupert pouts.

'I'm not sure that'll work,' Fitz says, rubbing Martha's back as she leans on the sofa arm, groaning. 'How long 'til the Uber arrives?'

Rupert checks his phone and whistles between his teeth. 'Twenty-five minutes.'

'Twenty-*what*?' Martha yells, in a voice that sounds absolutely nothing like Martha. 'That is literally impossible! There is always an Uber within five minutes! It is a law of physics! Where is Yaz? *She was meant to bloody be here!*'

'She's in America,' Letitia offers. 'What?' she says, noting my glare. 'Isn't she?'

'She's not picking up her phone,' Fitz says to me in a low voice. 'I'll keep trying her.'

Martha lets out a half groan, half scream, dropping into a crouch. Fitz flinches.

'I am not meant to be witnessing this,' he says. 'I'm supposed to be downstairs having a cigar and a whisky and pacing, aren't I? Isn't that what men do in these situations?'

I pat him on the shoulder. 'Let me take over.' I swing a cushion off the sofa for my knees and get down next to Martha. 'Fitz, you go and knock on the neighbours' doors. There must be someone with a car. Aurora, fetch some towels. Just in case,' I say to Martha when she turns panicked eyes my way. 'And Rupert . . . go and sterilise your hands.'

'In! In!' Sally from Flat 6 is yelling.

This emergency situation has been a wonderful bonding experience for the building. I can finally say I've met every single neighbour. I was astonished when Sally stepped up to the plate, though she was rather strong-armed into it: she's the only one in the building with a means of transport, and by the time we got to her the sound of Martha screaming blue murder was echoing down the halls.

'All I know about Sally is that she is a hedge-fund manager and lives in Flat 6, yet I have no qualms about getting in her enormous, serial-killer-style van,' Fitz observes wonderingly. 'Is this community spirit, Eileen? Trusting thy neighbour, and all? Oh, holy mother of God . . .'

Martha has his hand in a vice-like grip. She's leaning her forehead on the headrest of the seat in front; when she sits back, I notice she's left a foggy dark patch of sweat on the fabric. She's in a bad way. This baby is not dilly-dallying.

'Go! Go! Go!' Sally yells, though to whom I'm not sure – she's in the driving seat. She pulls out of her parking space to a series of outraged honks. 'Emergency! Baby being born in the back!' she shouts out of the window, waving her arm at an irate taxi driver. 'No time for niceties!'

Sally's definition of niceties is quite broad and seems to cover most of the rules of the road. She goes through every red light, clips someone's wing mirror, drives up three kerbs, and shouts at a pedestrian for having the gall to walk over a zebra crossing at the wrong moment. I find it fascinating that a woman so anxious about feeling safe in her own home drives as though she's on the dodgems. But, still, I'm delighted she's throwing herself into things. Though I've yet to get to the bottom of why she owns quite such a big van, as a woman living alone in the centre of London. I do hope Fitz's not right – I'd feel awful if she turned out to be a serial killer.

Martha startles me out of my reverie with a long, loud, agonised roar.

'We're almost there,' I tell her soothingly, though I haven't a clue where we are. 'You'll be in the hospital in no time.'

'Yaz,' Martha manages, a vein standing out on her forehead. She grabs my arm with that urgent, animal grip that only comes with pain.

'I can't get hold of her, honey,' Fitz says. 'I think she'll be on stage. But I'll keep trying her.'

'Oh, God, I can't do this,' Martha wails. 'I can't do this!'

'Of course you can,' I say. 'Just don't do it until we get to the hospital, there's a love.'

19

Leena

I'm on my fifth batch of brownies. I have discovered four entirely different ways of making brownies badly: burning them, under-cooking them, forgetting to line the tray, and missing out the flour (a real low point).

But *these* are perfection. All it takes is application. And practice. And possibly a slightly calmer mental state – I started this process in a fog of missing Carla and raging at my mother and wondering what the hell I was doing with my life, and I think maybe brownies are like horses: they can sense your stress levels.

Now, though, I am calmed, I have brownies, and – finally, at last, after so many missed weekends . . . Ethan is here.

He throws his bags down and swoops me up in a hug as soon as I open the front door.

'Welcome to the rural idyll!' I tell him as he lets me down.

'It smells like something's burned?' Ethan says, then, catching my expression, 'But delicious! Burned in a delicious way! Chargrilled? Barbecued? Those are great ways of burning things.'

'I made brownies. Quite a few times. But look!' I lead him proudly to the plate of perfect chocolatey squares on Grandma's dining-room table.

He grabs one and takes an enormous bite, then closes his eyes and moans. 'OK,' he says through his mouthful. 'That genuinely is delicious.'

'Yes! I *knew* it.'

'Always humble,' Ethan says, then he reaches to grab the drying-up cloth I'd slung over my shoulder. 'Look at you, baking! All domestic!'

I grab the cloth back and swat at him with it. 'Shut up, you.'

'Why? I like it.' He nuzzles into my neck. 'It's sexy. You know how much I love it when you do the fifties housewife thing.'

I blush and push him off. 'That was a murder-mystery party costume and I was not *doing a thing*, and even if I had been, it would not have been for you!'

'No?' Ethan says with a cheeky grin. 'Because I distinctly remember you doing a thing . . .'

I laugh, batting away his roaming hands, and move through to the kitchen. 'Do you want a tea?'

Ethan follows. 'I want *something*,' he says. 'But it's not tea.'

'Coffee?'

'Guess again.' He presses up against me from behind, hands snaking around my waist.

I turn in his arms. 'I'm sorry – I feel *so* unsexy right now. I've spent most of the day crying, and it's been such a weird week. Being back here is making me . . .'

'Turn into your grandmother?' Ethan says, with a teasing twitch of his eyebrows.

I pull back. 'What?'

'I'm kidding!'

'Where did that come from?'

'Spending your day baking, no interest in sex, wearing an actual apron . . .' He clocks that I'm really not laughing. 'Come on, Leena, I'm teasing!' He takes my hand and tries to twirl me. 'Let's go out. Take me to a bar.'

'This isn't a bar sort of place,' I say, awkwardly spinning into the twirl.

'There must be a bar *somewhere*. What's that little town nearby? Divedale?'

'Daredale. That's over an hour away. And anyway, I thought we could bob around to see Arnold this evening, my neighbour – he said he'd make us lamb for tea.' I try a smile. 'He's a bit grumpy, but he's a lovely guy at heart.'

'I should probably do some work this evening, really, angel,' Ethan says, dropping my hand and heading to the fridge. He pulls out a beer.

'Oh. But . . .'

He kisses me on the cheek as he reaches for a bottle opener from the drawer. 'You're welcome to chip in. I'm looking at white-space opportunities on the project I told you about last week – I know how you love a challenge . . .'

'I feel plenty challenged at the moment, to be honest,' I say, then blink as Ethan turns the TV on.

'Millwall's on,' he says. 'I thought we could have it on in the background.'

He didn't care about white-space opportunities or Millwall playing when he was asking to go to a bar. I swallow, reminding myself that he's come a long way to see me, and he's right – I'm in a difficult place at the moment, I've gone a bit . . . backwards on this grieving thing. I can see how it could be frustrating.

Still. He's not exactly getting in the spirit of the rural getaway, is he?

He looks up at me from the sofa, catches my expression, and softens. 'I'm being a knob, sorry,' he says, reaching up to take my hands. 'I'm not good at this rural-life schtick, angel. Give me a bit of time to adjust to the new you?'

'I'm not a new me,' I tell him grumpily, coming around to sit next to him on the sofa. 'And I'm not my grandmother.'

He pulls me in, tipping me so my head lies on his chest. This is my comfort place. I used to feel almost desperate if the fear and grief hit when Ethan wasn't there – I needed this, his arm around me, my ear listening to the beat of his heart. This was the only way it felt safe to stay still.

I soften into him. He kisses the top of my head.

'I'll tell Arnold we'll come around for lamb next time,' I say, as Ethan pulls me in closer, into just the right spot.

The next morning I get up early for a run and when I get out of the shower I climb into bed naked, pressing my still-damp body up the length of Ethan's frame. He wakes slowly, with an appreciative noise, his hand reaching for my hip, his lips finding my neck. It's lovely, just like it should be, and the weird tenseness of last night feels ridiculous – we joke about it as we bring our coffees back to bed, and he combs through my hair with his fingers as I lie against his chest, like we always do at home.

After that, Ethan's all conciliatory and agreeable; he says he'll come along to the May Day Committee meeting, even though it starts at eight a.m. today (why, Betsy?) and I give him a clear out ('if you need to work . . .').

When we walk into the village hall together every head swivels our way. Ethan, somewhat taken aback, mutters *Jesus* before plastering on his best taking-out-clients smile and working his way around doing introductions.

'Hi. I'm Ethan Coleman,' he says to Betsy.

He's speaking loudly and slowly, as if Betsy's deaf; I wince as her eyebrows rise. He does this with all the elderly people in the room – Penelope actually flinches a little, and she must be used to people yelling, given that she lives with Roland. Crap. I should have briefed him a bit before we got here.

Jackson is last to the meeting, as usual – not quite late enough to be *late*, but always last, and always greeted with a chorus of adoring hellos from the elderly in the room. He glances at Ethan, who clocks him and stands up again, stretching a hand out for him to shake.

'Ethan Coleman.'

'Jackson.'

'Good to know there's someone else under the age of a hundred around here,' Ethan says, dropping his voice and flashing Jackson a grin.

Jackson looks at him for a moment. 'These are good people,' he says.

'Oh, of course! Of course. I guess I just wasn't expecting so many grannies. I kind of imagine it to be all miners and farmers up here, you know, going *oh, aye* and *'ow do, love.*'

I wince. Ethan pulls a face when he does the Yorkshire accent, as though he's trying to look stupid – I'm not sure he even knows he's done it, but it's made Jackson's eyes narrow a fraction.

'Sorry,' Jackson says, 'you are?'

'Ethan Coleman,' Ethan repeats, then, faced with Jackson's blank expression, he straightens up a little more. 'Leena's boyfriend.'

Jackson's eyes flick to my face. 'Ah,' he says. 'You've come up to visit, then.'

'I would've come before, but it's not easy for me to get away from London,' Ethan says. 'People counting on me, millions at stake, that sort of thing.'

This is said entirely without irony. I blush, standing up and putting my hand on his arm.

'Come on, Ethan, let's sit down.'

'Remind me what you do, Jackson?' Ethan says, brushing me off.

'I'm a teacher,' Jackson says. 'No millions at stake. Just futures.'

'Don't know how you do it. I couldn't spend all day with kids without my brain going numb.'

We're in the centre of the room, now, and the May Day planning committee members are watching from their seats, utterly compelled, like this is a play in the round. I tug on Ethan's arm; he shakes me off again, shooting me a frown.

'Will you sit down, please?' I say sharply.

Ethan's eyes narrow. 'What? Jackson and I are just getting to know each other.'

'You're right, we should get started,' Jackson says and walks to his seat.

Only when he's sitting down does Ethan let me pull him back to his own chair. I stare down at my feet, heart thumping with embarrassment.

'Right!' calls Betsy, with patent delight. 'Well! How exciting. Ahem. Let's talk bonfires. Leena, are you ready?'

Deep breath.

'Absolutely,' I say, pulling my pen and notepad out of my bag. I try to collect myself. Ethan doesn't mean any harm; he just gets a bit macho and defensive when he thinks there's another Type A guy in the room, that's all. Everyone will understand when he's got his temper back. He can just charm them all another time. It's fine. Not a disaster.

'You're taking *minutes*?' Ethan says.

My cheeks heat again. 'Yeah. It's what my grandma does.'

Ethan laughs then, a too-loud laugh that gets everyone looking. 'When was it you last took minutes, Leena Cotton?'

'A while ago,' I say, keeping my voice down. I can feel Jackson watching us across the circle.

Betsy clears her throat pointedly.

'Sorry!' I say. 'Bonfires. I'm ready, Betsy.'

I ignore Ethan's glances and get on with my minutes. Having him here is making the meeting feel different – I'm seeing it from his point of view, like when someone watches your favourite TV show and all of a sudden you realise how rubbish the production values are. I can see Jackson watching Ethan, too, steady and unreadable.

I try to concentrate on the meeting. Betsy is explaining 'for any newcomers' (so, Ethan) that May Day is a traditional Gaelic festival celebrated here in Hamleigh for generations. She's getting really deep-dive on the mythology for something that is essentially just the usual quirky British fayre-type merriment, only with a maypole.

Astonishingly little is achieved in the meeting, except that I've got lumbered with finding a May Queen and a May King for the parade, which is going to be tricky when the only people I know in Hamleigh are present, and don't really like me. But I don't want to say no to Betsy, so I'll have to think of something.

I pack up and leave the meeting as soon as it's done.

'Leena?' Ethan says as I head for the door, dodging Piotr, who is trying to stop Penelope hauling Roland out of his seat on her own. 'Leena, slow down!'

'What were you *doing* in there?' I hiss, as we step outside. It's raining, thick sideways rain that gets under your collar right away.

Ethan swears. He hates getting his hair wet. 'God, this place,' he moans, looking up at the sky.

'You know, it also rains in London.'

'Why are you so pissed at me?' Ethan says, walking fast to keep up with me. 'Was it what I said about northerners? Come on, Leena, I figured Jackson was the sort of guy who could take a joke. And why do you care, anyway? You keep saying how everyone chooses his side over yours and how awful he's made you feel about the dog . . .'

'Actually, I keep saying how awful *I* feel about the dog. Jackson is a really good guy and he's not held that over me at all. *You* were the one acting all – all obnoxious and knobby, and I've been trying so hard to make a good impression on these people, and . . .'

'Whoa!' Ethan tugs my arm to pull me to a stop in the bus shelter. 'Hello? I'm obnoxious and knobby, now, am I?'

'I meant . . .'

'You're meant to be on my side, angel, aren't you?' He looks hurt. 'Why do you care so much what these people think of you?'

I sag. 'I don't know, really.'

What am I doing? First yelling at my mum, then at Ethan. I need to get a grip on myself.

'I'm sorry,' I say, taking his hands. 'I've been kind of crazy these last few days – weeks, maybe.'

Ethan sighs, then leans forward and kisses me on the nose. 'Come on. Let's get you home and in the bath, hey?'

Ethan has to head back to London pretty much as soon as we get back from the meeting, which is probably a good thing: I'm meant to be spending the day helping Jackson to decorate the Year One classroom as my penance for losing Hank. I'd hoped Ethan would muck in and help, but now I really don't fancy partaking of another Jackson–Ethan meet-up, at least not until Ethan's had longer to cool off and realise he needs to apologise.

Jackson's truck pulls into the car park just as I climb out of Agatha the Ford Ka, sweating slightly after a roasting from the air con. I didn't pack enough rough clothes, so I'm in skinny black trousers and a fleece I borrowed from Grandma, which I assume is fine for doing DIY as it already has an enormous purple paint splodge over one boob. (Interesting, as nothing in Grandma's house is painted purple.) Jackson is wearing threadbare jeans and a flannel shirt. He gives me a quick smile as he puts down the paint tins and brushes to unlock the doors.

'Hi. You better at the roller or the fiddly bits?' he says.

'Err, fiddly bits,' I say. I was expecting a frostier greeting after this morning; I'm a little taken aback.

I follow as he hefts the paint through to the classroom. It's strange seeing a school with no children dashing about – it makes you realise how small and flimsy everything looks, from the little plastic chairs to the brightly coloured bookshelf half full of tatty paperbacks.

'Jackson,' I say. 'I'm so sorry about Ethan being . . .'

Jackson's setting up, steadily laying out everything he needs; his hands pause for a moment. His eyes look very blue in the late morning sunshine streaming through the classroom window, and he's clean shaven today, the usual sandy grains of stubble gone from his jawline.

'He was trying to be funny,' I say. 'He's normally not like that.'

Jackson uses a paint-splattered screwdriver to lever up the lid of the tin.

'I'm sorry too,' he says. 'I could have been a bit more, you know. Welcoming.'

I tilt my head – that's a fair point. I relax a little, reaching for a brush. We start on the back wall, painting side by side. Jackson's forearm is lightly dusted with pale freckles, and when he moves past me to turn on the light I can smell the outdoors on him, cool air and a hint of earthiness, like the scent of rain.

'I never said thanks for helping out with Samantha when she was here for Easter,' he says eventually. 'She wouldn't stop going on about you afterwards.'

I smile. 'She's such a lovely kid.'

'She's already getting too clever for me,' Jackson says, pulling a face. 'She asks more questions than my class put together. And she's always *thinking* – bit like you, really.'

I pause, surprised. He glances over.

'Not a bad thing. Just the impression I get.'

'No, that's fair. Except I'd call it worrying rather than thinking, most of the time, so I hope Samantha's *not* like me, for her sake. My brain doesn't know when to shut up. I bet you I can think up twenty worst-case scenarios before you could even think of one.'

'Never been one for worst-case scenarios,' Jackson says. He crouches to dip his roller in the tray; his wrists are flecked with paint now, new, brighter freckles. 'When they happen, you cope. And it's usually one you've not thought of that gets you, so why worry?'

God, what I would give to think like that. The sheer *simplicity* of it.

'I just want to be sure I'm doing the right thing,' I say. 'I'm worried about – I don't know, you know those books you read as a kid, that let you choose what happened next, and you turned to a different page depending on what you picked?'

Jackson nods. 'I know the ones.'

'Right, well, I'm always trying to skip ahead so I can work out the best one.'

'Best one for what?'

I pause. 'What do you mean?'

'Best for you?'

'No, no, I mean just . . . best. The right thing to do.'

'Huh,' Jackson says. 'Interesting.'

I reach for a new subject, something more comfortable.

'Can I ask who was May Queen and May King last year? I've got to find someone to do it, and I'm thinking that'll be the best place to start.'

There is a very long pause.

'It was me and Marigold,' Jackson says eventually.

I drop my brush.

'Shit!' I reach for the wet cloth and dab at the vinyl floor – I've got there just in time to avert disaster.

'All right?' Jackson asks, gaze back on the wall again.

'Yes, fine. Sorry . . . you and Marigold? Your ex?' I realise belatedly I probably ought not to know about Marigold – it wasn't Jackson who told me. But he seems unsurprised. I suppose he does live in Hamleigh: he must be used to gossip doing the rounds.

'She always liked doing it when we were together.' His hand is steady and careful as he paints, but there's a muscle ticking in his jaw. 'She came back for it.'

'With Samantha?'

The roller pauses briefly.

'Aye.'

'Will they be coming this year?'

'I hope so. I'm lucky – Marigold's filming in London for a spell so she's in the UK for a few weeks.'

'That's great. I'm glad.' I chew the inside of my cheek. 'When I said about my flatmate Martha, the other day,' I say tentatively, 'I never meant – I know there are lots of ways to be a parent. Obviously. I'm sorry for upsetting you.'

He sluices more paint into the roller tray, and I wait, watching him carefully tilt the tin back without dripping any paint down the side.

'Marigold keeps saying they'll move back and set up in London,' he says, clearing his throat. 'But it's been over a year. And the visits are getting less and less often.'

'I'm sorry,' I say again.

'S'all right. You didn't mean any harm. You're just a bit – you know – direct in how you say things.'

'Mm. I get "forthright" a lot in appraisals at work.'

'Yeah?' His voice lightens a little. 'I get "good in a crisis". Code for "too laid back".'

'Whereas "forthright" is what they say now they're not allowed to call women bossy.'

'Doubt anyone would dare call you bossy,' Jackson says. 'Except Betsy.'

I snort. 'I'm sure Betsy's said worse than that.'

'You just need to give that lot time to get used to you.' He shoots me a wry glance. 'What did you expect? You swanned into Hamleigh with your city shoes and your big ideas, like this is small-town America and you're a New York bigshot and we're all in one of those Christmas films . . .'

'I did not swan! And I've been borrowing my grandma's shoes ever since I got here. *You*, on the other hand, Mister Not In My Town, with your devil dog and your big truck, scaring off my boyfriend . . .'

'I scared off your boyfriend?'

'No, I'm just kidding.' I shouldn't have said that – Ethan would hate that I had. 'I just mean, you know, you're pretty intimidating yourself. Everyone here hangs on your every word. You are unbeatably nice.'

The grin widens. 'Unbeatably?'

'I mean, unbelievably. Not unbeatably.'

The grin is still there, but he lets my Freudian slip slide. We switch over so I can do the edges on his side.

'Listen,' Jackson says after a moment, 'your theme for May Day. It was better than mine.'

'Oh, no,' I begin, then I stop myself. 'Yeah, it was, actually.'

'I feel a bit bad about how that went. I sort of, you know, played the daughter card a bit.'

'You also had a secret tropical cocktail session without me. And made me dress up as the Easter bunny and skip around looking like a twat.'

Jackson laughs. 'I wasn't trying to make you look like a twat. I thought you'd like to take part in an important Hamleigh tradition.'

'And you wanted to get back at me for winning Dr Piotr over to team medieval theme. Not that that lasted long.'

His eyes turn shifty.

'I'm right! I knew it!' I swipe at him with my paintbrush; he dodges surprisingly nimbly, grinning.

'I'm not proud of it,' he says, dodging my brush again. 'Oi!'

I get him on the arm, a big smear of pale green. He brandishes the roller at me and I raise an eyebrow, bouncing on my toes.

'Just you try it.'

He's a *lot* quicker than I expected him to be. He gets me right on the nose – I squeal indignantly.

'I didn't think you'd go for the *face*!'

Jackson shrugs, still grinning. 'The perfect attack, then.'

I lift my top to wipe my nose; as I drop it again, I see his eyes flick away from the bare skin of my stomach. I clear my throat. This is getting a bit silly; I turn back to the wall, sobering up.

'So anyway,' Jackson says, following my lead, 'I wanted to ask how open you would be to merging themes.'

I turn back to him, staring. 'Tropical Medieval? That is literally absurd. What are we going to do, falconry with parrots? Jousting with bananas?'

He looks thoughtful.

'No!' I say. 'It's ridiculous!'

'All right,' he says. 'How about medieval themed, but with cocktails?'

I squirm. *Gah.* It's so anachronistic! It's so messy!

Jackson looks amused. 'It's just a village fete – who's going to care if it's not perfect? And it's the only way you'll get Basil on side. Turns out that man loves a mango daiquiri. Besides, we've already booked the cocktail-makers.'

'Fine. But you have to get up in front of all of the committee and declare that you give my theme full support because it is much better,' I say, brandishing a finger.

'Apart from how it doesn't have cocktail stands.'

I growl. Jackson grins, dimples showing.

'It's a deal,' he says, stretching out his hand. I clasp it, feeling the wet paint between our fingers.

'Just so you know,' I say, 'you're going to have to be May King, and I will be ensuring that the outfit is totally ridiculous. Revenge for the bunny ears.'

He snorts at that. 'Ah, come on, I did you a favour, giving you the Easter bunny job – it's pretty much a Cotton family tradition,' Jackson tells me as we get started on the next wall.

I wrinkle up my nose. 'Don't tell me Grandma wears that outfit.'

'Not your grandma. Your mum's done it, though – and Carla, once.'

'Carla? Seriously? I never knew that.'

'When she was . . . seventeen, maybe?'

'Tell me,' I say, painting forgotten, because suddenly I'm hungry for it, this news about my sister, like she's still out there in the world, surprising me.

'Your grandma roped her into it, I think. You must've been at uni. I was doing teacher training, back for the holidays, and I bumped into her when she was out hiding the eggs. She looked at me absolute daggers. "You breathe a word of this to anybody," she said, "I'll tell everyone you smoke behind the allotments."'

I laugh, delighted. His impersonation of Carla is brilliant. He smiles back at me, blue eyes catching the sunlight again.

'She launched into it then, how it's all a Christian appropriation of a Pagan ritual or something, you know how Carla was about that sort of thing, and then around the corner comes Ursula – she must've been six or so, then – and suddenly off Carla skips, bunny tail flapping. She wanted the kid to think she was the Easter bunny. Preserving the magic. Kind of like you did, for Samantha.'

I breathe out slowly, my paintbrush suspended in mid-air. It's easy to forget, when you're missing someone, that they're more than just the person you remember: they have sides to themselves they only show when other people are around.

In the last few weeks I've spoken about my sister more than I have in the last year put together. In Hamleigh, people mention Carla without blinking; at home my friends stutter over her name, watching me carefully, afraid to say the wrong thing. I've always appreciated how Ethan will steer people off the topic if we're out for dinner – he says he knows talking about Carla will hurt me.

And yes, it does hurt, but not like I thought it would. The more I talk about her the more I want to, as if there's a dam in my brain somewhere with cracks forming and the water's getting through and the faster the flow, the more the dam wants to break.

20

Eileen

It's a long night, as any night spent in a hospital waiting room will be. I am reminded of Marian's birth, and Leena's, and Carla's. But most of all I'm reminded of the day when Carla was first admitted to hospital. The careful way the doctor cast his warning: *I'm afraid it's not good news.* The gaping, terrible panic on Marian's face, how her hands clutched at my arm as if she was falling. And Leena, doing what she always did, setting her jaw and asking all the questions. *What are our options? Let's talk about next steps. With all due respect, Doctor, I'd appreciate a second opinion on that scan.*

At about one o'clock in the morning Fitz suddenly seems to remember I'm old and might need to go home to sleep, but it doesn't feel right to leave Martha. So I sleep on the floor under a heap of Rupert and Fitz's jumpers and jackets. I haven't slept on a floor for a very long time; I ache everywhere. It's as if somebody has taken my body apart and jammed all the pieces back together again. My head is throbbing.

Fitz comes to fetch me at around lunchtime; I'm still dozing, but I've moved from the floor to a chair. He looks rather haunted, but happy.

'There's a baby!' he says. 'A girl!'

I try to stand too fast and clutch a hand to my head.

'Are you OK, Mrs C?' Fitz asks as he helps me up.

'I'm fine. Don't mind me. Did you get hold of Yaz?'

Fitz smiles. 'I held the phone so she could see Martha and the baby. She's on a flight back now.'

'Good.' Not quite good enough, in my opinion, but there we are. I get the impression Yaz is somebody whose gambles have so far always paid off – perhaps it will do her some good to realise that you can't always cut everything quite so fine.

We turn a corner and I inhale sharply, my hand going to the wall for support. There is a young woman in a bed. Her hair is curly and her face is drawn with exhaustion.

'Mrs C?' Fitz says. 'Martha's just through here.'

I turn away with a lurch of nausea. This place is not doing me any good.

'Are her family here now?' I ask. My voice shakes.

'Yes,' Fitz says hesitantly. 'Her dad's in with her.'

'She doesn't need me, then,' I say. 'I think I'd better go home.'

He looks as if he's thinking about going with me, but I'm glad he doesn't offer to when I walk away. It's impossible to find an exit in this endless place. At last I push my way out of the hospital and take a gulp of dry, polluted air.

I call Leena. My hand is almost shaking too much to find her number on this wretched telephone, but this is important. I can do this. I just need to – this blasted thing – would it – there, it's ringing, at last.

'Grandma, hi!'

She sounds lighter than usual, almost breezy. I was cross with her last night, but I'm worn out, and so much has happened since yesterday – I haven't the energy to argue with her. It's the traditional British solution to a family disagreement, anyway. If you act as if it didn't happen at all, eventually pretending not to be cross becomes actually not being cross merely through the passage of time.

'Hi, love,' I say. 'I'm just calling to say Martha's baby has been born. A little girl. They're both safe and well and her family is here.'

'Oh no!' She pauses. 'I mean, not oh no, but I missed it! This wasn't meant to happen for weeks! I'll call her – I should come down and visit! I'll check trains.' I can hear her typing away on the computer in the background. There's a pause. 'Are you all right, Grandma?' she asks.

'Just a little shaken, being back in a hospital. Thinking about our Carla. Silly, really.'

'Oh, Grandma.' Her voice softens; the typing stops.

I close my eyes for a moment and then open them again, because I can't stay steady on my feet with them shut.

'I think I should come home, Leena. I'm being daft, sitting around down here.'

'No! Are you not enjoying yourself?'

I stumble; I'd started walking, making my way to the taxis parked outside the hospital, but my balance is off with the phone to my ear. My spare hand grasps for the wall and my heart thunders. I hate the feeling of falling, even when you catch yourself.

'All right, Grandma?' Leena says down the phone.

'Yes, love. Of course. I'm fine.'

'You sound a bit shaky. Get some rest, we can talk about it tomorrow. Maybe even face-to-face, if I'm down in London seeing Martha.'

Leena coming back to London. Yes. Things are straightening up again, going back to how they ought to be. I'm glad. I think I'm glad, anyway. I'm so tired, it's difficult to tell.

Back at the flat, I sleep for a few hours and wake feeling awful: groggy and sick, like the start of the flu. There's a text on the mobile phone from Bee, inviting me out for tea. *I don't think I've got it in me*, I reply, then fall back asleep before I can even explain why.

An hour or so later, there's a knock at the door. I lever myself up out of bed. My head hurts the moment I'm upright; I wince, holding my palm to my forehead. I get to the door eventually, though it takes me so long I don't expect whoever knocked will still be there. I feel awfully old. I don't think I've quite shaken that feeling from when I stumbled outside the hospital.

It's Bee at the door, holding a large paper bag in her arms – food, by the smell of it. I blink at her, confused.

'Eileen, are you OK?' she asks with a frown.

'Do I look terrible?' I ask, smoothing my hair down as best I can without a mirror.

'Just pale,' Bee says, taking my arm as we move inside. 'When did you last eat or drink?'

I try to remember. 'Oh, dear,' I say.

'Sit yourself down,' Bee says, pointing to the chair Martha got me when I told her I couldn't cope with the ridiculous bar stools they sit at for mealtimes. 'I got comfort food. Sausages and mash with gravy.'

'Takeaway sausages and mash?' I ask, staring in bemusement as she begins to pull steaming Tupperwares out of the paper bag.

'The joys of Deliveroo,' she says, smiling and putting a large glass of water in front of me. 'Drink that. But maybe not too fast. Jaime always throws up when she drinks water too fast if she's poorly. Leena texted to say Martha's had the baby – she guessed you've been looking after her, not yourself. And now you're a bit wobbly?'

I nod, rather shamefaced. I've been daft, sleeping on floors, forgetting to eat properly. I'm seventy-nine, not twenty-nine, and I'd do well to remember it.

'We'll have you back to yourself in no time,' Bee says. 'How's Martha? Any sign of Yaz?'

'Martha's still in the hospital for now, and Yaz has nearly arrived.' I sip at the water. I hadn't noticed how thirsty I was; my throat is so dry it hurts. 'She seems to have conjured up a house that Martha likes after all – not to buy, but rented. They're getting the keys today.'

Bee rolls her eyes, fetching us plates from the cupboard. 'Well, *that's* impractical,' she says. 'You can't move in on the day you bring your baby home.'

'I know,' I say dryly, 'but there's no telling Martha that. Oh!' I say, straightening up. 'How was your date with the man from the library?'

Bee laughs. 'Half a glass of water and *there's* Eileen Cotton again.' She pushes a plate of steaming mash and sausages towards me. 'Eat that, and I'll tell you all about it.'

I scoop up a forkful of mash, chew, then look expectantly at her. She lifts her eyes in fond exasperation, an expression she usually only wears when she's talking about Jaime.

'The date was lovely,' she says, picking up her fork. 'He's smart and funny and . . . not my type at all. In a good way,' she adds, seeing me open my mouth to speak. 'But then he made a big thing of how he doesn't really get on well with kids once I mentioned Jaime.' She shrugs. 'I think we can agree that "must be cool with kids" is one part of my usual list we shouldn't throw out the window.'

How disappointing. But no matter. I was unlikely to get it right off the bat. 'You should try scouting around a nice expensive wine bar next. That's my recommendation.'

Bee looks at me shrewdly. 'Last week you'd have said you'd take me to one yourself. You're thinking of going home, aren't you?'

'Leena mentioned that, did she?'

'She was worried about you.'

'I haven't made up my mind yet,' I say. I put my fork down for a moment, taking deep breaths; the food is making me feel worse, though I'm sure it'll do me good in the long run. 'And she ought not to be worrying about me.'

'Oh, because you don't worry about her?' Bee asks, eyebrows raised.

'Of course I do. She's my granddaughter.'

Bee chews for a moment, looking serious. 'Can I tell you something I'm worrying about?' she says. 'About Leena?'

I swallow. 'Of course.'

'I think Ceci's up to something.'

'Ceci?' I narrow my eyes. She's the one that sent the text message to Leena's phone about the work project going from 'strength to strength'.

'I saw her having coffee with Ethan down by Borough Market. He's a consultant, she's an assistant – she's probably just networking,' Bee says, pouring me another glass of water. 'But still. I'd like to know if Ethan mentioned it to Leena.'

'You don't think . . .'

Bee swills her drink. 'I don't know what I think. But, I mean . . . Do you actually trust Ethan?'

'Not a jot,' I say, putting my glass down a little too hard; water splashes across the counter. 'Why does he have *three* phones? What's he really doing on all those fishing trips? How are his shoes always so shiny?'

Bee gives me an odd look. 'That's because he pays someone to polish them, Eileen,' she says. 'But on the other points: agreed. So, yes, he was there for Leena when Carla died. Give the man a medal. But he's been riding on that ever since – from where I'm standing, it looks like he's stopped trying. It's a huge time for her, and he's gone totally AWOL. Whereas, when *he* has a crisis at work, who's there to pick up the pieces and help out with the slide shows?'

I frown. 'She doesn't, does she?'

'*All* the time. The other day he suggested this brilliant idea for placating a tricky client and everybody loved it. It was only after the meeting that I clocked where I'd heard the idea before: Leena had suggested it to me when we were on the Upgo project. It was *her* idea, not his, but he never said a word to give her the credit.' She sighs. 'Doesn't mean he has it in him to cheat on her, though. Maybe it means the opposite. I mean, the man takes her for granted, but he must see his life would be a lot less cushy without her.'

In my experience, men do not think in this fashion. 'Hmm,' I say, attempting another mouthful of food as the nausea subsides a little.

'I don't know. I guess it was just . . . seeing Ethan in that coffee shop staring Ceci in the eyes . . .'

'There was staring?'

'Of the highest order,' Bee says.

'What do we do?' I ask, rubbing my neck, which is beginning to ache. 'Can you honeytrap him?'

'I think you've been watching too many crime dramas with Martha,' Bee says, shooting me an amused glance. 'I will not be honeytrapping anybody, thank you.'

'Well, I can't very well do it, can I?' I say. 'Come on. Step up.'

Bee laughs. 'There will be no honeytrap!' she says. 'I'll just . . . keep an eye on things.'

I wish I could stay here and do the same. He'd never suspect it if I was the one investigating. Nobody ever thinks it's the old lady.

'Oh, good,' Bee says happily. 'You must be starting to feel better. You've got your scheming face on.'

21

Leena

I'm all geared up to head back to London the next morning, but when Yaz answers Martha's phone she tells me – as kindly as a person can – that the two of them need a few weeks to get their shit together before anyone visits.

'She's even banned her own father from coming to stay,' Yaz says apologetically. 'Sorry, Leena.'

I hear Martha in the background. 'Pass me the phone!' she says.

'Hey!' I say. I've got the phone on speaker while I tidy Grandma's kitchen, but I switch back to hand-held. I need Martha's voice to be nearer my face – that's the closest I can get to hugging her. 'Oh my God, how are you? How is baby Vanessa?'

'Perfect. I know it's a cliché to say that but I really think she is, Leena,' Martha says earnestly. 'Though breastfeeding is a lot less Madonna-and-child than I was expecting. It *hurts*. She kind of . . . *chomps*.'

I pull a face.

'But the midwife says she'll come and help me with my latching position and we'll get it sorted in no time, won't we, my beautiful baby?' This is presumably addressed to Vanessa, not to me. 'And Yaz has found us a gorgeous flat in Clapham! Isn't she amazing? But anyway, none of this is what I wanted to say, sweetheart, I wanted to say . . . Oh, I'm sorry not to invite you down. I love you, but – I've just got Yaz back, and . . .'

'Don't worry. I completely get it. You need your time with Vanessa.'

'OK. Thank you, sweetheart. But that's also not what I wanted to say. What did I want to say, Yaz?'

God, this is like Martha after five glasses of wine and no sleep. Is this what people mean when they talk about 'baby brain', I wonder? But I'm smiling, because she's so *audibly* happy, just buzzing with it. It's so good to hear her and Yaz together again. I've always loved Yaz – when she's around, Martha opens out, like one of those flowers you see on fast-forward on the telly. Yaz just needs to be around a bit more.

'You wanted to tell her to stop her grandmother from going home,' Yaz says in the background.

'Yes! Leena. Your grandmother can't go home yet. It's so good for her, being here in London. I've seen her every day this last month and honestly, the transformation – she's blossoming. She's smiling ten times more. Last week I walked in and she and Fitz were dancing together to "Good Vibrations".'

My spare hand goes to my heart. The image of Grandma and Fitz dancing together is almost as cute as the picture of baby Vanessa that Yaz just sent me.

'You know she's dating an actor? And she's got us all turning the downstairs area of the building into this community space?' Martha continues.

'Seriously? The area with the miscellaneously stained sofas?' And then, processing: 'Is the actor called Tod? She won't tell me a thing about her love life, it's infuriating!'

'You are her granddaughter, Leena. She's not going to want to keep you up to speed on her sex life.'

'*Sex?*' I say, pressing a hand to my chest. 'Oh, my God, weird weird weird.'

Martha laughs. 'She's having an amazing time here, and she's working on this new project – a social club for elderly people in Shoreditch.'

'There are elderly people in Shoreditch?'

'Right? Who knew! Anyway, she's only just getting it off the ground, and she's so excited about it. You need to let her finish what she's started.'

I think of Basil, how he laughed about Grandma's projects never going anywhere, and I feel suddenly and very fiercely proud of my grandmother. This project sounds amazing. I love that she's not given up on the idea of making a difference, not even after decades of men like Basil and Grandpa Wade putting her down.

'It's talking to your mum that's got her thinking she has to come home,' Martha says. 'Something about an argument?'

'Ah.'

'Tell Eileen you'll sort things with your mum and I bet she'll stay here. And it'd be good for you, too, sweetheart. Talking to your mum, I mean.'

I pick up the cleaning cloth again and scrub hard at the hob. 'Last time we talked it ended in this horrible fight.' I bite my lip. 'I feel awful about it.'

'Say that, then,' Martha says gently. 'Tell your mum that.'

'When I'm with her, all the feelings, the memories of Carla dying – it's like getting bloody bulldozed.'

'Say that, too,' Martha tells me. 'Come on. You all need to start talking.'

'Grandma's been wanting me to talk to Mum about my feelings for months,' I admit.

'And when is your grandmother ever wrong? We've all fallen madly in love with Eileen, you know, Fitz included,' Martha says. 'I'm thinking about getting one of those wristbands people wore in the nineties, except mine'll say, *What Would Eileen Cotton Do?*'

I take a long walk after Martha's phone call, following a route I sometimes run. I notice so much more at this pace: how many greens there are here, all different; how beautifully those drystone walls are built, the stones slotted in like jigsaw pieces. How a sheep's resting face looks kind of accusatory.

Eventually, after ten unpleasant kilometres of thinking time, I call my mother from a tree stump beside a stream. It's about the most restful and idyllic setting imaginable, which feels necessary for what promises to be an extremely difficult conversation.

'Leena?'

'Hi, Mum.'

I close my eyes for a moment as the emotions come. It's a bit easier this time, though, now I'm braced for them – they own me a little less.

'Grandma wants to come back to Hamleigh.'

'Leena, I'm so sorry,' Mum says quickly, 'I didn't tell her to – I really didn't. I texted her yesterday evening and said she should stay in London, I promise you I did. I just had a moment of weakness when I called her, and she decided . . .'

'It's OK, Mum. I'm not angry.'

There's silence.

'OK. I *am* angry.' I kick a stone with the toe of my running shoe so it skitters into the stream. 'I guess you figured that out.'

'We should have talked about all this properly sooner. I suppose I thought you'd come to understand, as time passed, but . . . I only supported Carla in what she chose, Leena. You know if she'd wanted to try another operation or round of chemotherapy or *anything*, I would have supported that, too. But she didn't want that, love.'

My eyes begin to ache, a sure sign tears are coming. I suppose I know what she's saying is true, really. It's just . . .

'It's easier to be angry than sad, sometimes,' Mum says, and it's exactly the thought I was trying to form, and so Mum-like of her to know it. 'And it's easier to be angry with me than with Carla, I imagine.'

'Well,' I say, rather tearfully. 'Carla's dead, so I can't yell at her.'

'Really?' Mum says. 'I do, sometimes.'

That startles a wet half-laugh out of me.

'I think she'd be a bit offended to think you were refusing to yell at her, just because she died,' Mum goes on mildly. 'You know how big she was on treating everyone equally.'

I laugh again. I watch a twig caught behind a rock, fluttering in the flow of the stream, and think of playing Pooh Sticks with Carla and Grandma as a child, how cross I'd feel if my stick got stuck.

'I'm sorry for calling your grandma,' Mum says quietly. 'It was just a wobble. Sometimes I feel very . . . alone.'

I swallow. 'You're not alone, Ma.'

'I'll call her again,' Mum says after a while. 'I'll tell her to stay in London. I'll tell her I want you to stay and I won't have it any other way.'

'Thank you.'

'I do want you to stay, you know, more than anything, actually. It wasn't about that. It was just about needing – needing my mother.'

I watch the water churn. 'Yes,' I say. 'Yes, I can understand that.'

22

Eileen

I have to say, working with Fitz on the Silver Shoreditchers' space is making me see the man in a whole new light. He's working peculiar hours in his latest job – a concierge at some fancy hotel – but whenever he's home, he's down here painting something or hunched at his laptop reading about setting up charitable organisations on the Internet. He's handling all the Silver Shoreditchers' administration – he's even made some posters for the club, with a little logo. It's wonderful. I've been on at him for weeks about being more proactive in his career ambitions, but, if I'm honest, I'm a little shocked he's got all this in him.

'There!' he says, standing back from where he's just hung a large picture on the wall.

'Wonderful,' I say. 'The perfect finishing touch!'

The picture is an enlarged black-and-white photograph of the building from the 1950s, when it still operated as a printworks. There's a collection of people gathered outside, talking and smoking, their collars turned up against the wind. It's a reminder that this place isn't just a collection of individual homes, it's one building, too, with a history of its own.

I smile, looking around the space we've created. It's beautiful. There's a rich red sofa facing those glorious windows, a long dining table pushed to the back of the space, and lots of small tables with charmingly mismatched chairs, ready and waiting to host dominoes and rummy.

I'm so glad I'm here to see this. And I'm even gladder that the reason I didn't go home early is because Marian *asked* me not to. Hearing her say how much she needed this time with Leena, just the two of them . . . it was like something heavy lifting off my chest.

My phone rings. Fitz tracks it down and fishes it out of the side of the sofa. *Betsy calling.* Oh, damn, I meant to ring her. Until now I've called her every week – I just got rather distracted with all the renovating, and it slipped my mind.

'Betsy, I'd just picked up my phone to call you, what a coincidence!' I say as I answer, pulling a face to myself.

'Hello, Eileen, dear,' Betsy says. I frown. I am familiar enough with the tones of Betsy's false cheerfulness to spot the signs of a bad day. I feel worse than ever for forgetting to check on her.

'Are you well?' I ask carefully.

'Oh, bearing up!' she says. 'I'm calling because my grandson is down in London today!'

'That's lovely!'

Betsy's grandson is an inventor, always dreaming up ridiculous unnecessary contraptions, but he's the one member of her family who stays in regular contact with her, so that puts him high up in my estimation. If she knows his whereabouts, he's called her recently – that's good. Now he just needs to get his mother to do the same.

'And this is the grandson who invented the . . . the . . .' Oh, why did I start this sentence?

Betsy leaves me to stew.

'The hummus scoop,' she says, with great dignity. 'Yes. He's down in London for a meeting, he says, and I thought, gosh, what a happy coincidence, our Eileen is in London, too! You two must meet for lunch.'

THE SWITCH | 198

I purse my lips. I have a feeling Betsy may have forgotten that London covers more than six-hundred square miles and houses more than eight million people.

'I've already told him to call you and set it up. I thought you might be lonely there, and it would be nice to have someone to talk to.'

I don't have the heart to tell her that I'm far from lonely. I was at the start, of course, but now I hardly have a moment alone, what with seeing Tod, planning the Silver Shoreditchers' Club, gossiping with Letitia . . .

'He's *dating*, too, you know,' Betsy says. 'He might be able to give you some tips in that department.'

I pause. 'He's dating?'

'Yes! That's what he calls it, anyway. He's using all these funny things on his mobile phone,' Betsy says. 'Perhaps he could tell you about them.'

'Yes,' I say slowly, 'yes, that would be marvellous. Remind me, Betsy . . . what's he like, this grandson of yours? Relationship history? Hopes and dreams? Political views? Is he tall?'

'Oh, well,' Betsy says. She sounds rather taken aback, but then the grandmother in her kicks in, and she can't resist the opportunity. She talks nonstop for twenty-five minutes. It's perfect. Exactly the sort of intelligence I'm after. And, even better: he sounds very promising indeed.

'What a lovely man! How wonderful, Betsy,' I say, as she eventually runs out of breath. 'And he's going to call me?'

'He is!' There's a muffled sound behind Betsy. 'I must go,' she says, and I hear her voice tighten. 'Speak soon, Eileen! Do try and ring me soon, won't you?'

'I will,' I promise. 'Take care.'

Once I've ended the call, I open WhatsApp. I'm much better at using this phone now, thanks to Fitz's tutelage; he peers approvingly over my shoulder as I navigate the screen. There's a message waiting from someone I don't know. Fitz leans across and shows me how to accept him to my contacts.

Hi, Mrs Cotton, it's Betsy's grandson here. I think she's warned you about lunch! How is Nopi, one o'clock tomorrow? All the best, Mike.

I choose Bee's name before I reply to his message.

Hello Bee. Would you be free for lunch tomorrow? Nopi, one fifteen? Love, Eileen xx

Mike is not only very tall but also encouragingly handsome, though he has Betsy's nose – but he can't help that. He's got thick-rimmed glasses and brown hair that curls a little, and he's dressed in a grey suit, as though he's just come from a terribly important meeting. I try not to get too excited as we're seated at a perfect table: big enough to squeeze on another diner and in full view of the road so I can see Bee when she . . . Yes! There she is. Marvellous.

'Eileen?' she says, looking puzzled as she approaches the table.

She looks at Mike. The penny drops. Her eyes narrow.

'Bee!' I say, before she can start complaining. 'Oh, Mike, I hope you don't mind, I was supposed to meet my friend Bee for lunch today, so I invited her to join us.'

Mike takes this with the calm demeanour of a man who is used to surprises. 'Hello, I'm Mike,' he says, holding out his hand.

'Bee,' Bee says, in her driest, flattest, most off-putting tone.

'Well!' I say. 'Isn't this lovely? Mike, why don't you start by telling Bee all about your education?'

Mike looks rather perplexed. 'Let me go and ask for another chair, first,' he says, gallantly standing and offering Bee his.

'Thank you,' Bee says, and then, as soon as she's seated, she hisses, 'Eileen! You have no shame! You *cornered* that poor man into blind-dating me!'

'Oh, nonsense, he doesn't mind,' I say, scanning the menu.

'Oh? And how'd you figure that one?'

I glance up. 'He's fixing his hair in the mirror behind the bar,' I tell her. 'He wants you to like the look of him.'

She swivels, then tilts her head to the side. 'He *does* have a nice bum,' she says begrudgingly.

'Bee!'

'What! You wanted me to like him, didn't you, and I've not got much else to go on right now! Oh, hi, Mike,' she says as he returns to the table with a waiter and chair in tow. 'So sorry about this.'

'Not at all,' he says smoothly. 'Thanks so much,' he tells the waiter. 'I really appreciate you going to the trouble.'

'Polite to waiters,' I whisper to Bee. 'A very good sign.'

Mike looks amused. 'Eileen,' he says, 'you have the advantage over me and Bee – you're the only person at this table who has any idea who anybody else is. So. Why don't you tell us why you wanted to matchmake me and Bee today?'

I pause, a little startled. 'Oh, umm, well . . .'

I catch Bee's expression of rather wicked amusement. She shoots Mike an appreciative glance. I narrow my eyes at them both.

'I have spent a great deal of the last few years keeping my mouth shut about one thing or another,' I tell them. 'But I've come to realise lately that sometimes it's better just to stick your oar in, as it were. So you shan't make me feel embarrassed for trying to matchmake the two of you. As Bee put it – I have no shame.' I raise a hand as Mike opens his mouth to say something. 'No, no, let me finish. Bee is an extremely successful management consultant and plans to launch her own business any day now. Mike, you recently set up your own business about . . . hummus scooping.' I wave a hand at them both. 'Go on,' I say. 'Discuss.'

I return home feeling pleased as punch. I chaired the entirety of Bee and Mike's date and it was a roaring success. Well, they spent the majority of it laughing, at least – some of the time at me, admittedly, but that didn't matter. I've always been rather afraid of being laughed at, but when it's on your own terms, and you're laughing too, it turns out it can be quite fun.

I settle myself down at the breakfast counter with Leena's laptop. There are three new messages waiting for me on my dating website.

Todoffstage says: Tomorrow night, my house. The black lacy underwear.
I insist upon it.

I blush. Gosh. Normally I hate being bossed around, but somehow when Tod does it, I don't seem to mind at all. I clear my throat and write back.

EileenCotton79 says: Well, if you insist . . .

Whew. Well, this should calm me down again – a message from Arnold. I thought I'd told him to bog off and stop looking at my profile, hadn't I?

Arnold1234 says: I saw this and thought of you . . .

I click the link below his message. A video pops up. It's a cat, eating its way through a large patch of pansies.

I burst out laughing, surprising myself.

EileenCotton79 says: This proves nothing, Arnold Macintyre!

Arnold1234 says: There are bags of these cat videos on the Internet. I've been watching them for hours.
EileenCotton79 says: Have you seen the one with the piano?
Arnold1234 says: Brilliant, isn't it?

I laugh.

EileenCotton79 says: I thought you didn't like cats.
Arnold1234 says: I don't. But whatever you think, Eileen, I'm not a monster, and only a monster could fail to be amused by a cat who plays the piano.
EileenCotton79 says: I don't think you're a monster. Just a grumpy old man.

The dot dot dot lasts for ever. Arnold types so slowly. While I wait, I go back to his profile page. There's still very little detail there, but he has added a profile picture now, a shot of him grinning in the sunshine with a straw hat covering his balding head. I smile. He looks very Arnold-like, and I feel a bit guilty about my decade-old picture, taken in very flattering light.

Arnold1234 says: I'm not grumpy all the time, you know.
EileenCotton79 says: Just when I'm there, then . . .
Arnold1234 says: You ARE quite infuriating.
EileenCotton79 says: Who, me?
Arnold1234 says: And you can be a bit on the petty side.
EileenCotton79 says: Petty! When??
Arnold1234 says: When we found out my shed stretched a little over our boundary line and you made me rebuild the whole bloody thing on the other side of the garden.

I make a face. I did do that, I must admit. Arnold was apoplectic, it was ever so funny.

EileenCotton79 says: Property laws must be respected, Arnold. Other-wise, as my new friend Fitz likes to say . . . what separates us from the animals?

Arnold1234 says: New friend, eh?

EileenCotton79 says: Yes . . .

Arnold1234 says: New FRIEND, eh?

I laugh as the penny drops.

EileenCotton79 says: Fitz? He lives with Leena! He's young enough to be my grandson!

Arnold1234 says: Good.

Arnold1234 says: I mean, it's good that you've made friends with her housemate. What's their house like, then?

Belatedly I remember there's one more message waiting for me. This one is from Howard.

OldCountryBoy says: Hello, dearest Eileen! I've just finished reading The Mousetrap, *since you said it was one of your favourites, and I must say I loved it too. What an ending!*

Something warm blooms in my chest. I start typing back. Howard's always so attentive. It's rare to find a man who's more interested in listening than talking. We've discussed all sorts of things on this website – I've told him about my family, my friends, even Wade. He was very sweet and said Wade was a fool for letting me go, which I wholeheartedly agree with, I must say.

Arnold's next message pops up, but I press the minus button to shrink it away again.

23

Leena

When the doorbell rings I've only just got out the shower; I quickly tug on some jeans and an old blue shirt of Grandma's. It's probably just Arnold – he pops in for a cup of tea from time to time now, and, after much frustrated insistence from me, has started coming to the front door instead of the kitchen window. My hair drips down my back as I dash down the hall, still buttoning the shirt.

When I reach the door, I discover that it is not Arnold. It's Hank. Or rather, it's Jackson and Hank, but Hank really demands my attention first, standing on his hind legs at the full extent of his lead, desperately trying to reach me.

'Hello,' I say, as Jackson pulls Hank back into a sitting position. I hurriedly finish my buttons. 'This is a surprise!'

'Do you want to come for a walk with me and Hank?' Jackson says. His cheeks flush a little. 'This is a peace offering, in case you couldn't tell. From Hank, I mean.'

'I . . . Yes!' I say. 'Yes, absolutely. Thank you, Hank.' I do a weird sort of bow to the dog, then try to move on very quickly as though that didn't happen. 'Just let me . . .' I point to my head, then, realising this might not be sufficient: 'My hair needs sorting.'

Jackson looks at my hair. 'Oh, right. We'll wait.'

'Come in,' I tell him, as I head back inside. 'The kettle's still warm

if you fancy a drink. Oh, does Hank want one? There are plastic
bowls under the sink.'

'Thanks,' Jackson calls.

Drying my hair usually takes a good half an hour, so that's clearly
not an option. In front of Grandma's living-room mirror, with Ant/
Dec weaving between my ankles, I scrape it up into the bun I wear
for work instead – though, Christ, this is uncomfortable on the
scalp. Do I really wear it like this every day? It's like having someone
pulling my hair at all times. Never mind, it'll have to do.

'Did I leave my phone in there?' I call. I've grown accustomed to
the solid, heavy weight of Grandma's Nokia in the back pocket of my
jeans; I wonder if it'll take me a while to get used to my iPhone again
when I go back to London.

I drop my chin to finish tying the bun, and when I lift my head
Jackson's there, his face a little different in the mirror, that crooked
nose bending the other way.

I turn to face him; he smiles, holding out Grandma's phone. 'You
getting used to this old brick, then, are—'

There's a noise somewhere between a meow and the sound that a
birthing cow might make. Ant/Dec streaks by, and then, in a flash of
black fur, Hank comes bounding between us, nose outstretched, the
cat in his sights, his path cutting directly across in front of Jackson's
shins, so that mid step Jackson finds his left leg connecting with a
fast-moving puppy and the phone in his hand goes soaring and—

Oof. He tumbles forward into my arms, or rather he *would* tumble
into my arms, except for the fact that he probably weighs twice as
much as I do. It's more like being on the wrong side of a falling tree.
The back of my head connects with the cold mirror, my back heel
with the skirting board, and Jackson's pinned me against the wall,
his right arm taking the brunt of his weight, his belt buckle pushing
hard into my stomach.

For the briefest moment we're body to body, the lengths of us pressed close. My face is against his chest, turned aside so my ear can hear the thud of his heart. His arms frame me, and as he pulls back, his chest brushes my breasts. I breathe in sharply as the sensation zings. My cheeks flush; I should have worn a bra under this shirt.

Our eyes lock as he pushes off the wall, and he pauses there, arms braced on either side of me. His irises are speckled with darker flecks, and there are sandy freckles just beneath his eyes, too pale to see from far away. I find myself thinking about the muscles standing out in his arms, the way his T-shirt pulls across his broad shoulders, how it would feel to—

Hank licks my bare foot. I squeal, and the stillness between me and Jackson becomes a frenzy of awkward motion: he pushes off the wall and shoots backwards as I duck to the side and busy myself fetching Grandma's phone. Ant/Dec seems to have escaped unscathed; Hank is wagging his way around me, tongue out, as if I might produce another cat for him to chase if he hangs around a while.

'Are you all right?' I ask Jackson, twisting the phone between my hands. I've left it an awkwardly long time to meet his eyes again – I drag my gaze to his face and find him looking slightly ashen, fixed to the spot a few feet away.

'Aye, yes,' he says, in a strangled voice. 'Sorry about that.'

'No worries! No worries at all!' Too much exclaiming. Stop exclaiming. 'Shall we head out?'

'Aye. Yes. Good idea.'

We make our way out of the house and down Middling Lane. We're both walking extremely quickly. Too quickly to talk comfortably. Perfect. Silence is just what I'm after right now.

The walking seems to be working out some of the awkward tension between us. Hank's loving it – he's trotting right at Jackson's side, tail wagging. I take a deep breath of crisp, spring air as the Dales open out ahead of us. I can smell the sweetness of something blossoming in the hedgerows, hear the *chiff-chaff, chiff-chaff* of the little birds darting between tree branches above us. The beauty of nature. Yes. Focus on the beauty of nature, Leena, not the sensation of Jackson's broad, muscled body rubbing against your nipples.

'You ready to take him?' Jackson asks, nodding in Hank's direction.

I clear my throat. 'Yes! Sure!'

'Here.' He reaches into his back pocket and produces a dog treat. Hank smells it right away – he lifts his nose and glances towards us.

'Try saying "heel",' Jackson tells me.

'Heel, Hank,' I say.

Hank drops into step, looking up at me with the adoring expression I thought he reserved for Jackson. Turns out it's all about the chicken treats. I am much cheered by this.

'Hey, look at that!' I say, looking over at Jackson.

He smiles back at me, dimples showing, then his gaze slides away, uncomfortable.

We walk on; our footsteps are the only sound I can hear now, aside from the warbling birds. Hank is doing brilliantly, though I'm gripping the lead very tightly, just in case. Jackson takes us back on a route I don't know, passing through beautiful dense, cool woodland to the east of the village, until we're within sight of Hamleigh again. From here you can see the little cul-de-sac where Betsy lives, five or six white, blockish houses with their faces turned our way, windows blinking in the light.

'You're doing that thinking thing again, aren't you?' Jackson says, looking at me sideways.

'Do you honestly not think? As in, if you're walking around, you're just thinking of nothing?'

Jackson shrugs. 'If nothing needs thinking about, yeah.'

Astonishing. 'I was thinking about Betsy, actually,' I say. 'I wonder . . . I worry about her a bit.'

'Mmm. We all do.'

'Arnold said that too, but . . . why hasn't anyone *done* anything then?' I ask. 'Do you think Cliff treats her badly? Should we be helping her leave him? Offering her a spare room? Doing *something*?'

Jackson's shaking his head. 'It's about what Betsy wants,' he says. 'And she doesn't want any of that.'

'She's lived with the man for decades – if he has been mistreating her, how can you know she knows what she wants?'

Jackson blinks at me, registering this. 'What would you suggest?' he asks.

'I want to go around to see her.'

'She'll never invite you in. Even Eileen never gets to go in Betsy's house.'

'No way!'

Jackson nods. 'Far as I'm aware. Cliff doesn't like visitors.'

I grit my teeth. 'Well. All right. How about we enlist a little help from Hank?'

'Betsy, I'm *so* sorry,' I say, 'but I think Hank's in your garden.'

Betsy blinks at me through the inch gap in the door. Her house isn't at all what I'd expected. I thought it'd be all twee roses and perfectly polished doorsteps, but the house's gutters are hanging loose and the windowsills are peeling. It looks sad and unloved.

'Hank? Jackson's dog? How on earth did he get into our garden?'

Well, by me picking him up, Jackson giving me a boost, and me dropping Hank from a possibly quite dangerous height into the relatively soft landing of a large shrub.

'I really don't know,' I say, spreading my hands helplessly. 'That dog can wriggle his way in and out of everywhere.'

Betsy looks behind her. God knows what Hank is currently doing to her garden.

'I'll go and get him,' she says, and closes the door in my face.

Shit. I look behind me and whistle between my teeth; after a long moment Jackson appears at the end of the path to Betsy's front door.

'She's gone to get him!' I hiss.

Jackson waves a hand. 'She won't be able to catch him,' he says comfortably. 'Just stay put.'

I turn back to the door, tapping my foot. After about five minutes the door opens a crack and Betsy's head appears. She looks a bit more dishevelled than she did last time.

'You'll have to come through and get him yourself,' she says quietly. She glances behind her again. She seems older, more hunched, but maybe it's the setting of the worn-out house. The hall carpet is threadbare and stained; the lampshade hangs wonkily, casting strange lopsided shadows on the beige walls.

'Betsy!' yells a gruff male voice from somewhere within the house.

Betsy jumps. It's not a normal jump, the kind you do when you're startled. It's more like a flinch.

'One moment, love!' she calls. 'A dog's just got loose in the garden, but I'm getting it sorted! Come on through,' she whispers to me, ushering me past the closed door to our left and into the small, dark kitchen.

There's a door leading out into the garden; it swings open, and through it I can see Hank tearing through the flowerbeds. I feel a bit guilty. The garden is the one part of this place that actually looks cared for – the shrubs are carefully pruned and there are hanging pots on each fence post, overflowing with pansies and pale-green ivy.

'How are you, Betsy?' I say, turning to have another look at her. I'd never noticed how thin her hair is, how the whitish-pink of her scalp shows between the strands. There's thick, peach-coloured foundation caked under her eyes and gathering in the lines around her mouth.

'I'm well, thank you,' Betsy says, pulling the kitchen door closed firmly behind her. 'Now, if you wouldn't mind getting that dog out of my garden?'

I look outside again and wince: the dog is currently digging a hole in the middle of Betsy's lawn. I should probably put a stop to that.

'Hank! Hank, come!' I call, and then – this is the part Jackson gave me very firm instructions on – I crinkle the plastic packet of dog treats in one hand.

Hank's head shoots up and he freezes mid dig. Within half a second, he's bounding towards me. Betsy lets out a tiny shriek, but I am prepared: I grab him before he can change his mind, and fix the lead to his collar. He continues bouncing about undeterred – once he's collected his snack, of course – and I swivel to avoid him completely entangling me in the lead.

I can sort of see what Jackson means, now: Betsy isn't OK, is she, but what can I do to make her *say* it? This may not have been my finest plan. It's very hard to have a personal conversation with somebody when you're also trying to stop a Labrador from licking their face.

'And you're sure everything is all right?' I try, as Hank redirects his attention from Betsy to the bin.

'Everything is fine, thank you, Leena,' Betsy says.

'Betsy, what the bloody hell's going on?' yells a gruff male voice.

Betsy stiffens. Her eyes flick to mine, then away.

'Nothing, love,' she calls loudly. 'Be with you in a moment.'

'Is there somebody in here? Did you let somebody in?' A beat, then, low, like a warning: 'You didn't let somebody in, did you, now, Betsy?'

'No!' Betsy says, eyes flicking to mine again. 'Nobody here but me, Cliff.'

My heart thumps. I've gone cold.

'Betsy,' I begin, my voice low. I give Hank a hard yank on the lead and tell him very sternly to sit; blessedly, this time, he does. 'Betsy, he shouldn't speak to you like that. And you should be allowed to have friends around. It's *your* house as much as his.'

Betsy moves then, out into the garden, leading me to the passage running from the front to the back garden. 'Goodbye, Leena,' she says quietly, unbolting the gate.

'Betsy – please, if there's anything I can do to help you . . .'

'Betsy . . . I can hear voices, Betsy . . .' comes Cliff's voice from inside. Even I flinch this time.

Betsy meets my gaze square on. 'You're one to talk about needing help,' she hisses. 'Sort your own life out before you come in here and try to fix mine, Miss Cotton.'

She steps aside. Hank strains beside me, eyes on the pathway through the open gate.

'If you change your mind, call me.'

'You just don't take a hint, do you? Out.' She nods to the gate as if she's talking to the dog.

'You deserve better than this. And it's never too late to have the life you deserve, Betsy.'

With that, I go. The gate clicks shut quietly behind me.

I hate how little I can do for Betsy. The next day, I research local services that offer support for women who are in controlling relationships – I can't find much that's specific to older people, but I think there are some resources that might still help her, and I print them off, carrying them in my rucksack whenever I'm out in the village, just in case. But as the week passes, she's still as frosty as ever, and every time I try to speak to her she shuts me down.

I don't have much time left here. It's May Day next weekend, then I'll be back to London, and back to work the week after that. There is an email from Rebecca in my inbox to discuss which project I'll be working on when I return to the office. I keep opening the email and staring at it – it feels as though it's meant for somebody else.

For now, I'm just focusing on May Day. The final elements of the festival are falling into place. I have sourced a hog roast, I have worked out how to fix five-hundred lanterns to the trees around the

field where the main bonfire will be, and I have personally trans-
ported six bags of biodegradable green glitter to the village hall so
that it can be scattered along the parade route. (That, it turns out,
was what *glitter* meant on the to-do list Betsy gave me. My protesta-
tions that glitter is not very medieval were met with a firm, 'it's
traditional').

I can't step in and try to help Betsy without her consent, but I *can*
help her coordinate a large-scale project.

And there's something else I can do, too.

'Can't you look frailer?' I ask Nicola, straightening her cardigan
and brushing some lint from her shoulder.

She shoots me a glare that I make a mental note to imitate when
I next want to eviscerate a rude co-worker.

'This is as frail as I go,' Nicola says. 'I thought you said you were
taking me to Leeds to go shopping. Why do I need to look frail?'

'Yes, absolutely, shopping,' I say. 'We're just dropping in on a few
corporate law firms first.'

'What?'

'It won't take a minute! All our meetings are scheduled for twenty
minutes at *most*.'

Nicola glowers. 'What do you need me for?'

'I'm getting a sponsor for the May Day festival. But I'm all, you
know, Londony and corporate,' I say, waving a hand at myself. '*You*
are sweet and elderly and get the sympathy vote.'

'I'm not even from Hamleigh! And sweet my arse,' says Nicola. 'If
you think I'm going to sit there and simper for some fat-cat
lawyer . . .'

'Maybe just don't say anything at all,' I say, ushering Nicola
towards the car. 'Probably safest.'

Nicola grumbles the whole way to Leeds, but as soon as we get
into that first meeting room she's such a convincing doddery old
dear I find it quite hard not to laugh. *Such an important event for our*

poor little village, Nicola says. *I look forward to May Day all year.* They lap it up. Port & Morgan Solicitors sign up there and then; the others say they'll think about it.

It feels good to be back in a boardroom, actually. And it's especially good to be walking out of one victorious, instead of hyperventilating. I send a quick text to Bee as we head to the car.

You've still got it, she replies. *THAT'S my Leena Cotton.*

As we drive back to Knargill, Nicola cackles into the enormous mocha I bought her to say thank you.

'I had no idea it was so easy getting men like that to cough up some cash!' she says. 'What else can we ask them for, eh? Sponsor the mobile library? Sponsor a minibus?'

She might actually be on to something, there. My mind goes to the document still open on Grandma's computer: *B&L Boutique Consulting – strategy.* Corporate responsibility is more important than ever for millennials – businesses need to be building charitable work and volunteer opportunities into the heart of their business models, they need to . . .

'Leena? This is my house,' Nicola says.

I screech to a halt.

'Oops! Sorry! Miles away.'

She eyes me suspiciously. 'Don't know why I let you drive me anywhere,' she mumbles as she unfastens her seatbelt.

The next morning I pop around to Arnold's and knock on the conservatory door. He has morning coffee in here at ten-ish, and every so often I come around to join him. I'll be honest, the cafetière coffee is a big draw, but it's more than that. Arnold is lovely. He's like the granddad I never had. Not that I didn't have a granddad, but you know, Grandpa Wade hardly counts.

Arnold's already there, a full cafetière ready and waiting. It's sitting on his latest book, and I shudder as I step inside and spot the large brown ring spreading across the cover. I move it and spin the novel around: it's Dorothy L Sayer's *Whose Body?*, one of my grandma's favourites. Arnold seems to be on a detective novel thing of late. Discovering his love of reading has been one of my favourite surprises of my time in Hamleigh.

'How's your mother doing?' Arnold asks as I pour myself a coffee.

I give him an approving nod, and he sighs between his teeth.

'Would you stop acting like you taught me how to have a conversation? I wasn't *that* bad before you got here. I know how to be polite.'

Whatever. Arnold insists that his decision to 'clean up' (buy some new shirts, go to the barber's) and 'get out more' (start Pilates, go to the pub on a Friday) was his and his alone, but I know the truth. I'm his Donkey, he's my Shrek.

'Mum's good, actually,' I say, passing him his mug. 'Or, you know – a lot nearer to good than she has been for a while.'

Since that phone call after the argument, Mum and I have met up three times: once for tea, twice for lunch. It feels strange and tentative, as though we're rebuilding something wobbly and precarious. We talk about Carla in fits and starts, both afraid to go too close. It makes me anxious to the point where I'm sweating with it. I feel like I'm in danger of opening something I've fought very hard to keep closed. I want to do it, though, for Mum. I may not have really known what I meant when I promised Grandma I'd be here for my mother, but I get it now. Mum doesn't need errands doing, she just needs family.

I think part of what had made me so angry with my mum was the fact that I felt she should have been looking after me, not the other way around. But Mum couldn't be my shoulder to cry on, not when she was bent double with grief herself. That's the messy thing about family tragedy, I guess. Your best support network goes under in an instant.

I'm explaining all this to Arnold when I see his mouth twitch.

'What?' I say.

'Oh, nothing,' he says innocently, reaching for a biscuit.

'Go on.' My eyes narrow.

'Just seems to me that helping your mum has really got you talking about Carla at last. Which is what your mum wanted. Wasn't it?'

'What?' I lean back and then I laugh, surprising myself. 'Oh, God. You think she's doing all this talking about Carla for *me*? Nothing to do with helping her?'

'I'm sure you are helping her, too,' Arnold says, through a mouthful of biscuit. 'But you'd be a fool to think she's not getting her own way, that Marian.'

Here I am, making Mum my latest project, and there she is, making me the exact same thing.

'Maybe fixing one another is the Cotton family's love language,' Arnold says.

I stare at him, my mouth hanging open. He grins toothily at me.

'Borrowed a book about relationships off of Kathleen,' he says.

'Arnold! Are you thinking about trying to meet somebody?' I ask, leaning across the table.

'Maybe I already have,' he says, waggling his eyebrows. But, infuriatingly, no amount of bullying, cajoling or wheedling will get any more information out of him, so I have to give up for the time being. I take the last shortbread as punishment for his discretion, and he shouts such a florid string of old Yorkshire insults after me that I laugh so hard I nearly choke on it on my way out.

Mum texts me later to invite me around the next day. It's the first time she's suggested I come to her house, and I feel tenser than ever as I make my way over there, my fists clenching and unclenching beneath the sleeves of my hoodie.

As soon as she opens the door, I know she's pushed things too far this time.

'No, no no no,' Mum says, grabbing me as I try to bolt. 'Just come in, Leena.'

'I don't want to.'

The door to the living room is open. The room is exactly like it was when Carla died – all that's missing is that bed. There's even that chair where I used to sit, holding her hand in mine, and I can almost *see* the bed, the ghost of it, invisible blankets and invisible sheets—

'I'm trying something new,' Mum says. 'This podcast I've been listening to, by that professor – she says looking at photographs is a wonderful way to help you process memories, and I thought – I wanted to go through some photos with you. In here.'

Mum takes my hand and squeezes. I notice she has one of those old photo envelopes from Boots in her other hand, and I flinch as she pulls me in to stand on the doormat.

'Just try coming in, love.'

'I can hardly bear to look at that photo,' I say, pointing to the one on the hall table. 'I really don't think I can do a whole stack.'

'We'll just ease into it slowly,' Mum says. 'One step at a time.' She turns and cocks her head, staring at the photo of Carla on prom day as if she's seeing it for the first time. 'That photo,' she says.

She walks over to the hall table, picking up the frame, then looks up at me.

'Shall we bin it?'

'What? No!' I say, eyes widening, and I walk towards her to grab the picture.

Mum doesn't let go of the frame. 'Carla would *loathe* it. It's been there so long I've stopped seeing it – I'm not sure I even like it very much. Do you like it?'

I hesitate, then I let go of the picture. 'Well, no. I kind of hate it, actually.'

Mum links arms with me and marches me down the hall. As we move across the living-room threshold my eyes skit over the space where the bed would be, and my stomach drops with the same sensation you get when you go flying over a bridge in a fast car.

'It should go. It's a terrible photo. It's not Carla,' Mum says.

She drops it into the bin in the corner of the living room.

'There. *There*. Oh, that felt a bit strange,' she says, suddenly pressing a hand to her stomach. I wonder if her emotions tend to boil there, too, like mine do. 'Was that awful of me?'

'No,' I say, staring down into the bin. 'The photo was awful. You were just . . . impulsive. It was good. Mum-ish.'

'Mum-ish?'

'Yeah. Mum-ish. Like when you suddenly got cross with the green wallpaper one day and we got back from school to find you'd peeled it all off.'

Mum laughs. 'Well. In case you didn't notice . . . you're in the living room.' She tightens her grip on my arm. 'No, don't go running off. Here. Come and sit down on the sofa.'

It's not as bad as I thought, actually, being in the room. It's not like I forgot what this place looked like. It's seared on my memory, right down to the old stain in the corner by the bookcase and that dark splodge where Grandma fell asleep and let a candle burn down on the coffee table.

'Do you like this as it is?' I ask Mum as we sit down. 'This house, I mean? You've not changed it at all since . . .'

Mum bites her lip. 'Maybe I should,' she says, looking around the living room. 'It would be nice if it was a bit . . . fresher.' She flicks open the wallet of photographs. 'Now – looking at the photographs is supposed to move the memory into a different compartment of my brain,' she says vaguely. 'Or something.'

With enormous effort I suppress my urge to eye-roll. God knows which pseudo-science book she's got that one from, but I very much doubt there's a clinical trial proving the efficacy of such a technique.

But . . . Mum thinks it'll help. And maybe that's enough.

'Paris,' I say, pointing at the top photo. It hurts to look at Carla's smiling face, but I'm getting a little better at this – if you sit with the hurt it's a tiny bit easier, like relaxing your muscles instead of shivering when it's cold. 'Remember the boy Carla convinced to kiss her on the top of the Eiffel Tower?'

'I don't seem to remember him needing much convincing,' Mum says.

'And she never would acknowledge how awful her French was.'

'You were on at her about pronunciation all week,' Mum says. 'Drove her up the wall.'

We move along, photo after photo. I cry, messy snotty crying, and Mum cries a lot too, but it's not that choked sobbing I remember her doing after Carla died, when I had to hold it together on my own. This time they're the sort of tears you can brush away. Mum's doing so well, I realise. She's come so far.

We break for tea then finish the photos. I'm not sure any memories have moved brain compartments, but when I get up to switch on the light, I notice that I've walked right across the space where the bed used to be, as if it's just ordinary carpet.

I feel guilty, at first. Like not sidestepping that invisible bed is a betrayal of what happened in this room. But then I think of Carla in all those photographs – smiling, loud, piercings catching the camera flash – and I know she'd tell me I'm being fecking ridiculous, so I move back and stand there in that spot, right where she used to lie.

I stand still, and I let myself miss her. I let it come.

And I don't break. It hurts like nothing else, a keening raw hurt, but I'm here – no Ethan with his arms around me, no laptop in front of me – and I'm not running, not working, not shouting. And whatever I was afraid of – falling apart, losing control . . . It doesn't happen. The pain of missing her is scorching, but I'll live through it.

24

Eileen

Yesterday Bee sent me a text message to say she saw Ethan and Ceci slipping off for lunch together. It's been nagging at me all morning. I try distracting myself looking over the ads Fitz has made to stick up around Shoreditch – *Over seventy and looking to meet Londoners like you? Call this number to find out about the Silver Shoreditchers' Social Club!* But even that doesn't do the trick.

I think of Carla. She'd do something about this, if she were here. She wouldn't let Ethan run around on Leena. She'd be bold and brave and resourceful and she'd *do* something.

I push myself up and march over to knock on Fitz's bedroom door. Carla should be here for her sister. It's an unspeakable tragedy that she isn't. But I *am* here for Leena. And I can be bold and brave and resourceful too.

'I think this is the coolest thing I've ever done, Mrs C,' Fitz says, then promptly stalls the van he just borrowed from Sally of Flat 6. 'Whoops. Hang on. Yep, yep, got it, there we go! Don't tell anyone that happened when you regale them with stories of our stakeout, will you?'

'There will be no regaling, Fitz,' I say, in my sternest voice. 'This is a secret mission.'

He looks delighted. 'Secret! Mission! Whoops, sorry, didn't realise it was still in second gear. Oh, wow.'

We've turned on to the main road and it is chock-a-block. We both stare at the traffic stretching out ahead of us as people on foot weave between the cars.

'Let me check Google Maps,' Fitz says, reaching into the pocket of his bomber jacket to get his phone. 'OK. It's saying it'll be forty minutes to the Selmount office in this traffic.'

I deflate. We inch onwards. The traffic has rather taken the drama out of the whole affair.

Eventually we reach the vicinity of the Selmount offices, and Fitz parks – quite possibly illegally – so we can settle in a café opposite the Selmount building. Thanks to Bee, I happen to know Ethan is currently holding a meeting there. It's a surprisingly ugly street, a wide road lined with squat buildings that each have a few of their windows boarded up, like tarnished gold teeth. The shiny grey glass of Selmount HQ looks a bit over-the-top in the middle of it all.

I sip my tea and examine the doughnuts Fitz insisted on buying for us. Apparently one has to eat doughnuts on a 'stakeout'. They look very greasy – mine has already formed a bluish ring on its napkin.

'There he is!' Fitz says excitedly, pointing towards the building.

He's right: there goes Ethan, his briefcase in hand, tossing his dark hair as he strides out of the office. He is handsome, I'll give him that much.

'What now, Mrs C?'

'Now we play the little-old-lady card,' I say. 'Grab a few napkins, would you, there's a love – I don't want to waste this doughnut. I'm sure Letitia's cat will eat it. She eats everything.'

By the time I've managed to get myself out of the door Ethan's nearly disappeared down the road. I break into a fast walk, almost a jog; it takes a moment for Fitz to catch up with me.

'Jesus, you're rapid for an old lady!' Fitz says, matching his pace to mine. 'Hang on, if we cut down here, we can intercept him.'

I follow Fitz down an alley, barely wide enough for two people. It smells distinctly of urine and something else that it takes a moment for me to place, but which I eventually remember to be marijuana.

'There!' Fitz yells, pointing at Ethan across the street. 'Oops, sorry, secret-mission indoor voice, I remember.'

But it's too late – Ethan's looking over. I'll just have to work this to my advantage.

'Ethan! Dear!' I trill, barging through the flow of pedestrians and marching across the road. Behind me I hear Fitz inhale sharply and then apologise to somebody on a motorbike who had to swerve a little. 'What luck, bumping into you, here!'

'Hello, Eileen,' he says, giving me a kiss on the cheek. 'Are you well?'

'Very well, thank you,' I say. I'm rather out of breath; I look around, wishing there was somewhere I could sit down for a moment, but of course there's no bench in sight. 'Though, actually, I'm fair to bursting for a trip to the ladies,' I say in a confidential tone. 'I'm not sure I'll make it home! Once you're my age, you know, the bladder isn't what it was. Leaky, you know. Leaky.'

Ethan is wearing an expression akin to Fitz's when someone is maimed on one of Martha's crime dramas.

'My flat's just up here,' Ethan says, gesturing to the building at the end of the street. 'Would you like to pop up and, err, use our facilities?'

'Oh, you are a love,' I say. 'Lead the way.'

I find four clues in Ethan's flat.

1) A receipt on the hall table for a meal for two, coming to £248. Now, I know London is pricy – the amount they charge for things here is criminal – but that's an awful lot

of money to spend with someone if they're just a friend or colleague.

2) Two toothbrushes in the bathroom, both heads damp, suggesting recent use. Why would Ethan use two toothbrushes?

3) Alongside a couple of bottles of Leena's hair potions that I recognise – all designed to 'manage frizz' – there is a small bottle of serum for 'colour-protection'. Leena's never dyed her hair. Though I suppose it could be Ethan's. He is very proud of those dark locks of his.

4) No bathroom bin. This doesn't *in and of itself* suggest adultery, but I've found in my life that I rarely like a person if they've not had the consideration to put a bin in a bathroom. It's always men who do this, and almost always men you cannot trust.

Once Fitz and I are back at home, we compare notes. He found no clues at all, which is typical. I did tell him old ladies make the best detectives.

'You won't mention this to Leena, will you?' I say rather worriedly. I've fallen into a bad habit of sharing things with Fitz. He knows an awful lot about Tod now, for instance. I had two glasses of wine and he asked such candid questions it was a little disarming. I would never usually tell anyone these sorts of personal things, not even Betsy. Perhaps it's being down here living somebody else's life that's done it. Whatever the reason, it's been quite fun.

'My lips are sealed, Mrs C,' Fitz says. His face turns solemn. 'If you suspect there's dirt to be found on Ethan, I'm all for the digging. Leena deserves the best.'

'She does,' I say.

'And so do *you*, Mrs C.'

Fitz pushes Leena's laptop towards me across the sofa cushions.

Life in Leena's flat seems to circle around this sofa. We eat here, drink tea here; for a while, it was Martha's office.

'Any new messages?' Fitz asks. 'Oh, you've totally got a message from Howard, look at that smile! You are too cute.'

'Oh, shush,' I tell him. 'Go and make yourself useful – the washing-up needs doing.'

'Fine, fine. I'll leave you to your sexting.'

I haven't a clue what that means, but I suspect it's rude, so I shoot him a glare just in case. Fitz grins and disappears off into the kitchen, and I settle back into the sofa and read the message from Howard.

OldCountryBoy says: Hi Eileen! I just wanted to say that I'm ready to set up that website for your social club whenever you are. It'll only take me a day when you give me the go-ahead. Xxxxx

I'd forgotten all about Howard's offer to make us a website. I beam.

EileenCotton79 says: Thank you ever so much, Howard. What do you need to get started? Xx

I chew my lip in thought as I wait for his reply. Having a website will be very exciting, but it won't help bring members in for the launch event. I've started to fret about that a little, though Fitz's been plastering those posters all over the area. I just wonder if the people we're after really look at the posters on the walls around here. There are so many, and most of them are about bands and activism and things. We have said on the posters that transport to the venue can be provided – Tod has offered his theatre company's tour bus, bless him – but the people we want to reach might well not get out and about enough to spot the posters to begin with.

A thought occurs. I click away from the conversation with Howard, and press *Find a Match*. I fill in all the boxes, but I do it a bit differently, this time. Age: 75 plus. Locations: East London, Central London. Male or female? I click both boxes.

This is rather cheeky, but it's for a good cause. I press on the first person who appears on the list: Nancy Miller, aged seventy-eight. I click the little envelope icon to send her a message.

Dear Nancy,

I hope you don't mind me sending you a message, but I'm setting up a club in Shoreditch for over seventies, and I wondered if you'd be interested in coming along for our grand opening this weekend . . .

I spend hours sending out messages. There are over a hundred people on this list. I'm very glad Fitz showed me how to 'copy and paste', otherwise this would have taken all day; as it is, my eyes hurt, and my neck is stiff from sitting here at the laptop for so long.

I begin to get replies already. Some of them are a little nasty – *Take your advertising elsewhere! This isn't the forum for this sort of thing!* – and some of the men seem to be taking my invitation as an opportunity to start flirting, which I can't be doing with – I've got more important business to attend to now, and none of them are a patch on Howard or Tod, anyway. But there are already a few people who sound interested in the Silver Shoreditchers' Club. *I'd love to come along*, says Nancy Miller. *Will there be games?* asks Margaret from Hoxton.

Letitia pops around just when I'm at the end of my patience with replying to messages. She says she's dropping around a new herbal tea she wants me to try. I invite her in to drink it with me – I suspect that was the real intention of the visit – and fill her in on my new plan to advertise our club.

'I wish I was as nifty with that thing as you are.' She nods to the laptop.

'Oh, I'm sure you could learn!' I say. 'Ask Fitz, he'll teach you.'

'He's a good man, Fitz,' Letitia says. 'Has he found someone to take Martha's room yet? He was fretting about it when we last spoke.'

I smile. Letitia's been down in the communal area at least once a day, arranging vases of flowers, plumping cushions. These days when somebody comes through, they always stop for a chat. On Monday evening I saw Aurora and Sally down there playing cards with her. *We're trying out the tables!* Aurora had said. Then: *Boom! Full house!* went Sally, slamming her hand down and making Letitia jump.

'Not yet,' I tell her, reaching for a biscuit. 'I think he's going to put an advert up on the Internet somewhere.'

'Well whoever it is, they'll be lucky to live here.'

'Letitia . . . Have you ever thought about moving out of your flat?'

She looks horrified. 'Where to?'

'Not far. Over here. To Martha's old room.'

This is an excellent idea, if I do say so myself.

'Oh, no,' Letitia says, hiding behind her tea mug. 'I couldn't leave my flat. What about all my beautiful things! And anyway, nobody young wants to live with an old biddy like me.'

I push the last biscuit towards her. 'Nonsense,' I tell her. 'Though I do see your point about your lovely bric-a-brac. I mean,' I add hastily, catching her expression, 'your lovely antiques.'

'I couldn't leave the flat,' Letitia says, more firmly this time, so I don't push the point. It's a shame, though – she could do with the company, and I worry how she'll cope when I'm not here to nudge her along, even if we do manage to get the Silver Shoreditchers' Club running regularly.

Once Letitia has gone home, I nurse my empty teacup for so long the china goes cold against my palms. I can't stop thinking about the receipt on Ethan's hall table, the wet toothbrush in his bathroom. I know I'm inclined to jump to the conclusion that a man is unfaithful – it's quite reasonable in the circumstances, so I don't blame myself for it. But I need to know if it's clouding my judgement.

I reach for my phone and dial Betsy's number.

'Hello, love!' she says. 'How's your handsome actor?' She pronounces it ac-*tor*, which makes it sound even fancier.

I smile. 'He's as dashing as ever. May I ask your advice about something, Betsy?'

'Of course.'

'Leena's boyfriend, Ethan. You must have met him when he's been up to visit?'

'On the rare occasions, yes,' Betsy says.

'Has he not been up at the weekends?'

'One or two. I think Jackson scared him off.'

I blink, surprised. 'Jackson? Jackson Greenwood?'

'He didn't take much of a shine to your Ethan.'

'I always knew Jackson was a good judge of character,' I say darkly.

'Ooh, Ethan's not in your good books, then?' Betsy asks.

I tell her about my findings from my trip to Ethan's flat. Betsy inhales through her teeth. It's the same noise she makes when she's negotiating for something at the market in Knargill.

'It could be nothing,' she says. 'Not every man is like Wade.'

'Quite a lot of them are, though.'

'Mmm, well,' Betsy says.

I'm so close to asking her about Cliff, but she's started up again before I get the chance. This is how it always goes.

'I must say,' Betsy says, 'before I knew your Leena had a man, I would've said she had her eye on Jackson.'

How *very* interesting. 'What makes you say that?'

'She's spent half her time here squabbling with him, the other half twiddling her hair when he's anywhere in sight. At the last May Day Committee meeting she barely took her eyes off him. Ooh, and speaking of May Day – she's got a sponsor, you know.'

This is just about the only thing Betsy could have said to distract me from talk of Leena making eyes at Jackson. 'A sponsor for May Day?'

'Some big law firm. Very fancy. They're paying for almost everything, and she's come up with all these fundraising activities, bake-sale stands and treasure hunts and raffles.'

I beam. 'She's brilliant, isn't she?'

'Well,' Betsy says, 'she certainly gets things done, I'll give you that.'

25

Leena

For the first time, when I pick Nicola up and ask her where we're going, she says:

'Shall we go to your house?'

I'm absurdly flattered. Nicola is one of those people whose friendship you have to win the hard way – I feel I have been Chosen.

When we get to Clearwater Cottage, Arnold is weeding the front garden.

'I said I'd do that!' I tell him as I help Nicola out of the car.

'Well, you didn't,' he points out, waving a dandelion at me. 'Hello, Nicola, all right?'

I unlock the door and usher them both in. 'Tea?'

It's only when I'm waiting for the tea to brew in the pot that it occurs to me how odd it is that I don't find this situation strange. People are often telling me how 'mature' I am for twenty-nine (*Watching your sister die will do that to you*, I always want to snap back). But I've actually never been friends with anybody over the age of thirty before. And now I don't even bat an eye when Arnold pops around unannounced – in fact, I look forward to it – and I'm totally delighted that Nicola has decided she likes me enough to spend the afternoon with me. It's nice. I like how they change my perspectives, how widely our lives all vary. I'll miss this, when I go – I'll miss them.

There's a knock at the door. It's Betsy.

She looks a little crumpled. 'Hello, Leena,' she says stiffly.

'Betsy! Hi! Come in! We're just having tea,' I say. 'Let me get you a cup! Can I take your coat?'

I take her coat and hang it up, mind whirring. Betsy's not dropped around since that terrible first tea when I said all the wrong things. What's prompted this?

'I won't stay,' Betsy says. 'I'm just here for the spare key. Eileen keeps one somewhere.'

'Oh, sure!' I say, looking around, as though the key might be lying out on the dining-room table. 'Did you lock yourself out?'

'Yes,' she says.

I try to hold her gaze, but it skits aside. She's definitely lying.

Arnold looks back and forth between us for a moment, then gets to his feet. 'Nicola, I must show you the hydrangea at the bottom of Eileen's garden,' he says.

'The what?' Nicola says. 'I don't . . .'

But he's already helping her up.

'Oh, all right,' she grumbles.

I mouth *Thank you* at Arnold, and he gives me a small smile. Once we're alone, I turn back to Betsy, who is opening and closing drawers in the dresser.

'Can't Cliff let you in?' I ask her gently.

Betsy doesn't turn around. There is a long silence.

'It was Cliff who locked me out.'

I breathe in. 'Well, that's pretty awful of him,' I say, as neutrally as I can manage. 'Would you like to stay here for tonight?'

She looks around then. 'Stay here?'

'Yeah. You can have my grandma's room.'

'Oh, I . . .' She looks a little lost for a moment. 'Thank you,' she says. 'That's very kind. But I'd rather just find the key.'

'All right,' I say, as Arnold and Nicola make their way up the garden again. 'We'll track it down, between the four of us.'

I find all sorts of things, digging around for that key. My old school satchel (how did that end up here?); a photo of my mum when she was pregnant with me, looking movie-star gorgeous; and a recipe for mud pie in Carla's handwriting, which makes my eyes prick with tears. Carla seems to turn up all the time here in Hamleigh. She may not have lived in this village for long, but she's part of the fabric of the place. Maybe that's why I've finally been able to move forward a little while I'm here – or rather, to stop moving forward. Moving forward is my forte; it's standing still I'm not so good at.

I fold the recipe carefully and place it back where I found it. Maybe someday when I find a treasure like this, it won't make me tear up, it'll make me smile.

In the end, Nicola finds the key. It is carefully labelled in Grandma's spidery writing – *Betsy's spare* – and lodged in the back of a drawer in her hall table, along with a whole collection of keys for houses we've all long since left: Carla's flat in Bethnal Green, our old place in Leeds, and, much to my irritation, a bike-lock key I thought I lost approximately ten years ago. There's also a spare key to Mum's house, which I pinch for the rest of my time here – I've been using Grandma's one, but it always seems to get stuck in the lock.

I walk Betsy back to her house. I don't give her room to object to the idea, but I'm still surprised she lets me. I try to think what Grandma would say, and I decide she wouldn't say much at all – she'd leave Betsy room to talk. So as we make our slow way down Middling Lane in the rain, I just hold the umbrella and wait for Betsy to feel ready.

'I suppose you're thinking you know all about my situation, now,' she says eventually, looking straight ahead.

'No, not at all.'

'Good. Because it's – it's complicated.'

'I'm sure it is.'

I chew the inside of my cheek. Grandma would stay quiet. She'd leave it at that. But . . .

'Nobody should ever be afraid in their own home. And if you want to leave him, Betsy, everyone here in this village will have your back. Every one of them.'

We reach Betsy's house. She pauses in front of the gate – I'm supposed to leave, that much is clear, but I'd rather stay until I see she's safely inside.

'He'll have calmed down by now,' Betsy says, fiddling with the key. 'Off you go, Leena, you can't be hanging around here.'

'You deserve better. And I'm not going to stop telling you that, no matter how many times you kick me out or tell me to stop hanging around,' I say, with a little smile. 'I'm always here.'

'For less than a week,' Betsy points out.

'Oh, yes.' I'd genuinely forgotten for a moment that I was leaving at all. 'Well, after that you'll switch back to having the right Eileen Cotton at Clearwater Cottage again,' I say with a smile, but my stomach twists with something that feels a lot like sadness. 'That'll be even better.'

26

Eileen

Bu-bu-bu-BUH-BUH-bu-bu-bu goes Leena's mobile phone on the café
table.

'Oh, fuck, every time you get a text I think I'm about to have a
heart attack,' Bee says, clutching her chest. 'That is *so loud*.'

I intend to tell her off for swearing, but get distracted by my new
message.

'Who is it this time?' Bee asks. 'Old Country Boy or your sexy
actor honey?'

'It's my old neighbour,' I say, shaking my head. 'He's discovered
cat videos and has been sending them my way for weeks.'

'Oh, have you shown him the one where the cat pushes the child
into the swimming pool?' Bee asks, brightening. 'Jaime and I
watched that about six-hundred times.'

'I see your daughter shares your dark sense of humour,' I say, putting my phone down again. Arnold can wait. I need the gossip from
Bee. 'Well? How was your third date with Mike?'

Bee shakes her head incredulously. 'It was *good*, Eileen. He's . . .
well, he's a terrible dancer, he's *definitely* richer and more successful
than me, and he doesn't even live in London, so he ticks almost zero
of my boxes . . .'

'What did he say when you told him about Jaime?'

Her face softens. Ooh, I know that look.

'He said, "Tell me all about her." We talked about Jaime for like forty-five minutes straight. He didn't flinch or freak out or edge away, he listened.'

I smile. 'Now, "good listener" may not have been on your list, but it was on mine.'

'He was *so* helpful about setting up a business, too. He had loads of ideas, but in a really non-mansplainy way, you know?'

'Not really, but good,' I tell her. 'Have you spoken to Leena about these new ideas?'

Bee makes a face. 'I don't want to push her – last time we spoke about B&L plans she said her confidence had taken such a knock after Carla died, she couldn't really countenance it. I get it. I'm happy to wait until she's ready.'

'Mmm,' I say, as the waiter brings our coffees.

Bee raises her eyebrows. 'Go on. What is it you're trying not to say?'

'You're just not usually a waiting-around sort of woman.'

Bee stirs the foam on the top of her coffee. 'I am if Leena needs it,' she says simply.

'That's very good of you,' I say. 'But even Leena needs a shove now and then. In fact, now more than ever. I've never heard her happier than when she's talking about all those plans of yours, and it's been sad, not hearing her mention them for so long. Maybe it's just the thing she needs to keep her going.'

'Maybe,' Bee says, perking up a bit. 'Maybe I'll just . . . give her a little nudge again. I don't want us to lose momentum. I do sometimes worry we'll end up as Selmounters for ever.'

'You don't call yourselves that, do you? It sounds like the title of a smutty novel.'

'Oh, Jesus, I wish you'd not said that,' Bee says. 'Now I'm going to think that every time the CEO says Selmounter. Selmounter. Oh, shit, you're right, it does . . .'

That night I sit beside Fitz at the breakfast counter and sift through the replies I've had about the Silver Shoreditchers' Social Club. So far five people have asked for transport to come to the grand opening, and there are seven others who have said they'll confirm nearer the time, plus a handful who sounded interested. I'm trying not to get my hopes up, but it does feel rather exciting.

Every so often I check whether Howard's available on the chat page. His ideas for our website sound wonderful – his grand plan is that we'll use it for fundraising. I'm keeping it a surprise for now, but I already can't wait to show Fitz when it's done. The only downside is that Howard says he needs a little money to get things off the ground. He says he'll likely double it with fundraising within the week, so I'll get it back and more in no time, and it certainly still sounds like the website is worth doing. I'm just waiting to hear how much money he needs.

As I work my way through all my messages, I land on my conversation with Arnold, a series of cat videos interspersed with the odd bits and pieces about Hamleigh and the garden. I pause on his name, then on a whim I click to go to his profile.

There's some writing there now, as well as the picture. *My name is Arnold Macintyre, and I'm turning over a new leaf,* says his *About Me* section. *Is anyone out there doing the same? I'd love to chat to a like-minded soul . . .*

I rub my neck. I wonder if anyone has responded to Arnold's question. Is there a like-minded lady out there, chatting to him about turning over a new leaf? It hadn't really occurred to me that if Arnold's talking to me on this website, he's probably talking to other people, too.

I pause over the message button. There's a green dot by Arnold's name. It's funny to think of him up there in Hamleigh, sitting at his computer.

> EileenCotton79 says: Hello, Arnold. I've got to ask. What do you mean when you say you're turning over a new leaf?
> Arnold1234 says: Well, I felt a little inspired by you, actually.
> EileenCotton79 says: Me???
> Arnold1234 says: You've taken life by the horns again. I stopped doing that far too long ago. So now I've started again.

I stare at the screen for a while. Arnold starts typing.

> Arnold1234 says: I go to Pilates now, you know.

'Ha!'

Fitz turns away from his laptop screen and looks at me, eyebrows raised. I smile sheepishly.

'Nothing interesting,' I say quickly, swivelling Leena's laptop a little.

> EileenCotton79 says: What else??
> Arnold1234 says: Leena taught me how to cook Pad Thai for tea.
> EileenCotton79 says: But Leena is a dreadful cook!
> Arnold1234 says: Well, I know that now, don't I?

I laugh again.

> EileenCotton79 says: And Betsy told me you're on the May Day Committee, now, too . . .
> Arnold1234 says: I am. Though your granddaughter is refusing to make the May Day Eileen specials, so I doubt the day will be up to much.

I smile. Every year for May Day, I make toffee apples to sell on a stall outside my front gate. Arnold always buys three, grumbles about the price until I irritably let him have a discount, then gloats about it all evening. Usually with toffee in his teeth.

My fingers hover over the keys.

EileenCotton79 says: Well, how about I promise to make you some toffee apples when I get back?

His answer takes a long time to arrive.

Arnold1234 says: Special discount price?

I laugh, rolling my eyes.

EileenCotton79 says: Free, for looking out for Leena while I'm away, and as a thank-you for the cat videos. They've really kept me smiling.
Arnold1234 says: Well, how can I say no to that?

I smile.

Arnold1234 says: And how about the Silver Shoreditchers' Social Club? How's that coming along?

I forgot I'd mentioned it to him at all – it's sweet of him to remember.

EileenCotton79 says: It's the grand opening this weekend!
Arnold1234 says: I wish I could be there.

And then, as I'm absorbing that rather surprising sentence:

Arnold1234 says: Well, if I was invited.

EileenCotton79 says: Of course you'd be invited, Arnold, don't be daft.

Arnold1234 says: I've never even been invited into your house, so I wouldn't like to presume . . .

I frown at Leena's laptop, pushing my glasses down my nose.

EileenCotton79 says: You don't mean . . . ever?

Arnold1234 says: Ever. You have never once invited me around.

EileenCotton79 says: Well. I think you'll find I did invite you around once.

Arnold1234 says: Aye, well, not since that first day, then.

I bite my lip, then absent-mindedly dab at it to fix my lipstick.

It occurs to me, with the benefit of distance, perhaps . . . I have not been very charitable when it comes to Arnold.

I wait for a while, unsure what to say. After a moment Arnold sends me a video of a cat riding on a Hoover. I laugh.

Arnold1234 says: Thought I'd lighten the mood.

EileenCotton79 says: Well, Arnold, I'm sorry. When I am home, I would very much like to invite you in for tea and a toffee apple.

Arnold1234 says: I'd like that.

Arnold1234 says: Good luck with the grand opening, Eileen. We all look forward to having you back in Hamleigh again.

And, with that, the green dot disappears.

Tonight is my last night with Tod. I don't leave until Monday, but I want to reserve the weekend for goodbyes with my new friends.

I don't precisely feel sad, saying goodbye to Tod. We've known from day one it was coming, and when the moment would be. This is why I'm so very surprised when he sits up beside me in his plush white bed and says:

'Eileen, I'm not ready to say goodbye to you.'

I'm so taken aback I have to wait for the right words to come, and it takes so long that Tod's face falls.

'Oh, I'm sorry,' I say, reaching reflexively for his hand. 'I'm just surprised. We've always said . . .'

'I know.' He presses my hand to his lips. Disordered after an afternoon in bed, his silver-grey hair is fluffy and rumpled; I smooth it back to the way he likes to wear it, swept back like Donald Sutherland's. 'It's been extraordinary, really. There's no other way to put it. You're really one of a kind, Eileen Cotton.'

I smile, looking down at the sheets across my lap. 'We said today was goodbye.'

'Well, tomorrow can be goodbye. Or the next day. Or some distant day a long way off.' He smiles roguishly at me, linking his fingers with mine. 'Go on. Let me have a go at winning you round. Come to our cast party tomorrow. It's a barbecue on a rooftop in King's Cross. Good food, good conversation, the occasional West End star . . .'

'Skip the party,' I say impulsively. 'Come to the launch of the Silver Shoreditchers' Social Club.' I press a kiss to his cheek. 'It would be so lovely to have you there.'

He pauses. 'Well, I . . . I suppose I could.'

I beam. This project has been the most important part of my time here in London – it feels right to have Tod there for its grand opening. And perhaps what he says is true. Perhaps this doesn't have to be over, just because I'm going to move back to Yorkshire. It's only a couple of hours away on the train, after all.

It only occurs to me after I leave his house that Howard has said he will be at the grand opening, too. Oh, dear. I suppose this is when dating gets complicated.

27

Leena

'Absolutely not,' I say firmly.

'But Vera's got the squits!' Penelope wails at me.

I've got so much to do I don't even have time to find that funny.

'Penelope, I have to be out there making sure everything is running smoothly! Surely there is a young woman in this village who can be coerced or bribed into being May Queen.'

'I suppose . . . There's Ursula . . .'

Ursula is the sixteen-year-old whose parents own the village shop. She is usually to be found curled up with a book in the corner by the fresh vegetables. I have never seen her exchange a word with anybody.

'Perfect,' I say, turning back to the beautiful coat-of-arms garlands currently being slung between the lamp posts on Peewit Street. It's a chilly morning; the garlands are reflected in silver in the puddles on the pavement, and the flags we've fixed to the war memorial at the end of the street are flying beautifully in the wind. 'I leave it in your capable hands, Penelope.'

'That garland is wonky,' Roland says.

I close my eyes and breathe deeply. 'Thank you, Roland.'

'No trouble,' he says amiably, buzzing away after Penelope.

'It is, you know,' comes Jackson's voice.

I turn. In the end, I went very gentle on him with the May King costume. He's dressed in green trousers tucked into tall brown boots, and a loose white shirt belted at the waist, kind of like how I imagine Robin Hood, only as if he was a massive rugby player instead of a wily man of the forest. The May Day wreath is already around his neck. It's beautiful – Kathleen wove it out of wild flowers and leaves she found in the hedgerows.

The *pièce de résistance*, though, is the horns. Big green ones, curving like ram's horns, as tall as my Easter bunny ears were.

I went *gentle*, but I wasn't going to let the man off without some ridiculous headwear.

'Hey,' he says as I suppress a smile. 'I kept a straight face when you looked like Roger Rabbit.'

I press my lips together and adopt the most solemn expression I can manage. 'Very regal,' I say. When I turn back to the garlands, I feel something land around my neck. I look down; the May Queen wreath, the same as Jackson's, but with a few pink flowers woven among the white.

I spin on my heels to look at him again. 'Oh, no, you don't,' I say, moving to take off the wreath.

Jackson's hand catches my wrist. 'You know Ursula will never do it. Come on. Community spirit.'

'I can't be in the parade, I've got to organise everything!' I protest. 'The May King and Queen float has rotted through the middle – I need to either find a *very* talented carpenter or another float – and . . .'

'Leave it with me,' Jackson says, one dimple beginning to show in his cheek. 'Be my May Queen and I'll find you a way to travel in style, all right?'

I narrow my eyes at him. 'In case you're wondering, this is my suspicious face.'

'I've grown pretty familiar with that face, actually,' Jackson says.

His hand is still on my wrist; I wonder if he can feel my pulse fluttering. 'Leave it to me,' he says again, and when he drops my arm I can still feel the memory of his fingers on my skin, warm like sunlight.

I need Ethan to get here. It's been too long. I'm getting silly and distracted by this stupid – this whatever-it-is, this *crush* on Jackson. This week I've caught myself thinking about him when I shouldn't be, re-running our conversations as I make dinner, imagining what he might have been thinking. Remembering the sandy freckles under his steady blue eyes and the feel of his body pressed against mine as I was thrown back against the living-room mirror.

I check my phone – I'm waiting for Ethan to text and let me know when he'll get here – but I've got no signal, as per usual. I growl, turning back to the garland-arranging, my brain ticking its way through the list of jobs still to do: check Portaloos have arrived, deal with flooding in field currently planned for parking, ring the man about ice delivery, check in with Betsy on food stalls . . .

Penelope returns. 'Ursula said she'd rather let one of those falcons peck out her eyes than be May Queen,' she announces.

'God, that's . . . graphic,' I say. I have clearly misread Ursula. 'OK, I'll think of someone else once I've sorted food stalls and ice and flooding and Portaloos.'

'Breathe, dear,' Penelope says, laying a hand on my shoulder. 'You've done so much already! I'm sure Betsy won't mind if you take a little break.'

'Penelope,' I say, patting her hand, 'this is genuinely the most fun I've had in . . . God, I don't know, *ages*. Please don't make me take a break.'

She blinks those owlish eyes at me. 'You *are* odd, love,' she says.

I grin at her and check my phone again: three miraculous bars of signal, though still no text from Ethan. I shake off the thought and get Betsy up on speed dial (not joking: Grandma's phone actually still has speed dial).

'Sorry I missed your last call!' I say into the phone, gesturing leftwards to the men putting up the garlands (Rob and Terry? I think it's Rob and Terry? Or are they the ones I commandeered to block off traffic to Lower Lane?)

'Leena. The food stalls. They're not coming.'

'What? Why not?'

'I don't know!' Betsy sounds almost tearful.

'Don't worry, I'll sort it.' I ring off and dig out the number for one of the food stalls. They're all run by separate people, mostly local to the area; the cheese-toastie guy's number is the first I find.

'Sorry,' he says. 'Firs Blandon offered us double.'

'Firs Blandon?' The village that the Neighbourhood Watch are always bitching about? 'What *for*?'

'They're doing May Day too, I think. Got a sign up next to yours on the road, directing people their way. Bigger sign than yours, actually,' cheese-toastie man adds helpfully.

'Don't do this,' I say. 'I am already on my way to Firs Blandon' – I'm heading for Agatha at a jog – 'and I *will* be getting you all back to Hamleigh-in-Harksdale *as agreed*, but it's going to be messy, and I can promise you, it'll all be a lot nicer if you just come back and fulfil your contractual obligations here in Hamleigh.'

There's an uncomfortable pause. 'I didn't sign anything,' cheese-toastie man points out.

Feck, feck, feck. No, he didn't. We just contacted the food stalls that come every year and asked them to do a medieval theme this time, and they all said, *Oh, sure, we'll be there!* There might have been a contract once, when May Day was first organised, but God knows where that is.

'We still have legal rights,' I say coolly, though I haven't a clue if that's true.

'Right. Well . . . sorry, Leena. There's not a lot of money in the cheese-toastie gig, and . . . Sorry.' He rings off.

I unlock the car. Penelope appears beside me, her giant eyes wide with worry.

'There are no food stalls!' she says, clutching my arm.

'It's a *disaster*!' roars Basil, approaching at a very slow but purposeful jog. 'Bloody Firs Blandon! I should have known they'd be up to something!'

'All right, Leena?' calls Arnold from over the road, where he's checking the bulbs in the hanging lanterns.

'All of you: in,' I say, pointing to the car.

I chuck the keys at Penelope, who catches them, then looks extremely surprised her reflexes were up to the job.

'You're driving,' I tell her.

'Oh, but what would Dr Piotr say?' Basil asks. 'He said Penelope ought not to—'

Penelope's eyes twinkle. 'Bother Dr Piotr,' she says, opening the driver's door. 'This is *exciting*.'

I wouldn't say I feel *safe* with Penelope driving. But we certainly make progress.

'That was a red light,' Arnold says mildly, as we go sailing past it.

'It would have been green in a minute,' Penelope says, foot on the accelerator.

I, meanwhile, am glued to my phone.

'Who's in charge at Firs Blandon?' I ask. 'Is there a mayor or something?'

'What? No,' Arnold says. 'I suppose there's probably a chair of the parish council.'

'There might well be,' Penelope says shrewdly, 'but they're most likely not in charge.'

I glance up from my phone. 'No?'

'Eileen's chair of our Neighbourhood Watch,' Penelope says, taking a sharp bend at sixty. 'But we all know Betsy runs things, don't we?'

'Whoa, whoa, that was a thirty sign!'

'Well, I didn't see it,' says Penelope.

I roll my window down as we enter Firs Blandon. There are garlands! And lanterns! The bastards!

'Excuse me,' I say to one of the men hanging garlands. 'Who's in charge, here?'

'Take me to your leader!' Basil barks from the back seat, making himself chuckle.

'In charge?'

'Yes.'

'Well, the chair of the parish council is . . .'

I wave him off. 'But *really* though. Like, when someone starts parking a bit too near a junction or the pub starts charging an extra quid for fish and chips, who is it that gets things to go back to how they were?'

'Oh, you mean Derek,' the man says. 'He's down there, getting all the food stalls set up in the right spots.'

'Thank you,' I say, then let out a small shriek as Penelope puts her foot down again.

'I've never trusted men called Derek,' Penelope says rather mysteriously, as we come into view of Firs Blandon's Main Street, now filled with all our food stalls.

'You guys park up,' I say, already pulling the passenger door open. 'I'm going in.'

Derek is not difficult to spot. He is a man in his late sixties, wearing a very bright and entirely unnecessary yellow hard hat and brandishing a megaphone.

'Right a bit! Left a bit! No left a bit! No *left*!' he shouts into the megaphone.

'Derek?' I say pleasantly.

'Yes?' He barely glances around.

'Leena Cotton,' I say, stepping in front of him with my hand out. 'Here representing Hamleigh-in-Harksdale.'

That gets his attention. 'Didn't take you long,' he says, and there's a little smirk on his face that really gets my blood boiling.

'I have a very good driver,' I say. 'Is there somewhere we can talk?'

'I'm rather in the middle of things,' says Derek. 'Got a May Day festival to organise, and all. I'm sure you can relate.'

'Of course,' I say, smiling. 'I just wanted to say good luck to you.'

He blinks. 'Ta, love,' he says, that smirk widening. 'But we don't need luck. We've got the best food in Yorkshire served here today.'

'Oh, I don't mean good luck for today,' I say, 'I mean with the planning applications.'

Derek freezes. 'What?'

'Firs Blandon has some quite ambitious plans! That community hub on the edge of the village, you know, the one within the eyeline of several houses on Peewit Street in Hamleigh? It could be a wonderful addition to the local area, or, of course – depending on one's viewpoint – it could be an eyesore with an adverse visual impact on the iconic landscape of the Dales.'

I now have Derek's full attention.

'Oh, Penelope, Basil, Arnold!' I say, waving them over. 'Do come and meet Derek. We'll be seeing a lot more of him, now that we'll all be taking a much more active interest in the planning applications coming out of Firs Blandon.' I smile brightly at Derek. 'Basil and Penelope and Arnold all have very strong opinions on local issues. Don't you?'

'I should say so!' Basil says, puffing out his chest.

'Always been very engaged in village business, me,' says Arnold.

'All I'm saying,' Penelope says, with her gaze fixed on Derek, 'is there's something about the name Derek. Never met a Derek I've liked. Never.'

I smile brightly and take the megaphone from Derek's unresisting hand.

'Pack up, everybody!' I yell into the megaphone. 'We're off back to Hamleigh-in-Harksdale.'

The food stalls return to Hamleigh with their tails between their wagon wheels. Penelope drives back with the carefree abandon of a seventeen-year-old boy, and somehow gets us to the village at the same time as the food stalls even though she takes us via Knargill to pick up Nicola on the way. When we drive past Firs Blandon's May Day sign, Penelope swerves; I shriek, clinging to the door handle, as she clips the edge of the sandwich board and sends it toppling face down on to the verge.

'Whoopsie!' says Penelope.

'Get that one too!' says a trigger-happy Nicola, pointing to a sign for a farm shop further ahead.

As we approach Hamleigh, I figure I've just about got time to check the Portaloos have arrived before the drainage company get here to deal with the flooding. But when we pull up at the edge of the field assigned for food stalls, there's a small crowd gathered around the entranceway, blocking our view. Penelope and I frown at each other; she parks on a verge and we get out. I move to help Nicola, but Basil is already there, offering his arm with positively medieval chivalry. Arnold gives Agatha a pat as he climbs out – he's become very attached to my car since rescuing her from Grandma's hedge.

'What's all that then?' Arnold asks, nodding to the melee.

'No idea.' I check my phone as we make our way over towards the crowd. There's a message from Bee that makes my heart leap:

Leena, let's DO IT. B&L Consulting. I've been talking it all through with your grandma and I'm EXCITED. If you need more time you know

I'm here for you but what I'm saying is, let's not stall on it. Let me do the legwork if you don't have the headspace. But let's not lose sight of the dream, my friend! We're going to be bosses! xx

And one from Ethan that makes it sink.

Sorry, angel – things have gone crazy here. Going to need to spend a few more hours at the desk. Don't suppose there's any chance you could come down here instead? Xx

I swallow and tap out a reply as we make our way across the grass.

Ethan, you know I can't leave Hamleigh today, it's May Day. Hope you get everything done OK. Let's try and talk on the phone at least? x

'Ethan not coming?' Arnold says quietly.

I glance at him.

'You have a very bad poker face,' he explains.

I tuck my phone in the hoodie pocket. 'Not his fault. Work, you know.'

Arnold gives me a long, heavy look. 'Leena,' he says. 'I know he was good to you when you needed him. But you don't stay with somebody out of gratitude. That's not how to do it.'

'I'm not with Ethan out of *gratitude*!' I exclaim.

'All right. Well, good.' Arnold gives me another squeeze of the shoulder. 'I just think you deserve a man who treats you right, that's all.'

'I liked you better when you were a hermit,' I tell him, eyes narrowed.

He grins, then his smile drops. We've both heard the same thing.

'Don't you fucking dare!'

It's Cliff. I push through the crowd, now, into the field, where

Betsy and Cliff are facing one another like two cowboys waiting to draw. In fact, Betsy's already drawn – but it's not a gun in her hand, it's a television remote.

'I'm *sick* of it! You hear me! I'm *sick* of it!' She brings both hands to the remote as if she's about to snap it in two, and Cliff roars with rage.

Cliff looks pretty much exactly how I expected him to look. Red-faced, stocky, with sports socks and shorts on and a filthy sweatshirt stretched across his beer belly, he is in perfect contrast to neat little Betsy with her neckerchief and her pink cropped jacket. Only, of the two of them, I think Betsy genuinely looks the toughest right now.

'Cliff Harris,' she says, voice quiet and deadly. '*I. Deserve. Better.*'

And, with what I can only conclude is the superhuman strength of a woman who has put up with a lot of shit for a very long time, she snaps the TV remote in two.

Cliff comes towards her then, but Arnold and I are moving, and we're quicker than he is, and we've got him by the arms before he can reach Betsy.

'I want you out of that house by the end of the week, do you hear me?' Betsy calls across the field.

Cliff roars obscenities, awful things, so bad it makes me gasp. Arnold hauls him backwards, and gestures Basil over to help.

'We've got this,' Arnold says to me. I give him a nod. I'm needed elsewhere.

Betsy crumples into my arms as soon as I reach her. 'Come on,' I say, leading her away. I shoot a glare at the crowd around the entrance to the field and the bystanders scatter embarrassedly, letting us through. 'You were brilliant,' I tell Betsy.

She tries to turn around. 'Oh, I . . . I . . .'

I grip her arm. 'Now all we need to do is find you somewhere to stay. OK?' I chew the inside of my cheek. Clearwater Cottage is too close. She needs to get away for a week, until we've managed to clear Cliff out.

Penelope and Nicola are waiting by the car. Their eyes widen as Betsy and I stumble over, arm in arm. I help Betsy into the passenger seat, and by the time she's all strapped in, an idea has formed.

'Nicola,' I say quietly, once I've closed the car door. 'Betsy's given her husband a week to find somewhere else to live.'

Nicola's face softens. She glances at Betsy, mute in the front seat. She still has two pieces of remote control in her hands; she's clutching them tightly.

'Aye, she has, has she?'

'Do you think . . .'

'She can stay with me as long as she needs,' Nicola says.

'Are you sure? I know it's a lot for me to ask.'

'If a woman needs a place to stay, and I've got a bed to offer, then, well. That's that.'

Nicola is already opening the rear passenger door. I move to help her in, on autopilot.

'Let's get you back to my house, eh, love,' she says to Betsy as she settles. 'I'll put the kettle on, we can have a nice hot cuppa, then I'll do us fish pie for tea.'

It takes all my effort not to cry as I take the keys from a very worried-looking Penelope and sit myself down in the driver's seat. These people. There's such a fierceness to them, such a lovingness. When I got here, I thought their lives were small and silly, but I was wrong. They're some of the biggest people I know.

28

Eileen

The communal space is a whirlwind of activity. Fitz ducks just as Martha tosses Aurora a stack of napkins. Rupert catches the end of the tablecloth Letitia is spreading just in time to lay it flat. Yaz signs for the food delivery one-handed, Vanessa in the crook of her other arm. It's Yaz and Martha's first time back in the throng, after a few weeks of quality time as a family, and I must say they've hit the ground running. Not that I'd expect anything less.

We had hoped to give the Silver Shoreditchers a hot meal, but it got ever so complicated with allergies and the like, so for now it'll just be buffet snacks. Luckily I got to the supermarket order before Fitz pressed the 'Buy' button, because almost everything on there would have been quite the challenge for anyone with missing teeth or new dentures. Now there are much smaller piles of carrot sticks and crisps, and much larger piles of soft sausage rolls and quiche squares.

I fish out my mobile phone. Tod should be here any moment with the tour bus for picking up our Silver Shoreditchers; I'm expecting him to call when he's outside. And Howard said he'd get here right for the start time, too, so he's not far away either. I pat my hair nervously – Martha has pinned it all up, and it looks very smart, but I worry it's a bit much.

I have two messages. The first is from Bee:

*I'm stuck here with a client and I'm going to have to miss the launch
event. I'm so SO sorry. I feel terrible.*
*Will you come and see me before you go tomorrow morning if you can?
I'll be at Selmount, and I've not got any meetings. The Selmount office
is on your way, right, if you're heading to King's Cross?*

I type my reply.

*Hello, Bee. Don't you worry. How's 9 o'clock tomorrow morning? Per-
haps if you have time, we could have one last coffee and muffin
together. Not a problem if you can't, of course. Love, Eileen xx*

Her reply is almost instant.

Perfect. Sorry again Eileen xxx

The other message is from Howard.

*OldCountryBoy says: I'm glad you're happy with £300 to get us started.
I promise you, we'll have double that in donations within a week! xxx*
*EileenCotton79 says: I'll give you the cheque when I see you. I can't wait
to see our website soon ☺*

Up pops the dot-dot-dot that means he's typing something.

*OldCountryBoy says: I'm ever so sorry, Eileen, but I don't think I can
make it to the launch party. I've got lots of work to be getting on with
for the website! Could you transfer the money online?*

My heart sinks. I thought . . . I'd really . . . Well. Never mind. This
event wasn't about Howard and it's not the end of the world if he
can't come.

EileenCotton79 says: I'm not all set up for banking on the computer I'm
afraid. I can post you the cheque, though. Just send me the address.
All my best, Eileen xx

'Eileen?' comes a familiar voice.

I look up, and there's Tod – wonderful, handsome Tod. My heart lifts again. I suppose this is why it's handy to have several men on the go at once.

'You're here!' I stand on tiptoes to kiss him on the cheek.

He looks very dashing in an open-necked shirt and chino trousers. He surveys the hive of activity, looking rather dazed by it all.

'You did all this?' he asks.

'Yes! Well, we all did, really,' I say, beaming.

'Oh, *hi*, is this Tod?' says Fitz, popping up beside us. He stretches his hand out for Tod to shake. 'Pleasure to meet you. I fully intend to be you when I grow up.'

'An actor?' Tod asks.

'A proficient lover even in my seventies,' Fitz corrects him. 'Ah, no, that's not a vase, it's for walking sticks!'

That part was to Letitia. I make an apologetic face at Tod, who is looking very amused, thank goodness.

'Sorry about the chaos,' I say, at the same time Tod says, 'I have some bad news.'

'What bad news?'

'The tour bus. It's needed by the theatre company, I'm afraid.'

I clutch my chest. '*What*? You've not brought it? We've not got transportation?'

Tod looks worried. 'Oh, dear, was it very important?'

'Of *course* it was important! We've promised to pick people up!' I wave my mobile phone at him.

'Can't we just order them cabs?' he asks, nonplussed.

'So far the lovely people in this building have been funding this

BETH O'LEARY | 253

club out of their own pocket,' I snap at him, eyes narrowed. 'They can't be paying for who-knows-how-many cab fares on top of everything else.'

'Oh, right.' For a moment I think Tod might offer to pay, but he doesn't, which makes me narrow my eyes even further.

'Excuse me,' I say rather frostily. 'I had better go and sort this out.' Men. They always bloody let you down, don't they?

I know Sally isn't keen on the idea of the Silver Shoreditchers, and I'll bet she's planning on spending the afternoon firmly locked away in her flat. But we've got nobody else to ask. I wait nervously outside her door. She seems to take for ever to answer, and I don't know what we'll do if she's out.

Eventually Sally undoes the three locks on her door, takes one look at me, and ducks back inside.

'Hello?' I call, bewildered.

She bobs back up, this time holding her car keys. 'What's the emergency this time?' she says, already closing the door behind her.

She grumbles and sighs all the way out of the building, but I'm not convinced. I think Sally likes to be the hero.

Once she and Fitz have set off, complete with their list of names and addresses, I busy myself setting up dominoes and packs of cards on the tables, nervously glancing towards the door. I'm patting at my hair so often I'm at risk of ruining my lovely new 'do. I can't seem to stop fussing and fidgeting.

Just as I've run out of jobs to do, my phone beeps with a new message. It's from Arnold.

Dear Eileen,

I thought you'd want to know Betsy gave Cliff the boot today. Leena has sorted her out a safe place to stay for a while, with Nicola from Knargill, and we've had some choice words with Cliff, who has promised to move in with his brother in Sheffield by next weekend so Betsy can have her house to herself at last.

Sorry if I'm interrupting your grand opening, I know it's an important day. But I thought you would want to know.

Arnold.

I clutch the phone to my chest. My first instinct is to call Betsy, but then I remember how I felt right after Wade left, the humiliation, the shame. I didn't want to speak to a soul, not at first.

So instead, I send her a text message.

Thinking of you, I write. And then, on impulse: *You are a brave and wonderful friend. Lots of love, Eileen xxx*

I open Arnold's message again, but I'm not sure quite how to reply. It was so thoughtful of him to send me the news about Betsy. In a strange way, Arnold has been a comfort, these last few weeks, with his silly cat videos and his news from Hamleigh.

'Eileen?' Fitz calls. 'They're here!'

I turn to the door. He's right: the Silver Shoreditchers are coming, some with walkers to help them, some briskly strolling, but all blinking bright, curious eyes at the new communal area as Sally and Fitz help them through the doorway. I see it afresh through their eyes, the sage-green walls, the beautiful bare floorboards, and I beam with pride.

'Welcome!' I say, spreading my arms. 'Please, come on in!'

I asked myself, when I first met Letitia, how many other fascinating people might be pocketed away in little flats across London, never saying a word to anybody.

And now here I am, with a whole roomful of Letitias, all so different, all so extraordinarily interesting. There's Nancy, who used to play the flute in the London Symphony Orchestra. There's Clive, who's spent his whole life driving trucks at night-time, and now can only get to sleep if it's light. There's Ivy, who beats everybody at Scrabble and eats sausage rolls in two mouthfuls, then rather guiltily admits that she is, technically speaking, a genius, and probably ought not to be allowed to join in with the board games.

Rupert does a little half-hour art class – he had the foresight to put down a tarpaulin, which was very wise, because more paint seems to go on the floor than the canvases. Then there's food, and now music – Fitz's idea. Ivy and Nancy even get up to dance. It's glorious. I never want it to end.

'What a wonderful thing you've done, here, Eileen,' Martha says, kissing me on the cheek as she passes.

I take a breather on the sofa, watching Nancy and Ivy try out a slow foxtrot, dodging rummy tables as they go. Tod sits down beside me. I'm surprised to see him – he's spent most of the afternoon up in Leena's flat, taking calls. 'I guess this isn't really his crowd,' Martha said diplomatically when I complained about him not joining in.

It's true that he seems out of place here. Nancy and Ivy and Clive, they're all ordinary people, like me. It dawns on me that all the time I've spent with Tod has been in his world: his enormous house, his favourite coffee shops. This is the first time he's stepped into my world, and it's suddenly very obvious that it isn't a place he wants to be.

But then Tod takes my hand and runs his thumb to and fro across my wrist, the way he did on our first date in the café, and just like that, my heart jumps.

'It's goodbye today, isn't it?' he says. His voice is deep and smooth; that voice has given me shivers more times than I can count, these last two months.

'Yes,' I say. 'It's goodbye today.' If I didn't know it before, I know it now.

I don't want to spend the rest of my life with a man like Tod. I want to spend it with somebody who understands the things that matter to me, who's had a life with dark patches, like mine. I can't imagine Tod gardening with me or reading by my log-burning stove at Clearwater Cottage or helping out with Neighbourhood Watch business. He's part of my London adventure, and London is where he belongs.

'I have to go back to the theatre,' Tod says, his voice so low I can barely catch the words. 'But I could come back tonight. One last night. For old times' sake.'

That warm, butterfly feeling grows, and the rhythmic brush of his thumb on the skin of my wrist becomes more distracting than ever.

Well. Is it really an adventure if you don't make at least *one* rather ill-advised decision?

29

Leena

I do love a good bit of crisis management, but when I get back from Nicola's, I am a little bit apprehensive at how much has been left unattended in my absence. I mean, the fete is already officially open, now, and I'm not sure anyone's checked whether there are toilets yet.

But when I pull up in Peewit Street, I can hear the charity auction underway, I can smell hog roasting, and I can see the falconer setting up with his birds. It looks *amazing*. Someone's got the maypole up in my absence – it's nearly straight and everything. We've got lucky with the weather, too: it's that lemony pale sunshine you get when spring is just warming up, and the sound of chatter and children laughing carries on the light breeze.

I head straight for the Portaloo zone and am delighted to discover there are indeed toilets. Otherwise I was going to have to tell everyone to leave their doors unlocked and let visitors in if they needed a wee, and I had a feeling that was going to be a hard sell with the villagers.

'Oh, good, there are toilets,' says my mother from behind me.

I turn, surprised. She looks well – she's dressed in a long flowing skirt and a bell-sleeved blouse, and as she leans to kiss me hello I feel a little peculiar. It takes me a moment to clock: there's no wave of emotion, no follow-up panic, no fight-or-flight. I'm pleased to see her. That's all.

She pulls a list out of her skirt pocket – my list. I pat my own pockets, as if I might find it there even though I can literally see she's holding it.

'Basil picked it up after the scuffle with Cliff,' Mum says. 'I've been working my way through it as best I can. Sorry the maypole is wonky, I couldn't convince Roland it wasn't straight, and then I lost the will.'

'You . . . Oh, Mum, thank you,' I say.

She smiles at me. She's pulled her hair back in a loose bun, and her eyes look brighter. I'm so very grateful not to be angry with her, so glad to look at her and feel nothing but love, that I pull her in for a spontaneous hug. She laughs.

'Oh, this is lovely,' she says.

I kiss her on the cheek. Behind us, someone knocks on a Portaloo door from the inside, and a voice that I'm pretty sure is Basil's shouts, 'Hello? I'm stuck!'

I make a face at Mum. 'Back to work, eh,' I tell her. 'Will you be joining the parade?'

'I hear they've still not found a May Queen yet,' she says, lifting an eyebrow.

'Oh, God, I'm going to have to do it, aren't I?' I look hopeful. 'Unless you fancy it?'

Mum gives me a very motherly look at that, one that says, *Nice try, Leena.* 'Saving the day like you did this morning . . . that May Queen's crown belongs to you,' she says. 'Now. Are you going to let Basil out of the toilet, or shall I?'

Now that I'm actually in it, this May Day outfit looks less Queen Guinevere and more . . . bridal.

I adjust the bodice nervously, loitering in the doorway of Clearwater Cottage. The dress is high-waisted, falling in soft white chiffon from just below the bust, and Penelope has helped pin flowers in my hair, around the May Queen crown. I feel a bit ethereal. This is very new for me. I'm not usually the ethereal type.

I reach into my bag for Grandma's phone and send Betsy a quick text to tell her everything is going well. Arnold has taken Cliff home for now, on stern orders not to return to the fete, so I thought we might be able to bring Betsy back for the procession. But when she called to say she'd settled in at Nicola's, she sounded so wobbly I didn't even suggest it. It's easy to forget that Betsy's not Grandma: she's six years older, for starters, and though she's full of steely determination, she doesn't have Grandma's energy.

I'm not sure anyone else has that, actually. These last two months have reminded me of quite how remarkable my grandmother really is.

I smooth my dress with clammy palms. Out on Middling Lane, the procession awaits me. There was no selection process for joining the May Day procession – it pretty much includes anybody who wasn't busy doing something else, plus anyone Betsy would openly ostracise if she found out they didn't take part. My mum's there, laughing at something Kathleen says, and I can see the Neighbourhood Watch: Dr Piotr's bald head bowed as he speaks to Roland, Penelope winding a string of flowers around her neck and down her arms like a feather boa.

Then there's the kids. All thirty-eight of the children who attend the Hamleigh-in-Harksdale primary school are here, and they're gathered around Jackson in a circle, their faces turned up to his. They're holding bags of confetti, ready to throw rose petals out into the crowds, and they're dressed in white, like me, though most of their outfits are definitely made from bedsheets.

Well, all but one of them are dressed in bedsheets. One very special little girl is dressed as a satsuma.

'Easter bunny lady!' Samantha calls, breaking ranks to dash over and hug me around the legs. She bashes into me with an *oof*, bouncing off; Jackson steadies her. He looks up at me then, and I watch him double-take as he sees my white dress, my bare shoulders. His mouth opens a little, and then he's staring, really staring, can't-help-himself staring. I bite my lip, trying not to smile.

'You look like a queen!' Samantha says.

'Oh, thank you!'

'Or a ghost!' she says.

Hmm. Less good.

Jackson clears his throat. 'Ready to travel in style, as promised?' he asks, nodding behind me.

I turn. Parked up in front of Arnold's house is Jackson's pick-up truck, so heavily garlanded in ribbons and flowers that you can hardly see Arnold in the driving seat. He winds down the window, beheading a carnation in the process.

'Your carriage awaits!' he calls.

'Taking part in the May Day procession?' I call back. 'But Arnold, what about your reputation as the grumpy village recluse?'

'Go on with you, up in the back before I change my mind,' says Arnold.

Jackson kisses Samantha and sends her to join the other kids before helping me climb up into the back of the truck. We stand side by side and look at one another, the wind in our hair. I feel gladness, mostly – glad to be here, glad that I made this mad choice and stepped into my grandmother's life for a little while, glad that Jackson's smiling so broadly both his dimples are showing. There's excited chatter from behind us as everyone gets settled into position, then Jackson taps twice on the truck's roof and we're off, trundling along the glittering path ahead at three miles an hour, with a motley, merry May Day procession behind us.

I haven't been drunk in . . . I can't remember the last time I was drunk. Goodbye drinks for Mateo when he left to go to McKinsey?

And even then, I was too tired to really do the drunk thing properly; I just necked two Long Island iced teas then fell asleep on the tube, and nothing sobers you up like a long and expensive journey home from High Barnet.

But I am drunk on mango daiquiris and dizzy from very inexpertly dancing around the maypole, and I am *happy*. Happy happy happy. We reckon we've raised over a thousand pounds for charity today, and that money will go to help people like Carla, their families, their carers. Right now that feels like the most wonderful thing in the world.

I weave my way down to the big bonfire in the field where I first walked Hank. Most of the stalls are still up and running around me, lit with lanterns and the dappled light of the central bonfire; the tropical cocktail stands are the most popular, with queues snaking away from each one. The hills of the Dales stand dark and beautiful behind it all and I will miss this place, God, I'll really miss it. I don't want tonight to end.

'Someone's cheerful,' Arnold says, raising his glass to me as I approach the bonfire.

The fire spatters and crackles behind him; I walk forward and feel its warmth with a *whoomph*, stretching my hands out towards the heat. Jackson wanders over and passes Arnold a cup of something with a slice of melon floating in it. They stand together, comfortable, like father and son. I like that they've stayed that way even after Jackson's mum left Arnold. Family can be so complicated, but if you just pick your own way of doing it you can end up with something pretty perfect all the same.

Jackson squints up at the sky. 'Going to rain tomorrow,' he says.

'My stepson,' Arnold announces, 'here to rain on your May Day parade. The lady was feeling cheerful, Jackson! Don't ruin her good mood.'

Jackson coughs. 'Sorry.' He leans to put his empty cup down and staggers slightly as he straightens back up.

'Are you drunk?' I ask. 'Ooh, this is fun. What's drunk Jackson like?'

'Actually,' Jackson says, pulling loose flowers from his wreath, 'drunk Jackson tends to overshare.'

Arnold makes his excuses, waving vaguely at the treeline. Jackson and I move towards one of the makeshift benches set up beside the bonfire. It's dark; his face is starkly masculine in the firelight, shadows collecting beneath his browbone, below his jaw. As my heart starts to thunder, I know I shouldn't be sitting down with him alone – I'm thinking about this man too much, I'm too aware of him.

'Samantha loves you,' he says, pulling off his wreath and setting it down beside him. 'Though she definitely still thinks you're the Easter bunny. She explained to me that you're off duty until next year now.'

I relax a little – if we're talking about his kid, it doesn't feel so dangerous. 'That outfit. She's such a great kid.'

He looks sidelong at me. 'You know she got icing in your hair when you let her sit on your shoulders?'

I lift a hand to my hair and groan. 'God, that's going to be a nightmare to get out,' I say, picking at it. 'Why didn't anyone tell me?'

'I think everyone's too tipsy to notice. Except me.'

'Except you?' I raise my eyebrows. 'I thought you were at oversharing levels of drunk.'

'I am.' He turns to face me, his eyes bright and intense in the firelight. 'I just tend to notice you more than average.'

I go still. My heartbeat's in my ears now, in my throat, everywhere.

'Leena . . .'

'I should get back to–'

His hand covers mine on the bench between us. A flush of hot–cold energy goes through me as he touches me, like the moment when someone pulls you in for a deep kiss, but all he's done is place his fingers over mine.

'I think you're amazing, Leena Cotton. You are kind, and beautiful, and absolutely unstoppable, and God, that thing that you do, running your hand through your hair like that, it . . .' He rubs his mouth with his spare hand, jaw clenching and unclenching.

I lower my arm – I hadn't realised I'd even reached to touch my hair.

'I think you should know,' he says. 'I like you. Like I shouldn't. That sort of like.'

My breath is coming fast and shaky. I want to reach for him. I want to lace my fingers through his and pull myself towards him and kiss him hard on the mouth in the firelight, and he's so close, closer than he should be, so close I can see the pale freckles under his eyes, the dusting of stubble across his jaw—

'I've not known what to do,' he says, his voice so quiet it's almost a whisper. His lips are inches from mine. 'For weeks I've thought about it. I don't want to break up a relationship, that's wrong. But I also don't want you to leave without knowing.'

My brain kicks in the moment he mentions Ethan. I pull my hand away and back up, swallowing hard. My body's slower – I'm hot with wanting.

'I shouldn't – I'm sorry, Jackson, I should have stopped you the moment you started speaking. I don't see you that way. I have a boyfriend. You know that.' It comes out wobblier than I'd like; I try to sound firm and decisive, but my mind is foggy with tropical cocktails and my pulse is still pounding.

'And he makes you happy?' Jackson asks. He winces slightly as he says it. 'I'm sorry. I'm only going to ask you that once.'

I take a deep breath. It's Ethan we're talking about. Of course I know the answer to this question.

'Yes. He does.'

Jackson looks down at his feet. 'Well. Good. I'm glad. I'm glad he makes you happy.'

He seems to mean it, which makes my heart hurt.

'I'll be gone next week,' I say, swallowing. 'You'll . . . forget all about me. Life will go back to normal.'

We both look towards the fire, its flames torn by the breeze.

'I might just say goodbye now,' Jackson says.

I'm having a little gathering tomorrow in the village hall with the Neighbourhood Watch crew, maybe even Nicola and Betsy if they feel up to it. But I guess no Jackson.

'That's fine,' I say. 'Of course. I should . . .' I stand. One side of my body's hot from the bonfire, the other's cool from the breeze.

'I'm sorry,' Jackson says, standing too. 'I should have . . . Obviously, now, I can see I shouldn't have said anything.'

'No,' I say. 'I get it.'

It's better he said it. Now it's clear where the line is.

'Well. Goodbye,' he says.

I hesitate, and then,

'Come here,' I say, and pull him in for a hug. He closes his arms around me, my cheek against his chest, his hand almost spanning the width of my waist. He smells of open fires and wildflowers, the scent of his wreath still caught in the soft fabric of his shirt. I pull away as my pulse begins to pound again.

'Live a good life, Leena Cotton,' he says, in the moment we step apart. 'And . . . make sure it's the right one.'

30

Eileen

I leave Tod in bed with the sheets ruffled, his arm thrown wide as if reaching for me again. I like the idea of this as my last memory of him, and his last memory of me as the way I was last night: giddy, a little silly, and wearing perfect make-up because Martha did it for me.

My bags are all packed and waiting in Rupert and Aurora's hallway downstairs. Fitz carried them down for me before he left for work. I gave Aurora and Rupert a cactus as their goodbye present; Aurora was ecstatic. Really, that woman thinks anything shaped even vaguely like a penis is a work of art.

They've promised to keep the Silver Shoreditchers' Social Club going and to send me photos of each month's event. It's Fitz who's most excited about it, though: he has grand plans to expand the club already. It's been a joy, seeing him throwing his heart into it all – he reminds me a little of myself at that age. Though I had a good sight more common sense. The man just can't seem to learn how to look after himself – anything domestic goes in one ear and comes out the other. I've done what I can, though, while I've been here, and he's coming along. The other day I saw him pairing his socks after doing a wash.

I hail down a black cab to take me to the Selmount offices for my goodbye coffee with Bee. As we crawl through the streets, I remember how frightening this place felt when I first arrived. Now it's a second home. I'll miss the man in the market who gives me a discount on crêpes because he's from Yorkshire, too, and the *Big Issue* seller with the Alsatian who wears a pink bow.

We pull up outside the Selmount offices; it takes me a while to get out of the car, and I'm just getting my legs around to climb out of the door when I look up and freeze.

'Are you OK there, ma'am?' says the taxi driver.

'*Shh!*' I say, eyes fixed. I start swivelling, pulling my legs back inside the car again. 'Close your door! Follow that car!'

'Sorry?' he says, nonplussed.

'That cab there! The one two in front, with the lingerie lady on the side!'

'The one with the gent and the blonde girl getting in?' he asks, looking at me rather warily in the mirror.

'That is my granddaughter's boyfriend, and I'll bet you any money that's his bit-on-the-side,' I say. 'She fits the description down pat.'

The driver turns the key in the ignition. 'Right you are, ma'am. I'll stick to them like glue.' He cuts into the traffic smoothly enough that nobody honks. 'Can't stand cheaters,' he says.

'Nor me,' I say with fervour, as we pull in behind them. With difficulty – I don't want to take my eyes off that cab – I send Bee a quick message.

On to Ethan. So sorry to miss you. Lots of love, Eileen xx

She replies instantly.

I AM INTRIGUED.

I don't have time to fill Bee in. She'll have to wait. Ethan's cab is pulling in; my taxi driver stops behind them at a bus stop, looking rather nervously over his shoulder.

'I'll hop out,' I say, though it's more of a clamber than a hop, really. 'You've been wonderful. As soon as I've worked out how, I'll give you five stars.'

He looks bemused, but helps me climb out and gives me a friendly enough wave as I set off after Ethan, dragging my suitcase behind me.

I'm convinced that's Ceci. She's got straight blonde hair and long legs, which ticks off two of the things I know about the woman, and besides, there's just something about her that says, *I might steal your granddaughter's boyfriend.*

But I do lose my nerve a tad when they pause outside an office building. It occurs to me now that Ethan and Ceci could just be off to a meeting, in which case I have wasted a lot of money on a cab fare to . . . where exactly *am* I?

Then Ethan's hand brushes Ceci's arm, and I know I'm on to something. He ducks his head to speak to her. Then, quick as a flash, blink and you miss it . . . he kisses her on the lips.

For a moment I hesitate. I baulk. But then I remind myself of what I said when I first suspected Ethan was running around on Leena: Carla would never have baulked, and I shouldn't, either. So I hitch my handbag up my arm and me and my wheeled suitcase set off at a march.

Ethan and Ceci don't even look up as I approach. I tap Ethan on the shoulder. He spins.

'Eileen! Hi,' he says, taking a step back. 'What are you doing here?'

'Ceci, I presume?' I say to the woman.

She just raises her eyebrows. 'Excuse me?'

'Off you trot, lass.' I gesture her towards the building. 'My quarrel isn't with you. Though you ought to know that there's a special place in hell for women who set their sights on somebody else's man.'

'Now, hang on, Eileen,' Ethan says.

'I saw you kiss her.'

'What on earth has that got to do with . . .' Ceci begins.

'Are you still here?' I ask her.

Ceci looks at me with distaste. 'Ethan?' she says.

'I'll see you in the meeting,' he says. 'Stall them, would you?'

'Let's just go, Ethan. Who even is this woman?'

'I'm Leena's grandmother,' I say.

Her eyes widen.

'Oh.'

'Yes. Oh.'

'I'll . . . I'll see you inside,' she says to Ethan, and scuttles away on her high heels. She reminds me of a praying mantis. I look away. She doesn't deserve thinking about.

'So,' I say to Ethan. I wait.

He rubs his forehead. 'I think you've got the wrong end of the stick, Eileen.'

'I'm no fool, Ethan. Don't try to take me for one.'

'Look. You don't understand. In the nicest possible way, Eileen, modern relationships, they're not like . . .'

'No. Don't try that.'

He runs his fingers through his hair. 'OK. All right. I didn't . . . I didn't mean for things to happen with Ceci. The last thing I want to do is hurt Leena. But she's been so different lately. I don't know what's got into her. It doesn't even feel like I'm in a relationship with *Leena*, it's like this whole other person, and she wants to talk about the – the transport links in rural northern England, and making stew, and planning village parties. It's . . . It's just . . .' He reaches for my arm suddenly. 'Please. Don't tell her.'

'Ah, yes. I suspected we were going to get to that soon.' I remove my arm from his grasp with deliberation.

'Please. It'll mess everything up. I'll end it with Ceci, I'll do it right now after our meeting.' He's beginning to fray; his eyes are desperate.

'I won't tell Leena.'

He sags with relief.

'For two days. I'll give you that much. Though God knows you don't deserve it.'

I leave him there, then, because I can't hold my temper much longer and I can't stand the sight of him, withering, sorry for himself, sweating in his expensive shirt. A succession of kind strangers help me with my bags until I'm settled on the train in King's Cross, pulling out of the station into the open air, the wide sky, with the cranes pivoting steadily back and forth, building an even bigger London.

I'll miss this city. But it's not my home. As the train speeds its way up north I wonder if this is how it feels to be a homing pigeon, tugged onwards, as though someone's pulling on the threads that hold you to the place where you belong.

31

Leena

I wake up the morning after May Day in the customary manner (cat in face) but, instead of jumping out of bed, I go back to sleep for at least another three hours. On second wake-up, I discover Ant/Dec has taken up residence on my lower ribs, and is purr–snoring so gleefully I feel bad moving him. Also, moving sounds rubbish. I'm bloody *knackered*. And more than a little hungover, too.

Did my *mum* walk me home last night? I vaguely remember talking in great detail about my business plan with Bee, and then telling her I didn't want to leave Yorkshire, and her saying, *Why not set up your business up here? Why London? What's so bloody brilliant about London anyway?* And then I'd got into this big rant about the Central line, and . . .

My phone is ringing. It's Ethan. I rub my eyes and fumble for the phone on the side table.

'Hey.'

'Hey, Leena,' he says. He sounds tight, worried. 'How are you?'

'Bit hungover. You?'

'Listen, angel, I'm really sorry, but I need to talk to you about something. It might be a bit upsetting.'

I pull myself upright against the pillows. 'OK . . .'

'I bumped into your grandma this morning. I was with Ceci, from work – we were on our way to a client meeting. Your grandma . . .

I'm sorry, Leena. She went crazy. Yelling at Ceci and me, saying these awful things – saying I was cheating on you, it was mad, Leena. I don't know what got into her.'

'Oh my God,' I say, clutching at the duvet. 'What?'

'Do you think she's OK, Leena? Has she seemed a little . . . off to you lately, or anything? At her age . . .'

'What, you think she's losing her mind?' I've gone cold. My heart is beating in my ears.

'No, no,' Ethan says quickly, but I can hear the worry in his voice. 'I'm sure she was just . . . having a bad day, or something, and maybe took it out on me.'

'She said you were cheating on me?'

'Yeah.' He gives a breathy laugh. 'Leena, you know I'd never . . .'

'Of course,' I say, before he can even finish, because I don't even want him to have to say it.

'I think . . . can you come home, Leena?' He sounds so tired. 'Today, I mean? I need to see you. This has been . . . it's been a crazy morning.'

'Today? I'm supposed to be staying up until tomorrow lunchtime, to catch up with Grandma . . .'

'Right, of course.'

'Do you need me there?' I wipe my face; I've teared up a bit. This is horrible. Why would – how could . . . 'I'll come back now. If you need me. And I'll call my grandma and talk to her.'

'Don't be upset with her. Maybe it's about your granddad – I mean, he left her for another woman, right? Maybe she got a bit muddled and it all sort of came out. Maybe this trip to London was a bit much for her. She probably just needs some rest.'

'I've got to call her,' I say again. 'I love you, Ethan.'

'I love you too, Leena. Call me back, OK?'

I fumble with Grandma's stupid old phone; it seems to take for ever to get it ringing her.

'Hello?'

'Grandma, are you all right?'

'Yes, I'm fine, dear, I'm just on the train up to you now.' There's a pause. 'Are *you* all right? You sound a little . . .'

'Ethan just rang.'

'Ah. Leena, love, I'm so sorry.'

'What got into you? Are you OK? You're OK, aren't you?'

I can hear the train in the background, the rattle and whoosh as she makes her way here. I lean forward, bringing my knees up to my chest, staring down at the faint rose pattern of the duvet cover. My heart is beating too fast, I can feel it against my thighs as I curl in on myself.

'What do you mean, what got into me?' she says.

'Yelling at Ethan. Accusing him of – of – with *Ceci*, Grandma, what were you thinking?'

'Leena, I don't think Ethan has told you the whole story.'

'No, you don't mean that, don't say that! Why are you *saying* these things, Grandma?' I brush at my cheeks; I'm crying in earnest now. 'I don't know what to think, I don't want you to be going crazy and I don't want you to be in your right mind either.'

'I'm not losing my mind, Leena – good God, is that what that weasel told you?'

'Don't talk about him like that.'

'I saw him kiss her, Leena.'

I go still.

'He said things have been different while you've been away. He said you've been a different person, and–'

'No. I don't believe you.'

'I'm sorry, Leena.'

'I don't *want* you to say sorry because you're *not sorry for the right thing.*'

'Leena! Don't shout at me, please. Let's just have a civilised chat about all this over–'

'I'm going back to London now. Ethan needs me.'

'Leena. Don't. Stay in Hamleigh and we can talk.'

'I need to get back.' I scrunch my eyes so tightly it hurts. 'I'm not . . . I've let Ethan down. I'm not being his Leena, up here, in Hamleigh. I don't know *who* I'm being. I need to get back to proper me. Work, Ethan, my life in London. I shouldn't stay up here any longer.'

'You're not thinking straight, my love.'

'No,' I say, my finger already hovering over the red phone button, 'I'm not. This – this *stupid swap*' – I spit it out – 'was meant to help, but now it's messed up the one thing, the one good thing, and . . .' I start to sob. 'I'm done, Grandma. I'm done with all this.'

32

Eileen

I am home, at last, after what seems like an age. Even making a cup of tea feels beyond me. I shouldn't have stayed up so late last night, I ought to have known better. And now, after the long journey, and the difficult goodbyes, and that awful phone call with Leena . . . I feel heavy and sluggish, as if I'm moving through treacle.

There's a new distance between me and Leena. If we'd talked more about our experiences over these last two months, perhaps she would have believed me about Ethan. I thought we'd become closer, living each other's lives, but it's been quite the opposite. The house smells of her perfume mixed with the scent of home, and it's strange.

The doorbell rings. I lever myself up out of my armchair with effort, frustrated at the deep ache in my back and the fuzzy, quiet pain in my limbs.

I'm hoping it'll be Marian, but it's Arnold. He looks different, but I can't tell why – a new flat cap? A new shirt?

'Are you all right?' he says, with his usual abruptness. 'I saw you stumble, outside the house, and I wondered . . .'

I bristle. 'I'm quite all right, thank you.'

He bristles too. We stand there, bristling at one another, and it's just like old times.

Then his shoulders sag. 'I missed you,' he says.

'I beg your pardon?' I say, blinking, gripping the door frame to keep steady.

He frowns. 'You're not all right. You need to sit down. Come on. Let me come in, will you, and I'll make you a cup of tea.'

'Well,' I say, still reeling somewhat from Arnold's last declaration, 'I suppose you did come to the front door.'

He holds my elbow as we make our way back to the living room rather more slowly than I'd like. It's comforting to see him, or it was until he said he missed me. That was somewhat *dis*comforting.

'That confounded cat,' Arnold says, shooing Dec off the sofa. 'Here, sit yourself down.'

I just about refrain from reminding him that this is my house, and it ought to be me inviting him to sit. He's being very neighbourly. In fact he's being . . .

'Is that a new hat?' I ask abruptly.

'What?' His hand goes up self-consciously. 'Oh. Yes. You like it?'

'Yes, I do.'

'No need to sound so surprised. I did tell you I'd decided to turn over a new leaf. I got *three* new hats.' He's already off to the kitchen; I hear the sounds of the tap running, the kettle going on. 'Milk, no sugar?'

'One sugar,' I correct him.

'It'll ruin your teeth!' he calls back.

'Like toffee apples?'

'Those are fruit, aren't they?'

I laugh, closing my eyes and leaning my head against the back of the sofa. I'm feeling a little better, like the life's coming back to my limbs, tingling in my toes and fingers as if I've just come in from the cold.

'You know, Eileen, your cupboards are a state,' Arnold says, coming back into the room with two large mugs of steaming tea. 'There's a tin of broad beans in there from 1994.'

'Good year, 1994,' I say, taking my mug.

Arnold smiles. 'How was it, then? The big city?' He looks at me shrewdly. 'Did you find your one true love?'

'Oh, shut up.'

'What? You didn't bring a man back with you, then?' He looks around as if checking the corners for Romeos.

'You know I didn't,' I say, whacking his arm. 'Though I *did* have a rather torrid love affair.'

He looks back at me very quickly. 'Torrid?'

'Well, I think so. I've never actually been very sure of what that means.' I shrug. 'An actor, from the West End. It was never going to last, but it was good fun.'

Arnold is looking very serious all of a sudden. I suppress a grin. I've missed winding Arnold up.

'But it's over now?' he asks. 'And there wasn't anyone else?'

'Well,' I say coyly. 'There was *one* other man. But I was only chatting to him online.'

Arnold sits up a little straighter and begins to smile. 'Oh, aye?' he says.

'He's lovely. A really sensitive man. His life hasn't been easy, and he has his troubles, but he's so kind and thoughtful.'

'Sensitive, eh?' Arnold says, raising his eyebrows.

'He's been reading Agatha Christie because he knows she's my favourite author.' I smile, thinking of Howard tucked up in his flat, coming to the end of *The Murder of Roger Ackroyd.*

'Oh, he has, has he? How do you know that? Did someone dob him in?' Arnold asks, still smiling.

I tilt my head at him. 'He told me himself.'

Arnold's smile wavers. 'Eh?' he says.

'About the books. He lets me know when he finishes each one, and tells me when lines make him think of me, and . . .'

Arnold gets up so abruptly he spills tea down his shirt. 'Bugger,' he says, dabbing at it with his sleeve.

'Don't dab with that, you're just making it worse!' I say, moving to stand. 'I'll fetch you a—'

'Don't bother,' he says gruffly. 'I'd better be gone.' He puts down the half-empty tea mug and strides out of the living room. A moment later I hear the front door slam.

Well. What on earth's got into Arnold?

As soon as I have the energy, I get myself up and pull my shoes on and I walk rather more slowly than usual to Marian's house. This is the loveliest part of coming home, knowing I'll see her again. At least, I hope it'll be lovely. A little part of me is afraid she might be doing worse, not better, and I'll realise I shouldn't have left Hamleigh after all.

She knows I'm home today, but when I give her a knock nobody answers the door. I swallow uneasily and try calling her, but she doesn't answer. She's probably just nipped out. I'll see if she's down at the village shop.

I turn away from Marian's front door and then pause, looking down at the mobile phone in my hand. It's not mine. It's Leena's. We were supposed to swap back once I got home, but then she left for London.

Of course, we told everyone we speak to regularly that we'd changed our phone numbers, but I know for a fact that Leena didn't tell Ceci.

If Leena had proof that Ethan was being unfaithful to her . . . Surely then she'd believe me. And I could get proof. I just have to pretend to be Leena. Just for one little text message.

What I'm about to do is most certainly wrong. It's meddling of the worst kind. But if I've learned anything these last two months, it's that sometimes everyone's better off if you speak up and step in.

Hello, Ceci. Ethan has told me everything. How could you?

33

Leena

The journey back to London feels hazy, as though my ears have popped and everything's a little muffled. I find my way to my flat on autopilot; it's only when I step into the building that I really connect with where I am. It's all different. The whole downstairs space looks beautiful: exposed floorboards, a seating area, a dining table pushed to the back of the room. Grandma must have done this. There are bright, amateurish paintings stuck to the walls and a stack of bowls in one corner of the dining table; it seems lived-in, well loved.

Once I get to the flat, though, I forget all about the downstairs area. From the moment I open our door and smell that scent of home, all I can see is my life with Ethan. We cook in that kitchen, we curl up on that sofa, we kiss in this doorway, over and over, at the start and end of every evening we spend together. I can almost *see* him here, like the faint lines you leave in a notebook when you press down hard as you write.

He would never hurt me. He wouldn't. I won't believe it.

Fitz returns home half an hour later to find me sobbing on the floor, my back against the sofa. He's at my side in an instant. He pulls me against his shoulder and I cry into his cashmere sweater and he doesn't even tell me off for getting his dry-clean-only jumper all wet.

'Everything's a mess,' I say between sobs.

Fitz kisses the top of my head. 'What's happened?'

'Ethan . . . Grandma . . . He . . . She . . .'

'I think I need some of the linking words here, Leena. I was always shit at Mad Libs.'

I can't bring myself to tell him. There's this one particular thing Grandma said that I've been hearing over and over, playing on a loop over the train announcements, the saxophonist in King's Cross Station, the chatter of passers-by as I made my way here. *He said you've been a different person.*

I don't believe Grandma. I trust Ethan. I *love* him, *so* much, he's my happy place, my comfort blanket, he would never hurt me like that. He's *Ethan.*

Maybe it doesn't matter. Maybe if it's true I can just forgive him and we can go back to how we were before. I've had a crush on Jackson, haven't I? It doesn't mean anything. It doesn't mean I have to stop being Ethan's Leena.

But even as I think it, I know I'm wrong. If Ethan's – if he's – with Ceci–

'Jeez, Leena honey, stop, if you keep crying like this you'll run out of water,' Fitz says, pulling me in tighter against him. 'Talk to me. What's happened?'

'I can't talk about it,' I manage. 'I can't. Please. Distract me.'

Fitz sighs. 'No, Leena, don't do that. Let's talk about it, come on. Has Ethan done something bad?'

'I can't,' I tell him, more firmly this time, pulling away. I wipe my face on my sleeve; my breath is coming in quiet gasps even now the tears are stopping, and I try to steady my breathing as best I can. 'Is that my laptop?' I say, spotting it on the coffee table under a heap of Martha's old interior design magazines.

'Yeah,' Fitz says, in a tone that says, *I'm humouring your need to change the subject, but don't think I'm done.* 'How does it feel to be re-united? I could not live two months without mine. *Or* a smartphone.'

Shit, my phone. I never got to swap back with Grandma. I shake my head – I don't have the energy to worry about that right now. I pull the laptop on to my knees, the weight of it reassuring and familiar.

'How about I make you a smoothie?' Fitz says, stroking my hair.

I sniff, scrubbing my cheeks dry. 'Will it be brown?'

'Invariably, yes. I have not cracked that in your absence. They still always come out brown. Even when everything I put in is green.'

That's somehow quite reassuring. At least something hasn't changed. 'Then no thanks. Just a tea.'

I know it's a bad idea, but I need to look at Ethan's Facebook. He's coming over, but not for an hour, and I just need to reassure myself that . . . that . . . I don't know, that he's still my Ethan. And maybe that there aren't any pictures of him with Ceci.

I open the laptop. The chat page on Grandma's dating site is open on the screen.

> *OldCountryBoy says: Hi, Eileen. I just wanted to check whether you have had a chance to send me the money? I'm raring to go on the website!*
>
> *xxxxx*

'Shit,' I mutter. The page has timed out; I log in again after a few false starts, trying to remember the username and password I set up for Grandma.

'Isn't that like . . . identity fraud?' Fitz says as he places a cup of tea beside me.

'I'm Eileen Cotton, aren't I?' I tell him, scrolling back through her messages, skim-reading as I go. *Shit.* I should have warned Grandma about catfishing, I should never have just let her loose on this website – what was I *thinking*?

I reach for my phone; I only notice it's already ringing when it buzzes as my hand closes around it. It's Grandma calling.

'Grandma, did you transfer money to a man you met on the Internet?' I say as I pick up. My heart is beating fast.

'What? Leena, Leena – you need to get back here. Get back to Hamleigh.'

'What's going on? Grandma, slow down.' I scrabble to my feet, pushing my laptop on to the floor. I haven't heard that tone in my grandmother's voice since Carla was ill, and it makes me feel instantly sick.

'It's Marian. She's nowhere.'

'She's what?'

'She's not answering the door, and she's not anywhere in the village and nobody has seen her. It's just like the last time, Leena, she must be in there but she's not letting me in, and I can't find my key *or* the spare anywhere to get in and check she's . . . what if she hurts herself in there all alone?'

Right, step one: keep Grandma calm.

'Grandma, slow down. Mum's not going to hurt herself.'

I drag my laptop back on to my knees again.

Step two: check trains. Because I have just remembered I have both sets of keys to Mum's house in my purse.

'OK, I'll be there by seven, with the keys,' I say. 'I'm so sorry for taking them with me. Are you sure Mum's not just gone for a swim in Daredale or something?'

'I rang the pool,' Grandma says. She sounds on the edge of tears. 'They said she'd not been since last week.'

Step three: keep myself calm. Mum was doing really, really well when I left her, the antidepressants were helping, we did so much talking about Carla, it all felt so much healthier. I'm sure there's a totally reasonable explanation for all this.

But . . . the doubt's creeping in. After all, I underestimated how bad she was last time around, didn't I? I didn't even know about these depressive episodes until Grandma told me.

What if she really is in there, alone? Did I say something awful at May Day, when she walked me home drunk? Should I have done more to support her these last two months, like Grandma said from the start? I wish I was still there, I wish I'd left at least *one* bloody key, if she really is locked in that house having some kind of breakdown and there's nothing I can do, and not enough time and—

No, come on. Step four: recognise how much time you have, and how much you can do in that time. I remember a change-management seminar where the speaker told us that the doctors who handle real, every-second-counts emergencies move more slowly than doctors in any other department. They know the true capacity of a minute, just how much you can fit into it, and how much more fits in when you're calm.

'It's all right, Grandma. We'll talk it all through when I get there. Just stay at the house and keep knocking in case she is in there. And if you hear anything that makes you think she might be in danger, you go and get Dr Piotr, OK?'

'OK,' Grandma says, voice quivering.

I swallow. 'Right. Grandma, this man, did you send him a bank transfer?'

'A cheque. Why are you asking all this, Leena? Did you – why does this *matter*, did you not hear what I said? Marian's not coping again, she's gone, or she's hiding, she won't let me in, she—'

'I know. But I have twenty minutes in which I can do nothing about that. And I *can* use that time to stop you from getting scammed. You concentrate on Mum, and I'll be there as soon as I can.'

'What do you mean "scammed"?'

'I'll explain later,' I say shortly, and hang up. Grandma's bank's phone number is up on my laptop screen.

'Hello, there,' I say, when someone answers. 'My name is Eileen Cotton, account number 4599871. I'd like to cancel a cheque.'

'That's fine. I just need to go through a few security questions first before we can authorise that. What's your date of birth, please?'

'Eighteenth of October, 1939,' I say, with as much confidence as I can muster.

'Now *that* is definitely identity fraud,' Fitz says.

I am travelling north, at last. Across the aisle of the train a young family is playing Scrabble – I feel a bitter pang of nostalgia for the time when my family looked like that, happy in the ignorance of everything to come.

My legs jitter; I'm itching to run, but I'm trapped here on this train, crawling my way up to Yorkshire a hundred times more slowly than I want to be.

Breathe in, slow. Out, slow. OK. Yes, I'm stuck on this train, but that means I have two hours to get my head around this. Let's aim to reach calmness by Grantham. Mum is OK. Mum is OK. Mum is OK.

A new email appears in my inbox; my laptop is open in front of me, more out of habit than the need to do anything with it. Rebecca wants me to come in for a coffee on Friday to talk about my return to work. Ceci is copied in on the email, and I flinch when I see her name, even though I don't believe Grandma, of course I don't.

Shit, hang on. Ethan. I haven't told him I've left London.

I send him a quick message.

I've left – back to Hamleigh again – I'll tell you everything later xx

His reply comes almost instantly.

Leena? What's going on? Are you back on this phone?

And then, a moment later:

Can't we talk?

I respond straight away.

I can't talk now, I'm on the train, I have to go back to Hamleigh, I'm
*   sorry. I can't go into it now – it's about my mum. xx*

He replies.

Why did you text Ceci like that? I thought you said you believed me.

I go cold.

I didn't tex . . .

I delete the words and pause. My heart suddenly feels very high in
my chest, as though it's sitting at the bottom of my throat and the
air can't get past; my breathing is shallow.

I open my message thread to Grandma. We haven't texted much
at all these last few weeks. I hadn't even realised how little we'd
spoken.

Grandma, did you text Ceci from my phone?

I wait. The train pulls in to Wakefield; the family next to me gets
off and is replaced by an elderly couple who read their newspapers
in amicable silence. Everyone moves perfectly normally, turning
sideways to pass down the aisle, lifting their arms to take their suit-
cases from the overhead rack, but I feel as if I'm on a film set. All
these people are extras, and someone is about to yell *Cut.*

A reply from Grandma.

I'm sorry, Leena. I wanted you to see proof. I know it will hurt, but it will hurt more later, if you don't find out now.

I gulp in air, a rasping ragged noise that makes everyone in the carriage stare my way. I stumble out from behind the table and into the vestibule, then look down at my phone again through blurry eyes, and type as best I can.

Send me what she said to you – I need to see.

The reply takes for ever to come. I can imagine Grandma trying to work out how to forward a text on my phone, and I'm seconds away from sending her instructions before she finally responds with Ceci's message typed out.

Leena, I'm so sorry. I never planned for this to happen. All I can say is that it's been like a kind of madness. I can't stop myself when it comes to Ethan.

Another of those ragged gasps. It takes me a moment to realise it came from my mouth.

I know you must be heartbroken. After the first time I told him never again, but – well, I don't want to make excuses. Cx

That's all she's doing, of course. Ugh, that *Cx* at the end of the message, as if we're discussing weekend plans – God, I hate her, I hate hate hate her, I can taste the hate in my mouth, I can feel it clutching in my gut. I suddenly understand why men in films punch walls when they're angry. It's only cowardice and fear of pain that stops me. Instead I press the old brick of a phone into the palm of my left hand until it hurts – not as much as a split knuckle, but enough. My breathing finally starts to slow.

When I turn the phone over again my palm is almost purple-red, and there's a new message from Ethan.

Leena? Talk to me.

I sink down to sit on the floor, the carpet scratching my ankles. I wait for the emotion to hit again, a fresh wave, but it doesn't come. Instead there is a strange sort of stillness, a distance, as if I'm watching someone else find out the man they love has hurt them in the very worst way.

I gave him so much. I showed my rawest, weakest self to that man. I trusted him like I have never trusted anyone but family.

I just can't believe . . . I can't think of Ethan as . . . I gulp in air, my hands and feet beginning to tingle. I was so sure of him. I was *so sure*.

I don't hate Ceci – that wasn't hate. *This* is hate.

34

Eileen

I know as soon as I see her that Leena knows the truth about Ethan. She looks exhausted, bowed-down under the weight of it.

I can't help but think of the day when Wade left me. He was a good-for-nothing waste of space and I'd have kicked him out years ago if I'd had any sense, but when he left, just at first, the humiliation had hurt so keenly. That's what I'd felt: not anger, but shame.

'Leena, I'm so sorry.'

She leans to kiss me on the cheek, but her eyes are on Marian's front door behind me, and the key is in her hand. We both pause for a moment, just a second or two, bracing ourselves. My heart's going like the clappers, has been all afternoon – I keep pressing my hand to my chest as if to slow it down. I feel nauseous, so much so the bile rises in my throat.

Leena unlocks the door. The house is dark and quiet, and I know right away that Marian isn't here.

I stand there and try to absorb it while Leena moves through the rooms, flicking on lights, her face drawn and serious.

Marian isn't here, I think, with a peculiar sort of detachment. I was so sure she would be, I hadn't even thought of alternatives. But she's not here. She's . . .

'She's not here.' Leena comes to a stop in the middle of the hall. 'Is that good, or bad? Both, maybe? Where *is* she?'

I lean back against the wall, then jump as both my phone and Leena's phone let out a succession of beeps. She's quicker at pulling hers out of her pocket.

Dearest Mum, and my darling Leena,

Sorry it's taken me a little time to compose this message. I'm at Heathrow airport, now, with three hours until my flight and plenty of time to think.

Something Leena told me last night stayed with me when I woke up this morning. Leena, you said, 'I couldn't have figured myself out if I'd not been someone else.'

These last few weeks have been some of the happiest in recent memory. I have loved having you back, Leena, more than I can express – it's been wonderful for me to be able to look after my daughter again. And Mum, I've missed you, but I think perhaps I needed you to leave me for a little while, so I could realise I can stand on my own, without you holding my hand. Your absence has made me appreciate you all the more. I'm so grateful for everything you've done for me.

But I'm ready for something new, now. I don't know who I am when I'm not grieving for Carla. I can't be the woman I was before my daughter died. I couldn't, and I wouldn't want to be. So I need to find the new me.

My yoga mat and I are going to Bali. I want quiet, and sand between my toes. I want an adventure, like you've each had, but one that's mine.

Please look after one another while I'm away, and remember that I love you both very much xxx

'Bali,' I say, after a long, shocked silence.

Leena looks blankly at the picture on the hall wall and doesn't answer me.

'I don't understand,' I say, fretfully scrolling to the top of the message again. 'She's far too fragile to be going off on her own in some foreign country, and . . .'

'She's not, Grandma,' Leena says, turning to look at me at last. She breathes out slowly. 'I should have kept you in the loop more, then you'd realise. She really isn't fragile. She's been doing great, this last month or so.'

I can't quite believe that, but I want to.

'Honestly, Grandma. I know you think I didn't see how bad things were for Mum, and . . .' She swallows. 'You're right, for a long while I didn't, because I wasn't here, and that's on me. I should have listened to you when you said she was struggling instead of just thinking I knew best. But I can tell you that while I have been here I've seen her make so much progress. She's been doing so well.'

'I don't . . . But . . . *Bali*?' I say weakly. 'On her *own*?'

Leena smiles and tilts her head towards that picture on the wall. 'She's going to her happy place,' she says.

I stare at the image. It's a photo of a lady doing yoga in front of some sort of temple. I've never really noticed it before, though I vaguely remember it hanging in their old house in Leeds, too.

'Do you really think it's a good idea for her to go away all on her own?'

'I think we should have told her to do it a long time ago.' Leena steps forward and rubs my arms. 'This is a good thing, Grandma, just like your time in London and my time in Hamleigh. She needs a change.'

I read the message again. '*I couldn't have figured myself out if I'd not been someone else.*'

Leena looks embarrassed. 'I have no recollection of saying that. I was a bit drunk, if I'm honest.'

'You said something like that, though, when you thought I'd lied about Ethan.' I hold up her hand to stop her protesting. 'No, it's all right, love. It was a shock – you just needed time. But you said you weren't being *his* Leena.'

'Did I?' She's looking down at her feet.

'I want you to be *your* Leena, love.' I reach for her hands. 'You deserve to be with somebody who makes you feel *more* yourself, not less.'

She starts to cry, then, and my heart twists for her. I wish I could have protected her from this, that there'd been another way.

'I thought that person was Ethan,' she says, leaning her forehead on my shoulder. 'But – this last two months – I've felt – everything's been different.' Her shoulders shake as she sobs.

'I know, love.' I stroke her hair. 'I think we all got a bit lost this last year, didn't we, without Carla, and we needed a change to see it.'

Bali, I think, still reeling, as Leena cries in my arms. I'm not quite sure where that is, precisely, but I know it's a long way away. Marian has never been further afield than the north of France. It's so . . .

It's so *brave* of her.

There's a knock at the door. Leena and I both pause. We're sitting here in Marian's house with every single light switched on, both blubbering, make-up down our faces. Goodness knows what who-ever's at the door will think.

'I'll get it,' I say, wiping my cheeks.

It's Betsy.

'Oh, thank goodness,' she says, reaching to take my hands. 'I came as soon as I heard Marian was in trouble.'

'Betsy?' comes Leena's voice from behind me. 'Wait, how . . . how *did* you hear?'

I just hold my dearest friend's hands between my own. She looks wonderful. Her usual neckerchief is nowhere to be seen, and she's wearing a loose, polka-dotted blouse that makes her look like the Betsy Harris I knew twenty years ago. There's too much to say, and I falter for a moment, unsure, until she squeezes my hands and says, 'Oh, I've missed you, Eileen Cotton.'

That's the way with old friends. You understand each other, even when there's not enough words out there for everything that should be said.

'I'm so sorry I've been away when you needed me the most.' I raise my hands to her cheeks for a moment. 'Marian's fine, it turns out. Come on in, won't you?'

'Neighbourhood Watch,' says a voice behind Betsy. Basil and Penelope appear in the doorway and follow Betsy through. Dr Piotr comes by, giving me a gentle pat on the arm before stepping inside.

'Are you all right?' Kathleen pops up next. Goodness, are they all out here? Oh, yes, there's Roland parking up his scooter. 'I came as soon as I heard.'

'How *did* you hear?' Leena asks again from behind me, sounding completely flummoxed.

I watch them all file past her and suppress a smile. It's the Neighbourhood Watch. Knowing is their job.

'All right, Eileen?' comes a familiar voice. Arnold hovers with uncharacteristic uncertainty on the doorstep. Last time we spoke, he went off in a huff, but I find I haven't the energy to hold a grudge about it.

'Arnold! Come in,' Leena says.

Arnold's eyes flick to mine for permission.

'Yes, of course, come in,' I say, stepping aside.

I watch in surprise as he gives Leena a quick kiss on the cheek before he moves past her into the kitchen. He did say they were seeing each other for coffee, now and then, but it's still peculiar to see them acting like old friends.

'How did the rest of them even get here?' Leena asks me as I close the front door. 'Betsy's staying in Knargill!'

'I wouldn't put it past Betsy to hitch-hike, for a real emergency,' I say, with a little smile at Leena's expression. 'Is this all right, love? Everyone being here?' I give her arm a rub. 'I can tell them to go if you want some time just the two of us.'

'I'm OK. I think.' She takes a deep, shaky breath. 'What about you, though? You had quite a scare, with Mum, and then – with that Howard guy turning out to be . . .'

I shudder. I've been trying very hard not to think about that.

'So it wasn't . . . real?' I say, lowering my voice so the Neighbourhood Watch won't hear. They're bustling around in Marian's kitchen; someone's put the kettle on. Presumably they've figured out that Marian isn't here having a crisis after all, but they're showing no signs of departing. 'Everything he said about how he felt . . .'

'These scammers, they do it all the time, Grandma,' she says gently. 'They're lovely and friendly and things move really fast, and it seems like they're falling for you . . . and then they ask for money. Then they keep asking. So we were really lucky to catch it before it got too far.'

I shudder again, and Leena grips my hand.

'At first I hadn't been at all sure about how over-the-top and friendly he was,' I tell her. 'But then I got used to it, and it had felt quite . . . nice.' I sigh. 'I'm an old fool.'

'You're not! I'm so sorry, Grandma, it's my fault. I should have prepped you a bit more before letting you loose in cyberspace. But scammers like that trick everybody.'

'I *liked* him,' I say in a whisper. 'Was he even real? Was his name Howard?'

'I don't know, Grandma. I'm sorry. I know it's horrible, being tricked like that. Do you want me to tell this lot to go so we can have a proper chat about it all?' Leena says, glancing towards the kitchen.

I shake my head. 'No, I want them here,' I say, pushing my shoulders back. 'Come on, it ought to be me looking after you, with the day you've had. I'll make hot chocolate and you can have a good cry on my shoulder.'

'You can cry on mine too, if you need to, Grandma,' she says. 'I've figured that out this past two months.' She pulls me in for a hug, and then, in my ear, she says, 'If you're holding someone close enough, you can be the shoulder *and* the crier. See?'

I can hear the smile in her voice; she's laughing at herself as she says it, but she's saying it all the same. The Leena of two months ago would never have said something like that.

'God, this is what happens when I spend too much time with my mother,' Leena says, half-laughing, half-crying. 'I'll be collecting bloody crystals next.'

'Leena!' I scold, but I pull her in tighter as I say it, and that strange distance that grew between us while we were apart disappears as she leans her cheek on my shoulder.

There's another knock at the door.

'I'll get it,' Leena says, clearing her throat. 'You get the hot chocolate going.'

I glance back as I step into the kitchen.

'Leena,' says a deep, steady voice. 'Are you all right?'

35

Leena

It's Jackson. He stops at the threshold; he's taken his cap off, and he's holding it between his hands. I look up at him, his broad, open face, those kind blue eyes, the raggedy worn-out shirt too tight across his shoulders. I want to collapse on him and sob into his chest, but I feel that probably wouldn't be wise.

'Come in,' I say instead, stepping aside. 'The whole fecking village is in here.'

I lead him into the living room, where the Neighbourhood Watch committee members are now assembled, all perched on sofas and armchairs.

Jackson stands for a moment, looking at the room.

'Why are the chairs all facing that way?' he asks.

I follow his gaze to the empty space where Carla's bed once stood. Grandma's looking, too, and I see her eyes shutter, the emotion quivering in her face. Then I look at the bin in the corner of the room, and there it still is, that awful old photograph of Carla. I should have clocked then how desperate Mum was for change, how much she needed it.

I'm seized by that familiar urge to *do* something, that same sensation that got me switching lives with Grandma in the first place.

Maybe something less drastic this time. But something for Mum.

'Let's redecorate,' I say. It comes out a bit too loud; I clear my throat. 'While Mum's away. She said she wanted to, a while back. We could do it all for her, a full overhaul, not – not clearing Carla out of the house, but just . . . making space for the new Mum.'

Eileen smiles up at me. 'That's a lovely idea. I've been practising my redecorating skills, too. Martha taught me all sorts.'

'What *have* you been up to, Eileen?' Penelope asks, in a hushed tone. 'Was it all ever so exciting?'

Grandma folds her hands in her lap. 'Well,' she says. 'I hardly know where to start . . .'

I stay up in Hamleigh for another night, planning the redesign of Mum's house, catching up with Grandma, helping her unpack . . . everything except thinking about Ethan. The next morning I get up early so I have time for a run in the hills – I borrow an old pair of trainers from Kathleen. There is nothing like running here. It's breathtaking, and as I round the bend on my favourite route, the one that gives me 360-degree views across Harksdale, I feel my heart ache. A thought pops into my head, and it makes me a little afraid, because it says, *This place feels like home.*

But it's not home. I have a life in London, regardless of Ethan – I've got a career to salvage, a flat, friends.

You have friends here, too, that little voice says. Still, I get myself back to Daredale station, and I take that train back to London, and I walk back to my empty flat, where my real life is, because that's the sensible thing to do.

The misery hits as soon as I'm home again. It's worse than the first time, because this time I know for sure: the life I've had with Ethan here, it's gone. There's the cushion I bought from Camden Market with him one Saturday, and there's his usual seat at the breakfast counter, and there's the scuff on the floor from when we silly-danced to jazz music after a long day at work, and all of it means nothing now. I slide down the door and let myself cry.

This is where I am when Bee comes around to see me.

'Oi!' she calls through the door. 'Leena, let me in!' A pause. 'I know you're in there, I can hear you crying. Let me in, will you?'

She bangs on the door.

'Let me in, Leena, I can hear you!'

She's like a little London Arnold. I shift to the side and reach up to open the door without standing. She steps inside, takes one look at me, and then pulls a bottle of wine out of a supermarket bag in her hand.

'Come on, you,' she says, pulling me up by the arm. 'We need to start talking, which means we need to start drinking.'

It's at approximately one a.m. the next morning that Bee and I finalise our business plans. This life-altering conversation goes something like this.

'It's just like my mum says, why's it got to be *always about London* anyway, I mean *God* I don't even fucking like this city, do you like this city, Bee?'

'There's no men here.' This comes out a little strangled, because Bee is currently hanging upside down from my sofa, her feet up the back, her hair splayed on the floor. 'All the good men are in Leeds. All the good men. Oh my God, do I have a babysitter?' Bee sits up with a gasp and clutches her head.

'Jaime's with your mum,' I remind her, for the fifth or sixth time since the second bottle of wine was opened.

She flops back down again. 'Mmkay good.'

I take another swig of wine. I'm on the rug, legs spread-eagled; my brain is whirring through the drunken fog. 'Shall we just *go*, Bee? Shall we just go and fucking do it? Why are we even *here* anyway?'

'You mean like ... philosophicalilly?' She narrows her eyes and tries again. 'Philosophocally?' Then, with great amusement: 'Philofuckitally?'

'I mean like, why are we in London anyway? Who says we have to run our business from here?' I rub my face hard in an attempt to sober up. I have the vague sense that what I'm saying is very import-ant, and also, possibly, the cleverest thing anyone has ever said in the whole wide world. 'We'll end up travelling all over anyway. And there's so much business around Leeds, Hull, Sheffield . . . I want to be up in Yorkshire where my family is. I want to be with Hank the dog and all the gang, and those *hills*, God, they make my heart fuck-ing sing, Bee. We can get an office in Daredale. Bee, you'll love it, Bee. Bee. Bee. Bee.'

I poke her. She's gone very still.

'Oh my God,' Bee says suddenly, pulling her legs down and then swivel-rolling so she ends up in a heap on the floor. 'Oh my God that's such a good idea I'm going to be sick.'

We hash out the details in slightly more depth over the next two days – there are some issues to overcome, not least the massive life-change for Jaime. But we figure it out, bit by bit, so that when I walk back into Selmount HQ for the first time since that awful panic attack, I'm doing it with a letter of resignation in my hand.

Rebecca takes one look at me once I walk into her office and sighs. 'Fuck,' she says. 'You're going to resign, aren't you?'

'I'm sorry.'

'It was always a risk, sending you packing for two months.' She peers at me. Rebecca needs glasses, but will not acknowledge this sign of human weakness in herself – she prefers to squint. 'Though you look better for it, I've got to say. Nothing I can say to change your mind?'

I smile. ''Fraid not.'

'Where'd you go, then, for your two months of self-actualisation? Bali? Bali seems to be a popular one.'

I try not to laugh. 'Actually, I went to the Yorkshire Dales. Where my family lives. That's where I'm going, when I finish up here – I'm going to move in with my grandma, hopefully, and B –' I stop myself just before I mention Bee's plans to buy a house in Daredale for her and Jaime. Bee has yet to hand her notice in. In fact, I suspect she is hovering outside the door, ready to come in as soon as I come out.

'Huh.' Rebecca narrows her eyes. 'Smart.'

I blush, and she gives me a knowing look.

'Thank you,' I say. 'Really. Thank you for everything.'

She waves me off. 'Give me your absolute everything for the next two months, if you really want to thank me,' she says. 'Oh – and tell that ex-boyfriend of yours to stop hanging around when he should be client-side.'

'Ethan?'

'He's been mooning around your desk since seven this morning.'

I wince, and she grins.

'I told him you were on a project in Milton Keynes. 'Spect he's trying to find the right address for sending a box of chocolates as we speak.'

'Thanks,' I say, rather wearily. 'He's trying to make amends, I think. Only . . . it's something chocolates can't fix.'

There's a quiet knock on the door, and Ceci pokes her head around it. I freeze. We look at each other, and I watch the colour creep up from her neck to her cheeks.

'Great to have you back, Leena,' she says nervously. 'So sorry to disturb you. I'll . . . I'll come back.'

I watch her scuttle away. My heart pounds, half loathing, half adrenaline. Some deeply instinctual part of myself wanted to claw at her face, but now she's retreating I'm glad I didn't let her see how thoroughly I loathe her. Let her scurry away from me for the next two months on those absurdly long legs of hers. She doesn't deserve a moment's thought.

'Whatever you did to earn *her* respect at last, it definitely worked,' Rebecca comments, flicking through a pile of papers on her desk.

'I think she met my grandmother,' I say. 'That's probably what did it.'

36

Eileen

For the first time in over a decade, I go to Betsy's house.

At first we handle Betsy leaving Cliff the way we've always handled these sorts of things.

'Tea?' she asks, and then she says she got scones in for us as a treat, and we talk about the progress we're making with doing up Marian's house.

But then I think of Martha crying on the sofa, telling me how unprepared she felt to be a mother. Bee confessing how hard it's been for her to find a man. Fitz letting me write him to-do lists and teach him to cook. How honest and open my young London friends were.

'How *are* you, Betsy?' I say. 'Now that Cliff's gone? I can't imagine how you must feel.'

She looks a little startled, glancing at me as she stirs the milk into the teas. Then, rather cautiously, she says, 'I'm . . . bearing up.'

I wait, taking the tea tray from her and making my way into her front room. I can't have been here since, oh, the late nineties? She's still got the same patterned carpet, but the armchairs are new, two matching soft pink ones that I can't imagine Cliff would have liked much.

'The hardest part is the guilt,' she says eventually, settling into an armchair. 'I can't shake the feeling I ought to be looking after him.' She gives a little smile, reaching for the jam for her scone. 'And I keep thinking of how horrified my mother and father would be, if they'd seen me screaming at my husband out there with everybody watching.'

'I for one wish I'd been there. I would have cheered you on,' I say fervently.

She smiles. 'Well. Our Leena did a good job stepping in for you.'

We eat our scones and sip our tea.

'We ought to have done more,' I say. 'For one another, I mean. I should have done an awful lot more to help you leave Cliff, and I'm very, very sorry I didn't.'

Betsy blinks for a moment, then sets her scone down. 'I should have told you to give Wade the boot thirty years ago.'

I consider the point. It probably would have made a difference, that. I'd always rather thought Betsy would say I ought to stay with my husband through thick and thin, the way you're supposed to.

'We've got a few years left in us,' Betsy says after a moment. 'Let's promise to meddle in each other's business as much as we see fit from now on, shall we, dear?'

'Let's,' I say, as she picks up her scone again. 'More tea?'

The following week I bump into Arnold on my way home from painting at Marian's; Leena was here at the weekend, and we got almost all the downstairs rooms painted, so I was only finishing up edges today. I'm dressed in my shabbiest painting clothes, threadbare old trousers and a T-shirt that shows rather more of my upper arms than I'd like anybody to see.

Arnold gives me a stiff nod. 'Ey up,' he says. 'How are you, Eileen?'

'Oh, fine, thank you,' I say. Things have been peculiar ever since I got home. In fact, aside from the day Marian left, I've hardly seen him. After years of Arnold popping up in my kitchen window and calling out to me over the hedge, I can't help wondering whether this sudden absence is significant.

'Good, good. Well, I'll be on my way.'

'Arnold,' I say, catching his arm. 'I wanted to say thank you. Leena said what a help you were, while I was away in London.'

'Tell you about the car, did she?' Arnold says, looking down at my hand on his arm. He's in a short-sleeved shirt and his skin is warm beneath my palm.

'The car?'

'Oh.' His eyes flick to the dent in the hedge I've been wondering about for weeks. 'Nothing. It was no trouble. She's a good'un, that Leena of yours.'

'She is,' I say, smiling. 'Still. Thank you.'

He moves away, back towards his front gate. 'See you when I see you,' he says, and I frown, because that seems to be hardly at all, these days.

'Will you come in?' I call, as he walks away. 'For a cup of tea?'

'Not today.' He doesn't even turn; he's through his gate and gone before I can clock that he's turned me down.

This is irritating. As much as Arnold and I have always been at each other's throats, I've always thought . . . I've always had the impression . . . Well, I never invited him for tea, but I knew that if I did, he'd come. Let's put it that way.

Only now it seems something's changed.

I narrow my eyes at his house. It's clear that whatever is wrong, Arnold's not going to talk to me about it any time soon.

Sometimes, with obstinate people like Arnold, you have no choice but to force their hand.

'*What have you done?*' Arnold roars through the kitchen window.

I put my book down, carefully popping my bookmark in the right place.

'Eileen Cotton! Get in here now!'

'In where?' I ask innocently, stepping into the kitchen. 'For you to ask me *in* anywhere, Arnold, you'd have to be *in* there too, and you seem to be outside, to my eye.'

Arnold's cheeks are flushed with rage. His glasses are a little askew; I have a strange desire to open the window, reach through, and straighten them up again.

'The hedge. Is gone.'

'Oh, the hedge between your garden and mine?' I say airily, reaching for the cloth by the sink and giving the sideboard a wipe. 'Yes. I had Basil's nephew chop it down.'

'*When?*' Arnold asks. 'It was there yesterday!'

'Overnight,' I say. 'He says he works best by torchlight.'

'He says no such thing,' Arnold says, nose almost pressed to the glass. 'You got him to do it at night-time so I wouldn't know! What were you *thinking*, Eileen? There's no boundary! There's just . . . one big garden!'

'Isn't it nice?' I say. I'm being terribly nonchalant and wiping down all the surfaces, but I can't help sneaking little glances at his ruby-red face. 'So much more light.'

'What on earth did you do it *for*?' Arnold asks, exasperated. 'You fought tooth and nail to keep that hedge back when I wanted it replaced with a fence.'

'Yes, well, times change,' I say, rinsing out the cloth and smiling out at Arnold. 'I decided, since you were so reluctant to come around, I'd make it easier for you.'

Arnold stares at me through the glass. We're only a couple of feet apart; I can see how wide the pupils are in his hazel eyes.

'My God,' he says, stepping backwards. 'My God, you did this just to brass me off, didn't you?' He starts to laugh. 'You know, Eileen Cotton, you are no better than a teenage boy with a crush. What next? Pulling my hair?'

I bristle. 'I beg your pardon!' Then, because I can't resist: 'And I wouldn't like to risk what's left of it by giving it a tug.'

'You are a ridiculous woman!'

'And *you* are a ridiculous man. Coming in here, telling me you missed me, then marching off and not talking to me for days on end? What's the matter with you?'

'What's the matter with me?' His breath is misting the glass. 'I'm not the one who just hacked down a perfectly serviceable hedge in the middle of the night!'

'Do you really want to know why I did it, Arnold?'

'Yes. I really do.'

I chuck the wet cloth down. 'I thought it would be funny.'

He narrows his eyes. 'Funny?'

'Yes. You and me, we've spent decades fighting over who owns what, whose trees are shading whose flowerbeds, who's responsible for pruning which bush. You've got grumpier and grumpier and I've got snarkier and snarkier. And do you know what we've *really* been talking about all that time, Arnold? We've been talking about what happened the very first time we met.'

Arnold opens and closes his mouth.

'Don't tell me you've forgotten. I know you haven't.'

His mouth closes, a firm line. 'I've not forgotten.'

Arnold was married to Regina, Jackson's mother. A strange woman, blocky-shouldered like she was most at home in the eighties, her hair tightly curled and her fists usually clenched. And I was married to Wade.

'Nothing happened,' Arnold reminds me.

My hands are spread, leaning on the worktop on either side of the sink. Arnold is framed in a pane of glass, cut off at the shoulder like a portrait.

'No,' I say. 'That's what I've always told myself, too. No point dwelling on it. Certainly no use talking about it. Since nothing happened.'

'Quite right,' Arnold says.

'Only it almost did, didn't it, Arnold?' My heart is beating a little too fast.

Arnold reaches up to adjust his cap, his hands weathered and callused, his glasses still slightly askew. *Say something*, I think. *Say it.* Because I *am* like a teenage boy – I'm painfully self-conscious now, terrified he'll tell me I was reading something that wasn't there.

'It almost did,' he says eventually.

I close my eyes and breathe out.

We'd been in this kitchen, not far from where I'm standing. He'd brought around an apple pie Regina had made, with custard in a little milk jug; we'd talked for so long in the hallway my arms had started to ache from holding the plate. He'd been so charming, such a thoughtful, engaging man.

Wade and I had just bought Clearwater Cottage. The house was barely furnished, half falling to pieces. Arnold and I had walked through into the kitchen – I remember laughing very hard, feeling ever so giddy – and I'd opened the new fridge to pop the custard in there, and when I'd closed it again he'd been very close, just a few steps from where I am now. We'd stayed like that. My heart had raced then, too. I'd not felt giddy in so long I'd thought it was gone from my repertoire for good, like touching my toes.

Nothing happened.

But it almost did. And it was enough to make me want to keep Arnold as far away from this house as possible. Because I had made a vow. It meant nothing to Wade, it seems, but it had meant something to me.

'We got into the habit, didn't we,' Arnold says, as I open my eyes again. He's smiling slightly. 'We got so bloody good at hating one another.'

I take a deep breath. 'Arnold,' I say, 'would you like to come in?'

*

In the end, it's not a stolen kiss between new neighbours. It's a slow, lingering one between very old friends, who, as it happens, have only just realised that's what they've been all along.

It's an extraordinary feeling, wrapping my arms around Arnold's shoulders, pressing my cheek to the warm skin of his neck. Breathing in the cut-grass and soap smell of his hair and his collar. It is strange and wonderful. Familiar and new.

Afterwards, when my lips are left tingling, we sit together side by side on the sofa and stare out at the hedge, or what remains of it. Arnold is smiling. He seems energised, almost jolted into life – he holds his spine very straight and the hand that isn't in mine is flicking and fidgeting in his lap.

'Bloody hell,' he says, 'just think what Betsy and the rest of them will say.' He turns to me and grins, a cheeky, fiendish grin that makes him look like a little boy.

'You won't say a word,' I tell him sternly, raising a warning finger. 'Not a word, Arnold.'

He grabs the finger so fast I yelp.

'That tone of voice won't work on me any more,' he says, bringing my hand to his lips for a kiss that doesn't dislodge his grin for a moment. 'Now I know what you're *really* saying when you tell me off.'

'Not *all* the time,' I protest. 'Sometimes you really need telling. Like with the rabbit.'

'For the last time!' Arnold laughs. 'I did not poison your bloody rabbit.'

'Then how did it die?' I ask, flummoxed.

'Eileen, it was seven years ago. I imagine it's too late for an inquest.'

'Damn. I hate an unsolved mystery.'

'You really thought I did it?'

'It didn't occur to me that it could have happened any other way, quite honestly.'

He frowns. 'You think that little of me?'

I smooth my thumb across the back of his hand, tracing lines between the marks age has left on his skin.

'Perhaps I wanted to,' I say. 'It was easier if you were an ogre.' I glance up. 'And you did such a good job playing the part.'

'Well, you made a pretty stellar old harpy, too,' he says.

I lean forwards and kiss him. It's sweet and warm and his lips taste of tea, no sugar. I didn't even know that's how he took it until today.

37

Leena

'And you're sure about this?' I ask, panting.

Bee and I are on the spin bikes – I've realised over the last six weeks that the best way to survive the stress of Selmount life is to exercise daily and aggressively. Sitting in an air-conditioned gym is a bit crap after running through the Dales – kind of like taking vitamin tablets instead of, you know, eating. But it'll do for now.

'I'm done with you asking me if I'm sure,' Bee says, glancing across at me. 'Never been surer, my friend.'

I grin and slow down, sitting up to wipe my face with my T-shirt. We wobble our way to the changing rooms together, breathing hard.

'How's Jaime feeling about the move?' I ask, heading for my locker.

'Ridiculously happy. Apparently Yorkshire has loads of dinosaur fossils or something.' Bee rolls her eyes, but she doesn't fool me.

'Has she met Mike yet?' I ask.

'No, no,' Bee says, frowning. 'She doesn't even know there's such a thing as a Mike.'

'The man you're moving up north for? She doesn't know he exists?'

She whips me with her towel. I yelp.

'While I am glad that you have dragged yourself out of the pit of Ethan-related despair enough to start taking the piss out of me again, will you *stop* with that please? I am not moving up north for Mike. I mean, I'm basically moving up north for you, actually.'

I look chastened. 'Right. Sorry.'

We head for the showers.

'Only it is a happy coincidence that Mike will be there too,' I say very quickly before locking myself in the shower cubicle.

'You are as bad as your grandmother!' Bee shouts through the wall.

'Thanks!' I yell back, grinning as I turn the water up to hit me full blast.

When I get back to the flat that night, the place is full of boxes, and the balding cat lady from next door is sitting in front of the television watching gory true crime on Netflix.

I pause in the doorway. I tilt my head. I swivel to look at Fitz, who is standing in the kitchen, leaning over a pile of boxes to reach the bottle opener.

'Oh, Letitia?' he says, in response to my perplexed expression. 'Yeah, we're like besties now.'

'You . . .' I swivel back to stare at Letitia. 'Sorry, hi,' I say, remembering my manners.

She looks up from the television, gives me a polite smile, and then returns to the story of a young woman's dismemberment. I look back at Fitz.

'And the boxes?' I ask him, when he offers no further information. 'I thought you hadn't found anywhere to move to yet?'

This has been a source of some stress to me these last few weeks. Fitz was showing no signs of actually sorting out getting new flatmates or finding himself somewhere else to live; with Martha gone and me heading up north, there's absolutely no way he can cover the rent here.

'Oh, yeah, I chatted to Eileen about it actually,' Fitz says, opening his beer.

'My grandma Eileen?'

'Yeah?' Fitz looks at me as though I'm being extremely dim. 'Obviously? She suggested I move in with Letitia. Her flat's *amazing*, full of antiques and vintage stuff. All the Silver Shoreditchers' Club furniture comes from there.'

I got my first glimpse of the Silver Shoreditchers' Social Club a couple of weeks ago. It was hands down the loveliest thing I have ever witnessed, and I've seen Samantha Greenwood dressed as a satsuma. The moody artists in Flat 11 taught painting, the intense woman in Flat 6 gave people lifts, and Fitz coordinated everything with astonishing proficiency. I honestly hadn't realised how brilliant he could be when he was working on something he actually felt was important. Last week he applied for a job as an event manager for a major charity. When I told Grandma that she let out the most un-Grandma-ish whoop and started dancing.

'So you're moving ... next door? With ... Letitia?' I say, absorbing.

'I've decided old ladies make the best flatmates,' Fitz says. 'They can usually cook, because in the fifties women had to do that shit and they've still got all the skills. They're always blunt and will tell me if my outfit isn't working – or at least the ones I've met will. And they're in all day, which is perfect if you're getting a parcel delivered!' He lifts his beer bottle in my direction. 'Thank you for enlightening me, Ms Cotton the Younger.'

'You're welcome,' I say, still processing.

'What are you wearing for tonight?' Fitz asks.

I make a face. 'I'd normally just get Martha to pick something for me, but she's, you know, a bit busy.'

It's Martha and Yaz's engagement party. Having Vanessa seems to have turned Yaz from free-spirited wanderer into full-time relationship committer in a matter of weeks. Yaz proposed to Martha with Vanessa in her lap, and they have already detailed exactly how cute the baby's flower-girl outfit is going to be.

'You know Ethan's going to be there?' Fitz says.

My stomach drops. 'Shit. Really?'

Fitz offers me a conciliatory beer. 'Sorry. Classic Yaz. She had him on the invite list before you guys broke up and then just hit send on the email, and there's no way that man's missing a chance to see you.'

I rub my face hard. 'Can I not go?'

Fitz lets out a positively theatrical gasp. 'To Martha and Yaz's engagement party? Leena Cotton! Even your grandmother is coming! All the way from the wilds of Yorkshire!'

'I know, I know . . .' I groan. 'Right, come on, you. We need to find me a bloody phenomenal outfit. Bye, Letitia!' I say as we walk past her. 'Nice to see you!'

'*Shh*,' she says, pointing at the television.

'Told you,' Fitz says as we head for my wardrobe. 'Blunt.'

38

Eileen

I'm off to the party. But I'm taking a little detour, first, to pick some-body up.

I have learned many surprising things about Arnold in the last two months. He sleeps in purple silk pyjamas that look like they belong to a Victorian count. He gets grumpy if he goes too long with-out a meal, and then gives me a kiss whenever I remind him. And he loves reading Charles Dickens and Wilkie Collins, but he'd never read any Agatha Christie until he started working his way through my list of favourite books from the dating website. When he told me about that, it was so damn lovely I took him straight to bed.

But the most interesting fact of all is that Arnold Macintyre is a *fountain* of Hamleigh gossip. As a result of one of his particularly fascinating titbits, I am now on Jackson Greenwood's doorstep, dressed in my London get-up: leather boots, bottle-green culottes, and a soft cream sweater Tod bought me as a goodbye gift.

'Hello, Eileen,' Jackson says when he answers the door. He doesn't seem especially surprised to see me standing on his doorstep dressed up to the nines, but then, now I think about it, I'm not sure I've ever seen Jackson looking surprised about anything.

'May I come in?' I say. It's a little blunt, but I'm rather tight for time.

He steps aside. 'Course you can. Would you like a tea?'

'Yes, please.' I make my way through to his living area, which is surprisingly tidy and well decorated. The wooden coffee table is a new addition since I was last here; there's a book there, splayed out on its front with the spine up, called *Thinking: Fast and Slow*. Behind a stairgate, Hank wags ecstatically in the conservatory. I give his ears a fond scratch, careful not to let him anywhere near my lovely cream sweater.

'Milk, one sugar,' Jackson says, placing my mug down on a coaster as I head for the sofa. I'd never have pinned Jackson as a coaster sort of man, I must say. I run my finger over the wood of the table and reflect on just how little you can know about your neighbours, even when you are extremely nosy.

'Ethan's out of the picture,' I say, once I'm sitting down.

Jackson pauses midway to the armchair. Just a momentary falter, but enough to send a trickle of tea down the side of his mug to the rug under the coffee table.

He sits down. 'Huh,' he says.

'He was having an affair with Leena's boss's assistant.'

His hands flex convulsively. This time the tea spills in his lap – he swears quietly, getting up again to fetch a cloth from the kitchen. I wait, watching his back, wondering.

'Leena found out?' he asks eventually from the kitchen, still facing away from me.

'I found out. I told her. She finished with him right away.' I look down at my tea. 'Adultery is one thing Leena will not tolerate.'

He looks at me then, a sympathetic glance. I don't acknowledge it. I'm not here to talk about me and Wade.

'I'm going down to London, to a party, and she'll be there. I thought you might want to come.'

'Me?'

'Yes.'

Then Jackson sighs. 'Arnold told you,' he says.

'Yes. Though I had to wring it out of the man, so don't blame him.'

'S'all right. Half the village knows how I feel about her anyway. But . . . go to London?' Jackson says, scratching his head. 'Isn't that a bit much?'

'That depends. Are there things you wish you hadn't left unsaid?'

'Actually, I . . .' He sits down again, those giant hands wrapped around his mug until all I can see is the curl of steam rising from the tea. 'I told her at the May Day festival. How I felt.'

'Did you?' *This* Arnold did not tell me. 'What did she say?'

'She said she doesn't look at me that way.'

Hmm. That's not Betsy's account of things, and I trust Betsy's eye when it comes to a brewing romance. Rumours that start with Betsy are rarely wrong.

'I was ashamed of myself, after,' Jackson says. 'She's got – she had a boyfriend.'

'Yes, well,' I say briskly. 'No need to worry about that any longer, we made quick work of him.' I reach forward and pat his arm. 'If she doesn't see you that way, then you need to change the way she sees you. Come to London. Wear something smart. You know how, at the pictures, when the girl gets dressed up for a party and walks down the stairs in slow motion with her glasses off and her hair up and a bit of leg showing and the man is standing at the bottom, mouth open wide, as if he can't believe he's never seen her that way before?'

'Yeah?' Jackson says.

'You need to be that girl. Come on. Have you got a suit?'

'A suit? I . . . There's the one I wore to Davey's funeral.'

'You haven't got a less . . . funereal option?'

'No. I've got smart trousers and a shirt?'

'That'll do. And wash your hair, there's half a tree in there.'

He raises an experimental hand to his head and pulls out a sprig of something evergreen. 'Oh,' he says.

'Shower, get dressed, then it's go-time. You can drive us to Daredale station in that truck of yours?'

'Yeah, I can. I'll . . . but . . .' He swallows. 'Is this a good idea?'

'It's an excellent idea,' I tell him firmly. 'Now come on. Chop, chop.'

Fitz kisses me on the cheek when I arrive, then double takes when he sees Jackson.

'Is this Arnold?' he says, clutching at his chest.

I laugh. 'This is Jackson,' I say. 'Arnold's stepson. In love with Leena,' I add in a whisper, though it might not be as quiet as I thought it was because, behind Fitz, Martha goes *oooh* and before I know it, she's grabbed Jackson's arm and started what looks like a very personal conversation.

The party is a heaving mass of bodies; I wince despite myself at the barrage of thumping music as we move inside. We're in a bar under the arches by Waterloo station, and the noise echoes from the high, cavernous ceiling as stylish youngsters mill about holding beer bottles.

'Oh, bloody hell,' Jackson mutters beside me, having escaped Martha's well-meaning clutches. 'This is . . .'

'Don't worry,' I say, patting his arm. 'If you feel out of place, just imagine how I feel.'

He looks down at me. 'Somehow you fit right in, actually.'

'I know,' I say breezily. 'I was just trying to make you feel better. Come on, let's find Leena.'

We make an unusual pairing as we move through the crowds, one old lady and one giant young man walking arm in arm through the throng. Jackson has smartened up well, I'm pleased to see. His shirt is open at the neck and just the right fit across the shoulders, and even though he's wearing a very battered pair of brown leather shoes, the overall effect is very impressive.

Combined with the clean hair and the smart trousers, it's all bound to get Leena's attention.

'Eileen?'

I turn, surprised, and am faced with the rather hunted expression of Ethan Coleman.

'What on earth are you doing here?' I hiss at him.

Beside me I can feel Jackson drawing up, getting even taller, even broader. It's all very manly. I look around quickly, hoping Leena is within view, but no such luck.

'I'm here for Leena,' Ethan says. 'Eileen, please, you have to understand . . .'

'I have to do no such thing,' I say, pulling on Jackson's arm. It's like trying to tug at concrete. 'Come on.'

'You're here sniffing around after Leena, are you?' Ethan asks Jackson, lip curling a little. 'I thought as much when I first met you. But she's not your type, mate. Or, rather, you're not hers.'

Jackson is very still. I yank at his arm, but again, nothing – he is firmly rooted.

'What's that meant to mean?' Jackson asks Ethan.

'Don't worry about it,' Ethan says, moving to pass us. 'I'll see you around.'

Jackson's arm shoots out. Ethan walks right into it with a quiet *oof.*

'If you've got something to say, say it,' Jackson says. He sounds very calm.

Well. This is all rather thrilling. Where *is* Leena when you need her?

'I've got nothing to say to you,' Ethan says, rattled. 'Get out of my way. I'm going to find Leena.'

'What do you want with Leena?'

'What do you think?' Ethan snaps.

'I'll have a guess,' Jackson says. 'You still think you have a chance with her. You think Leena will come around and forgive you – you're her blind spot, aren't you, and you can get away with pretty much anything. You don't see why now should be any different.'

'You don't know what you're talking about.'

Jackson shrugs. 'I hope you're right about that. Good luck to you, *mate*, but I hope she tells you where to shove it.' He turns to me. 'Eileen, shall we?'

'Let's,' I say, and we head on through the crowd, leaving Ethan behind.

'So,' Jackson says to me, 'who do you think is going to find Leena first?'

I scoff. 'I'm Eileen Cotton and she's Eileen Cotton. I've lived her life and she's lived mine.' I tap the side of my head. 'It's a sixth sense, Jackson. You wouldn't understand.'

'No?'

'No. It's a complex bond, like the one between a—'

'We seem to be heading to the gin bar,' Jackson remarks.

'Where would you be if you'd just found out your ex was at your friend's engagement party? It was this or in front of the bathroom mirror, fixing her hair – ooh, doesn't she look *beautiful*!' I breathe, catching sight of her at the bar.

She's wearing a long black dress that leaves her arms bare; there's a striking silver bangle on her wrist, but that's all the adornment she needs. Her hair is stunning – worn as it should be, loose and large and full of life.

I glance at Jackson. He's staring at Leena. I watch as his Adam's apple bobs. You'd have to be a fool not to tell what that man is thinking.

'Leena,' Ethan calls out to our left, pushing through the crowd.

I curse under my breath. 'The little weasel!' I hiss, trying to shove Jackson forwards. 'Quick, before he . . .'

Jackson holds his ground and shakes his head. 'Not like this,' he says.

I huff, but stay where I am. At the bar, Leena's brushing Ethan off. Her cheeks are flushed – she's getting up now, trying to walk away – towards us . . .

'Look, Ethan,' she says, spinning on her heels just a few feet away. 'I gave you a free pass, didn't I? I didn't even know I'd done it, but *you* did. I decided you were the guy for me and that was it. Well, turns out that pass *does* expire, Ethan, and there *is* a line, and you fucking *crossed it.*'

'Leena, listen to me –'

'I don't know what was worse! Sleeping with my arch-bloody-nemesis or telling me my grandmother was losing her mind! Do you *know* how messed up that was?'

'I panicked,' Ethan wheedles. 'I didn't mean –'

'Do you know what? Do you know what? I'm almost *pleased* you slept with Ceci. There. I said it. I'm glad you cheated on me because thank God I came to my senses and realised you weren't right for me at all. Not this me, not the me I am now, not any more. We're done.'

And with that she turns to storm off and walks right into Jackson.

He catches her arm as she stumbles backwards. Their eyes meet. Her cheeks are flushed, his lips are parted. Around us the crowd shifts, closing Ethan from view, leaving a small quiet island just here. Just the two of them.

Oh, well, and me, I suppose.

'Jackson?' Leena says, baffled. She looks him up and down. 'Oh, wow, you look . . .'

I breathe in, hand at my heart. Here it comes.

'Weird,' Leena finishes.

'Weird?' I blurt. 'Oh, for goodness' sake, girl!'

They both turn to me then.

'Grandma?' Leena looks between me and Jackson, then glances over her shoulder as if remembering Ethan. Her eyes narrow. 'What's going on?'

'Nothing,' I say quickly. 'Jackson just fancied a trip to London, and so I thought, oh, there's a party this evening and . . .'

Her eyes are narrowed to slits.

'Oh, look,' I say brightly, as a member of staff heads out of the storage room to the side of the bar. 'Just come this way a minute.' I grab Leena and Jackson by the hands and pull. Thankfully they follow me. I lead them into the storage room.

'Wha – Grandma, where are we –'

I duck out and close the door behind them.

'There,' I say, brushing my hands down on my culottes. 'Not many seventy-nine-year-olds who could be quite that nimble, if I do say so myself.' I tap a nearby gentleman on the shoulder. 'Excuse me,' I say. 'Would you mind leaning on this door, please?'

'Grandma?' Leena calls through the door. 'Grandma, what are you doing?'

'Meddling!' I yell cheerfully. 'It's my new "thing"!'

39

Leena

This cupboard is extremely small. It's also lined with shelves, so there's nothing to lean on; Jackson and I are standing very close together but not quite touching, as though we're on a tube train.

What *is* Grandma playing at? I look down at my feet, trying to shuffle backwards, and my hair brushes against Jackson's shirt. He inhales sharply, raises a hand to his head, and elbows me in the shoulder.

'Sorry,' we both say.

I laugh. It comes out far too high-pitched.

'This is my fault,' Jackson says eventually. I risk a look up at him; we're so close together, I have to crane my neck to see his face. 'I shouldn't have let her talk me into coming.'

'Did you . . . come to see me?'

He looks down at me then. We're so close our noses almost touch. I'm not sure I've ever been quite so aware of somebody, physically, I mean – I hear every rustle as he moves, feel the heat of his body inches from mine.

'Course I did,' he says, and just like that, my pulse is thundering again.

There's just something about Jackson. Even with his hair all fluffed up, and dried-out shaving foam behind his ear, he's so *sexy*.

It's the unintentional confidence he has, as if he's wholly himself and couldn't possibly manage being somebody else even if he wanted to.

'Though,' he goes on, 'this is not how I imagined we'd see each other again. Bit of a last-minute plan change. Think I got Eileened.'

His hand brushes mine. I inhale sharply, and his eyes search my face, but it's not an objection, it's a reaction to the sharp shot of heat that comes when his skin touches mine. I let my fingers twine with his, and I feel like a schoolkid doing seven minutes in heaven with the guy I've been crushing on all year.

'What had you planned? Beforehand?' I ask. My other hand finds his.

'Well, I didn't know how long I'd have to wait before you binned that ex of yours. But I thought you'd see sense eventually, and when you did, I'd wait an appropriate amount of time . . .'

His lips touch mine, very gently, not even quite a kiss. My whole body responds; I can feel the hair on my arms stand on end.

'Like six weeks?' I say.

'I'd imagined six months. But it turns out I'm impatient,' Jackson whispers.

'So you'd wait six months, and then . . .'

Our lips are touching again, another almost-kiss, a little deeper now, but his lips are gone before I can kiss him back. I shift my fingers between his, holding him tighter, feeling the calluses on his palms.

'No shame – I'd make full use of all the tools at my disposal,' he says, his voice husky. 'Get the schoolkids to sing you that Ed Sheeran song, "Thinking Out Loud", send Hank around with a bunch of flowers in his mouth, bake you heart-shaped brownies. Burn them, in case you make them that way because that's how you like them.'

I laugh. He kisses me then, a real kiss, lips parted, his tongue tasting mine. I melt into him, our hands still linked at our sides, and I stand on tiptoes to kiss him better, and then, when I can't resist it any longer, I let go of his hands to thread my arms across those broad shoulders and press my body against his.

Jackson breathes out. 'You have no idea how many times I've imagined how it would feel, holding you like this,' he says, pressing his lips against my neck.

I sigh as he kisses the sensitive skin behind my ear. 'I might've thought about it too,' I confess.

'Oh?' I feel him smile. 'You *did* fancy me, then. Could've given me a clue. I've been shit-scared all evening.'

I laugh. 'You've been distractingly fanciable for months. I'm surprised you didn't figure out I had a crush on you.'

'Ah, was that what losing my dog and crashing the school van meant?'

I press a kiss to his jaw, feeling that sandy stubble beneath my lips. 'No,' I say. '*That* meant I was a mess.'

He pulls back then, rests his forehead against mine. 'You weren't a mess, Leena Cotton. I've never met a human being who is less of a mess than you are.'

I move away a little to look up at him properly.

'What do you think people do when they lose someone? Just . . . plough on?' He smooths my hair back from my face. 'You were healing. You're still healing. You'll maybe always be healing. And that's OK. It'll just be part of what makes you you.'

I rest my face against his chest. He kisses the top of my head.

'Hey,' he says. 'Say the distractingly fanciable thing again.'

I smile. I don't know how to explain the way Jackson makes me feel, how freeing it is to be around somebody so completely themselves, so utterly without guile.

'When you're here, *I'm* here, too,' I say, turning my face up to his. 'Which is amazing, because most of the time, I'm always somewhere else. Looking back or looking ahead, worrying or planning or . . .'

He kisses me on the lips until my whole body is humming. I want to take that shirt off him and feel the hair on his chest and the broad, firm muscles of his shoulders and count the pale freckles on his arms. Instead I kiss him again, hungrily, breathlessly, and he walks me backwards half a step so my back is pressed against the cupboard door, his body flush to mine. We kiss like teenagers, his hands tangling in my hair, mine clenching fists of fabric at the back of his shirt.

Then – *oof* – the door opens, and we're thrown backwards. All that stops us falling is Jackson's arm thrown out to catch the doorframe – I cling to him, my hair in my face, as the music of the party blares around us. I can hear laughter and whoops, and even once I'm steady on my feet, I keep my face buried in Jackson's neck.

'Leena Cotton!' I hear Fitz call. 'You're just as much of a minx as your grandmother!'

I laugh, pulling away a little and turning to look at the crowd around us. I see my grandma's face – she's beaming at me, a large gin and tonic in her hand.

'Are you going to tell me off for meddling?' she calls.

I lean into Jackson, my hands linked around his waist. 'You know what? I can't fault you on this one, Grandma. Switch places, and I would have done the exact same thing.'

EPILOGUE

Eileen

It's been almost six months since Leena moved to Hamleigh; eight months since Marian left. And two years to the day since Carla died.

We're at Leeds Airport, awaiting the arrival of the last member of our party. Leena's organised it all: the village hall is decked out in moon daisies and lilies, Carla's favourite flowers, and we're having shepherd's pie then brownies for pudding. We even invited Wade, though thankfully he took the invite as it was meant – purely a gesture – and declined.

Here in Leeds Airport, Samantha comes tearing around the corner, eyes scanning the gaggle of people waiting around us. She spots Jackson first, and that's it, she's flying towards him, her blonde mop of hair bouncing as she darts her way through the crowd and throws herself into his waiting arms.

'Daddy! Daddy!' Samantha cries.

Marigold follows her daughter more slowly. In her defence, nobody could move at speed in those ridiculous heels.

'Leena, hi,' she says, leaning to kiss my granddaughter on the cheek. Marigold looks relaxed, and the smile she shoots Leena seems genuine.

This is all Leena's doing. Samantha will be spending the next four weeks here, then going back to America with Marigold after Christmas. Leena worked on Marigold for weeks: softly softly, placating, easing her into the idea, removing each obstacle one by one. I was there for the moment, one month ago, when she told Jackson that Marigold had agreed to a longer visit at Christmas. If it is possible for a man to look both broken and healed at the very same moment, then that's how Jackson looked. He hugged Leena so tightly I thought she'd suffocate, but instead she came up red-cheeked and beaming, turning her face up to his for a kiss. I have never been prouder.

We make our way back to Hamleigh-in-Harksdale in convoy, Jackson's truck in the lead, and me in Agatha the Ford Ka, who now – thanks to Arnold – has functioning air conditioning. There's snow on the hilltops and dusting the old stone walls crisscrossing the fields. I feel a fierce, intense love for this place that has always been my home, and I watch Leena smile out at the Dales as we pass the sign saying *Welcome to Hamleigh-in-Harksdale*. It's home for her, now, too.

The Neighbourhood Watch are setting up the village hall when we get there. They greet Marigold and Samantha like returning war heroes, which just goes to show that absence really does make the heart grow fonder, because Basil and Betsy used to harp on about Marigold like she was Mary Magdalene before she moved to America.

'You guys! You've done an *amazing* job,' Leena says, bouncing on the spot.

Betsy, Nicola, Penelope, Roland, Piotr, Basil, and Kathleen are all beaming back at her, and, behind them, Martha, Yaz, Bee, little Jaime, Mike, and Fitz are doing just the same. *Everyone's* here – Betsy's daughter, Dr Piotr's ex-wife, even Mr Rogers, the vicar's father.

Arnold walks in behind us, arms full of napkins waiting to be distributed on the long table running down the centre of the hall. 'Eyeing up Mr Rogers, are we?' he asks, following my gaze. 'Probably very dull in bed, remember.'

I whack him on the arm. 'Oh, would you shut up? I can't believe I let you talk me in to showing you that list!'

Arnold chuckles and returns to napkin duty. I watch him go,

smiling. *Hates me almost as much as I hate him,* that's what I'd written on Arnold's list. Well. That was about right, in the end.

'Grandma? Did you want to say a few words before the food?' Leena asks, as everyone takes their seats.

I look towards the door. When I turn back, Leena's expression is a mirror of mine, I imagine – we both had our hopes up. But we can't wait any longer before starting the meal.

I clear my throat and make my way to the head of the table. Leena and I are at the centre, an empty chair between us.

'Thank you, everyone, for coming here today to celebrate our Carla.' I clear my throat again. This might be harder than I'd thought it would be. Now I'm standing here, talking about Carla, it occurs to me how tricky it'll be not to cry. 'Not all of you knew her,' I say. 'But those who do will remember what a bright, fiery person she was, how she loved to be surprised, and how she loved to surprise us. I think she'd be surprised to see us all here, now, as we are. I like that.'

I sniff, blinking rapidly.

'Carla left a . . . I don't know the words for the sort of hole she left in our lives. A wound, a crater, I don't know. It seemed – it seemed so utterly *impossible* that we were expected to go on without her.' I'm crying now, and Arnold passes me one of the napkins. I take a moment to collect myself. 'A lot of you know that earlier this year, Leena and I took a little sabbatical from each of our lives, and we stepped into one another's shoes for a while. That time showed me and Leena that we were each missing a part of ourselves. Perhaps that part left us when Carla did, or perhaps it was gone long before, I'm not sure. But we needed to come back together again – not just to each other, but back to ourselves.'

There's a sound from the doorway. I breathe in. Heads turn. I can't look, I'm so hopeful it hurts, but then I hear Leena breathe out, a half-gasp, half-smiling laugh, and it tells me everything.

Marian looks so different. Her hair is cut short and dyed white blonde, stark against her tan; she's wearing patterned trousers cuffed at the ankles, and though her eyes are full of tears, she's smiling. I haven't seen that smile – *that* smile, the real one – in so long that for an instant I feel like I'm seeing a ghost. She stands in the doorway, one hand on the frame, waiting.

'Come in, Mum,' Leena says. 'We saved you a seat.'

I reach blindly for Arnold's hand as the tears come in full force, sliding down my cheeks and misting my glasses as my daughter takes the empty chair beside me. I was a little afraid she'd never come home again, but here she is, and smiling.

I take a shaky breath and go on. 'When people talk about loss, they always say that you'll never be the same, that it will change you, leave a hole in your life.' My voice is choked with tears now. 'And those things are undoubtedly true. But when you lose someone you love, you don't lose everything they gave you. They leave something with you.

'I like to think that when Carla died, she gave each member of her family a little of her fire, her bravery. How else could we have done everything we've done this year?' I look at Leena and Marian and swallow hard through the tears. 'As we've muddled onwards, trying to learn how to live without her, I've felt Carla here.' I tap my heart. 'She's given me a push when I've almost lost my nerve. She's told me I can do it. She's led me back to myself. I can say now with certainty that I am the best Eileen Cotton I've ever been. And I hope – I hope . . .'

Leena stands then, as I lean forward against the table, tears streaming down my cheeks. She raises her glass.

'To being the best woman you can be,' she says. 'And to Carla. Always to Carla.'

Around us, everyone choruses her name. I sit down, my legs shaking, and turn towards Marian and Leena. Those big, dark, Cotton eyes look back at me, and I see myself mirrored there, in miniature, as Marian stretches out her hands and links us all together again.

ACKNOWLEDGEMENTS

It's thank you time, which is exciting, because it means I really did manage to write a second book! Whew. Don't tell Quercus but I wasn't *totally* sure I could do that.

First up, I could not have written *The Switch* without the support of Tanera Simons, my agent, who has an uncanny ability to make everything better with one phone call. I also couldn't have written it without Emily Yau, Christine Kopprasch, Cassie Browne and Emma Capron, all of whom have been my editors during this novel's journey, and all of whom have made it stronger in countless ways. Special thanks to Cassie, who picked up this novel when it was barely a half-formed thing and loved it so enthusiastically – you really kept me going, Cassie.

Publishing a book takes a village, and Quercus is a village lovely enough to rival Hamleigh-in-Harksdale. They constantly amaze me with their dedication and their creativity. I'd like to give a special thank you to Hannah Robinson, for always being straight with me and for having my back, and to Bethan Ferguson, for dreaming so big with my books. And as for the brilliant Hannah Winter and Ella Patel . . . what can I say? Without you ladies I'd be lost. Probably literally. You are both stars.

To the Taverners: thank you so much for welcoming me in, for making my writing stronger and for being so supportive. Peter, thanks for answering endless work questions with such patience;

Amanda the dragon, and all my other lovely consultant friends, sorry if I've pinched bits of your job and then got them wrong because it suited the narrative better. The perils of being friends with a writer . . .

To the volunteers and diners of the Well-Being lunch club: it's an absolute joy to see you every Monday. You've inspired me, both for this book and my life in general – I feel lucky to know you all.

Thank you to my grandmothers, Helena and Jeannine, for showing me that women can be incredibly brave and strong whatever their age. And thank you to Pat Hodgson, for forgetting about the gardening to read a typo-riddled print-out of an early draft, and for your enthusiasm at meeting a character of 'your vintage', as you so brilliantly put it. You're a total inspiration.

Mum and Dad, thank you for reminding me to trust my ski. And Sam, thank you for keeping me smiling. I am beyond lucky to be marrying a man who can laugh at a funny scene even when he's already read it five times over . . . *and* help with the medical stuff.

I also want to thank the book bloggers, the reviewers, and the booksellers who do so much to spread the word about the stories they love. Authors would be lost without you, and I'm so grateful for your support.

Finally, thank *you*, lovely reader, for giving this book a chance. I hope you have been well and truly Eileened . . .